THE
Shadowed Land

ALSO BY SIGNE PIKE

The Forgotten Kingdom

The Lost Queen

*Faery Tale: One Woman's Search
for Enchantment in a Modern World*

THE
Shadowed
Land

❧ A NOVEL ❦

SIGNE PIKE

ATRIA BOOKS

New York London Toronto Sydney New Delhi

ATRIA
BOOKS

An Imprint of Simon & Schuster, LLC
1230 Avenue of the Americas
New York, NY 10020

First Atria Books hardcover edition December 2024

ATRIA B O O K S and colophon are trademarks of Simon & Schuster, LLC

Simon & Schuster: Celebrating 100 Years of Publishing in 2024

For information about special discounts for bulk purchases,
please contact Simon & Schuster Special Sales at
1-866-506-1949 or business@simonandschuster.com.

The Simon & Schuster Speakers Bureau can bring authors to your live event. For more
information or to book an event, contact the Simon & Schuster Speakers Bureau
at 1-866-248-3049 or visit our website at www.simonspeakers.com.

Interior design by Jill Putorti
Map by David Lindroth Inc.

Manufactured in the United States of America

1   3   5   7   9   10   8   6   4   2

Library of Congress Cataloging-in-Publication Data
Names: Pike, Signe, author.
Title: The shadowed land : a novel / Signe Pike.
Description: First Atria Books hardcover edition. | New York : Atria Books, 2024. |
Series: The lost queen
Identifiers: LCCN 2024019298 (print) | LCCN 2024019299 (ebook) |
ISBN 9781501191480 (hardcover) | ISBN 9781501191497 (paperback) |
ISBN 9781501191503 (ebook)
Subjects: LCSH: Arthur, King—Fiction. | Great Britain—History—To 1066—Fiction. |
BISAC: FICTION / Historical / General | FICTION / Sagas | LCGFT: Historical fiction. | Novels.
Classification: LCC PS3616.I425 S53 2024 (print) | LCC PS3616.I425 (ebook) |
DDC 813/.6—dc23/eng/20240816
LC record available at https://lccn.loc.gov/2024019298
LC ebook record available at https://lccn.loc.gov/2024019299

ISBN 978-1-5011-9148-0
ISBN 978-1-5011-9150-3 (ebook)

For my mother, Linda Johanson,
every word.

There are no goodbyes for us.
Wherever you are, you will always be in my heart.
—Mahatma Gandhi

Three great ages;
the age of the yew tree,
the age of the eagle,
and the age of the Cailleach Bhéara.

—Proverb from West Connacht

P

THE
ORCADES

Moray Firth

Gray Mts.   CRAIG   BURGHEAD
             PHADRIG   FORTRESS

DUN   DUNADD
MONAIDH

Firth of Clyde

PICTLAND

MANNAU
STIRLING

GODODDIN

STRATH-
CLYDE   BERNICIA

The
Narrow
Sea   SELGOVAE

RHEGED

SCOTIA
(THE
WESTLANDS)   CAER
                  GREU

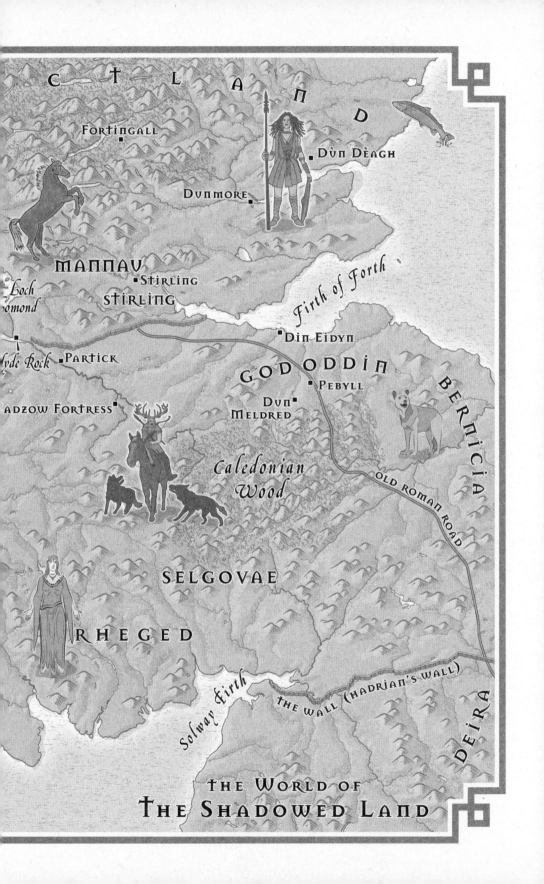

THE WORLD OF
THE SHADOWED LAND

THE PEOPLE

The Angles
Ælle: King of Deira
Æthelfrith: son of Æthelric, grandson of Ida
Æthelric: Angle lord of Bernicia, son of Ida
Hussa: King of Bernicia
Ida: Angle conqueror
Theobald: son of Æthelric, grandson of Ida

The Britons
Kingdom of Strathclyde
House of Morken
Brodyn: Languoreth's cousin, former captain of her guard
Eira: Lailoken's wife, born Gwendolen, daughter of Urien of
    Rheged
Gwenddolau: Uther Pendragon, Lailoken and Languoreth's
    foster brother
Lailoken: Counsellor of Strathclyde, Languoreth's twin brother
Languoreth: Queen of Strathclyde, Rhydderch's wife
Torin: captain of Languoreth's guard

House of Tutgual
Angharad: second daughter of Rhydderch and Languoreth
Cyan: second son of Rhydderch and Languoreth
Tutgual: King of Strathclyde

Elufed: Queen of Strathclyde, a Pict

Gladys: firstborn daughter of Rhydderch and Languoreth

Morcant: eldest son of Tutgual

Rhydderch: King of Strathclyde, Languoreth's husband, second
    son of Tutgual

Rhys: eldest son of Rhydderch and Languoreth

The Christians

Brother Anguen: head monk in Mungo's order

Brother Thomas: culdee

Mungo: Counsellor of Strathclyde, former bishop of Strathclyde

Kingdom of Selgovae

Maelgwn: Dragon Warrior and the 3rd Pendragon

Fendwin: Dragon Warrior

Diarmid: Wisdom Keeper

Archer: Chieftain of the Selgovae

Kingdom of Ebrauc

Peredur: King of Northern Ebrauc

Gwrgi: King of Southern Ebrauc, Peredur's brother

Euerdil: Urien of Rheged's sister, Gwrgi and Peredur's mother

Kingdom of Gododdin

Cywyllog: wife of Meldred

Meldred: Chieftain of Southern Gododdin, Aedan's grandson

Kingdom of Rheged

Urien: King of Rheged

Eira: Urien's daughter, birth name Gwendolen, fostered by
    Euerdil

Owain: Lord of Rheged, Urien's eldest son
Elffin: Lord of Rheged, Urien's son
Penarwan: wife of Owain

The Picts
Ariane: priestess, the Orcades, Languoreth's former counsellor
Bridei: High King of the Picts
Briochan: head Wisdom Keeper, Bridei's foster father
Gogfran: King of Stirling
Eachna: High Priestess at Fortingall Muirenn: chieftain of Dùn
     Dèagh
Imogen: Briochan's wife
Talorcan: warrior, Muirenn's lover
Rhainn: Pictish commander
Vanora: Gogfran of Stirling's daughter

The Scots
Aedan mac Gabrahn: King of Mannau and Dalriada
Ana: daughter of Aedan, Meldred's mother
Artúr: Aedan's son
Bedwyr: warrior of Mannau
Bran: son of Aedan, Artúr's brother
Cai: warrior, Artúr's foster brother
Chaorunn: Wisdom Keeper in Dalriada
Domangart: son of Aedan, Artúr's half-brother
Eiddilig the Small: warrior of Mannau
Eochaid Bude & Eochaid Find: twins, Artúr's half-brothers
Gabrahn: Aedan's father
Gartnait: son of Aedan, Artúr's half-brother
Maithgemma: daughter of Aedan
Young Ewan: Artúr's ghillie

PRONUNCIATIONS

Angharad: "An-HA-rad"
Arderydd: "Ard-dur-ITH"
Ariane: "Ah-REE-AH-nee"
Artúr: "ar-TOOR"
Bedwyr: "BED-oo-eer"
Bridei: "BRI-dee"
Briochan: "BREE-o-can"
Brodyn: "BRO-din"
Cai: "k-EYE"
Cyan: "KY-ann"
Cywyllog: "Coo-ETH-log"
Eachna: "AUCK-na"
Eiddilig: "ETH-il-egg"
Eira: "EYE-ra"
Elufed: "El-LEAF-ed"
Eochaid: "YOCH-id"
Gladys: "GLA-diss"
Gododdin: "God-DO-thin"
Gogfran: "Gog-VRAN"
Gwenddolau: "GWEN-tho-lye"
Gwrgi: "Ga-WHERE-gi"
Lailoken: "LIE-lo-kin"
Languoreth: "Lang-GOR-eth"

Maelgwn: "MILE-gwinn"
Peredur: "PEAR-REE-dur"
Rhainn: "RAIN"
Rhydderch: "RU-therk"
Rhys: "REEse"
Tutgual: "TOOT-gee-al"

In the 1830s, a group of quarrymen discovered a body buried on a hilltop east of Dunipace, Scotland. The skeleton had been laid to rest in an ancient coffin of unhewn stone. No weapons, jewelry, mirrors, or combs were found in the grave. The only accompanying artifacts were a simple earthenware vase and, inside it, the decayed remains of what looked like parchment. A report was published in the *New Statistical Account of Scotland* and the body was removed so quarrying could continue.

Where the skeleton was sent, or whether it was reburied elsewhere, no one knows. The body, the coffin, and the earthenware vase have all been lost.

Along with the parchment, and whatever had been written upon it.

CHAPTER 1

Languoreth

Dùn Meldred, Southern Kingdom of Gododdin
Land of the Britons
2nd of July, AD 580

It began with a dream.

Those were the first words my daughter uttered after eight years missing. Angharad was dead. Or so I'd been told. When I sat at my weaving, eyes touched upon me with pity. *Look at the woman who has lost both daughter and son.* I met their gaze, unflinching. Yes, I am still here. It is a wonder, is it not, what the heart can survive?

I heard them whisper, *Some say she still keeps counsel with their ghosts.*

Perhaps they were right. For only yesterday I had watched my lost daughter glide like a specter across a battlefield. Who was this woman who kept company with Pictish warriors, ink marking her body and hair falling down her back in a mass of ruddy coils? She wore a cloak made of feathers, beaded and slick from driving rain.

From a distance, I'd not known her at first, my own child. The relentless churn of time can do such things. After all, how could I have imagined the woman she'd become?

Now she stood beside me high upon the ramparts of a fortress, her gray eyes somber as we looked out across a field of the dead. On the muddy expanse below, warriors prodded the fallen, hoping to finish any enemies who yet lived. Soon, the corpse birds would come.

Lord Meldred's Hall sat like an eagle's nest high above the Tweed River Valley, commanding views of the Dreva Hills. Spears of summer sun pierced the blue-black clouds overhead. It was the sort of light that followed a storm, casting the grassy lands of Dùn Meldred in a gilded light that belied the massacre below, where men lay like effigies, eyes unblinking. My body still thrummed from the terrors of war, but I pushed it aside, reaching instead for Angharad's hand. Along the creamy underside of her wrist, a trail of birds had been pricked in black ink.

"Crows?" I asked. Had she remembered what I'd told her of my old teacher Cathan, or how our hearts were like birds, pricked full of feathers? But the look she gave me was veiled, unyielding.

"We cannot speak of our markings," she said.

I felt a stab. *We cannot speak.* My daughter was a stranger, no longer a Briton. Last evening I'd overheard her speaking with the Picts, their tongue rushing from her lips like water. Now, when she spoke Brythonic, it was with the cadence of one who came from the north. I did not want to ask how long she would stay, for I knew she would not. I looked at our joined hands.

"You must forgive me. I cannot help but touch you," I said. "This morning when I woke, I worried it all was a dream, your returning."

Angharad looked at me, her gray eyes taking my measure, but said nothing. If she was angry, she had every right: I was her mother, meant to protect her, yet I'd sent her away when she was just a child. My reasoning had been sound. Angharad had a gift. But what did that matter? I had sent her away, and she'd been lost to war. She and her elder brother, Rhys, whose first battle had been his last.

"You must know," I said, "not a day went by that we did not search for you. I carry the loss of your brother like a boulder. But a child gone missing is worse than any death. The trickery of hope is enough to drive a mother mad. We searched for you in kingdom upon kingdom, our search sputtering out again and again on the shores of either sea. I am shamed to say, the days I woke and wondered if you might be dead, I felt the smallest relief. For at least in death I knew you could not be suffering."

Angharad looked out over the hills.

"There are those who call the kingdom of the Picts the Shadowed Lands," she said. "I cannot blame them. One can scarcely imagine its vastness. There are mountains upon mountains, countless rivers and lochs that furrow the land. It is a world unto itself. Deep and hidden. As a child, I feared it. But now I cannot imagine who I might have become had I not known it. Now there is no other place that feels like my home."

I could not help but marvel at her—this young woman who'd dreamt that an army of Angles was marching to make war upon the Britons. She had returned to us with a band of Pictish warriors who had turned the tide of the battle. I had been headstrong and impetuous at her age. Angharad's training had wrought her into a woman far wiser than her seventeen winters.

After the Battle of the Caledonian Wood, as our celebration had cooled to embers, I'd listened with a tortured sort of rapture as Angharad described what had become of her as a child all those winters ago, in the Battle of Arderydd. She'd run to my brother's hut in the woods to find his wife, Eira, waiting. They'd escaped the fighting only to be taken by Gwrgi of Ebrauc. Though he said he meant to deliver Angharad to her father, Eira knew he could not be trusted. Their attempt to escape left Angharad alone in the forest. There she met a monk who promised to deliver her to safety, but their boat was set upon by Picts, and Angharad found herself held captive once more.

Since that day, she'd been hidden away in the shadowed lands of the Cruithni, the first people. Over time, her memories of home grew distant. She began her training as a priestess. She woke one day to find that she no longer wished to escape.

"Angharad . . . ," I said now. But for some things, there are no words. She turned to me, reading my face.

"It wasn't your fault, Mother. All that passed was meant to be. I do not blame you for it."

I reached out with my free hand to smooth her coiled hair. "You are so at ease in the hands of the Gods. They have snatched you up as if you were their treasure, when always you have been mine." I reluctantly lowered my hand from her hair as if she were a thing forbidden. "I strive to be devoted. I have even felt their touch. But giving you up was one of the most difficult demands they have made of me. And now, knowing all the misfortune you suffered, I do not know if I can ever be at peace."

Angharad looked at me as if I'd somehow disappointed her. "It was not misfortune, Mother. Can't you see?" She took a breath as if to say more, but the moment was broken by a shout from the battlefield. She lifted her hand to block the sun, squinting into the distance.

She pointed. "There."

Far across the fields, where the river Tweed snaked beneath the Dreva Hills, a cluster of warriors was racing to surround a wounded man. They'd discovered him as they were rooting through the nearby heap of dead warriors, no doubt. But from the way he loped, half crouched as he attempted to run, he appeared close to death himself.

"He must have hidden beneath that pile of the dead," Angharad said.

"Yes," I agreed. "And that standing stone will be Drumelzier Haugh." I nodded at the specked stone in the distance. Our warriors closed on him like a pack of hunting dogs, but not before he'd reached the tall gray stone beside the river, falling against it as one embraces a mother.

The man was claiming sanctuary.

The warriors stepped aside as Torin, captain of my guard, pushed through. I did not know much of the ancestral stones here; these were the lands of our neighbors, the Britons of Gododdin. But sanctuary was a right by law, and—enemy or no—our warriors would not risk dishonoring the dead.

Torin turned and looked up, searching out the place where I stood, and I motioned impatiently, my voice carrying across the pasture from the great height.

"Bring him," I called out. They snatched up the prisoner, tossing him onto a nearby cart, and I took my daughter's elbow.

"Come, we'll meet them at the lower gate," I said. "I am curious about this man. He may be of value."

Angharad nodded. I glanced over my shoulder at the fort as we trod the mud-slick path, wary of meddling. My husband, the high king of Strathclyde, was out hunting survivors with Lord Meldred and the Dragon Warriors. With Rhydderch away, my word was held highest. But the battle was scarcely over, and Lord Meldred's swineherds still milled the grounds with their wolfhounds close at heel. The wayward warriors would be all too eager to wet their blades with Angle blood.

The sturdy doors of the outer gate eased open and my warriors urged the mule-drawn cart through. I studied the wounded man as the cart rattled closer. Older than twenty winters, yet still younger than thirty. His hair was the color of ash bark, his beard trimmed to a point, darkened by blood. His eyes were a pale blue and his skin was waxen. He'd lost much blood. He grunted in pain as my men hoisted him, propping him against the back of the cart so I might look him in the eye. Torin was already frowning. It seemed the man had tested his patience.

"We discovered him skulking beneath the dead. He claimed sanctuary before we could spear him," he said.

"Has he given his name?" I asked.

"He has refused, my lady."

"Is that so?" There was something distinctive about him, something in his bearing that made me wonder if he might be nobility. I moved to stand before him. "Tell me, then. What is your name?"

The man turned away.

"Obstinate," I observed.

I looked to Torin, giving a slight nod, and he jabbed the butt of his blade against the man's weeping stomach wound. The man expelled an animal sound, collapsing in pain.

"Your name," I said.

He looked up, eyes searching the sky overhead. "My name . . . is Ealhstan," he said.

Beside me, Angharad shook her head. She leaned in, speaking softly in my ear. "Ealhstan is not his name."

I did not question my daughter's gifts.

"My daughter is wise," I said. "Lie to me and I will discover it. And it will be far the worse for you, Angle."

"I have given . . . my name."

I tossed him a reproachful look, and Torin leveled his blade at the man's throat as I leaned over the splintered edge of the cart.

"You have claimed sanctuary," I said. "However, I wonder: Is sanctuary to be honored in times such as these? What honor have your people shown in slaughtering good Britons, in burning our homes as you swarmed from your stolen lands at the edge of our eastern sea? And not for the first time," I added. "I was a child of ten when Ida the Angle took the kingdom of Bryneich. I saw what 'honor' the Angles were made of then. Babies smashed against rocks. Children made motherless, limping to my father's gates in states of gore. I wrapped their wounds with my own two hands."

I gestured and Torin pressed the point of his blade to the skin.

"You wear the clothes of a footman, yet I sense you are learned. I am learned, too. Do you know who I am?"

He coughed, his look dismissive. "You are Languoreth of Strathclyde. Wife of Rhydderch. They call you the 'Lioness of Damnonia.'"

I glanced at Torin. *The Lioness of Damnonia?* This was a name we had not heard.

"Yes, I am Languoreth of Strathclyde. But who are you?" I said. "I possess some knowledge of Anglisc, thin as your tongue may be. *Eahl-Stan.* It means 'sacred stone,' does it not? Come, now. You insult me."

"I have claimed sanctuary," he said. "Kill me, and you do so before the eyes of the Gods."

"Your sanctuary means nothing to me. The Morrigu rode with the Britons today. I'm certain she would not deny me the satisfaction of your death." I considered him. "But I believe you to be a noble. You do not wish me to know your value, should I offer you up for trade. Despite our victory, there can be no doubt that your people have prisoners, too. I assume, then, that you are worth a good deal to your king."

His face betrayed nothing, which only made me keener.

"I will discover who you are. But should you die of your wounds before I come to it? Well. The decision shall be made for me. Who is to say? Perhaps I am as dim-witted as you think."

I turned to Torin. "He'll give us nothing more now. Take him to the prison hut."

Torin gave the order. As the cart rolled uphill, Angharad stared after it as if figuring a puzzle.

"What is it?" I asked.

"That man. He looked familiar. As if I have seen him somewhere before."

"The Angle? Are you certain?"

Her gray eyes were distant, her fingers fidgeting along the inside of her palm. "Yes, I'm certain. Perhaps it will come to me."

"It will, my love. I do not doubt it." If I was right, and the man was indeed noble, he could not be traded in such a state. He would likely die on the journey, which was no use to us at all. I paused, torn between a mother's caution and the desire to allow my daughter to ply her gifts.

"Will you tend to him?" I asked. "You're a strong healer. Far better than I ever was. His life could be worth ten or even twenty of our own warriors in exchange."

"Yes," she said. "I will see to it."

"Good," I said. "But I do not trust him. I'll send two of my men to keep watch at the door."

"If you wish it," she said, seeming unworried. "I'll go and gather my basket."

"Thank you, Angharad."

"Of course, Mother."

Mother. The word sounded strange coming from her lips. I watched as she followed the cart up the steep slope of the fortress to fetch her supplies. There was a chasm between us now, and I felt the rift like breaking earth. She was a child of the Gods, I reminded myself. I had given her up long ago.

"My lady?" Torin's deep voice stirred me from my thoughts.

"Yes. What is it?"

His blue eyes held concern. "Will you return to the Hall, then?"

"No." I frowned. "The man is a noble, don't you agree? He must have swapped garments with a footman. Let's return to the battlefield. Perhaps we'll find something that gives him away."

"Well enough." Torin nodded, offering his arm. My boots squelched in the muck as we followed my men back through the open gate, and I yanked at the hem of my dress impatiently as it caught in the slop, tangling about my feet.

"What Angle lords are accounted for? I cannot remember," I said.

"Quite a few," he said. "Come, then. I will show you."

We strode side by side, easy in our silence. It had been seven winters since I'd plucked the fair-haired sentry from his place guarding
Tutgual's prison pits, and he'd become invaluable to me since. I felt
closer to Torin than I did to my only living son, though it saddened
me to think it. Now twenty-two winters, Cyan carried too much of
Tutgual's blood. Where Cyan was prone to rage, Torin was level as
a woodworker's plane. Smart and precise, Torin was, above all, honorable. Too often now when I looked at my son, I sensed a growing
darkness, as if something within him twisted as he grew.

I took a breath as we neared the place where our trophies had been
thrust upon pikes beyond the outer rampart of the fortress. Fifteen in
all, each bearing an Angle's head, gruesomely severed. This is what became of those who waged war upon the Britons. But it was not the gore
I need steel myself against; rather, it was the memory it summoned.
My cousin Brant's head, taken as a trophy by Rhydderch's brother,
Morcant, after the battle of Arderydd. I closed my eyes against it, but
it tore through me all the same, the way his blood-blackened hair had
crackled beneath my fingers as I'd drawn his head from the pike.

"Are you well?" Torin asked. "You needn't look if it troubles you."

"No, Torin. It isn't that. Go on."

"If you're certain."

"It would be a help to see their bodies. Where are they?" I asked.

"Piled to be burnt. The men have already gathered any plunder."
He turned to them. "Find the corpses and line them up here, brothers."

As the men struck out to pair bodies with heads as best as could be
managed, I lifted my gaze to the faces of the dead. I had thought, by
my age, I would be more accustomed to it. But each face was night-
marish. Motherhood changed a woman more than becoming a queen
ever could. Each of these men had been a babe once, no less beloved
than my own.

Torin gestured to the pike bearing the head of an old, balding man. "That will be Rawdon. And there is Wacian, or I'm a fool," he added. Despite his measured tone, Torin's eyes were lit like a child's on a festival day. In passing winters, Torin had excelled in his position. As volunteers came to join my guard, he quickly distinguished their gifts and put them to good use, for not all were warriors—some were even women. I now possessed not only a strong and loyal guard but also a growing number of men and women who kept close watch from other kingdoms, sending news and information. So it was that the features of every high-ranking Angle lord was known to Torin. He'd seen to it. But he had seen few of them himself.

I gestured to a man's head with long strands of tangled black hair. "And this man? Who is he?"

Torin leaned closer, his blue eyes keen. "Him I do not know." He called to the men, now returning with bodies. "Who took this trophy, then?"

A thick, freckled warrior with ginger hair stepped forward. "It was I."

"Did you slay him in battle?" Torin questioned.

"Nay, I cannot claim it. I found him by the river," The man gestured toward the standing stone.

"What was taken off him?" I asked. "I would see what he was stripped of."

The warrior reached into his padded leather vest. "His was not the armor of a king, my lady. A lesser nobleman, perhaps. He wore this." He withdrew a brown leather belt with a golden buckle, handing it to me. The delicate metalwork gleamed in the sun, interlacing knots of Angle craftsmanship. Amidst the swirling nest of gold a lion bared its teeth.

"Æthelric of Bernicia and his kin claim the lion, do they not?" I asked.

Torin looked over my shoulder. "Aye. The lion belongs to Æthelric, a son of Ida."

Ida the Angle had ruled in my youth and had issued twelve sons. Those twelve bore countless sons of their own, and I confess I knew only a scattering by name. I glanced at the corpse head. "This man seems too young to be Æthelric. What of his sons?"

"He has two who are grown. Theobald and Æthelfrith." Torin examined the dead man's head. "Theobald's head is shaven, I am told. Æthelfrith is said to be brown of hair, but it is light in color. Not nearly so dark as this."

"The man in the prison hut has light brown hair. What if he swapped clothing with this fellow, hoping to escape the battlefield unnoticed? This could very well be the head of a footman. "

"If we do hold a spawn of Ida, no doubt they'll be eager for his return," Torin said.

"You are right." I handed the golden buckle back to the warrior. "Thank you. You may keep this."

The warrior bowed and I turned to Torin.

"Dead men can't be traded. It is good, then, that Angharad will see to him. When Rhydderch and the men return, I'll speak to him about the prisoner exchange. I'm certain they've found others."

"We mustn't keep him long lest he hear or see too much," Torin said.

"Yes," I agreed.

A spawn of Ida, the first Angle to bring ruin to our lands. I could not forget the horrors I'd witnessed as a child at his hands. As we turned back to the fortress where the Angle now lay, the girl I'd once been pounded in my marrow, demanding revenge. But she was impetuous; the woman I'd become was measured. Any grandchild of Ida was worth a great deal, and we would need all our leaders returned, if indeed they yet lived. This man's life was not mine to take.

"I should have known him on sight," Torin said.

"Torin, he was much disguised by blood. You could be one of Mungo's Christians for how you flagellate yourself."

Torin only frowned.

"If you'd like, I could arrange for a goat's-hair shirt," I said. "I hear Mungo wears just such a one beneath his robes."

"You should not jest of Mungo, my lady," he said. "He watches you. And now that he returns in our company to Strathclyde, there is no telling what he may do."

"I must find humor where I can, else I would weep," I said. "I still cannot fathom that my own husband would bring such a dangerous man back to court. Believe me, Torin, I above all know what Mungo is capable of."

We fell into silence, the echoes of my past rumbling in my head. As we neared the upper gate, I stopped.

"I saw a spider this morning as I was dressing," I said. "She was sat high in the corner of the guest quarters, silent, building her web. I watched her awhile, her delicate legs working. 'How beautiful it would be, to be a spider,' I thought. Sticky is her silk; there is nothing that passes that she cannot catch."

I looked at him sidelong, dropping my voice so only he might hear.

"It was a sign, Torin. Sent from the Gods. For now that I am queen, I need a *gwyliwr*. A watcher. My brother is to be head counsellor, along with Mungo. Lailoken is in danger, too. We must build a greater web, one that catches every whisper. I must have eyes ever watchful, ears pressed to every door."

"You . . . wish me to be your *gwyliwr*?" Torin asked.

"I can imagine no other."

"But I am no spymaster. I know far too little of the craft."

"Torin, you have done as much already. Your aptitude is beyond argument. You have learnt the image of nearly every Angle lord in

Bernicia. How came that to be?" I did not wait for his answer. "You have placed men and women among the Angles—no simple feat. There is no other I would trust. Please. It must be you."

He considered it. "We would need more scouts. That will require barter and coin. And in Partick, we must have someone among the Christians."

I thought of my chamberwoman Desdemona, her dark head bowed before the blade, and an old wound twisted in my gut. I did not wish to speak of it—not her betrayal, nor the choice I'd had to make.

"I tried as much, once," I said. "It did not fare well."

"Then we must try again," Torin said.

"It is not so simple."

"No," he said. "In this realm, nothing is simple. But it *can* be done," he said. "There is that man we spoke of. That hermit in the wood. Perhaps we should begin there."

"Do you mean to say you agree?" I asked. "You will do it?"

He took a breath, then blew it out. "Aye. I'll do it."

I clasped his arm and squeezed it, unable to keep the emotion from my voice. "I am grateful for you, Torin of Mann."

He nodded, clearing his throat. "The men will soon return. We must quicken our pace."

Up ahead, the fortress loomed from its perch on the hill like a hungry bird. Torin urged me on, his light eyes unwavering.

"You say you are in need of a greater web, my lady. Together, we shall build it."

CHAPTER 2

Angharad

A ngharad followed the narrow path toward the prison hut, her palms throbbing. Curious. They were such old wounds. Yet sometimes, in sunlight, she could still see the places where the thorns had embedded at the Battle of Arderydd as she tumbled from the heights of Caer Gwenddolau. So many winters had passed. It was strange that her body begged her to remember now, and the sensation plucked at her as she passed the kitchen house, where spits were being tended by hollow-eyed servants hungry for meat.

Brother Thomas had warned her, hadn't he?

Pluck the thorn, and it is gone from you. The hole will heal, and your skin soon forgets. Let it linger and, in time, your body may eat the thorn away. But the thorns will be in your blood, going round and round within you, forever.

A shiver traced her arms despite the warmth of the day, causing the willow basket hanging from the crook of her arm to slip. In a world made of war, every novice learned healing, and despite the fact that it wasn't Angharad's calling, even she had to admit she had a knack for it. She hoisted the basket as she spotted the dank wattled hut where four men stood guard before a padlocked door. Two belonged to her mother, the others to Lord Meldred.

The taller soldier stepped forward. "We are to accompany you. The man might well be dangerous," he said. But a gaming board was set on the small pine stool between him and one of Meldred's men, and the other two held ale horns. All looked worn through.

"The man is more dead than living," Angharad said. "Listen out if you will."

"Aye, then." The soldier twisted the key in the iron padlock and waited as she ducked into the dim confines of the chamber. As Angharad's eyes adjusted she was met by the smell of rot. The prisoner was curled upon a dirty sheepskin, his back to the door.

"I've come to dress your wounds," she said. The man stirred only slightly, grunting as he turned with some effort onto his back. Of course he would let her. Otherwise he would die. Alone in the hut with him, the prickle of knowing she'd felt would not leave her. But her mind was a sluggish thing, her senses weakened from long days on foot and the immediate onslaught of battle.

Return, she commanded her memories as she set down her basket. But the memories in which this man might be found had long been banished to the bottom of a waterfall. She squatted but did not touch him—not yet. Angle or no, each touch would be agony. She didn't wish to poke and prod until she'd seen the entirety of his injuries.

"You are cavalry, even if you are not a nobleman," she observed.

The man scoffed but said nothing.

"Oh, come. I can see it here. Nearly all of the blows were dealt to your legs. You were mounted, on horseback. Until someone speared you, that is, in your stomach. Then you fell from your horse." Angharad peered at his stomach. "You had good armor as well. The spear did not pierce all the way through. Perhaps it is true what they say: fortune favors the rich."

The man lolled his head to regard her with what looked like a grudging respect, and Angharad rolled up her sleeves. "Are you ready, then?"

He nodded, closing his eyes, and she reached for him. But as the tips of her fingers met his clammy skin, memories crashed back in a torrent: There she stood upon the grassy banks of the river Tyne, Brother Thomas at her side. Upriver, a small currach glided toward them, four figures at oar and a captain. His eyes were pale and his hair ash brown. His beard was groomed and trimmed to a point.

Angharad yanked back her hands as if she'd been burned.

"You," she said. "You were the Angle trader from the river Tyne."

It was astonishing how his face shifted then. He shot up onto his elbows, eyes widening as if Angharad were an adder.

"You . . . ," he breathed. "You were that girl, a *wicce*! You cursed my sister and she died!"

"Your sister, was she?" Angharad stiffened. "She stole my mother's torque. Stole from a child."

I curse you, she'd shouted at the oarswoman. *I curse you to die!*

"*Wicce*," he repeated.

Angharad threw him a disapproving look. "I am no witch. I'm a Wisdom Keeper. One would think you would know the look of one. After all, you are certainly not a Christian."

He'd tossed the beautiful wooden cross Brother Thomas had carved into the river.

"Besides," she added. "Your sister died by a Pictish spear."

She narrowed her eyes. "The question is, who are you? You are no simple trader. You've taken great pains to keep yourself secret. Traded clothing with another soldier, no doubt. Was he dead already, or were you the one to kill him?"

The man's jaw twitched and he looked away.

"That's fine. You needn't speak," she said, setting to work on his wounds.

Words were a distraction in any case. Visions would come if she bade them. His body would turn traitor.

The Angle watched her with a withering look of a warrior who'd suffered injuries far worse than these. But behind his practiced gaze, Angharad sensed a subtle pulsing: a longing for home.

Tell me more, she invited. But the wounded man seemed curious of her, too.

"Your mother is queen," he observed.

"Yes," Angharad allowed, packing a poultice. "And the torque your sister stole was a family treasure. It was given to my mother by her father when she was a child."

The man only shrugged.

Angharad paused, looking up. "I must commend you on your mastery of Brythonic. As I recall, you scarcely spoke a word at all." She lifted her hands in imitation. "*'I . . . am . . . Angle trader!'*"

She'd expected the man to bristle, but he laughed instead, coughing.

"Amusing, is it?" She raised a brow. "What were you doing on the river, then?"

He looked at her a moment, deciding something. "Scouting," he said.

"Of course. The Angles knew war had been waged upon Uther Pendragon. You wanted to see the destruction for yourself." Angharad was surprised by the anger in her own voice. She had thought herself healed, but the presence of this man was picking at scars.

"Uther was a great warrior," he said.

Angharad fell quiet. She'd loved her uncle, with his two great golden eagles. She'd admired him. Though to her, he would always be Gwenddolau. The Angle mistook the softening in her eyes for opportunity.

"Listen," he said, lowering his voice. "You are a Wisdom Keeper. Surely you know the Gods have put you before me. You must help me escape."

"You know I cannot," Angharad scoffed.

"Then your healing is wasted."

"No healing is wasted."

"Hussa will only kill me," he said.

"Hussa your king? But you fought for him in battle."

"Indeed. He placed me where I most certainly would die."

"But you lived."

The thought did not console him. He turned to stare at the wall. In the silence that settled, the vision Angharad had sought came at last, weaving its dreamlike filaments between her skin and his. It whispered of the man he was and, possibly, the man he would become. Angharad saw a wooden Hall perched upon a steep, grassy mount, surrounded by the sea. The great room breathed with hearth smoke beneath high beams of sturdy timber. The man sat on a bench at the edge of the Hall, a woman by his side. Her hand rested on his thigh, but his pale eyes were fixed upon the throne.

"You wish to be king," Angharad said aloud. If the man startled, he recovered quickly.

"What I wish is no matter, for soon I will be dead," he said, baiting her. But Angharad would not offer up her visions to the enemy.

She secured the last of his packings with a knot. "I am finished. If you should die, it will not be by my hands."

The man sank back onto the dirty sheepskin, and Angharad glanced round the putrid hut. Blood stained the earthen floor. How many had met their end here? Enemy or not, she could not help but pity him. This was the curse of the healer. Angle, Pict, Briton, Scot— their wounds and pale bodies all looked the same. They were all once children, loved by their mothers.

Returning the supplies to her basket, she stood. "Rest, then. I will send someone to change your poultices."

"You will not return?"

"No, I will not."

The man coughed and looked up. "I must thank you, then," he said stiffly. "I . . . shall think of you with kindness for what you have done."

They regarded each other for a moment. His words felt like oak.

"I wish you well," Angharad said, then thudded on the door. As the sentries secured the iron padlock behind her, a name came in a whisper.

Flesaur. The Twister.

Not his given name, perhaps, but it left her ill at ease. She'd share it with her mother. Angharad followed the cobbled path up to Meldred's Hall, deep in thought. The aching in her palms had ceased, yet the memory of the oarswoman still lingered behind closed eyes.

I curse you. I curse you to die! She could still taste the bitterness in her mouth as she'd shouted it, still hear the woman's scream as the Pictish spear sailed from the trees overhead, piercing the woman through the eye. Brother Thomas had assured her the woman's death was not her doing, but even then, Angharad had known the power of her Gods. A curse was a serious matter. If wrought without cause, it would harm its creator. Cursewomen bartered on such business and oft paid the price. She'd seen them as she traveled through settlements: age fell upon them more quickly. Illness, too. There had been lovesick girls at both Fortingall and Woodwick who had dabbled in tablets, symbols of malice carved into wood. No good ever came of it.

But a curse uttered from the mouth of the righteous? It was the call of a fledgling, demanding its mother. The Gods did not suffer injustices done to their children.

She stopped on the hilltop not far from the Hall, looking out over the distance. Clouds piled like fleece over the Dreva Hills. Angharad looked out over the wide green- and yellow-grassed valley to the place where the dark river bent and the ancient stone stood.

Why has this man come to us? she wondered. Bird flesh pricked her arms, the kind that arrived on the tail of paths and their alignments. Whatever his purpose, it would be revealed only in time. But Angharad sensed him in days to come. *Flesaur*. His spirit cast a long shadow.

She stood a long while, hoping for a sign: a flicker of sunlight over the hills, or the far-off swoop of a bird. Instead, the only things she saw were the distant specks of men upon horseback. She rubbed her eyes, tired of the sort of dreaming that left her wondering whether what she was seeing belonged to this world or the next. But no. The men were quite real. They were streaming into the valley from the Old Roman Road. And as the wind caught their banners, the fabric pulled taut.

Red and black.

Angharad's stomach soured. These were the banners of Ebrauc. It seemed Gwrgi and Peredur, the kings of Ebrauc, had survived the battle after all.

"Angharad. There you are."

Angharad spun to see Eira emerging from Meldred's Hall. Her hair gleamed golden in the sun and her cheeks were flushed from the Hall's summer heat.

"Angharad, what is it?" Her uncle's wife looked puzzled. "You look as if you've seen a shade."

"The men of Ebrauc have returned."

Eira's face fell. She looked out over the fields.

"I thought Gwrgi might be dead," she said. "I should have known better. Evil is no easy thing to kill."

Run, Eira had told her, that night. *I will follow right behind*.

But Eira had not followed. Angharad had concealed herself in the bushes just beyond the tent. Eira did not know that Angharad had heard her cries that night, heard what men thought they could get away with in times of war, as if true darkness could ever be banished by morning's light.

In fact, Angharad had not spoken of it to anyone. She had left it in the pool at the base of the falls. She had been healed by Eachna at Fortingall by tree and by stone. But just like the thorns, the echoes thrummed still.

As the warriors of Ebrauc reached the lower gate, Eira's face paled. Angharad took her arm.

"Lailoken and the others will soon return," she said. "Until then we must hide you away, somewhere you'll be safe. My mother's quarters. Come, I will take you."

"Hide me away?" Eira stiffened and drew back. "Whatever do you mean?"

Angharad cursed. It was delicate, this dance of pretending. Eira would suffer if she realized what Angharad truly knew.

"Gwrgi has not set eyes upon you since putting you on the prison cart," Angharad said quickly. "Forgive me, Eira. My mother told me as much."

Eira glanced down at the line of men on horseback winding their way up the hill. Angharad wanted to beg. *Eira, you needn't face them.* But Eira's back was straight as a rod.

"We needn't speak of it." Eira reached for her hands, her lips wearing a smile that did not match her eyes. "It was you and I, wasn't it, when they came upon us, after the battle. It is right that we are together now."

"Yes," Angharad said, pressing Eira's fingers in hers. "It is right."

Turning, they strode briskly uphill, Gwrgi's arrival chasing like a shadow at their backs. Hand in hand, they thrust open the doors of the Hall like children wishing to prove they no longer held a fear of the dark.

CHAPTER 3

Languoreth

The Hall smelled of oil smoke, of wicks burnt too low, and the acrid taste settled in the back of my throat as I entered. Mungo turned from his conversation by the hearth with Lord Meldred's wife, Cywyllog. His gaze felt like winter, but I met his blue eyes unflinchingly. *I am no longer the child you frightened in the wood.* How it must rankle him that of all the Britons it was I, Morken's daughter, who now reigned over Strathclyde. After all, it was my father who brought about his exile. And I was determined to see him banished again.

Across the room, Ariane, my former counsellor, leaned against the wall in her blue cloak, watching the men and women of Meldred's court with an idle disdain, and I slipped round the outskirts of the great room to join her. This Hall, and nearly all of those in it, had become repellent after so many days in cramped quarters. I would have clawed from my own skin if it promised escape.

"You look as I feel," I told her, nodding at the room.

"Gatherings like this are quite unnatural," Ariane said. "Britons hide behind high stone walls with good reason."

"You are right. I suppose the last occasion that thrust together Britons, Picts, and Scots was the coming of Rome." I smiled, but the thought was sobering.

"I imagine you are eager to return to your far-flung isle," I said. "Gatherings of any sort have always been unnatural for you."

Her pale, delicate face eased at the thought of it. "Yes, I will return to the Orcades, at least for the time being," she said.

It was still a shock to see her standing before me, close enough to touch, though Ariane had never been one for embraces. I had loved her and trusted her above all, and she had left me without so much as a farewell. Her departure had wounded; it felt a betrayal. And I had not seen her since. Now she'd returned in the company of my daughter, but neither would stay. Wisdom Keepers answered a call beyond my hearing.

"All these winters passed, and I still do not know the reason you left," I said. I meant to speak evenly, but it came hotly, an accusation.

"You knew the conditions of my counsellorship, Languoreth. I did not leave because I did not care for you. I left because it was time." Ariane's eyes were a mild summer evening, and her words made me feel like a child. After all, she'd told me when she arrived at Cadzow that she would not stay forever. I swallowed the thickness in my throat.

"It cannot be an easy life, living at the whim of the wind," I said.

"No life is easy." Ariane eyed my torque. "It is only a matter of which difficult task we are summoned to do. Is that not so, Queen Languoreth?"

Her words held a weight that left my stomach feeling heavy. "I cannot say I have fulfilled the hopes of those who placed me here," I said. The Angle man had called me the Lioness of Damnonia, but in truth I did not know what I had done to earn that title. I'd rescued a slave cart of Gwenddolau's people—people of the Old Way—many of whom were still safe in my service at Cadzow. I kept the old festivals. I prayed to the Gods and kept watch for their signs. But while battles came and went, and loved ones died, I could not help but feel I was little more than a figurehead, put in place to placate my people while the Christian power grew. I searched Ariane's face for the answer I'd been grasping after all of these years. But her gaze was fixed upon Mungo as he joined the cluster of monks near Lord Meldred's table.

"Perhaps your summons had not yet arrived," Ariane replied. I followed her gaze.

"It has always been him, hasn't it? My purpose and his—they have always been intertwined."

Ariane did not answer; she needn't. She reached instead to tuck a wayward strand of her dark hair back into her plait, and I spotted streaks of silver sprouting at her temples. A desperate sort of loneliness struck. *Do not age, do not leave this earth, I cannot lose you*, I wanted to say. The day she'd left, I'd fractured. Ariane had always known the Gods' map, and my place on it, and without her I'd felt adrift. But in a deeper place, I'd known that wherever Ariane might be, she was ever wakeful, listening to the wind, working in shadow to keep the ways of our people alive.

She turned then as if she could yet read me, and I nearly startled as she reached for my hand. Her skin was smooth and cold to the touch, but the power of mountains thrummed through her fingers. I would have stood there, soaking in her strength for ages, had she not suddenly stiffened.

"What is it?" I asked as she released me.

"Something foul."

A clamor sounded from the entryway and a sunburnt watchman appeared, rushing to Cywyllog to murmur in her ear. Meldred's wife stood abruptly, her skirt snagging beneath a stool leg.

"Make ready," she called to her servants. "The warriors of Ebrauc have returned. Even now they are at our gate!" Her smile was broad, as if they were heroes. I wanted to spit.

It was not that I hadn't considered this moment; rather, it had been easier to consider in the face of battle, when it was uncertain any of us would survive long enough to face it.

"I must find Eira," I said, hurrying toward the door. I rounded the corner of the entryway, only to nearly collide with her, Angharad following close behind. From the looks upon their faces, they'd spotted the warriors from the hilltop. I wrapped Eira beneath my arm.

"We needn't see them. Come, hurry. I'll take you to my chamber."

But Eira slipped from my grip, shaking her head. "No, Languoreth."

I stopped in disbelief, whispering fiercely. "Eira. Gwrgi is mad! There is no telling what he might do."

"I will not hide. I am sickened to death of hiding!" she hissed. My chest tightened with dread. I could see that she was resolved. What else could I do? It was she who had suffered.

"If that is your decision, I will not fight you. But I am here. Torin and the men are here. We will keep you safe, I swear it."

Angharad's hands were clasped, white-knuckled. I turned to her to offer comfort, but she looked past me in search of Ariane as Meldred's men—those who could leave their posts—arrived in a bright gust of summer wind, their faces pink from the heat. As we trailed behind them into the great room, they dealt impatient looks to the servants scurrying to the tables with platters of cheese, bread, and heaps of roast meat, for yesterday we had defeated the Angles, and now more celebration was in order. Hospitality demanded that the men of Ebrauc be lavished with food and drink, and that they receive their share in spoils. Meldred's warriors jostled round the ale barrels with their drinking horns in hand.

Then, from outside, the hollow blow of a horn, the rumbling trudge of boots.

"They're coming," Angharad said. Eira flinched as a sudden thunder of fists struck up, pounding a welcome upon the heavy oak tables.

"*Ebrauc. Ebrauc.*"

The doors to the hall were thrust open, and the warriors of Ebrauc flooded into the great room like rats in a storm. Red and black were their banners, their shields. The reek and gore of battle was still upon them, their foreheads anointed with rusty streaks of Angle blood. Cywyllog's wry smile dropped at the sight of them. Beneath her façade I glimpsed a flicker of uncertainty.

Aye, Cywyllog, I wanted to tell her. *They are unpredictable. You're wise to be afraid.* The warriors did not smile. They did not even acknowledge their welcome. Such were the men who served Gwrgi and Peredur, the kings of Ebrauc.

As a girl, I'd first found the brothers to be comically ill-matched: Peredur was tall and slender with gray-streaked, thinning hair, while Gwrgi was short and muscled, the hair beneath his helmet kept close-cropped, blackened with lead to disguise his years. I soon learned there was nothing humorous about them. Each was his own breed of monster.

"*Ebrauc. Ebrauc!*" The chant rose to a roar as Gwrgi yanked off his war helmet, tossing it upon a table. It was almost funny then, how the brothers looked round the hall with indignance, searching for a king. But no man present possessed a higher nobility than I.

"Where is Rhydderch?" Gwrgi called out. The din dropped. Before I could speak, Mungo stepped forward in a swish of robes. He was over fifty winters now, his flaxen hair shifting to gray, which lent him an irritatingly learned look.

"Rhydderch King is off scouting," he said. "But I am here."

"Bishop," Gwrgi bowed.

I strode into the center of the hall, leveling Mungo with a look. "This man is no longer a bishop. A counsellor of Strathclyde, only. I am your host. I and the lady Cywyllog."

Gwrgi regarded me, sniffed, then rubbed at his nose. His fingers were still crusted with blood.

"We imagined you returned to Ebrauc," I said.

Peredur raised his thin brows in a show of surprise. "Return to

Ebrauc? Not whilst Angle dogs yet cower in the wilds." He gestured to his men. "Come. Bring the trunk."

Two warriors shuffled forward, dragging a wooden trunk and dropping it unceremoniously before me with a thud. Peredur stood impassively as they unfastened the lock, thrusting it open, and a sea of precious metals glinted in the lamplight. Silver brooches and hand pins. Daggers. Rings. Armlets.

"Our spoils." Peredur waved at the trunk. "We will await your husband, the king."

"Of course. In the meanwhile, the lady Cywyllog will see to your comfort. Perhaps she might also arrange for finger bowls so that you might refresh yourselves." I looked pointedly at Gwrgi, who found this delightful, braying with laughter.

"Oh, there's no need," he said, waggling his fingers. "It seasons the meat."

A look of disgust crossed Cywyllog's face. Yes, idols and feet of clay. Was that not from the Christian book?

"Let us have music," she said quickly, clapping her hands. As the musicians struck up, she leaned toward a passing servant, catching her arm. "And you. See to bowls."

I let out a breath as the men dispersed, filling their horns with drink, and the kings of Ebrauc took the seats of honor at Cywyllog's table. Across the room, Eira stood, taut as a bowstring. I knew her as a sister, could sense she was about to do something.

I tried to catch her eye. *Please be careful, Eira.* But she did not see me. Her eyes were locked on Gwrgi. I could only stand, helpless, as she lowered her head and plunged into the river of men like a minnow fighting the current. It seemed an eternity before she reached the far side of the great room where Gwrgi sat, drinking deeply from a white horn of ale.

"I would speak," she said. Eira's voice was swallowed by the din,

and neither Gwrgi nor Peredur possessed the good graces to acknowledge her. I glanced worriedly at Torin, who stood watching just beyond Cywyllog's table, and he gave a slight nod, touching a finger to
his blade. They had still not given Eira any notice. Her cheeks flamed
as she looked between Gwrgi and Peredur, her anger mounting. And
then, in one swift movement, she lifted her arm, slamming her fist like
an anvil down upon the table.

"I would *speak*!" she said.

Warriors lowered their horns, stunned silent by this woman's brash-
ness.

She had Gwrgi's attention now, and I did not like the look upon
his face.

"What is the meaning of this?" Peredur turned to Cywyllog. "Who
is this woman?" Cywyllog's mouth opened like a stranded fish.

Eira cut in before she could speak. "Do you mean to say you do not
recognize your own kin, Lord Peredur?" she asked. Peredur frowned.
But Gwrgi—oh, how he loved a game. His dark, glittering eyes fixed
upon her like a weasel eyeing a field mouse. Beside him, Peredur
scoffed.

"Recognize you? You insolent woman. Go away."

It was alchemy, the way she drew herself up then.

"You insult me," Eira said tightly. "It has been many winters since
I was a foster in your mother's care. I may have grown into a woman,
but surely my face remains unchanged. I am Gwendolen, daughter of
King Urien of Rheged. And you are my cousin."

I'd heard Eira use her birth name only once before, when she'd told
me of her past. She had discarded that name when she chose a new
life. But like some strange incantation, it seemed to return a certain
power to her now.

"It is funny you should not know your own fosterling," she continued. "I can still recall the morning you and your brother returned from

raiding, the way the banners flapped in the wind. 'We must welcome our heroes home, Gwendolen,' your mother told me. What a horrible mistake that was. To think you heroic."

A woman gasped. The people of the great room were riveted, shameless with expectation.

"What is it, then," Peredur asked with impatience. "What is it you would say?"

Eira took a breath. "I stand before you to seek justice for a horrible wrong done by this man." She thrust a finger toward Gwrgi. "For Gwrgi of Ebrauc did beat me, abuse me, and leave me to die."

A wave of murmurs traveled the room. It could not be a shock to see Gwrgi of Ebrauc accused of lawbreaking. It was only that no woman had ever dared accuse him. Eira paused, looking uncertain.

"Continue," I called out, sending her strength. She glanced at me, then carried on, her voice remarkably even.

"'Throw her body into the river,' Gwrgi told his man. He thought me dead. But his warrior took pity upon me. He brought me to a woman who hid me away and healed me. She raised me as her own, and my family was deceived. They were told I died from fever."

"Lies," Gwrgi pronounced flatly. But his eyes danced with amusement.

"You will allow her to speak," I warned.

"I left the girl called Gwendolen behind," Eira went on. "Even as I undertook a life of servitude, I was thankful to start anew. At least I should never have to look upon his face again."

"And next she will say she bore his bastard," Peredur cut in. "I tire of this. Give her one head of cattle. She is but a chamberwoman. Pay her and be done with it. Our men have earned their ale."

"I am no chamberwoman!" Eira shouted. "I am a daughter of Rheged, of Urien King, and I have not *finished*."

Gwrgi tilted his head and passed off his drinking horn, peering at her. "Come now . . . *Eira*, is it? Even I tire of this game. Is this how Ebrauc is rewarded for our efforts? Had I injured my own kin—a child of Rheged, as you say—surely my uncle Urien would have brought war."

He might have said as much, but Gwrgi knew her; I could see it plainly on his face.

Eira's jaw was tight. "Each moment you have lived has been by my grace," she said. "But I will keep silent no longer. I would have the Song Keepers sing for a thousand ages of what a disgraceful and piteous man you are. You did not know me today, just as you did not know me when you encountered me after the Battle of Arderydd. When you commanded your men to defile me and then sent me off in the prison carts."

Lady Cywyllog stiffened as Peredur shot to his feet. "You cannot make such accusations! This is no assembly. There is no jurist present."

"How you must tire of keeping after a madman," Eira snapped.

Things were spinning dangerously out of control. I closed the distance between me and Eira.

"Let it be an assembly, then," I pronounced. "This woman has called for justice. The law states that in absence of a jurist, a king or queen may administer."

Peredur's laugh was humorless. "Ridiculous. This chamberwoman is clearly in your service."

"*Enough*," Mungo thundered, stalking into the center of the great room. "I am counsellor to Rhydderch of Strathclyde, the kingdom where this woman now dwells. I will act as jurist in this matter."

My mind raced. I did not trust it. What reason could Mungo have to speak on Eira's behalf?

"Now is not the time," I said. "If Lord Peredur demands jurists, we must bring the matter to assembly."

Mungo turned to me. "Why should the matter not be settled now? As you say, this woman has called for justice. If she speaks the truth, she has nothing to fear. What say you, Gwrgi of Ebrauc?" Mungo waited. Peredur shot his brother a silencing look.

"Do not consent," he said.

"I do not address you, Lord Peredur. I am speaking to your brother," Mungo said evenly.

Tension crackled like dry moss underfoot. I could see what played behind Gwrgi's eyes; he could not resist the temptation to harm. He would risk it, if only to watch Eira suffer.

Gwrgi stood, bowing with a flourish. "Very well. I consent."

"And you, Lady Eira?" Mungo asked. "Do you wish to settle this matter forthwith?"

Eira glanced at me, squaring her shoulders. "I do."

"Then it shall be so." Mungo clasped his hands, walking prayerfully in a show of contemplation. "Lady Eira. The events you recount transpired many winters ago. It is customary to ask: Do you possess a living flame? One who perhaps bore witness, who might speak on your behalf?"

My stomach dropped. Without a living flame, it was Eira who would suffer. I had not borne witness, and Angharad had escaped into the forest.

Eira blinked. Gwrgi's warriors watched with triumph in their eyes. The very men who had defiled her. *Please, Gods*, I prayed. *Show your hand in this. Protect your daughter.* Silence billowed, weighted with the promise of ruin. But then a shuffle sounded from the corner of the hall.

"Please. Let me through." The crowd parted, and my daughter stepped forward.

"Angharad?" I breathed. Her eyes darted to me, then fixed upon Eira. Eira shook her head ever so slightly, as if she did not want to be-

lieve it. After all, Angharad had not been there. Eira had assured me
she had escaped into the wood.

"You bear knowledge of these supposed events?" Mungo demanded.

"Yes, I do. I am a living flame."

"Speak, then. We would hear your account."

"I cannot speak to the first accusation," she said. "But I bore witness to the second."

Sickness rose in my throat. Sweet Gods, she'd been only a child.

"Go on, then. Give your name." Mungo said. If you knew nothing
of him, you would not even catch the distaste in his tone. But I knew
that Mungo had a particular dislike of priestesses. It had been his sil-
very tongue in Tutgual's ear when I was a girl: he'd seen to it that female Wisdom Keepers were exiled from court. But Angharad was also
the daughter of his king. Mungo could not dismiss her out of hand.

"I am Angharad. Daughter of Rhydderch," Angharad began. "I was
but a girl when we were taken against our will by Lord Gwrgi after
the Battle of Arderydd. Lady Eira was then my nursemaid. She was
struck with fear at the sight of Gwrgi. I thought it strange, for he said
he intended to return me to my father. But he soon enslaved her. He
allowed her to accompany me only when I insisted. Eira told me we
were in danger, that we must escape."

"And did you escape?" he asked.

A shadow darkened her face. "I did, but only thanks to her cour-
age. Lady Eira was captured ensuring it." Angharad paused. A look
passed between them.

"Continue," Mungo said. "We must know all."

Anticipation played in the twist of Gwrgi's lips. The hall hung upon
Angharad's every word, and yet, suddenly, she seemed frozen. Her chest
was rising and falling too quickly. I knew she was prone to visions.
Was she seeing it all again? Across the hall, Ariane murmured something, shifting her weight, a reminder—of what, I could not say. But I

watched Angharad's resolve return, color rushing to her freckled ivory cheeks. It was fury rising; I could feel it mounting like thunderheads.

"Speak." Mungo was losing his patience. Angharad's voice shifted, deepening with anger.

"It was night, and dark, the forest beyond the tent was only blackness. Eira shouted for me to run, but I was too afraid. Instead, I ran into the brush. I hid myself away." She paused, closing her eyes as if seeing it replay on the backs of her lids.

She spoke then, revealing the horrors that had transpired that night.

I watched the men of Ebrauc as the shame they hadn't felt then gripped them at last, smothering. They shrank back upon their benches, darting glances round the room.

"I heard such suffering that night," Angharad concluded. "No god shall ever forgive Gwrgi of Ebrauc and his retinue for what they have done."

The great room was silent as a tomb. A tear slipped down Eira's cheek. Mungo looked at Gwrgi as if seeing him anew. And then, out of the stillness, a rumble sounded. I looked round in confusion before recognizing the source.

Thunder.

Just as the others recognized it too, a boom sounded so near overhead that the timbers rattled, startling the monks near Cywyllog's table. Mungo craned his neck, glancing up at the rafters, then back down at Angharad, his face full of a newfound curiosity. But Angharad took no notice of nature's judgment. Her gray eyes were fixed upon Gwrgi as if a look alone could burn him to the ground.

In the wake of the thunder, the people in the great room were dumbstruck. I gripped my skirts beneath the table and broke the silence.

"I think we have heard quite enough," I said, turning to Mungo. "Speak, then. What is your judgment?"

Mungo's chest rose with a breath. Bowing his head, he spoke, as if to himself. "I have heard the words of a living flame. However, this young woman cannot speak to the distant past. Therefore, regarding the matter of the woman as a fosterling, I can pass no judgment."

Gwrgi laughed. My stomach wrenched. Mungo continued.

"Regarding the events that took place following the Battle of Arderydd, I believe this woman's account to be truthful." Mungo turned to address the kings of Ebrauc. "Lord Gwrgi. In commanding your warriors to harm this woman, you have committed a most vile evil. It is an act that utterly disgraces you in the sight of God. The law states: For the defilement of a daughter of a king, the guilty will offer forty-two milk cows."

Peredur slammed his fist down, nearly upending the table. "This is an outrage!"

Mungo waved a hand unworriedly, turning to me. "I understand Lady Eira is wife to Lailoken, son of Morken. Is this true?"

"Yes," I said carefully. "Lady Eira—Gwendolen, as she was once called—is my sister by marriage."

Gwrgi clapped his hands, grinning with delight. "Lailoken's bride? If only I had known. I would have ordered my men to defile her twice."

I wanted to rip out his eyes. Across the hall, Lady Cywyllog's mouth fell open and the monks seated beside her murmured in alarm. I stifled my fury and leapt upon the opportunity Gwrgi had granted with his madness.

"He has *admitted* it!" I scoffed. Mungo's placid expression fell away, replaced by something dark and more familiar.

Lord Gwrgi, baptized a Christian, had just demonstrated his vileness in such a way that no lavish gifts to the church or prowess in battle could persuade one to overlook it.

Mungo crossed the great room in a few short strides, towering over Gwrgi. For a moment I thought the former bishop might strike him.

"It would seem my judgment is not yet complete. The wife of a counsellor holds an honor price of twenty-six milk cows," he said. "Therefore, in recompense for this most egregious act, you shall pay a debt of sixty-eight milk cows.

"Furthermore," he went on, his voice low but deadly, "you are hereby exiled from all rituals, celebrations, and observations of God. No church—nor churchman—shall ever again offer you sacrament. Nor shall you be entitled to the God-given mercy of sanctuary."

Mungo leaned in, a hairsbreadth from Gwrgi's face. "Your soul shall be banished from the afterlife. On the day you breathe your last, you shall yet be condemned, not to join the exalted in the kingdom of God but to languish as a shade, wandering the earth in disgrace and in suffering, forever."

I had never imagined Gwrgi to be a pious man. But it would seem my judgment was in error, for Mungo's words seemed to strike him to his core. His face reddened. He blinked. Whispers buzzed round the room. I did not wish to lose the moment. I stood and moved to the place where Eira stood, taking her hand.

"Sixty-eight milk cows and exile from the church is a sound judgment. And yet the Lords of Ebrauc possess no cattle here at present." I glanced at the trunk. "I do, however, see a generous quantity of silver."

The warriors of Ebrauc bristled. I pinned them with my eyes, daring them to speak as Mungo considered it.

"Lady Eira. Would you accept these spoils of war in exchange for Lord Gwrgi's debt?"

Eira's reply was plain upon her face: neither silver nor cattle in any amount could ever undo what had been done. But I hoped she saw my intent. Cows were of great value. However, cattle belonged only to the kings of Ebrauc. Their warriors stood before us, and they cared for nothing so much as their plundered silver and gold.

"I accept," Eira said.

"It is done, then. This matter is settled." Mungo nodded. Across the hall, Torin gestured and two of my men stepped forward, lifting the trunk by its leather handles and hefting it off to my temporary quarters. The warriors watched their battle spoils being dragged off like wolves eying a stolen carcass. I knew the way of beasts. It was their leader who would be blamed, he who allowed their kill to be so readily taken. Soon there would be murmuring in the mead halls. In the distant corners of Ebrauc, they would plot to remove their kings.

Only one final task remained. I crossed the great room to stand before Gwrgi.

"There is no hospitality owed to lawbreakers. Your judgment has been pronounced. Now you will leave."

For a moment he regarded me with a vague stare of disbelief.

"Did you not hear me? I said you will leave."

Gwrgi's eyes were like knives. I waited, unyielding, as he got to his feet, ale horn in hand. As Gwrgi reached out, Torin rushed to my side, but Gwrgi only chuckled and lifted his brows, tipping the contents of his horn onto the ground. A shuddering of benches scraped through the great room as his warriors followed suit, standing to splatter their ale upon Cywyllog's tidy flagstone floor.

It puddled like urine and Cywyllog stood, enraged by the sight of their indignant, bloody faces. "How dare you? You dishonor us all. The queen of Strathclyde has given an order. You will leave—now! At once!"

Boots squelched as the warriors of Ebrauc clattered for their weapons. My men raised their spears. Cywyllog's men followed suit. For a moment, we stood motionless. Had a flint been struck, Meldred's Hall might have burst into flame.

Then Gwrgi hurled his empty horn to the floor and nodded at his brother. My shoulders sank in relief as the kings of Ebrauc strode from the hall, their warriors following close at their heels.

Cywyllog looked as if she might faint.

"Thank you," I told her.

"You would have spoken for me," she said, looking after them. But there was little warmth in her voice.

"I would have done," I agreed. She'd been hostile upon my arrival at Dùn Meldred, and I did not trust her, but I could offer her at least some grace.

"I fear I have made an enemy of Ebrauc," she said.

"Ebrauc was an enemy already, Lady Cywyllog. Only now you are aware of it, too. This will not come down upon you. You were a most gracious host. And you were within your rights by law."

The silence in the great room was stifling. I looked to the bards. "Let us have music, please."

The musicians struck up dutifully, a somber tune. Servants came with buckets and cloth, sopping up the spilled ale, and the warriors and nobles turned to one another, talking in low voices. They averted their eyes from Eira, an offering of kindness. I wanted to go to her, but there was one with whom I needed to speak first.

Mungo stood in the center of the great room, regarding me. I cut through the crowd, closing the gap between us. I could not bear to thank him. But it could have gone very badly for Eira indeed.

"Your declaration was just," I said.

"Why is it you seem surprised, Lady Languoreth? I am a man of God."

"Forgive me," I said. "I did not imagine murder and mutilations were Christian acts."

Mungo stiffened. "I would advise you to better guard your tongue. I may forgive your slander, but I can assure you, there are many who love me. And they? Possibly not." A threat lurked in his shadowy blue eyes. Then, like the weather on a mountain peak, his mood shifted.

"Your brother and I both have spent long years parted from Strathclyde," he said. "Now that we both return, I would have peace. Your husband, the king, has invited me to be his counsel. Rhydderch only seeks the balance his people demand. It would seem that God has thrust us together. Do you not find it curious, after all of these years? I am willing to leave the past behind for the sake of our kingdom. Are you, my queen?"

He looked at me, expectant. I softened my gaze.

"I would do anything for my people," I said. For that wasn't a lie.

"I am gladdened to hear it." Mungo smiled, but his eyes were unchanged. "I think I shall retire until the king returns."

"Then I bid you good evening."

"Good evening." He turned and, signaling to his monks, strode to the door.

Eira looked as if she'd been spat out by a storm. I wanted to go to her, but Angharad was crossing the great room to join her. This was not a moment meant for me. I stopped a short distance from them, watching as something passed between them. Eira reached with the tenderness of a mother, cupping Angharad's face between two slender hands. They stood like that a long while. Above the murmur and scrape of the servants righting the room and the soft strains of music, I confess I leaned closer, hoping to catch a scrap of their words.

"You must know I would suffer it again, Angharad," I heard Eira say. "I would suffer it all again, for it granted you your freedom."

CHAPTER 4

Angharad

There are laws more ancient than the judgments of men.

That night, Angharad met Eira outside the gates of the outer rampart. The bodies of the fallen were no more, their blood gone back to the earth. The moon's light was meager, but nonetheless the two women found their way through the field to that dark twist of river. Angharad glanced up at the sky.

"The moon is right," she said. "We need a dark moon."

Brother Thomas once said that enough evil would find its way. Did Angharad truly wish to aid it? But she also believed that the Gods she loved were just. Were they not the lawgivers? Was it not their systems that the Wisdom Keepers divined?

Yes, there were laws more ancient than the judgments of men.

"Are you certain, then?" Angharad asked.

Eira nodded.

"Good. Take my hands, and we will remember. One last time, together."

The women closed their eyes, intertwining their fingers. Angharad opened herself, allowing the memory to swallow her once more so she might do its work.

Suddenly, Angharad could hear the echo of Eira's cries again, piercing the night forest, as if she still lay concealed in the bushes. Anger rose, slow and burning, churning in the vat of her stomach. She made herself hollow so that it might fill her, rising with the force of a flood from the soles of her feet to the top of her skull. Through the meeting of their hands, she felt Eira's fury, too.

The curse would be strong.

The muscle of Angharad's heart began to grow dull with ache, like slowly rotting fruit. Still, she did not cease.

More. Let me feel more. The rage became a pulsing, with no beginning, no end. They trapped it there, on the banks of the night river. The Old Ones bore witness, lending it their breath.

Then, pressing Eira's hands, she gathered their fury and sent it to the sky.

"I curse you, Gwrgi of Ebrauc. I curse you to die."

Her voice rang in the night, and she felt the curse fly. Beside her, Eira's breath was coming fast. The venom was so bitter, Angharad leaned forward and spat. She lowered their arms, their fingers still joined. Her body was spent, empty as a snail shell. A dark wisp of cloud raced over the moon.

"It is done, then," Eira said.

"Yes. It is done."

CHAPTER 5

Languoreth

R hydderch and the men returned to Dùn Meldred at sundown.
Bone weary and sore, they threw more prisoners into the prison
carts, the glow of victory drained from their faces. Eira drew my
brother away. When Lailoken returned, he sat in silence, his blue eyes
fixed stonily on the fire.

Later, in the quiet of our chamber, Rhydderch listened as I told
him all that had taken place. His dark hair was still damp from his
bath, his knuckles bruised in brown and purple blooms from battle.

"You did as I would have done," he said at last. "And as you say,
you have broken no law."

"But what of Ebrauc? What if we should once more need their
allegiance?"

He ran a hand over his tired face. "It is they who are pressed by
Angles, both north and south. They rely upon my honor and expect
reciprocity, no matter their actions. They will find me sorely mis-
judged. I am finished with Ebrauc. If they should fall, so be it."

It was not like Rhydderch to offer up Britons. I lowered my voice.
"You would sacrifice Ebrauc, see it settled by Angles? And what of the
people of Ebrauc? They are innocents, Rhydderch."

"Let them come. We will shelter them." He took my hand gently, tracing my knuckles with the calloused pad of his thumb, then glanced up at me.

"I must travel south tomorrow with the prison carts," he said. I drew back.

"What? Must you? Can you not send someone?"

"No, it must be me. The Angles . . . they have my brother."

I straightened. "Morcant has been captured?"

"Aye. The Angles would meet at the boundary stone beyond Rheged. I know you do not care for him, but he is my brother. I must ensure all goes to plan."

"You are king of Strathclyde, my love. What if it's a trap? The risk is too great. Every man on that field will be looking to kill you."

Rhydderch's smile was halfhearted. "I have not grown this aged in being careless, wife. I will keep far back. And we shall be in the company of Urien of Rheged and his men. They have been walloping Angles since the days of Emrys Pendragon." He paused. "This Angle you found, Æthelfrith. Will he survive the journey?"

"I cannot say. Angharad has tended him, so if he has any chance, it is due to her." I hesitated. "She is leaving tomorrow. She hasn't said as much, but I know she will not stay."

Rhydderch looked down. "Her place is with the Picts now. In the Shadowed Lands. We knew when we gave her up that she was no longer ours to keep."

I bit my tongue. There was no sense in speaking with Rhydderch of matters he did not understand.

"I would travel with you to Rheged," I said. "Gladys is there. She sent word she is once again with child."

"Is she?" Rhydderch smiled, pleased. He was fond of our eldest daughter, Gladys. He was fond of all of our children, but he had no need to clutch them. Perhaps it was because his own mother had never left him; Elufed was still at court in Strathclyde. Rhydderch knew nothing of the want of a mother's touch, the ache for that cool hand that can soothe any fever.

"You must return to Clyde Rock," he said. "But I will give Gladys your love."

I could not keep the frustration from my voice. "But she will want to know of Angharad, that she is alive and well."

"Mungo and your brother cannot be left to themselves," Rhydderch pointed out. "And I cannot be in two places at once. The Angles must see me at this trade, Languoreth. They must see that I am hale and in power, and know that Strathclyde is far beyond their reach. You may visit Gladys when the babe is born."

The unseen collar tugged at my neck. *You may.* But like any old dog, I'd learned that no good came of straining at my lead.

I swallowed my disappointment and reached to tuck a curly strand of gray behind his ear, pushing thoughts of freedom and Maelgwn Pendragon away, looking into the wide-set wintry eyes that these many years had become my home. In them I could see the battle's reflection, haunting like a waking dream.

"You did not visit the *fulacht fiadh* by the river," I said. I'd seen the Dragon Warriors building the large wicker frame in which to have their post-battle ritual. They fashioned it in the shape of a dome, covered overtop with hides. River water was channeled into a nearby stone-lined pit and heated to boiling with red, glowing rocks from a fire. Inside the makeshift hut was a holy place where steam, herbs, and oils cleansed far more than battle grime from the bodies of warriors. Wisdom Keepers sang over the hiss of hot mist, taming the memories of split skin and the frenzied panic to survive. In my father's time, men did not return to their wives before they had visited the *fulacht fiadh* and were soothed of their memories of war. They were a place of giving over, of rebirth.

"I had no time for such ceremony," Rhydderch said. "Mungo spoke a blessing."

"Ah," I said, worn too thin for strife. Rhydderch might be tolerant of the Old Way, but he was born a Christian, and it was the Christian lords and chieftains of Strathclyde that had tipped the scale in winning him the throne. He was meticulous about preserving his Christian image.

Soon, Rhydderch was asleep. I wrapped myself in a shawl and tiptoed through the dark hut. As I eased the door open, Torin stirred from his bedroll beside the hearth.

"I'm only stepping outside," I whispered. Torin said nothing, only picked up his blade and followed as I stepped out into the clear summer night. Night insects called to a slim hanging moon. Torin watched from a distance as I walked the stone line of the upper rampart, my gaze fixed to the starry sky. I was remembering a song my mother had taught me. And then I felt another presence.

Have you ever stood with your back to a mountain?

You might be standing on a moor amidst sprays of sunny gorse, the waters of a loch shimmering in the distance, but it is the mountain you feel, towering behind you. Vast and rooted. Full of hidden caves.

This is what it was to stand with your back to Maelgwn Pendragon.

I could hear the startle in his voice as he stopped a few paces away. "Sleep has not found you, either," he said.

We had not spoken since before the battle. Rhydderch had been commanding the men of Strathclyde and hadn't seen the Angles creeping along their flank, hoping to capture the fort—and kill any sheltering there. It was Maelgwn and my brother who'd broken from the battle haze. They'd fought with their backs to the rampart, protecting those of us inside. It was his voice I first heard, fists pounding upon the door, shouting, "Open! It is Maelgwn Pendragon!" It was his green eyes that caught mine as he stumbled into the Hall. His face was bloodied and covered in grime, his eyes still wild from the battle's coursing. But he lived. My relief was a feral thing. I wanted to run to him, soothe away the wounds of the words I'd spoken the last time we had met. But we were surrounded by prying eyes, and I was a queen.

Rhydderch's wife.

A glance across the room later that evening was all I could risk. And now there was Torin, watching, guarding my honor as was his duty.

"I hoped it might help to look at the moon," I said. Maelgwn looked up.

"Aye, she's a comfort," he agreed. But his tone was proper, formal.

"You cannot imagine my relief in seeing you whole," I ventured.

"Is that so?"

"It is."

"It seems it was not my day to visit the Summerlands."

"Come, now," I said. "You are Maelgwn Pendragon, chosen leader of the Dragon Warriors, protector of the Britons. You cannot fail."

"I am a man of five and forty, Languoreth," he said solemnly. "Already my hair is threading with white, and I am the chosen leader of a forgotten kingdom. Gwenddolau's lands have long been eaten by Rheged and Strathclyde."

I couldn't bear the defeat upon his face.

"It is true, the lands may now belong to other kings. But you needn't live in exile any longer. There is a place for you in Strathclyde."

"What," Maelgwn scoffed, "among King Rhydderch's guard? Come, now, Languoreth. Do not insult me."

"I would never insult you."

It had been I who'd made an end of things. I didn't want to pick and prod at the scabs upon his heart. But nor did he seem to understand. So I spoke the words.

"I only mean to say that the Britons still require you." I paused. "I still require you."

Maelgwn said nothing. I could feel the churning of his emotions.

I did not say as much to be cruel. I couldn't bear it if either of us died without Maelgwn truly understanding how I felt.

"You, too, are a leader," I went on. "You know well what it demands. Yet, whilst men may take multiple wives and lovers at will, women are not afforded such luxuries. You cannot tell me you've not sought comfort in the arms of others through the years. I do not thrill to the thought, but I accept it. But I am a woman, and queen of the most powerful kingdom of the Britons. I am a woman of the Old Way, married to a Christian. Adultery is not tolerated. Should we be discovered, our people would lose an irreplicable advocate. You know as well as I, there is nothing that would delight Mungo more. Perhaps I did not say it so well when last we met, but I hoped you might know: I did not sever our ties because I do not love you."

Maelgwn was quiet a moment, thinking. "I cannot come to court. Not now. And not only for the reasons you say. Lailoken is leaving the Caledonian Wood, but there are yet men who are arriving, pledging us their blades. I cannot abandon them. I must stay with the Selgovae to receive them and train them."

"More Dragon Warriors come?"

He shook his head sadly. "Nay, Languoreth. The days of the Dragon Warriors are over. But perhaps in our exile we have become something greater. Our numbers are larger now than any retinue Gwenddolau possessed. With this strength, Lailoken intends to draw further support from the lords and chieftains of Strathclyde. Languoreth, don't you see? Your brother and I—we are building an army."

"An army? To what end?"

"To preserve the Old Way. To stave off the Angles, if need be, too. There will be none so loyal as these men will be unto you—you and your brother—for he has known them and offered them shelter and friendship these past many years. You are the last lights of our people. Your beacon must not flicker."

For a moment I was speechless. An army, one that did not belong to Rhydderch but to me. My brother and me. I was still turning it round in my head when Maelgwn shifted, his green eyes warm in the dark. "You must be very glad to see your daughter."

"You searched for her," I acknowledged. "I never thanked you."

He waved it away. "Many of us searched for her. Angharad had been with us only a year, but she had become the better part of our hearts."

"She is a Pict now."

"She is a Wisdom Keeper," he said. "This is what you wished for, the path you could not follow. Now you can see that you did not re-lease her to that fate in error, for look at what she has become."

"She is magnificent," I whispered.

"Aye." He smiled.

"But it is so painful. Becoming."

"Aye, it is painful. But we have survived it," he said. "And so shall she."

We stood still in the thick summer air. I could feel the warmth of his hand at his side, knew it was no accident when it gently brushed mine.

Standing so close to the love I had given up, the girl in me tugged at her bonds and the ropes chafed, blistering. But I had no choice. And there was still one thing that lay unfinished between us. I turned, soaking in the sight of his profile in the dark even as I reached into my garments, snapping the golden ring with the green stone from the thread that kept it close to me. The jewel was cold in my palm as I clutched it.

"Our beginning seems so very long ago now," I said. "Yours and mine."

Perhaps it was the touch of the Cailleach that had chased the in-nocence from me, ushering in my queendom. Or perhaps it was merely the passing seasons. But I understood now there were many kinds of love. Flint sparks and oil lamps both make fire, but only one has fuel enough to burn through a long winter's night. My pull to Maelgwn existed outside of reason and beyond possibility. Because of that, it had never had the opportunity to grow and to build, to become what that wild-haired Midsummer girl once believed it could be.

"I should have returned this when last we met, in the Selgovian lands," I said. "This ring has been a great source of comfort to me. Not a day has gone by that I haven't worn it. But I think you understand, I can no longer keep it."

I took Maelgwn's hand gently, unfurling his fingers, and pressed the ring into his palm. He nodded slowly, looking down in the darkness.

There had been so many severings. Battered hearts bear them better than most. But I knew both his and mine had grown weary.

"I understand," he said.

He closed his fist round the ring, tucking it away.

I could feel Torin's gaze at my back, willing me indoors, away from the night, away from this warrior and the dangers of scandal, but I still startled when he cleared his throat.

"If you should change your mind about joining us in Strathclyde, or if anything should happen," I said, "you need only send word."

"And we will await any such word from you," Maelgwn said, reaching briefly for my hand. His palm was tough as a turtle shell from ceaseless winters of gripping spear and blade, and the same sweet humming passed between us. I did not want to draw away. But I had tarried too long already.

"Gods keep you," I said.

I pressed his fingers and let them go, releasing Maelgwn to his destiny.

CHAPTER 6

Languoreth

The next morning was bleak and unseasonably cold. I held Angharad. Breathed her in. She smelled of strange new scents now,
earth and spice. I placed one hand upon each side of her smooth,
freckled cheeks and kissed her. Could she feel the power in that gesture? It was a mother's gift, built of a thousand shields.

We parted at the river. My retinue would ride northwest to
Strathclyde, while Angharad traveled with the Picts northeast to Din
Eidyn. As my party reached the crest of a hill I glanced over my shoulder one last time, but Angharad did not look back. Instead, it was
Ariane who turned. Our eyes met across the pebbled wash of the river
and she tilted her head ever so slightly. A bow. Only once before had
a Wisdom Keeper made such a gesture to me. It had been Cathan, my
beloved friend and teacher. I nodded, bowing in return. A merciful
wind kicked up, blowing my hair about, obscuring my tears.

Our company traveled north along the Old Roman Road. We Britons kept tidy the road that they'd built to subdue us, following in their
boot prints as we reopened old wounds, fighting now amongst ourselves. I'd forgone the cart to ride with my brother and Eira on horseback, where the wind could reach me and clean my sorrow away. Torin
rode ahead and, behind us, Mungo's monks traveled with the footmen,
those who were wounded in open carts of their own. Eira sat before

Lailoken in the saddle, and Fendwin, one of my favorite of the old Dragon Warriors, rode beside us. Lailoken's long sandy hair was freshly clean and loose about his shoulders, his white robes pristine. Seven long winters I had been without my twin. His return to Strathclyde made me feel whole again, a comfort much needed. Feeling my scrutiny, my brother smiled, squinting at me. "You look at me as if I might melt from view."

"Truth be told, I fear it." I smiled. "How is the horse Rhydderch gifted you?" I asked, nodding at his muscled gray warhorse.

"Eos," he said, reaching to pat her neck. "It's a fair name and she answers to it, though I haven't had much chance to test her. I gave her to a man before the battle, his need was greater than mine. He said she served him well, but she likes to bite." Eos's ears flicked back and she swiveled to glance at him with one dark eye, as if she considered it now.

"She'll need to get accustomed to you," I said.

"Aye." He laughed. "Though, in truth, I pray it'll be some time before we find ourselves back in battle."

"Yes," Eira cut in. "You require a soft, boring life at court, Husband. After seven years in exile, you have earned it."

Fendwin turned, glancing over his shoulder somewhat uneasily at the road behind us.

"And you have been missed," I told Lail. "Not only by us, but by our people. You shall see, my brother. All of Strathclyde will celebrate your return with gifts and mead . . ." I frowned as Fendwin twisted in his saddle, looking back once again.

"Fendwin. You're making me quite nervous."

He looked up, startled. "I?"

"Yes. You. Why is it you keep looking over your shoulder?" I smiled. But the old Dragon Warrior's face was grim.

"Are we in danger, you think?"

"Nay, not that." His blue eyes narrowed into the distance.

"What is it, then?" I prodded.

"I can't exactly say. Only, it feels as if I travel in the wrong direction."

My brother turned to him. They exchanged a look; it was something weighty. Leaning from his horse, Lailoken reached to grip Fendwin's arm, then nodded.

"If you'll excuse me, Sister," Lail said. "It occurs to me I must have a word with Torin."

"Of course," I said, glancing between them. Fendwin and I rode on in silence awhile as Lailoken and Eira rode ahead. It was as if there were something he would speak of. I waited patiently. After the Battle of Arderydd, it was Fendwin who'd risked his life to steal into Cadzow with a message from my brother. A warning of their raid on Clyde Rock. I knew him to be a kind and honorable warrior. But he had the look of a man who carried a burden.

"Fendwin. Is there something you wish to tell me?" I said at last.

He looked at me sidelong. "There is, aye. In truth, I should have told you already, but I could not find the moment."

"I'm beginning to worry," I said, though I could scarcely imagine what the old warrior might have to say. Fendwin took a breath.

"I'm powerful glad for the return of Angharad," he said. "But there is something you must know. In the Battle of Arderydd . . ." He paused.

Sweet Gods, I could not take it. "Please, Fendwin. Out with it."

He rubbed a thick hand over his plaited hair, his words coming in a rush. "It was I who killed your boy. Your son, Rhys. He died by my hand."

Beneath me, my horse kept plodding along the road. But for a moment, the world shrank round me, closing out every sound but the thudding of my heart. Seven winters had passed, but when it came to losing a child, time did nothing to deaden the pain. In small hours of the night, I'd imagined my son's death in a thousand different ways.

I suppose I'd always known Rhys had died by the hand of a Dragon. But in all my imaginings, I'd been unable to conjure a face until now.

Fendwin watched with a warrior's compassion, allowing me to choose. How much did I want to know? How much could I bear? Everything. Nothing.

"Lailoken knows?" It was not really a question.

Fendwin nodded. I fell quiet a long moment, absorbing it, then came to it. The only question that truly mattered.

"Did he suffer?" I knew Fendwin would not lie.

"No death is painless," he said. "But I swear to you on my sword, he did not suffer long."

A crow rattled and cawed as it flapped over a field, disappearing into the leafy branches of an oak. I remembered to breathe.

"The Battle of Arderydd was a wicked sort of beast," I said. "Uncle against nephew. Brother against brother. It should never have come to pass. I hope we shall never see the likes of it again." I turned to look at Fendwin. "Seven years is a long time to carry such a weight. I pray you are able to release it."

"Perhaps that's the trouble." Fendwin fixed his eyes on the road ahead, but I could see his torment. "I find I cannot."

"But you have my forgiveness," I said. "Surely that must be some help."

"It was a different sort of battle, like you say. We Dragon Warriors had loved Angharad like our own. If only the Gods could spin the hand of time. I would—"

"Had it not been you, it would have been another," I said. "Such is the way of war."

Fendwin looked down at his reins. "Perhaps. But a life taken in such a way is a debt unsettled." He glanced up. "I'm not young as I once was. But if you will have me, I would offer my service."

I had not expected this. Such a proposal was not to be taken lightly. It was no less than his own life he offered up, should circumstance demand it, and Fendwin was a strong, loyal tower of a warrior. I thought on it. He would do well in my guard. But Gladys was with child, and so near to the land of the Angles. And I was unable to go to her, except by my king's pleasure.

My conversation with Rhydderch yet echoed. Rhydderch was ready, he declared, to see Ebrauc fall. But I knew he could have no hand in it. I drew my horse closer to Fendwin's. Perhaps here was a way I might see Gladys safe as well as bring an end to Gwrgi and Peredur after all.

"I accept," I said. "I will tell you my plan. And if you agree, all shall be settled."

He listened intently as I spoke in low tones, then nodded.

"I will protect her as my own. I swear on my life."

"I trust that you will," I said. Reaching beneath my light summer cloak, I pulled a golden cuff from my arm. "When you see Gladys, give her this. She will know you are sent by me."

"I'll keep it safe," Fendwin said, tucking it into his saddlebag.

"Will you say goodbye to my brother?" I asked.

Fendwin glanced ahead. "I'll see him soon enough." He gave me a nod. I watched as he urged his horse round, disappearing back down the Old Roman Road.

"Are you going to tell me what you are thinking?" Lailoken asked, easing his horse back alongside mine.

"Dragons need posts," I said.

"And what post have you given him?" There was an edge to Lail's voice, and I realized it had been too long since he and I had been together. And all the while he'd been watching the backs of his brothers, hiding in the woods.

"You must remember, you trust me," I said firmly. He softened. I did, too.

"I have sent him to Gladys, and on another errand as well. But we'll speak more of that in closer company, my lord counsellor," I said, inclining my head in the direction of the monks.

The road took us through damp pastures and low, skulking hills. We'd won a battle that had seemed impossible. So many lives had been lost. Yet, as the day wore on and twilight fell like a curtain, I did not weep for the fallen in the Battle of the Caledonian Wood, cruel as it may seem.

I wept for my dark-haired boy, who'd died at the hand of a Dragon Warrior. I wept for my gray-eyed, freckled little girl, who'd once danced in circles round oak trees, quietly singing.

I wept for the dreaming. From the very beginning, it was disaster it foretold, time and time again.

CHAPTER 7

Artúr

The Dimwood, Kingdom of Strathclyde
Land of the Britons
3rd of July, AD 580

In Artúr's dream, he was a boy again. It was summer, and the high
hills were blanketed in purple sprays of heather and broad tufts
of buttery gorse. He and Cai were racing barefoot up the steep path
of Coire Gabhail. The Lost Valley. They knew the path like the figure of a friend. One leap over the fast-rushing burn. Up the wooded
ravine, their bodies light-boned as birds, boots splashing through
pebble-bottomed puddles. The rare summer sun was hot on their
backs, the only heaviness the heaving of their breath as their fingers
gripped root and rock, pulling themselves up as if they might fly,
each fed by the fire to beat the other to the great boulder standing
sentinel at the entrance to the corrie, that giant guardian that kept
the valley a secret.

Artúr! Cai called out, laughing. *Artúr!*

Artúr mac Aedan woke to find himself lying upon the spongy forest
floor of the Dimwood. He rubbed the crick in his neck, newly aware of
the damp woolen bedroll beneath him, beaded with morning dew. He
kept his eyes closed a moment, longing for that impossible feeling of
lightness; it was as if they had been little more than spirits of the glen.

But the ground had turned boggy overnight and the gnats had stirred with the sun, swarming with biting teeth.

"*Meanbh-chuileagan*," Artúr mumbled, slapping at his neck, and looked up to see his foster brother leaning over him, his hazel eyes disapproving.

"You'd sleep through a siege if I didn't wake you, " Cai said.

Artúr arched his back stiffly and stretched. "I was dreaming of summer in the Lost Valley."

Cai's face softened at the memory, filling with that same, familiar longing: to be boys again, fetching the cattle down from the corrie. Battle had seemed a glory then. The faces of warriors, with their polished shield bosses and silver-tipped spears, shone brighter than any sun.

It passed between them like water, washing away some of the gore from the Battle of the Caledonian Wood, and Cai offered a hand, hoisting Artúr up.

"Don't you miss it?" Artúr asked. "Your father would be glad for the sight of you."

"Home is on horseback now," Cai said. "Yours and mine both. Come and eat. We should be off."

Over by the fire, the men of Mannau were heating gruel in a cook pot. While the warriors from other retinues had lingered at Dùn Meldred for feasting and celebration, Artúr and his men had swung back upon their horses to return to their kingdom. They'd come to fight and seen it won. Summer was the season of raiding and of war, and Artúr had been absent too long already. His father had entrusted him with the protection of Mannau, a small, landbound kingdom, pressed on all sides by enemies. Coire Gabhail was only a dream.

Cai passed Artúr a wooden bowl, gruel topped with salt pork. They'd lost eighteen men in battle. And as the warriors of Mannau boiled their oats that morning, the absence of their brothers hung like foul vapor.

"That messenger who found us on the road," Cai said. "You haven't spoken of it."

Artúr looked round, lowering his voice. "I've been summoned to Dùn Monaidh."

Cai lifted a brow. "It's not every day your father summons."

"Nay, it is not."

Artúr licked his bowl to clean it. The gruel tasted of fish despite being here, in the forest. It was always better to choke it down before one could taste it. He looked round to pass the bowl to his ghillie, Young Ewan, but the boy was nowhere to be found.

"Where has he— Young Ewan!" he shouted. The men shook their heads as the youth came running, half out of breath, his fair hair sticking up with sweat and his face somehow appearing more freckled.

"Aye, aye!" Young Ewan said.

"Where is it you've been?" Artúr asked.

"Scouting, Sir!"

"Scouting? Nay. You're to help with the washing up and ready the horses."

"Aye," Young Ewan said, looking disappointed.

Artúr held out the bowl. "Young Ewan."

"Aye, m'lord."

"Do not leave this company again without my command."

"I won't, sir. I swear it," he said. At least the boy possessed wit enough to look ashamed. Young Ewan was the son of one of Mannau's wealthiest lords. The boy had set his mind to become a warrior but lacked any skill whatsoever with a blade, and so had been made a ghillie, a steward serving the warriors.

Cai watched the boy take the bowl to the streamlet, carrying on from where they'd left off. "Don't like dividing the men," he said.

"Nor do I," Artúr agreed. "But we cannot all travel there. The whole of our company would draw too much notice, and they've earned their rest. The men and the horses must return to Mannau. You and I will hire a vessel at Clyde Rock."

Artúr and his cavalry had ridden to the rescue of the Britons in the Caledonian Wood. But he'd need a boat to reach Dalriada, and travel by water left him with the problem of what to do with the bulk of his men and their exceedingly valuable horses.

"You mean to hire a boat at Clyde Rock?" Cai frowned as he reached to lash his bedroll to his horse's back. "Two coins Rhydderch of Strathclyde learns the purpose of your visit before you, then. Departing from his fortress?"

Artúr looked at him. "Have you a better idea? Rhydderch's a clever king. He'll learn it soon enough, whatever it may be."

Across the clearing, Eiddilig the Small was leaning against the trunk of a silver birch watching them, his muscled arms cradled casually behind his head.

"Can't tell what you're saying, but you argue like brothers," he called out. Eiddilig might've stood only chest high to others, but despite his shortened limbs, he'd already become a warrior of legend by the time he'd arrived in Mannau, a pack of bards trailing him like hunt hounds, enraptured by the smell of his fame. He'd come in search of Artúr, declaring he craved challenge and adventure, and had offered up his blade.

Across the clearing, Bedwyr threw Eiddilig an exasperated look. "Do quit lazing about and ready your horse," he said. "Can't you see we're breaking camp?"

Eiddilig slipped the axe from his belt and hurled it with a thunk into the elm just above Bedwyr's head.

"Terrible aim," Bedwyr muttered, smoothing his mane of golden hair.

"Young Ewan, ready my horse," Eiddilig hollered.

Bedwyr shook his head as he strode through camp, organizing the men. "Right, then, let's put out the fire. Just because the days are long doesn't mean we've got all morning."

Artúr glanced at Cai, returning to the matter at hand. "Rhydderch was grateful for our aid and has granted us passage from Clyde Rock. I would take it."

"Well enough," he agreed. "Who would you bring to Dalriada, then?"

"You, Bedwyr, and Eiddilig," Artúr said. "We need men enough to guard the horses on their return to Mannau."

"We need men enough to guard Artúr, son of Aedan." Cai nodded at the golden torque round Artúr's neck. "There is more than one who'd gladly see you buried in peat."

"The three of you, brother. We'll leave it at that."

"And me," Young Ewan cropped up from behind their horses. "You'll need your ghillie, won't you, m'lord."

Artúr looked at him. "Young Ewan. I have asked—nay, commanded—you not to listen to words not meant for your ears."

"I am ever so sorry, m'lord."

Eiddilig pushed off the silver birch and crossed the clearing. "You're lucky your father's important, Young Ewan," he said. Then, leaning in, he murmured, "We *will* need a ghillie, Artúr. You can't expect *me* to gather kindling and wipe your arse."

"And to think, only days ago, I stopped a spear from striking you on the battlefield," Artúr mused, clasping his shoulder.

Despite their banter, the men were somber as they set out into the damp summer morning.

Rhydderch may have granted safe passage through Strathclyde in thanks for their aid, but Cai did have reason to be cautious. Artúr and his father had raided the Britons at Clyde Rock some winters ago, leaving their Great Hall in cinders. Britons had long memories, and their peace with Rhydderch Hael was a fragile one. Still, as they moved deeper into Strathclyde, it seemed word had spread of

Artúr's cavalry and their heroism in the battle, for Britons rushed to the muddy road with Brighid's knots and bannocks, flasks of ale and creamy, cloth-wrapped cheeses, pressing them into the warriors' battered fingers. These settlements were not in the path the Angles had burned on their way to Din Eidyn, but, for many, their husbands and fathers, lovers and sons, had gone off to fight and not yet returned.

"My brother is Eld of Blackwood," a boy said. "Have you seen him?"

Artúr's men frowned—most spoke only Goidelic—and the people flocked to Artúr, for all knew his mother had been a Briton.

"Carwin? Have you seen a lad called Carwin? He's tall and favors a leg, can't mistake him." This from a mother.

Artúr shook his head, answering in their tongue. *"Mae'n ddrwg gen i."* I'm sorry.

At the crossroads he sent his mount off in care of his company and watched as his men disappeared down the road to Mannau. The five of them would now continue on foot.

As they twisted west toward Clyde Rock, away from the desperate eyes of strangers and the questioning looks of his men, Artúr drew up his hood, feeling a tide of relief. How could he tell them the reason for his errand when he did not know it himself?

Artúr had not aided the Britons in the Battle of the Caledonian Wood because it was honorable, nor because his mother, long dead, was a Briton. He'd not ridden south because Lord Meldred was the son of his much elder sister, nor because Lailoken and the Dragon Warriors were allies.

He had ridden south because if the kingdom of Gododdin should fall, it would not be long before the fiery torches of the Angles licked the borders of his own kingdom. And Mannau guarded the passes that led into Dalriada, the kingdom of the Scots. The Scots had trouble enough from Bridei and his Picts without facing an Angle invasion to boot.

Tuath and *clann*, Artúr's father always said. *The land and the children.*

"*Tuath* and *clann*." Artúr and each of his five brothers had repeated it as they took their first meat from the point of a sword.

A king ruled over nothing without loyal kin. And yet, if it came to a knife's edge, each of Aedan's sons knew which his father valued more. It was land, above all.

Artúr could feel Eiddilig's eyes on him as they walked on in silence.

"Aedan's picked his tanist at last," Eiddilig ventured. "Why else would he summon you?"

Eiddilig might believe it, but Artúr wasn't so certain.

"Aedan has a keen nose. He can sense when the weather is shifting," Eiddilig said. "The Angles may be beaten, but they'll rise again, and he's still not chosen a tanist."

"It *has* been six winters since Aedan claimed the throne of Dalriada," Bedwyr said. "Perhaps the council has demanded he choose."

"No one demands anything of Aedan," Cai said.

"Perhaps they've *suggested*." Bedwyr smiled.

"Perhaps Aedan mac Gabrahn has no plan to die," Artúr said. He'd meant to lighten the mood, for if Aedan mac Gabrahn did not wish a thing to happen, it simply did not. But in his core, Artúr knew the real reason his father had not yet chosen a tanist.

Indecision was its own sort of power.

With no tanist yet named, Aedan's many sons were forced to vie and claw amongst one another. And Aedan mac Gabrahn sired nothing but warhorses. So his sons would continue to drive themselves from battle to battle, bridled at their father's command.

Cai ducked a low-hanging branch, a twig catching in his curly dark hair. "Could be Gartnait," he said, extracting it gently.

"Gartnait is eldest, but Domangart is just as strong." Eiddilig tossed Cai a wink as he passed beneath the branch without ducking. "One of the benefits of my stature," he added.

Gartnait and Domangart were Artúr's half brothers, and Picts. Their mother was Aedan's first wife, who still remained at court. Artúr's mother was a Briton of Strathclyde, but she'd died on the childbed, birthing his younger brother Bran. The twin boys—born of Aedan's newest wife, a Scot—were blond and leggy tusslers called Eochaid Bude and Eochaid Find.

Artúr's sisters, too, were good warriors for their father. His eldest sister, Ana, had been wedded twice already, and was mother to Lord Meldred of the Gododdin. His other sister, Maithgemma, had been married off to a powerful king of the Ulaid in Scotia to keep the peace and now dwelled across the Narrow Sea.

Night fell.

As they neared Clyde Rock, Rhydderch's warriors directed them to the fortress, but Artúr asked if they might camp instead on the outskirts, by the river.

Later, by the fire, Bedwyr glanced up at the mount, rising like a whale back against the darkening summer sky. "I wouldn't mind the comfort of a fleece-lined couch," he said. Artúr shot him a look.

"Nay, you're right, of course," Bedwyr said. "Poor taste, really, accepting their hospitality when they've only just rebuilt it."

Cai almost smiled.

As stars pricked the black sky overhead, Bedwyr sang the tale of Blodeuwedd, the woman made of flowers.

"I should like to meet a woman made of flowers," Eiddilig mused, stroking his beard. "Most I've known are made of nettle."

"Speaking of flowers"—Bedwyr glanced at Artúr—"did you know it was Angharad of Woodwick Bay who summoned the Picts to battle? Wasn't she the priestess who tended you in the Orcades?"

"Angharad?" Artúr sat up. "You mean to say she was there? Did you see her?"

"Nay, not I," Bedwyr said, but his blue eyes flicked to Cai.

"I saw her through the haze of battle. She seemed unharmed," Cai said.

"And you said nothing?" It came more sternly than he'd intended. The warriors round the fire lifted their brows.

"Angharad? Is she flowers or nettle?" Young Ewan asked.

"She is Queen Languoreth's daughter," Bedwyr explained. "So I'd say a bit of both."

Eiddilig picked at the dirt beneath his nails with a knife. "Our Lord Artúr is clearly keen on her. Did you tickle her bits?"

"Come, now, Eiddilig." Artúr shot him a dangerous look. Gods, their eagerness. It was like being pricked with bone needles. "She was a novice. They're meant to be chaste."

Artúr didn't know why it rankled him. He'd known Angharad only a handful of days. But he had felt an ease in her company, and her hands—they had pulsed with power, like a heartbeat. It was a gift of prophets, the laying on of hands, and she had done it to ease his wound. He supposed he found her fascinating. How strange that fate had brought them both to Dùn Meldred. How confounding that he had not seen her. He pictured her fair, freckled face, her gray eyes and rich reddish hair. The Keepers believed those with yellow hair were closest to the Gods. Brown hair was of the earth. But *rua*. Those with red hair were meant to have power in their blood. Artúr knew the feel of it, for Artúr was *rua*, too.

But his power was war.

"He won't speak of it," Eiddilig observed. "Like squeezing water from a stone."

"A song, then," Bedwyr declared, lifting his drink horn. "It's your turn, Artúr. You love the Songs."

Artúr held up his hands, warding it off, and took a deep draft from his horn.

"Let's have the tale of your father, then," Eiddilig said.

"Aye," said Young Ewan. "I can scarcely believe we've been summoned to Dùn Monaidh."

"*You've* not been summoned anywhere," Eiddilig pointed out. "But I'd just as soon hear the tale once more."

"I'll tell it," Bedwyr said. "I rather like that one."

Young Ewan straightened, listening, as Bedwyr cracked his knuckles and began.

"Six and forty-odd winters ago, a boy called Aedan was born in Aberfoyle, in the kingdom of Mannau. He was the son of Gabrahn and the Pictish princess Luan, and theirs was a legacy of seafarers. Aedan was born early, impatient, they say—all freckle and bones and wild, curling hair. But Gabrahn showed him no favor. He was the last of four boys, and regrettably . . . he was small."

"Careful . . ." Eiddilig lifted a finger.

"Well enough," Bedwyr acknowledged. "But small Aedan was. So he trained at weapons and swimming and horse racing, harder than any of his brothers. Soon Aedan built muscle on bone. He learned to be quick, where brawn made his elder brothers slow."

"But when one is small," Eiddilig said, "one learns that brawn alone cannot make one a king. Ears and eyes. Watching. Listening. Faces and gestures give so much away. It was all too easy for Aedan, that game."

Artúr wearied of this tale. "Soon, all Aedan's brothers had died in fighting their father's wars," he cut in. "And when at last an aging Gabrahn turned his gaze upon his youngest, Aedan was ready. And so it was that Aedan mac Gabrahn at last became king. Now, when Aedan seeks wives, he favors tall women. For tall women birth strong, tall boys."

Across the fire, Cai was watching.

"You skipped all the good parts. The fighting bits," Young Ewan pointed out.

"We do enough fighting," Cai said.

Artúr wrapped himself in his plaid and took first watch. While the other men breathed, muttering in their sleep, he sat wakeful, listening to the wind rustling the leaves overhead. Tomorrow they would board a vessel bound for Dalriada. It would be good to be in a currach again, for the tale told no lies: Aedan's was a legacy of seafarers. His forefather, Fergus, had been the first to strike out from Scotia to settle the western reaches, crossing the Narrow Sea. When Artúr conjured his father, his memories, too, were of water. Of salt spray and rock and the rise and swell of waves. Of currachs gliding, speeding toward land. Then, drums pounding. The rush of blood and battle. The slam of metal and shield. The acrid smell of burning thatch. A clap upon the shoulder. His father's gray-green eyes surveying a wasteland from a battle-proud face.

Perhaps their legacy had once been that of seafarers. But they held two kingdoms now: the massive, watery reaches of Dalriada, and the landlocked kingdom of Mannau.

Theirs was now a legacy of conquerors.

"*Tuath* and *clann*." Artúr lifted his horn to the sky. The stars above flickered, as if they knew what lay in store.

CHAPTER 8

Languoreth

Cadzow Fortress, Kingdom of Strathclyde
Land of the Britons
3rd of July, AD 580

Elufed stood waiting high upon Cadzow's warrior's walk, her rich purple cloak stark against the flat silver sky. It was odd; Rhydderch's mother had always seemed ageless. But in the gray light of afternoon, I saw the worry lines on her face and the naked look of relief at the sight of me.

"You should have kept to Clyde Rock," I admonished her. "I travel there tomorrow."

She gave me a sour look. "I could not spend one more day behind those forsaken walls. And I've a pretty new horse, eager to stretch her legs. Besides. I knew you'd stop here. You always do."

I greeted the servants, and the two of us settled onto a fleece-lined couch in the great room.

Elufed leaned in. "So, then? Tell me the state of things."

"Rhydderch travels south with the prisoners," I began.

"Does he?" She frowned. "I'd prefer he come home." She had not heard, then, of Morcant. It was no secret I detested Rhydderch's elder brother, but I, too, was a mother.

"He would have done," I said gently. "Only . . . Morcant's been taken."

Elufed blinked. "By the Angles?"

"So they say. Last I knew, Morcant was barring the road to Din Eidyn. The Gododdin won the contest, but many lives were lost."

"Of course," she said. Her voice was measured, but I felt the worry that lay beneath.

"The Angles will trade for him," I said. "We have many of their men. High-ranking ones, too."

"Yes, I'm certain they will. They must . . ." Her voice trailed off as she stared into the fire. "Morcant is so very like his father," she said softly. "Some children, like trees, grow crooked. It does not mean we stop loving them."

At twilight I excused myself and went to visit my own father at his place beneath the oaks. The grass-covered mound where he lay buried had sprouted small white flowers. Nearby, my mother's healing hut sat, shuttered and dark, a vacant tomb of wattle and daub. Damp soaked my skirts as I knelt upon the earth.

"For seven years, it has felt as if I've been sleeping," I told them. "Grass grows and seasons spin. Battles come and fall away. I have sacrificed love so that I might better rule. I have been blessed by the Cailleach. And yet I remain unchanged. I long for a new season. This feeling of waiting seeps into my bones. But what is it I wait for?"

I sighed. An owl hooted from the nearby wood, but all else was still. I told them of Angharad's return, and the Battle of the Caledonian Wood. Of the health of our snowy-white cattle and the repairs to the stable and kitchen keep. I told them of the prisoners we held, now traveling south to Rheged, and the tension that lived buried within silence. The air had gone cold by the time I'd finished, and clouds hovered low, heavy with rain. The dead speak in feathers, in whispers and found things. I closed my eyes as a gentle rain began to fall.

Sometimes, that is all one needs.

Elufed and I had just finished supper when the guards called out the alarm and Torin stood, nearly spilling his stew.

"Someone is at the gate," he said. His words echoed, stirring a memory that swallowed me in its tide. It had been those words uttered at this very table, some thirty winters ago, in rain just like this. Lailoken and I had been left in the care of our cousins. That was the day I'd first trained with a knife. The day the wounded people of Bryneich had come pouring through our gates.

Torin startled me back to the present. "My lady, the gate!" My men were rushing from the Hall as Torin slung his sword hastily over his shoulder.

"Yes, of course." I stood, snatching my cloak. Elufed shot from her seat.

"Languoreth, whatever are you doing?" she demanded. "Keep to the Hall. You are the wife of Rhydderch Hael, Strathclyde's queen!"

"I'm sorry but I cannot," I told her as I rushed to the door. "I may be Strathclyde's queen, but Cadzow is my home."

The night was pitch-black and pelting with rain. In the courtyard the charred, wet wood of the guard fire hissed smoke, clouding our vision. Shouts echoed: Brythonic and a foreign tongue. I blinked against the hammering drops as I hurried up the steps to the guard tower.

"Who is it?" I shouted.

"Gauls," one of my men called up. "We caught them scaling the rampart!"

Gauls? Whatever were Gauls doing here? Down below my warriors circled round a cluster of rain-drenched men, holding them at spearpoint. They wore long hair and cloaks made of otter pelts that slicked off the rain. Their tunics were made of coarse cloth, patched beyond repair. Four stood, arms lifted, their weapons gathering mud at their feet. But the fifth man—he was feral. I watched in alarm as he thrashed and cursed, straining in the grip of two of my strongest men.

Gaulish traders came to Cadzow from time to time, especially when I was in residence. But these were not traders. These were warriors, rough men. Torin caught the man by the collar of his cloak just as he'd managed to wrench free. His wet hair was plastered across his face as he shouted.

"Unhand me, you spotted cock!" His battered leather boots slipped in mud as he jerked in Torin's grip.

I squinted into the rain. That voice. I would know that voice among three hundred men.

Torin grit his teeth as he fought to keep his hold. "You'll mind your words in front of the queen."

"The queen?" the man exclaimed, squirming to look up. "I *told* you, I'm her kin!"

"Keep still!" Torin demanded, sending the wooden butt of his spear into his gut.

"Stop! Do not harm him," I shouted, already rushing down the stairs.

Moments stretch when you dwell in uncertainty. It could not be. After all this time? I held my breath, nearly slipping in mud as I dashed through the gate.

"Please, let him go," I told them. He straightened as Torin released him, pushing the curtain of wet hair from his face. Age and circumstance make heavy masks, obscuring the man who once lay beneath. But despite his thick, graying beard, there could be no question. I was looking into the warm brown eyes of my cousin.

"Brodyn!"

I raced to close the gap between us, flinging myself at him, nearly toppling us both. He smelled of woodsmoke and forest, of unwashed travel musk. It had been Brodyn and I, alone for so many years at

Rhydderch's court. In that time, I had grown closer to him than perhaps my own brother.

"You're here! You've come home." My voice muffled against wet
otter pelt as I gripped him. "Are you hurt? Let me see you."

I drew back to look at him. His weathered skin spoke of travel and
sun, of wind and water. Passing winters had deepened the creases on
his face. But his eyes were unchanged: kind and playful, wet with tears
disguised as rain.

"Whyever didn't you come to the gate?" I demanded.

"I was hoping to surprise you."

"You might've been killed!"

"Ha," he laughed dismissively, and Torin stiffened in offense.

"Never mind him, Torin," I said.

"Truly, little cousin," Brodyn looped his arm round my shoulders.
"Your men *should've* cut the boughs of that elm. We scaled it in a heartbeat."

Torin's jaw twitched. "I can assure you our defenses are—"

Brodyn stopped and looked at him, narrowing his eyes. "Oi. I know
you. I never forget a face . . ."

Of course. I glanced nervously between them. Torin had been one
of the prison guards who'd kept Brodyn captive at Tutgual's command.
Perhaps he wouldn't remember.

"I never forget a face"—Brodyn jabbed at the air—"especially
when it belongs to a cocky child soldier who *pissed* on me in the prison
pits!"

"I'll remind you that you would be dead were it not for me," Torin
replied.

"Och, aye! Because you turned traitor." Brodyn eyed him with disdain. "Languoreth, I must know. How has this man a place in your
guard?"

"Cousin. Much has happened since the day you and I last saw each other. I trust Torin with my life. And you must trust me. Come, now. He was scarcely more than a boy then."

"He's scarcely more than a boy now," Brodyn said. But then one of his men called out something in Gaulish.

"What does he say?" I asked. Truth be told, I'd forgotten they stood there.

"He says your men should lower their spears, else he shall make them," Brodyn said.

"Some company you keep," I murmured. "It's all right!" I shouted. "These men are our guests."

My men lowered their spears and the Gauls bent to pick up their arms. As we followed my armsmen in from the rain, Brodyn looked them up and down, leaning in with a broad, conspiring smile.

"So, is this the best of Strathclyde, then? Because I thought surely they'd be taller."

"Hush," I said, reaching for his hand.

"You're right," he said. "Never mind it. Truth be told, I imagined Brant would've taken up my station. Captain of the Guard isn't a bad post for an old warrior with as many lives as a cat. Where is he, then, that stuffy old sack?"

His voice was bright, but behind his eyes lurked a warrior's grim worry. He knew the Battle of Arderydd had been a devastation for the Dragon Warriors. But there was always a chance that some had survived. Especially his brother.

Seeing the look upon my face, the light faded from his eyes.

He cleared his throat. "Was he given a warrior's honor, then?"

I hesitated. I could not tell him that his brother's head had been carried to Strathclyde as a trophy by Morcant—that I had wrested it from the end of a pike and brought it home to Cadzow in a sack. But I could still answer truthfully.

"I saw to it myself. Tomorrow, I will show you the place."

In the great room, Elufed was waiting anxiously by the hearth.

Her slim fingers flew to her lips as we came through the doors. Her face was caught fetchingly in the warm light, and Brodyn nearly tripped at the sight of her. He stopped, smoothing his dark hair as if suddenly self-conscious. I had not told him Elufed was there.

Her face, at first, was a picture of surprise. Then her wide gray eyes softened. She moved round the table, still cluttered by the remains of our supper, coming to stand before him.

"You are late," she said. "As you can see, we've already eaten."

"Late," Brodyn scoffed, looking at her.

She had been Tutgual's queen when the two of them were lovers. Now her husband was dead. At last she was free to love whomever she chose. I watched as she closed the distance between them, and Brodyn reached out, pulling her in. The Gauls whooped. After a moment, Elufed drew back, resting her forehead upon his. He traced a thumb lightly over her cheek.

"Seven winters gone, and that's all you would say?" he asked.

"Yes, that is all I would say," she answered. "Perhaps I shall say more, once you have taken a bath."

CHAPTER 9

Lailoken

Buckthorn Hall, Partick, Kingdom of Strathclyde
Land of the Britons
3rd of July, AD 580

Beyond the center of town, Buckthorn stood waiting, its white-washed walls like the pale face of a friend. My father's Hall. The sight of it summoned him so powerfully for a moment, I wondered if he mightn't still be waiting in his chair on the other side of the iron-banded door. He did not visit in dreams. Perhaps he waited here, for my homecoming.

Eira twisted in the saddle to look at me, her bright eyes hopeful. "Is it as you remember it?"

I smiled, looking round the property. The servants were hurrying from the hall at the sound of the horses to greet us. The stables in back still had life in their thatching, the hedgerows for the livestock stood sturdy as they'd always been, and my mother's medicinal garden still thrived in its neatly ordered patches, though some of the white stone quartz from its borders was missing.

"Aye, it is just as I remembered." I reached round to squeeze her. "You've kept it well in my absence, my lady Eira."

Eira smiled, but I should have known better than to assume my arrival would be all celebration. As we drew nearer, Eira stiffened, looking toward the Hall. "Something's wrong, Lailoken. Look."

The servants were stopped at the Hall's entrance in a cluster, voices raised. We dropped from the horse, hurrying on stiff legs toward the Hall. An older woman with light eyes and weather-beaten cheeks turned as we neared, half beside herself, using the bulk of her body to block the main door.

"Oh, don't look, don't look! Give us a moment, m'lady, we'll clear it away!"

"It's all right, Ceindrech," Eira assured her as I pushed through the throng.

"What is it? Please. Move aside," I said. The servants exchanged heavy glances as they stepped away. There upon our door was the Christian sign of the Chi-Rho, painted what looked like rather hastily, the color reddish-brown. I touched the dried paint, flaking off a chip of it with my finger, and brought it to my nose. It smelled rusty, of blood.

My jaw tightened as the older woman, Ceindrech, burst into tears. "It isn't right, it isn't right," she cried. "And on the day our master's only just come home!"

"Come, now, Ceindrech." Eira took the woman in her arms. "This isn't your fault."

I glanced at Eira, lowering my voice. "How it is no one has seen this until now? It's midday. It's dried. Clearly it's been here awhile."

"We've been busy preparing for your arrival, m'lord," Ceindrech said. "We hadn't come out this way. We'd been in the kitchens round back!"

"Lailoken," Eira said. "You needn't be so stern."

"This is Morken's Hall!" I snapped. Then took a breath, regretting it. I had known such nonsense awaited upon my return to Strathclyde. I just hadn't imagined it would arrive so soon. But in my anger, I was only allowing who'd ever done it a triumph. The servants traded worried glances, but some looked angry on behalf of their mistress, and who could blame them? It was Eira who'd cared for Buckthorn these past seven winters. I might've been their lord, but I was a stranger.

"It's nothing that can't be cleaned," I said more kindly. "Please, someone, fetch soap and a bucket. Chicken's blood, no doubt," I muttered, stepping past the servants into the Hall.

Eira followed, closing the door.

"I'm sorry," I told her. "I did not mean to shout." She said nothing, just hung up her cloak.

"I have been in exile seven winters, nearly lost my life in battle, and then traveled two days in a caravan with Mungo and his blasted monks for company," I said. "If finding a Chi-Rho upon my father's door was meant to rankle me, it did."

Eira cast me a withering look. From the other side of the door came the hushed sounds of scrubbing. "You are not the only one who's suffered trials and tribulations, Lailoken. Ceindrech and the others, they came from Arderydd's prison carts."

I nodded, bowing my head. She said nothing of herself, of course. My fierce and noble wife. Too much battle had addled my head—a Wisdom Keeper. I reached to stroke her cheek and she allowed it. I hoped Eira could see I was also a man.

"We never imagined your return would be easy, only that it was necessary," she said. "Necessary for all of us."

I nodded again and, taking her hand, drew her gently into the great room. It was empty, too quiet. We'd not been given children, though in the beginning we'd hoped. Weaving still sat upon her loom. I felt all her emptiness here, seven winters and more. *Home*, I thought, trying to make it feel right. Across the great room my father's chair sat empty. Eira followed my gaze.

"Come and sit," she said, guiding me there. "You are your father's son. That chair has long been waiting for a master."

I eased myself down. Cathan had stood just here, to my right, leaning to speak low into my father's ear, watching me and my sister chase
round the room, bickering. Blood from my battle wound had soaked
through the bandage and into my trousers, and my leg was still hammering. So many gone, and yet I lived. I let the chair take my weight,
setting my arms along its arms, tracing the wood where my father's
thick fingers had worn the curling knobs smooth. I missed him and
Cathan then with an ache that was nearly sickening.

"Perhaps we need more men," Eira said. "The Christians who back
Mungo, they know where you are. If a mob were to come . . ."

"There will be no mob," I assured her. "At least, not yet. This was
a harassment—or, at worst, a warning. For all we know, it was the act
of a zealous, wayward boy."

"When your sister arrives tomorrow, you must tell her."

"Yes, I'll tell her tomorrow at Clyde Rock. She'll want to know." I
turned, searching her eyes. "Do you feel unsafe?"

"No," she answered. "Not now."

I wrapped my arms round her. "I will keep you safe, I swear it. You
have nothing to fear, not ever again. We have waited so long for our
life to truly begin. I will let no danger come between us."

The door opened as the servants dragged my trunk into the Hall,
what few things I'd managed to gather in exile.

"They are good people," I said, watching them. "I was too sharp."

"Yes. They are good people. *Our* people, those who once dwelt on
Gwenddolau's lands. They have been so eager for your return, Lail.
You remind them of home. They will soon learn what a kind and just
lord you are."

Just then Ceindrech appeared in the doorway, cheeks flushed and
eyes bright. "My lord, you must come look!"

Eira and I exchanged a worried glance, following Ceindrech outside. I was not prepared for the sight that met me. The door was yet

stained a watery wash of red. But beyond the porch, people were coming through the field, mothers and fathers with their children, three old women. They were not loud, but rather came quietly into the courtyard.

"*Croeso, croeso, Lailoken. Croeso adre.*" Welcome, Lailoken, welcome home. Their eyes set upon me, gentle smiles upon their faces. They bore wildflowers and Brighid's knots, clay jars of honey and morning's bread. One by one they came, setting their gifts reverently by the door.

This was the way of the Britons.

My chest swelled at the sight of those who had so little, offering so much. I stepped out to greet them, Eira by my side. An old woman reached fondly for my bearded face, patting my cheeks as if I were her son. Behind her, a bead of water slipped down the bloodstained door. Looking into her wise, weatherworn face, I remembered again what it was all for. These were my people, the people of the Old Way.

And we might have defeated the Angles, but the battle for Strathclyde had only just begun.

CHAPTER 10

Languoreth

Cadzow Fortress, Kingdom of Strathclyde
Land of the Britons
4th of July, AD 580

The road was quiet the next morning as our caravan set out for
Clyde Rock.

To grow old was to dwell in a world of echoes, I decided, as I slipped
into a trance timed by the plodding of horses. At forty winters, I was
accustomed to such visitations. But something had shifted since Angharad's returning, as if the dreaming she spoke of clung to her, leaving
its vestiges on all that she touched. Perhaps it was the shadowy return
of Mungo, too, that had memories revisiting with a voraciousness that
left me reeling.

Here we were traveling the road to Clyde Rock, another caravan of
nobles and soldiers. I am a woman grown who has borne four children,
yet I am also a child again, riding my white horse Fallah on my first
visit to the capital with my father. How magical Partick had seemed
to me then! Were it not so sad, I could laugh at my innocence. But on
that journey, I'd met an ailing monk named Fergus. And when he'd
died, it was his body Mungo and his followers had buried beneath the
slaughtered oaks of Bright Hill.

"Have you made up your mind about the Gauls, little Cousin?"

Brodyn stirred me from my thoughts, drawing his horse up beside mine. "They're good fellows, quite happy to ride with the trunks. They don't often complain. Look." He gestured.

I glanced back at them, laughing and singing as they bounced along in the open cart that followed Elufed's sleek chariot. Something about them made me smile. And yet . . .

"I only wonder why they should offer their allegiance," I said. "They have no loyalty to me."

"Well. I told them you possess a most excellent cook." When I did not smile, Brodyn looked at me sidelong. "I find you much changed, Languoreth. I would not bring you men you cannot trust. You must know that."

"Yes, Cousin, you will find I'm much changed. I must be careful," I said sharply. "And I have plenty of men in my guard. Ones I have already furnished with clothing and horses."

"Surely the queen of Strathclyde can part with four horses," he said.

"Five, counting you." I looked back at the cart again with a sigh. "Go on, then. Tell me their tale."

"Truth be told, they were bandits when I met them, come here from Gaul," Brodyn said. "But across the water, they'd been honorable men, warriors in the retinue of their king. There are few places now in Gaul for people of the Old Way. When their king took his baptism, they refused to follow. For their loyalty to the Gods, they were banished. They've been here ever since. Upon our first meeting, they beat me within a hairsbreadth of my life. But not by any fault of their own. They thought me one of Tutgual's men, you see. And when they discovered their error, they patched me up and shared their supper." He smiled encouragingly, then, looking at me, turned solemn.

"Tales are swimming the seas, you know. Stories of you and Lailoken. They say you're beacons of the Old Way. These men are proud to serve you. And in fact they already have."

"What do you mean?"

"They aided in my search for Angharad," he said. "We searched the Caledonian Wood for days on end. I had no payment to offer; they did it because they are good men. They're amongst the fiercest fighters I've seen. Let them frighten people on your behalf. They'll be happy to. As you say, you must be careful. And these men cannot be bought."

"Thank you," I said earnestly. "Brodyn, I am so happy you've returned. It feels as if life can begin again now that we are all home together. Lailoken will be overjoyed to see you."

"Aye." Brodyn nodded. "It'll be good to see Lailoken, too."

We reached Clyde Rock at midday and I climbed the many steps only to find my son Cyan standing on the watch mount, brooding, looking out over the salt waters of the firth. A vast merchant ship drifted in the distance, angling toward the fortress.

"You've come back," he said without turning. I bade the others carry on to the Hall. I wanted to wrap my arms round him, pull him close, as I had done when he was little, but he was a man of twenty-odd winters now, and a lord, as he never failed to remind me. I touched his slender shoulder, turning him to me. His blue eyes were stormy. He was angry so much of the time.

"Are you not happy to see me alive and returned from war? I'm happy to see you. I feared for your safety," I said.

"Of course I am safe," he snapped. "I had Elufed as my keeper, did I not? You kept me to Clyde Rock with my *nain* like a boy." The bitterness in his voice made me shrink. He would be treated as a man, yet still spoke with the petulance of a child.

"You were kept at Clyde Rock to protect the oldest known fortress of the Britons," I said.

"Yes, Mother." His laugh was humorless. "Whilst the Angles attacked Din Eidyn, some sixty leagues off. You know as well as I that we at Clyde Rock had nothing to fear."

I could not stop my mouth. "If you wish to accompany your father into battle, you must first learn better how to fight." It was as if I had struck him.

I let out a sigh. "You do not wish to be coddled, Cyan. So let me speak plainly. You are the sole living heir to the kingdom of Strathclyde. And whilst you possess many gifts, warriorship is not among them. Your father kept you to the mount so that you would not die."

"Yes." Cyan looked out to sea. "I thought as much."

"We did not wish to insult you or cause you embarrassment."

He turned, and I saw the hurt plain in his eyes. "You swore never to lie. To Gladys and me."

My shoulders sank. "I'm sorry, Cyan. You are right." I reached to smooth his shaggy blond hair. "Between a mother and her child, there should never be lies. We must always tell the truth, you and I."

"Yes." He nodded. "That's what you said."

I drew him to me, speaking low as I held him. "I know you suffer, Cyan. It isn't your fault. You are not your brother; you needn't be. You are your own man."

He leaned into me a moment. Not long enough, but it was something. Then he sniffed, drawing away.

"I know Angharad yet lives. Half the kingdom has heard it by now."

I brightened. "I hadn't the chance to tell you yet. Oh, Cyan. You should see her. She looks so well. Grown to a woman. She'll soon be a priestess. She asked after you. You and your sister. I'm certain she'll visit before too long."

"A priestess," he murmured, casting his eyes to the sky. "You must be proud."

"I am proud of all my children. Not the least of all, you."

My words were as nothing.

"Not every king is a warrior," I insisted. "Your fascination for learning will serve kingship well. You are Rhydderch's eldest son, now. There are always good men willing to fight for a leader who is wise."

This was not what Cyan wished to hear. It seemed no matter how I tried, I could never say the right thing to ease him. I looped my arm into the crook of his elbow.

"Your uncle has returned. And Mungo. Your father means to make them joint counsel."

"I am well aware, Mother. After all, who do you think advised him?"

I stopped. So this had been Cyan's doing? I had not realized the extent to which he'd learned to bend his father's ear. Then again, it was not so much Rhydderch's ear as it was his heart. He, too, worried over Cyan's place at court. Rhydderch sought only to help Cyan find meaning. But to what end? Riot? Civil war? It was not like Rhydderch. Age was making him far too tender.

The look I gave Cyan was heavy with warning. "Since you had the mind to summon them both here, I trust you will help foster peace between them in the coming days. You underestimate Mungo if you think him a kind and faithful old man."

"Oh, you've told me, Mother. A murderer, and worse." I did not like his cavalier tone.

"Please, Cyan. Mind your voice."

"I will form my own opinion," he said lightly. "Despite what you say, his reputation precedes him as a devout man of God and a great leader of the Christian way. They say six hundred monks wept when he left Hoddam, where he'd lived in exile these past years."

"Tears of joy, no doubt," I muttered. But I would not argue with Cyan, not about Christ. At least not now. I had allowed my children to choose their own gods. Still, it stung, the compassion Cyan lavished on Mungo, the man who had scarred his uncle's face.

"Come inside," I said. "Lailoken is my only brother, and your blood. You must greet him and make him feel at home."

We ate that night, a small gathering. I could not help but notice how Mungo tracked Cyan. Such eagerness lay beneath the strict wash of decorum. I watched as Mungo looked up, catching Cyan's gaze, and inclined his head.

Glancing away, I drank deeply from my cup and pardoned myself from the table. I found Lailoken and Brodyn staring thoughtfully at a gaming board.

"I was hoping you'd be lured by the prospect of seeing me whipped at gaming," Lail said.

"There are games enough afoot," I said darkly. Lail's face betrayed nothing, but I could sense that he, too, was upset. Such was the curse of twins.

"You would tell me something," I guessed, low-voiced.

"I arrived at Buckthorn to find a Chi-Rho marking the door."

The news struck like a dart. But across the hall, Mungo and his spies were watching. Brodyn, all too aware, let out a boorish laugh, pronouncing loudly, "Your sister has brought you luck, but I shan't be bested. Let's go again!"

"This is my fault," I whispered. "I should have had men posted. Whoever it was might've been caught."

"No, Sister. How could you know?"

"Would that I'd been there," Brodyn said. "It's enough to make Morken turn in his grave."

Lail glanced up. "I pity the man who stirs him."

I could find no humor in it. "Is this how it will be? My very blood boils at the sight of him. And now I must host him in my hall?"

I'd kept my distance from Mungo as best I could. But his presence

resurrected traumas that thrummed at the backs of my eyelids each time
that I blinked. A grove of ancient oaks in splinters and the putrid boil
of a freshly dug grave. The acrid burn of smoke in the back of my throat
as my father's granaries blazed on the banks of the river. The tortured
scream of my brother as I welded shut the knife wound that would forever mar Lailoken's cheek. The lifeless body of Brother Telleyr. Cathan's
purpled face as he hung from a tree, his white robes twisting in the wind.

Exile had not been near enough consequence for the horrors
Mungo had wrought. And now my own husband welcomed him back
to court.

I could not help but wonder what thoughts had occupied Mungo in
the long winters he had languished in exile.

More than once, I looked up in the Hall to discover Mungo watching me. His sunken blue eyes tracked me calmly, with patience, casting shadows as he built a web all his own.

Lailoken moved a game piece. "We made a pact long ago, you and I.
Together, we are stronger than any might imagine. We need only find
a way."

"If I cannot provide a more suitable influence, my son will soon
turn to Mungo. Did Cyan speak to you?"

"Little more than pleasantries," Lail said. "It cannot be me, Sister.
I pray to the wrong gods, you see."

"He's not yet a Christian," I said. "He's not yet been baptized." But
I could tell my brother found it an empty hope. "Remember how fond
we were of Brother Telleyr?" I asked. "There is a man Torin spoke
of—a Christian hermit who lives in the woods. By all accounts he is a
good man, and reasonable. If I can persuade him to come to court, he
could be an opposition to Mungo."

Lail considered it. "You think Rhydderch would agree? The Christian lords of Strathclyde belong to Mungo."

"We have heard whispers of nobles who visit this hermit in his wood," I said. "The Christians who supported Brother Telleyr, it would seem. If they had a champion, a man of balance and reason, Rhydderch would be inclined to support him. He has brought Mungo back only because he believes he must."

"I feel the divide; it will grow worse than before," my brother said. "If this man is indeed reasonable, perhaps he could be the one to ensure peace amongst our people."

"We are agreed, then," I said. "As soon as I'm able, I'll make an excuse to go riding. It is high time I met this hermit in the wood."

CHAPTER 11

Artúr

Dùn Monaidh, Kingdom of Dalriada
Land of the Scots
6th of July, AD 580

At Clyde Rock, Artúr was provided a seagoing currach with a small crew at Rhydderch's behest, and from there they set sail onto the salty Firth of Clyde. The journey took them skirting along the coast, until at last they reached the lochs, the watery heartland of the Scots.

As they drifted past crannogs and wooden watchtowers, fishermen and their loch-side steadings, Artúr breathed in the air. The kingdom of Dalriada was a place that smelled at once of sea and of swamp, where hills rose like fists, lording over sea-lochs that brought vessels not only from Scotia but from distant lands, ones whose borders could not be fathomed from shore.

The rain was coming in sheets by the time they reached Aedan's fortress of Dùn Monaidh. Only moments before, it had seemed a fine enough day. But later that morning, the wind had switched direction.

The weather in Dalriada was as changeable as his father.

The hulking mount of Cruach Mhòr was buried in cloud, but Artúr knew that behind it the warm, dry Hall of Dùn Monaidh awaited. As the boatmen drew in their oars, easing the currach into the quay,

Artúr spotted the large, open-air Gathering Place just beyond the dock, with its stately painted posts and thatched gabled roof. Its usual hum of activity was dampened by driving rain, the only people a scattering of tradesmen and rain-weary seafarers. They stood in an orderly line beneath the shelter of the pavilion, waiting to pay a balding Wisdom Keeper their tax in goods for their travels through Dalriada. At the edge of the pavilion, a hulking warrior with eyebrows like caterpillars stuck his arm into the rain to dampen his whetstone and carried on sharpening his knife. Artúr pushed back his hood, wiping the water from his face. At the sight of him, an excitable murmur traveled the crowd.

"It's Artúr and the Eastlanders. Hail the Men of Mannau!"

Hail, hail. The echo traveled like water.

Eiddilig sniffed. "*Eastlanders*. As if there aren't a hundred kingdoms east of Dalriada."

Artúr only smiled, lifting a hand in greeting. "Don't see why it bothers you. You're no Eastlander."

"It isn't respectful."

"Mannau and Dalriada may both be under Aedan, but they are two separate kingdoms," Cai said. "They mean nothing by it."

Bedwyr clapped Eiddilig on the shoulder. "You needn't be so serious. Look. There's Chaorunn waiting, looking like the Morrigu herself."

At the far end of the Gathering Place, Aedan's chief counsellor stood in her white robes, her long gray hair plaited and studded with delicate clasps of gold foil. Horses were waiting beside her, shifting their hooves with a bored sort of impatience, their long, curling lashes still beaded with rain. Chaorunn had been a great warrior once. Legend had it she'd trained at the school begun by the great female warrior Scáthach in Scotia, across the Narrow Sea. Killing was an art, and Chaorunn knew much of war and its counsel. Artúr bowed, and the Wisdom Keeper broke into a smile, gripping his arms.

"Artúr. It is good to see you. Are you well?" It brought him comfort to hear her deep voice.

"Aye, Chaorunn. Well enough."

She eyed him with a warrior's kenning. "You are just returned from battle. Tomorrow you should visit the loch. It will bring you comfort."

He nodded. "I will, then. Thank you."

Chaorunn glanced at the small crew of Britons lent by Rhydderch as they came striding up the quay and signaled to the warrior with the whetstone. No Scot wanted Britons hanging about.

"Feed the oarsmen and let them dry by the fire," she said. "Then be certain they're off."

"Aye, Chaorunn." He nodded and stood, sheathing his blade.

"Come, then. Your father waits."

They set off from the Gathering Place, crossing the frothing white burn that skirted the base of Cruach Mhòr, its mossy green boulders bright from rain. As the horses hurried uphill toward the promise of grain and a dry stable, they passed beneath a lofty oak, and something round and hard pelted Artúr upon the top of his head. He frowned, looking down to see an acorn, still green, burrowed in the folds of his cloak. Funny. Acorns didn't drop in summer; they weren't fully grown. Twisting in his saddle, he glanced up at the tree and flicked the acorn from his thigh.

The horses bent their necks to the growing pitch of the hill. *Eastlander*, they called him. But perhaps Eiddilig's point was fair, for while Artúr made his fame as a warrior of Mannau, Artúr's forefather Fergus had founded Dalriada. Gabrahn, Artúr's grandfather, had made a home for himself in Mannau, but he'd battled the whole of his life to become the king of Dalriada. It would come to pass that Dalriada was a fickle bride, for the middle-aged Gabrahn ruled only a short time before he was killed on the battlefield by Bridei, king of the Picts.

The throne of Dalriada had not passed to Aedan then, but to Aedan's uncle.

Aedan retreated back east, to Mannau, to the very fortress where Artúr now dwelled, and had schemed the whole of his life to become king of Dalriada like his father. It was a bloody legacy of short-lived kings. Thankfully, Aedan mac Gabrahn had no plans to die.

As they reached the heights of Cruach Mhòr, the rain stopped and the clouds blew off. Artúr looked out over the marches of Dalriada. To the east, rising from the Moine Mhòr, the Great Moss, Artúr could see the sacred mount of Dunadd. The place kings were made. Young Ewan's eyes widened at the sight of it.

"Is that the place where the future king takes the sword from the stone?" he asked.

"Aye," Artúr said. Turning from the view, he dropped from his horse and passed it off to the waiting groom. As they strode through the high gate into the upper citadel, Artúr was knocked back on his heels by a careering little boy with floppy blond hair.

"Artúr! You've come!"

Laughing, Artúr righted himself and hoisted up his little half brother, holding him, legs dangling, at arm's length so he might look at him.

"Could this be my brother Eochaid Bude?"

"Nay," Cai frowned. "He is far too tall."

"No, it *is*! It *is* me!" Eochaid Bude cried out.

Artúr squinted and jiggled him, making him giggle. "Aye, then, you are. For surely, you *sound* like a Scot." Eochaid Bude gripped Artúr's ears, his blue eyes bright with mischief.

"Put me down or I'll wallop you!" he shouted.

"A son of Aedan, indeed!" Artúr pronounced, dropping his brother onto the grass. Eochaid Bude took off in a run, shouting over his shoulder.

"They're all waiting. The giant man, too!"

Artúr and Cai glanced at each other as they moved past the huts and toward the wooden Hall, which dominated the citadel. The Hall itself was sturdy and simple. While other kings fussed over woodcrafters renowned for ornamentation, Aedan mac Gabrahn was far more concerned with strong defenses and good metalsmiths: iron spikes for ramparts and jeweled bird-headed brooches for his men.

They stepped into the great room only to be accosted by a shrill cry and the frenzied flapping of a giant sandy-gray-feathered bird, startled by Eochaid Bude as he'd thrust open the doors. Had they been less familiar, they might've ducked, but it was only a crane, one of his father's pairs. His father kept them for luck. It settled indignantly in the far corner of the room, and Chaorunn dealt a harsh look to Eochaid Bude, pointing to the Hall's back chambers, where he was sure to find his twin brother.

Music raced, bodhran and pipe, and the Hall was hot, crowded with Keepers, warriors, lords, and their wives, all making merry as they kept from the rain. Hanging bowls—jewel-toned oil lamps covered with glass tile from the Mediterranean—shimmered as servants hurried with dry linens, helping the men with their rain-drenched cloaks.

Artúr spotted his father at the far end of the Hall, his elbows resting on the king's table just beyond the central hearth. Aedan's curly hair had grown longer since Artúr had last seen him. It settled on the gold torque at his neck, making him almost appear a young man again. His deep-set hazel eyes were intent as he spoke to the hulking, richly dressed Pictish man sitting beside him.

"That's Gogfran Gawr, king of the Round Table at Stirling." Artúr nodded to the man beside his father. His dark blond hair was streaked with gray, and his blue eyes were sharp. His nose was bulbous, as if it had been smashed by a metal shield boss and never quite mended. Gogfran was a Miathi Pict, part of a confederation that had been frac- tured when the Romans came and built their most northerly wall.

The Antonine Wall hadn't lasted more than one generation, but the wound it had left plagued the Miathi still. Their once-great tribe had shattered like glass, forming countless new *tuaths* across Pictland. Those nearest to Mannau and Dalriada paid tribute to Aedan mac Gabrahn. But those farther east were loyal to Bridei, high king of the Picts, Aedan's greatest enemy. Gogfran paid tribute to neither. Why, then, was he here at court?

Young Ewan screwed up his face, clearly pondering the same ques- tion. "M'lord, Gogfran's lands are less than half a day's ride from Mannau, yet your father has summoned us all here. Surely it might've been better for the king to visit *our* fortress in Mannau."

"You cannot be serious," Cai said.

"And you've not been summoned anywhere," Bedwyr reminded him.

Eiddilig was eyeing the Pictish king Gogfran, measuring him up. "They say he's descended from giants," he said.

A giant. Artúr could almost believe it. The Pict was four heads taller than any other in the room. Gogfran's fortress at Stirling pro- tected the only ford of the river Forth. The citadel's bustling harbor was the entry point into the entirety of the great isle for any merchant or trader, whether they traveled north into Pictland, or south into the land of the Britons. Through wisdom, wealth, and ferocity, he'd man- aged to keep his small but powerful kingdom his own.

Sensing his scrutiny, Gogfran looked up, meeting Artúr's gaze.

"Come, then, Artúr," Chaorunn urged. "Mustn't keep them wait- ing."

Aedan's warriors grinned as Artúr made his way to his father, lift- ing their ale horns or thudding him fondly on the back. His father stood as Artúr reached him, opening his arms.

"Artúr, my son." Aedan gripped him. "You've made me proud."

"Father." Artúr breathed in the familiar aroma of myrrh oil as Aedan drew back to look at him, his hands warm on Artúr's shoulders.

"Severing the supply line. Taking the battle into the woods," he said. "It was smart, Artúr. Something I might have done." He beamed, turning to Cai and the men. "Welcome, welcome. You've done well, all of you. Go and take your comfort." Aedan nodded toward the feast tables, then turned to his guest.

"Gogfran Gawr, king of Stirling. Meet Artúr, my son."

Gogfran set down his cup and stood. "I know Artúr," he said. His Goidelic was deep and flecked with the northern tongue. His grip on Artúr's forearm was crushing.

"Good, very good," Chaorunn cut in efficiently. "Are we ready, then? Come. Follow me."

Aedan tossed Artúr a wink, and his stomach dropped. He was a commander of battle—he detested surprises—and he'd seen this look on his father's face before. Gogfran nodded to his advisor, a fierce-looking Wisdom Keeper, and they followed Chaorunn from the great room. Artúr glanced back at his men, happily ensconced on the benches, arguing over the best joint of meat. Just beyond the great room, his father stopped before a closed chamber door. It was the chamber his father kept for his personal doings, intimate, set only with a long oaken table, a sideboard for drink, and a scattering of benches.

"Enter, Son." Aedan's smile was broad, as if he were presenting Artúr with a new courser or a particularly fine steer. Perhaps Artúr should have suspected that now his father was gifting him a woman.

She sat straight as a rod, her features hidden behind a creamy linen veil. Her pale fingers were stacked in gold rings and folded neatly upon the table. Three attendants stood close behind her. Artúr stepped into the chamber caught out, speechless. He knew a bride was only a matter of time, but surely his father might've given him some warning.

Chaorunn made a sweeping gesture. "Gogfran Gawr, king of Stirling, offers his daughter, Vanora, to be your wife."

"My lady Vanora." Artúr bowed, stiff as a puppet. Vanora did not move, but he could feel her attention pricked like a deer in a meadow.

Her father, Gogfran, lumbered forward. "I am certain you realize the weight of this bond, Artúr, son of Aedan. Since the days of my forefathers, Stirling has had no overking. But now our borders are ever tested. I have no sons. I can no longer protect the pass alone. I, Gogfran, have pledged to join my kingdom with the kingdom of Mannau. Together, we are stronger. May you protect my lands as you protect my daughter."

Aedan looked at Artúr, expectant.

"Gogfran Gawr, you have my word, and my sword," Artúr replied.

"Good, then." Chaorunn smiled. "Artúr, would you look upon her face?"

Nerves kicked in his stomach. He who held Stirling was the gatekeeper of the north, Picts and Scots alike. This being a political match, Vanora's fairness was of little consequence. But hers was the face he would see in hearth light, upon waking, and returning from battle. This woman would bear his children. Like any man, he hoped her face would be a pleasant one.

"If it pleases the lady," he said.

Gogfran offered his hand to his daughter and she rose gracefully to stand before Artúr. She was nearly as tall as himself; his father had seen to that. Artúr caught the scent of flowers as Gogfran lifted his strong hands to gently draw back her veil.

Her skin was the pale milk of a noblewoman, unexposed to elements. Her brows were blondish brown, but the hair beneath her veil lightened to nearly white, in the way of some Miathi Picts. As she

lifted her chin, she met Artúr's eyes. Hers were the green of a mountain loch and wiser than her years.

"Lord Artúr."

Her voice held the northern richness of her father's. She offered her
hand and Artúr took it. *She is close in age to Angharad*, he thought. Blast
the men for uttering her name. He straightened, sending Angharad
from his mind as Chaorunn moved to place her hands atop their own.
Something was happening. Something Artúr was unprepared for.

"I can see no sense in delaying the handfasting," Aedan spoke up
from the corner. "If Gogfran agrees."

Wait just a moment, Artúr wanted to blurt out.

"I agree." Gogfran nodded. Rain still dripped from the soggy sleeve
of Artúr's tunic, but he caught no reflection of panic in Vanora's
steady green eyes. Aedan placed a hand upon his shoulder as if to trap
him there as Chaorunn drew a thick ribbon of forest green silk from
the satchel at her waist and began to wrap it round Artúr and Vanora's
hands. His palm went damp in hers as he battled to keep his compo-
sure, his cheeks growing hot.

Artúr scarcely heard the words Chaorunn uttered. He came back
to himself to find the Wisdom Keeper blinking at him, impatient.

"Artúr. Do you swear?" she repeated.

He found his voice. "Aye, I do swear."

She turned to his future wife. "Vanora. Do you so swear?"

"Aye, I do swear," Vanora echoed.

As Chaorunn stepped back, Aedan looked between the two of
them, satisfied, placing his hands heavily on their own.

"It is done," he said, releasing them.

The words rang within Artúr with the gravity of a death bell. He'd
known this day would come. His father had waited longer to betroth
Artúr than he had any of his elder sons. *It is a good thing, to have a wife,*

Artúr told himself. And with Vanora came Stirling. He was now a landed lord, no matter who his father should choose for tanist. But as the two kings embraced, all Artúr felt was relief as he regained possession of his hand.

Aedan leaned to kiss Vanora tenderly upon the forehead.

"Daughter. You shall be as my own," he said. Then, with a triumphant smile, he turned to Gogfran.

"My friend, I would speak with my son. May we join you in the great room shortly?"

"Well enough," Gogfran agreed. Chaorunn gave Aedan a knowing look as she guided the Picts from the chamber, closing the door behind her.

Artúr felt as if he'd just been spat out by a storm.

His father leaned against the wall, crossing his arms over his chest. "Well? Are you contented?"

Artúr shot him a look. "You could not send word that you intended to bind me in handfasting?"

Aedan looked surprised by his tone. "I cannot see how that would make any difference. I summoned you here. It is never without reason."

Artúr glanced away. It was no use. It was done now, wasn't it? "We gain the kingdom of Stirling," he replied evenly. "You have made a skilled match."

Aedan only laughed. "Never fear, Artúr. She's only your first wife. We are not Christians! She needn't be your last. But your first wife *must* be a Pict. Both I and my father wedded the Picts before any other. Surely you knew you were bound to the same fate?"

"Why would you say so?" Artúr asked. "It is not my intention to speak against your match. I seek only to understand. You have two sons already—Gartnait and Domangart—both wedded to Pictish brides."

"Aye," Aedan allowed. "You are right. But Gartnait and Domangart are Picts, born by a Pictish mother, and thus they must lay claim to Pictish thrones. They cannot rule Dalriada. The Scots would not have it. You are both Briton and Scot. Already you have better ties to Strathclyde and Rhydderch Hael than any of my other sons. Strathclyde is a powerful neighbor."

Am I your tanist? Artúr wondered. His father still had not said it. Beyond the wooden walls of the chamber the bodhran thudded in time with Artúr's own blood. He dared not speak as Aedan moved to the sideboard to take up the pitcher of wine and pour out two cups.

"I have given much thought as to who shall lead Mannau and Dalriada when I am dead," he said, passing a cup to Artúr. "I have delayed my decision longer than I might. Longer than other kings, perhaps. But a decision such as this, well, I had to be certain. You have proven your might and your military cunning, my son, countless times over. The raid at Clyde Rock. The Battles of the Black Water—four campaigns in which you have punished the Picts. Now you have beaten the Angles in the Caledonian Wood."

He stopped a moment, his hazel eyes softening. "Artúr, your mother named you after her favorite beast. You have proven yourself to be as wise, stalwart, and formidable as any bear. It can only be you, Artúr. I would make you my tanist."

Artúr blinked.

"Well? Speak, then. Do you accept?" His father raised his brows, breaking the spell.

"It would be my honor, Father. Of course, I accept." Artúr bowed.

"Good," Aedan pronounced. "For you, me, and your brothers; together we will end the reign of Bridei. We will sever his head and avenge my father at last."

Artúr lifted his cup to his father's. Together, they drank. The wine rolled over his tongue, viscous with its memory of sunnier climes.

"This is why you would have me wed Vanora," Artúr said, setting down his cup. "She is Miathi. You hope that together with my brothers, we can unite the Miathi once more. Draw those who support Bridei under our sway. For even if we kill Bridei, Gartnait could never rule Pictland without their support."

"You understand!" his father exclaimed. "Indeed, you are right. In killing Bridei, we shall win all of Pictland for Gartnait. He will rule as high king, supported by Domangart. Bran and your younger brothers shall become faithful men in your armies, governing trusted posts in Dalriada and Mannau with lands and brides of their own."

It was then that Artúr realized. "You mean to rule the entirety of the North," he said, unable to hide his disbelief.

"Aye." Aedan's voice was hard. "All the lands, from the river Forth to the isles of the Orcades, shall belong to and pay tribute to the sons of Gabrahn. Dalriada. Stirling. Mannau. All of Pictland! United, our armies will be undefeatable. No other king possesses such numbers. The Angles will not dare to come against us. Can you not see? You, my keen strategist?"

Aedan took his hand, his voice thick with emotion.

"With my sons in their places, our kingdoms would no longer be plagued by war. At long last we shall have *peace*."

Peace? Artúr had never known it. It was a beautiful dream. But the words sank like a stone in a silted river. The ambition. It was impossible. His father demanded too much.

Even as the thought struck him, the warrior in him reasoned. Hadn't his father achieved the impossible before? Aedan mac Gabrahn was one of the greatest warlords of their age. What single king had ever claimed both Mannau and Dalriada before Aedan took the throne?

And when he became king, Dalriada had still been a client kingdom, owing tribute and service to the kings of Scotia across the Narrow Sea. Aedan had won Dalriada's independence at the Council of Drumceatt, returning in a blaze of triumph.

"We must wait until autumn for the tanistry rite," Aedan was saying. "The *cenéls* must have time to gather; the *clanns* will want to come
to Dunadd. They will want to watch you lift the sword from the stone.
Until then, drain your cup. A toast between father and son. We will
announce your tanistry and your handfasting to all. *Slàinte mhath.* We
have much to celebrate this night!"

"*Slàinte mhath.*" Artúr drank deeply, as if the wine might drown the
clamoring of his head. His father could sense it, Artúr's unmooring.
Aedan leaned in, drawing him close so that they rested forehead to
forehead, nose to nose. His father's hands were warm and steady, his
grip strong as a vise.

"When it comes to battle, we will not lose. Will we, Son?" he asked.

"No," Artúr said. "We will not lose."

Aedan lowered his battled-scarred hands to Artúr's face a moment,
then patted his cheeks fondly.

"The Keepers have foreseen it," he said. "Artúr mac Aedan will be
a hero long remembered."

CHAPTER 12

Artúr

At first light, Artúr tossed a linen over his shoulder and left to visit the loch. His head was clouded from drink, his shoulders heavy beneath the weight of all he could not tell his men. Cai knew something troubled him, and he'd rather escape his foster brother's gaze. If they succeeded, his father's ambitions would soon become plain enough. Until then, it was a secret that must be kept by Aedan's sons alone.

The day was warm as he followed the herdsman's path through the forest, the one that skirted the sea-lochs, traveling on into gently knuckled hills.

Chaorunn had once told him, *We carry the dead upon our shoulders*. Now Artúr traveled to the place where the dead might enter the Summerlands. The eighteen brothers of Mannau—their bodies were buried in southern soil, but here, in traveling the fingers of underground lochs, they could at last find their way home.

By the time he'd reached the loch, a sheen of sweat slicked his skin from the undulating footpath, making his tunic cling, and he draped his linen over a boulder, stripping his clothes off gratefully and stepping onto the earthy bank. The forest rose round him in a wall of green, circling the loch where the water rippled in a shiver, blurring its reflection of the sky.

Artúr closed his eyes, intoning a prayer, then dove beneath the skin of the loch. The water was an icy slap, leaving a burn in the wake of its touch, but he welcomed it, the cleansing. Could the Gods see him now? His battle-scarred skin and hairy legs, shivering in the violent peace of their waters?

He let them come then—the visions he'd been beating back into the recesses of his mind. Faces and screams, the sounds of piercing flesh. No two battles were alike. Only the wild rage to face one man and the next, each time to be the one who survived—that was always the same. Artúr had killed in a thousand different ways; a master of splitting skin. Such was the art of war.

Make me clean once more, he begged.

With a kick he descended farther into the murky water and felt the cold beat at his chest, rushing in his ears. He felt the weight of his men still upon his back, their deaths flashing behind the blackness of his lids.

Go now, my brothers. Please, be at peace, he bade them.

For a moment he worried they might cling to him forever, their last living host, their captain, the man who'd charged ahead blindly, leading them to their deaths. But then he sensed the slightest shift; a giving way. His lungs near bursting, Artúr kept himself submerged as their diaphanous filaments dissolved like snow in water, sinking down into the depths to begin their long journey home.

He broke the surface with the snort of a water horse, standing waist-deep in the loch as he sucked in a greedy breath of late summer air.

A musical laugh sounded from the water's edge and he spun, startled to see Vanora standing upon the bank, watching. Caught unawares, he thought her at first to be some lady of the waters, the way her hair was lit gold by the early morning sun, the shafts of light revealing the shape of her legs through her thin scarlet robes. But pretty as she was, she was not a welcome sight.

"How long have you stood there?" he asked.

"I'm sorry. I did not mean to startle you," she said. "It's only . . . well. You looked so innocent. Like a child."

Artúr said nothing.

Vanora looked out at the water. "I was told there was a loch here, beautiful and long held sacred."

"Aye, it's a sacred loch. For the lords of Dùn Monaidh." He glanced round the bank. "You have no warriors to escort you?"

"I kept my warriors to the fortress. Your men assured the way was quite safe."

"Bedwyr and Eiddilig, no doubt," Artúr said. A rather obvious strike at matchmaking, sending lady Vanora unattended to interrupt his swim.

"Yes, those were their names. They told me the warriors of Dalriada do well at keeping the wild Picts at bay." She smiled, but Artúr did not return it.

"So they might say. Yet here stands one before me now."

Vanora's smile faded. Artúr knew he ought to be kinder, but he was desperate for solitude, and Vanora had broken his ritual. The woman ought to have known better. He raised his brows impatiently, waiting for her to leave. His legs were unfeeling from cold, not to mention his other parts, standing as he was, half-submerged in water. And yet, still she stood. *So be it*, he thought. Running his hands over his wet hair, he strode from the loch, standing naked and dripping before her on the bank.

Vanora blinked. Her pale cheeks flamed but she did not look away.

"Would you hand me that linen, then?" he gestured, fighting to keep the annoyance from his voice.

Vanora did as he asked, thrusting it at his chest with more force than was necessary.

"Am I to play the part of meek?" she said. "I am sorry to disappoint you, my lord, but there is little you might do that could startle me."

Artúr scoffed, toweling his hair. "First I find you here in the wood, unescorted, and now you declare my nakedness does not startle you. Am I to assume you are not chaste?"

"Do not mistake character for a lack of propriety," she replied. "My father is Gogfran Gawr, the Keeper of the Ford. Do you think he's not taught his daughter how to protect herself?"

He wrapped the linen round his waist, tucking it at his hip. "You are indeed an innocent if you think your strength equal to any band of men who might stumble upon a lone woman in the wood," he said.

"As I say, I was assured—"

"Never mind it," Artúr said tightly. "You are here now, are you not? I will see you safe. After all, I've given an oath."

"Your oath," she echoed. "Of course."

Artúr felt like a buckish colt. The more she sought to gentle him, the more he wanted to beat at the air with his hooves. Silence stretched, and he made no effort to fill it. At last Vanora spoke, looking out over the sheen of summer water.

"It was strange, was it not? The handfasting. I know it is custom. But it is not my custom."

Artúr gave, if only a little. "Do you mean to say that Picts do not bind and promise to one another?"

"We do. Only, not in that way." Vanora glanced up at him. "I suppose I could show you. If you like."

Artúr hesitated, then gave the slightest nod. Vanora took a step closer. They stood face-to-face now. In the morning sun he could see the delicate blue veins on the underbelly of her wrist as she reached for his hand.

"Two of your brothers are Cruithni, are they not?" she asked. "So surely you know that when one offers their name, we tap here, above our heart." She looked up at him, tapping two fingers gently to her breastbone.

"Yes," he allowed.

"It is only natural, then, when a union is made between two people, that we take our hand and place it upon the other's heart."

Gently, she unfurled Artúr's fingers. Taking his open palm, she placed it flat, just beneath her collarbone. Her skin was smooth and sun-warm beneath his cold, calloused fingers. The thrumming of her heart padded, the way a rabbit runs. Vanora kept her hand overtop his a moment, as if he might startle, then placed her own over his heart. Artúr did not expect the sensation that moved through him as her fingers met his chest. They stood so close, he could feel the soft puff of her breath against his neck, raising bird flesh. Her hair smelled of meadowsweet.

"Then we lean in," she whispered, "touching our foreheads. Like this."

Their eyes locked, Vanora leaned forward. Artúr found himself bending toward her like a tree toward sunlight.

"Picts, too, believe that the head is the seat of the soul," she said. "And the heart the soul's cauldron. The Old Ones say that if two stand together long enough like this, their two hearts will begin to beat singly, as one."

The touching of their foreheads was tender, more intimate than any kiss, and her long pale hair fell forward, tickling his naked chest. Artúr felt a rush of heat at the nearness of her. His hand pressed flat above the curves of her breasts, he could feel the delicate rise and fall of her breathing.

Did Vanora feel this, too? She was his; they'd been handfasted. And here they stood, alone in the wood, with only a thin linen cloth between them. He need only tilt his head and he could take her. He imagined letting his hands roam, searching beneath her summery scarlet robes to find the wet heat of her with his fingers, making her gasp. His member twitched at the thought of it, causing the linen to slip from his hips. But his reflexes were too keenly honed; he jerked without thinking to catch it, slamming his forehead painfully against hers.

"Oh!" she exclaimed, wincing.

"Sweet Gods! I'm sorry," Artúr said, pulling away. Vanora's hand was on her head.

"No, you needn't apologize," she said, stepping back. But her heel caught on the crimson hem of her skirts, and the next thing he knew, Vanora lost her balance. Stumbling back, her arms flailing ungracefully, she slammed down onto her bottom on the hard, rocky bank.

For a moment they only looked at each other—Vanora sprawled clumsily on the ground, Artúr standing over her, clutching the soggy linen to his groin. It spread like a ripple, the absurdity of it. And then Vanora burst into laughter.

Artúr's snort was unstoppable. Vanora's green eyes widened at the sound and she doubled over, consumed yet again. They could not stop themselves. Tears streamed down Vanora's face as she clutched at her stomach. At last they took a breath, recovering. Artúr swiped at his own face, then offered his hand. They looked at each other for a long moment. She clasped his hand, allowing him to draw her up.

"Well," Artúr said. He bent to pick up his tunic, pulling it over his head.

"Well," Vanora echoed, clasping her fingers together. She glanced at the nearby boulder. "Your trousers."

"Aye, I'll need those, I suppose." Artúr smiled, yanking them on. "We should return to the fort. They'll be wondering what's become of you," he said.

"Yes." She turned to the path, seeming reluctant. Artúr draped the wet linen over his shoulder. But it no longer seemed like just a scrap of fabric. It carried a memory now, and he felt a rather foolish attachment, as if he might keep it.

"My men and I are returning to Mannau on the morrow," he said.

"Are you?"

"Aye. And you're bound to Stirling."

"I am."

"Well, it seems my men and I should escort your caravan."

"Very well, then." She raised a brow. "But only because you've made an oath."

"Good." Turning from the loch, he gestured for Vanora to walk ahead on the narrow path. Funny. He hadn't welcomed the intrusion, but now, as they left the water's edge and slipped beneath the leafy cover of trees, Artúr did notice that the weight upon his shoulders had lessened. As Vanora ducked beneath an overhanging branch, he called out to her.

"Perhaps we shall stumble upon some rough men and you can show me this strength you boast of."

"You should be so fortunate," she said. "I'm certain you've heard, but the Miathi of Stirling are born from the stock of giants."

CHAPTER 13

Gladys

The Old Roman Road, Kingdom of Rheged
Land of the Britons
8th of July, AD 580

All little girls want to be princesses.

Fools. What do they know of it? They see luxury and mistake it for happiness. Silken robes and cosmetics ground from jewel dust. Each morning, someone to plait your hair. In fact, there was a servant for every need that required tending. Gladys could see it when she rode in the procession, the ways the eyes of the little tenant girls shone.

We've come to consume the harvest your mothers and fathers have broken their backs for, she wanted to tell them. *In turn, my husband has sworn to protect you from blade and from fire.* It was a hollow promise in days such as these. The Angles were bent upon conquest. And if not the Angles, a raiding party of Britons just might do the same. Gladys never dared speak such things aloud, for she was not ungrateful for her status; it was only that Gladys sometimes wondered, had she been given the choice, if she might have preferred the life of a tenant over this narrow and lonely life of pain.

The cart she was riding in rocked, and Gladys's hands went instinctively to her gently rounded stomach, cradling it. Mothers loved their children. But not always in like ways. Gladys knew, for she was a mother of two babes already, with a third in her belly. She'd written her mother hoping that this time she might visit. Each time Gladys found herself swollen with child, she spoke to the quickening. *Who will you become?* Each love was full, full to bursting, yet different. Her own mother had carried on as best as she could since losing the two children who'd always drawn her brightest gaze: her eldest brother, Rhys, and her little sister, Angharad. Were they alive, Angharad would be nearly eighteen winters now, most likely a Wisdom Keeper. Rhys would be four and twenty, a handsome lord with lands and children of his own.

A lady must sound comforting and full of good grace when she told her children, *This is your duty*. Bear a boy and watch him march off to war. Bear a girl and watch her undertake a life of imprisonment, far from her kin.

This was how Gladys became married to a man of Rheged. This was her bitterness. She had been a good daughter. She loved her mother. She had doted on her father, and Strathclyde was her home. Marriage to Rheged had felt like a banishment.

Daughters fair of face and figure were raised to be jewels, sparkling little peacekeepers. Daughters less fair, whose fathers were graced with power and position, were kept for their breeding, supplemented in their duties by the presence of concubines or second and third wives. Gladys, with her nut-brown hair, wintry eyes, and simple yet pleasing features, existed some place in between.

The wheels of the cart jostled and crunched over a stretch of hardened earth. The swaying and rumble had sent her drifting again, and her woken dreams were always haunting memories of home.

"Gladys. I am speaking to you." Elffin leaned in, covering the hand that rested in her lap.

"I'm sorry, Husband. What did you say?" She drew her gaze from the rumbling road, pitted with muddy puddles in places that needed repair, and took in his face. Sea-blue eyes, a straight, equine nose, and barley-colored hair that fell to his shoulders. Perhaps she should be grateful that Elffin hadn't yet chosen another wife.

"We are nearly there," Elffin replied. "Are you frightened? You needn't be. The Angles have been defeated. They have no force left with which to sting us."

"Thank you, my love, but I am mother to two children. I promise you, there are few pains any Angle could inflict greater than that of childbirth."

Elffin allowed a small smile. He was not witty, but Gladys liked when he smiled, the way his eyes softened and his mouth curved invitingly. There were plenty of reasons she continued to bear his children. Elffin, for his part, was not the cause of her pain.

"Are you certain you are well?" he asked, leaning over in the cart. "You look rather pale. You've been too long in this cart."

"Yes, I am well. As I told you, I don't mind it. My mother would never forgive me if I didn't come. It has been so long since I've seen her."

"I know you wish to see your mother and father, but, with any luck, this visit will be brief," Elffin said. "The prisoner exchange will take place at dawn tomorrow. We shall be riding back home before you know it. In the meantime, I beg you be careful. Gods willing, this one shall be a boy."

"Of course," Gladys said. She'd borne him two daughters, their skin smooth as apples. What a price they would fetch: king catchers both. The thought made her queasy. It had been worse with this babe, the sickness. That was how she knew that this time she might indeed carry a boy.

Elffin turned, gazing at her in admiration. "Sometimes I think you fear nothing," he said.

"Mmm." Gladys forced a smile, searching for the right thing to say. Nay, she could not say her husband was the brightest of Urien's sons. But he was certainly the kindest.

"If that is so, it is only because you are by my side," she said, catching herself against him as the cart drew to a stop.

"Ah. We've arrived." Elffin leapt out and offered his hand. Gripping it, Gladys stepped down carefully into a rocky field, blinking in the sudden sun. Scores of tents were pitched in the grass, cook fires scattered throughout, wooden spits pricked with hot, roasting meat. Her tent would be well-appointed, as if for a festival. Were they not gathered here to exchange prisoners from battle, it might have been difficult to believe that, only days ago, Hussa, king of the Angles of Bernicia, had murdered and burned his way across their land. Perhaps that was the problem with Britons these days: they were far too eager to forget.

But as she and Elffin made their way through the grounds, she noticed no music or cheer. The Battle of the Caledonian Wood had been bloody. Many lives had been lost. The Britons who sat waiting round camp looked beaten and embittered. Beside one of the tents, a young man fumbled to break a bannock with bandages on his hands.

"Here, let me." Gladys bent down and tore it to pieces, setting them gently on his wooden trencher.

"Thank you, m'lady." He looked up, his cheeks going pink.

"May the Gods heal you quickly," she said. As she moved through the camp, offering help where she could, it seemed to cheer the warriors to see that their world was not made only of warring men but contained wives and mothers besides. As they glanced at her stomach, she saw hope spark in their eyes. New leaders would yet be born to the Britons.

A murmur traveled through the camp and Elffin straightened, taking her hand. "Look, my love. Over that rise. Strathclyde comes."

Gladys lifted her other hand to shield her eyes from the sun. Yes, just there, coming over the crest of the hill, she spied her father's banner. Rhydderch's pearl-white swan fluttered on the rich lake-blue cloth like a promise as the warriors of Strathclyde thundered down the hill, prison carts rolling behind. She reached to adjust the bone comb in her hair, a gift from her mother.

Gladys spotted her father at the head of the cavalry. His beard held more gray than she remembered, and there was exhaustion in his eyes. He motioned and his men fell in line, slowing as they neared the camp.

"My father looks tired," she remarked. As much as she wished to see him, he should have sent someone in his stead. Urien of Rheged was a valiant king but kept himself and his heroic son Owain to Rheged, sending Elffin, the son he valued least. Gladys scoured her father's retinue as it came into view.

"Funny, but I can't see my mother's horse. Perhaps she rides in one of the covered carts," she murmured. But there were only men-at-arms and the open-aired prison carts, heavily guarded. Gladys bit back her disappointment as Elffin turned to her with a frown.

"What is it, Wife? You look like you might weep. Are you not happy to see your father the king alive and well?"

He wanted her to smile. She blinked the tears from her eyes.

"Yes," she said. "I am happy. 'Tis only . . . it is a terrible thing, war."

As the men of Strathclyde dismounted, Gladys leaned in, brushing her father's bearded cheek with a kiss.

"Gladys. You look well." Rhydderch stepped back to look at her. "Thank you, Elffin, for keeping her safe," he said, clasping her husband's arm in greeting.

"It is no easy task. I would have her at Rheged," Elffin said in a conspiring tone. "But Gladys would not hear of it."

"She is her mother's child." Rhydderch smiled.

"Where is Mother?" Gladys asked lightly. "Has she not traveled with you?"

"We are only narrowly returned from battle," Rhydderch said. "I must be here, and Strathclyde needed its queen."

You might've sent Cyan, Gladys thought but did not say. She knew better than to press when it came to her brother. Likely they'd kept Cyan to Clyde Rock, charging him with protecting the "oldest known fort of the Britons," and then, in secret, doubled his guard.

"It saddened your mother that she could not come," Rhydderch said. "But Languoreth did send someone in her stead."

An older, flaxen-haired warrior stepped forward, clearing his throat. "Lady Gladys. I am Fendwin. A friend to your uncle and a warrior in your mother's service." He reached into his padded vest and drew out her mother's favorite gold cuff, passing it to her. "Your mother gave me this to offer you. She sends her blessings."

"Fendwin is a Dragon Warrior," Rhydderch said with respect. "Your mother has asked that he join your personal guard."

Gladys did not care for strangers, and this one looked rather rough. It had taken her a while to grow comfortable with the men in Elffin's guard already. She had no wish to add another, Dragon Warrior or no.

"That's very kind. But my guard is well attended by my husband's men, I assure you." Gladys cast Elffin a pointed look, willing him to speak.

"All the same . . ." Fendwin bowed, a gesture that seemed unnatural.

"Truly. There's no need." Gladys's smile was strained.

"Daughter," Rhydderch's voice held warning. Gladys felt that same sinking, as if she had swallowed a sack of pebbles.

Beside her Elffin was eyeing Fendwin as if he were some curiosity. "A Dragon Warrior, eh? Well, I can see no harm in it. Fendwin, is it? You are most welcome," he said.

Fendwin nodded and turned to his horse, fiddling with his saddle-bag, and Elffin leaned in.

"They need a purpose, my darling, since the Battle of Arderydd," he whispered. "There's no place for the ones that yet live."

Easy for you to say, Gladys thought. In some months she would be birthing again, and until then she cherished her privacy. Now, thanks to her mother, she had a strange new warrior trailing her like a dog.

"It is settled, then," her father said.

"Yes. Please give our thanks to your wife," Elffin said. "Come, Rhydderch king. Dawn will rise early, and you must be weary. Let us show you to your tent."

There wasn't a breath of wind the next morning as the Britons massed on the hill at sunrise, weapons in hand and banners slack. It was uncommonly hot. Gladys, craving bread and having no stomach for meat, had eaten three bannocks before bed and woken with no appetite. It was a little over a league to the boundary stone that marked the border between Rheged and the newer Angle kingdom of Bernicia. The meeting place was a vast, boggy, flat-bottomed field with a hill rising on either side. Gladys slapped at a fly on her neck and guided her horse forward to better glimpse the Angles massed on the opposite slope, but they had not yet arrived.

"You swore to keep to the rise," Fendwin reminded her, taking her horse's reins in hand. Gladys glanced down at him, annoyed. It did not seem there was any way she'd be rid of him; she thought perhaps he'd have changed his mind, but she'd stepped from the tent that morning only to trip upon him. He'd slept outside their tent, wrapped in his cloak.

"This waiting is interminable," she said. And not only because she worried for her father and Elffin, but also because it left too much time for her to knock about in her mind all that her father had told her last night.

Angharad yet lived. Why, then, did Gladys feel so angry?

If she lived, why did she not return to us? she thought. *We imagined her dead. Had she no care for those she left behind?*

No, of course she did not. When they were young, Gladys had fussed after Angharad like a little mother. But even then, there had been a distance. Angharad had known things she oughtn't; she'd seen shades in their chamber and hummed songs to the trees. Gladys was proud knowing that Angharad was special.

She lives, Gladys, Rhydderch had said. *She was so little when war took her. She follows her own path now. She was bound to become a Keeper.*

His words had meant to soothe, but they'd only salted her wounds. Of course he would take her part. Gladys might've been the picture of their father, bearing his same chestnut hair and wide-set gray eyes. But he'd always rejoiced at the sight of his little red-haired girl.

Angharad was Chosen by the Gods, and I was her sacrifice. There was not a day that Gladys had not thought of this, the order of things. Her mother had sacrificed for Lailoken. She'd never said as much, but Gladys had seen the way her mother's gaze trailed after Wisdom Keepers, heard the heaviness in her voice when she spoke of healing.

Gladys was her mother's miniature. And so Gladys had yoked herself to a nobleman while her sister roamed free. As if the gift demanded a price.

A single blast of a horn sounded and the Angles appeared over the rise. The men on the hill bristled as Gladys peered into the distance.

"There are a few in fine helmets; the rest look dirty and ill kept."

Fendwin looked at her sidelong. "Have you ever been in battle, my lady?"

"Say what you will, but the Britons take pride in their appearance." She frowned. "I was only attempting to make conversation."

Elffin's steward had been up late into the night polishing his lord's armor, and it gleamed under the hot sun as Elffin and her father leaned back on their mounts, guiding them slowly downhill. The Angles, too, were slipping downhill, white banner held aloft. A cluster of prisoners stood upon their hill, awaiting the moment the exchange would take place.

Gladys told herself that she wasn't afraid, but as she stood with the modest forces of Rheged and Strathclyde, watching her father and Elffin, her pulse thrummed and fear became a living, creeping thing. In need of diversion, she turned back to Fendwin.

"You never did tell me why she sent you," she said. "My mother."

Fendwin was watching the men below, his light eyes steady. "I owe your mother a debt."

"What kind of debt?"

"A debt that stays between me and your mother."

"Obviously not. For now you are here, with me."

Fendwin only blinked.

"Very well. Keep what is yours. It is an honor to have a Dragon Warrior in my guard, I suppose," Gladys said flippantly. But then she remembered Gwenddolau and felt a wave of regret. She'd loved him and her uncle Lailoken. When they were little, she and Rhys were convinced the men had fashioned the moon and stars.

"I can still recall that day, before the Battle of Arderydd," she mused. "Angharad and Cyan and I helped our mother send warning. Then Tutgual locked her away in her chamber like a common prisoner. And I watched my brother Rhys ride off to war."

"Some things are better left unremembered," Fendwin said.

"Oh, I don't know." Gladys looked at him. "My mother always said memory is the one thing that can never be taken."

Fendwin only grunted. "Watch, then. It's nearly time." He pointed down below.

Rhydderch stopped midway downslope, while Elffin and the banner-men carried on to the middle of the plateau, where the bannermen planted their white flags in the tufted bog.

"That's as far as your father will go," Fendwin explained. "He's well out of shot. But he wants the Angles to see him, to know that he's come."

Gladys scanned the hill. "Has their king come? Hussa?"

"Ach, no," Fendwin said. "He wouldn't dare. There isn't a Briton here who wouldn't take aim at him."

"Do you think they will keep their word?" she asked.

"Aye," Fendwin said. "We've got one Hussa's eager to get back. Æthelfrith." He nodded over at the prison cart. "See that one there?" He gestured to a scraggly-looking man who sat slumped but alert against the slats of the wooden cart.

"He looks like a wolf," she said.

Fendwin shook his head. "No, not a wolf. A lion. I'd have killed him if I'd had the chance."

"Then why didn't we?"

He squinted at the prisoners on the opposite hill. "They have Rhydderch's brother."

"Morcant?" she asked.

"Aye."

"Would that the Angles had killed *him* when they had the chance," Gladys whispered. Beside her, Fendwin's mouth twitched, nearly a smile. It was clear that Fendwin did not care for her uncle Morcant any more than she did. Morcant struck his wife. When her mother became queen, she'd seen him remarried, and his first wife had joined a nunnery. Morcant's new wife was a lady of Gododdin, whose lands bordered the Angles just southeast of Din Eidyn.

Elffin urged his horse forward now, alone, as a warrior on horseback broke from the Angles and struck out to meet him. Gladys held her breath as they stood only paces from each other, their peace fragile as an egg. Elffin's face was full of contempt as the two men spoke words that were swallowed by distance. Then Elffin glanced over his shoulder and nodded, and his men unlatched the prison cart, freeing the Angle prisoners to stumble downhill. Gladys watched the man called Æthelfrith step down from the cart stiff legged. As the Angles released the Britons in return, Gladys searched their faces for any she might know, her eyes catching upon Morcant. Some of the men were so badly wounded they could scarcely stumble, yet her dark-haired uncle strode seemingly unharmed, his face tight with fury at the indignity of being bound and marched like a common slave.

"It's done, then," Fendwin said.

As the Britons' bonds were cut, Morcant stalked uphill toward her father. On the far hill, Gladys watched, curious, for the bindings round Æthelfrith's wrists were not cut along with the others.

"How strange," she murmured.

"What, then?" Fendwin asked.

"That man called Æthelfrith. You said the Angles were keen to have him, but look. They've not set him free."

Fendwin looked on, unsurprised. "Hussa, the king, is no blood of his. He's from a rival family. I reckon the king hoped battle would finish him. Now he'll be making sure of it himself."

"Well, it appears the king mightn't need to waste a blade," Gladys observed. "Look. He's fallen over."

Æthelfrith lay motionless upon the ground. The footman nearest him called out and a captain frowned, dropping from his horse.

It happened so quickly that Gladys scarcely saw it: Æthelfrith snatching a weapon off the footman leaning over him, slitting his throat. The warrior closest to him dispatching the captain and the two nearest men. Gladys gasped as blades and shields clashed in a fury. Men from Hussa's retinue were backing Æthelfrith. Amidst the chaos, two warriors catapulted the young lord onto the back of the captain's horse and, slapping it, sent it galloping.

Hussa's Angles, caught on their heels, scrambled off in pursuit. The Britons looked on, champing at the bit.

"Nay, leave off," Elffin commanded his men. "Let them kill one another. Our battle is won."

Gladys blinked, reeling in the wake of the violence. Surely they'd catch him. What was the use? But as Æthelfrith looked back over his shoulder, Gladys could have sworn he smiled. The lion kicked his horse, disappearing over the rise.

CHAPTER 14

Anharad

The Northern Sea
Land of the Picts
10th of July, AD 580

Waves slapped against the vessel's hull as it rocked at the whim of a fathomless sea. The milky blue waters were restless, but they were not angry.

Home, they whispered, *home*. Beside her on the vessel bench, Ariane had closed her eyes, but Angharad could tell the priestess was not sleeping.

Sailing the skin of the ocean had once been frightening, but Angharad had been a child then. Never could she have imagined the journey that would take her deep into the heart of this strange and mysterious land. Picts, the Britons called them. But unto themselves, they were simply the Cruithni. The People.

The Cruithni commanded all the northern reaches. Their kingdoms were vast, innumerable forts keeping close watch over their seas, riverways, and high mountain passes. No ship, cart, nor rider passed into the land of the Cruithni without their knowledge—or their blessing.

The Britons called these vast northern reaches the Shadowed Land, for nowhere did winter's bleakness cling longer than here. But

Angharad held no fear of the dark. In darkness, she'd learned, one only traveled deeper.

The sky was tarnished silver. She tasted ocean salt at the back of her throat and breathed in the sea, naming its color. *Gwyrddlas*, she decided. But, no, that was a Briton's word. This was a color built for a northern tongue, and though she'd lived seven winters among the Cruithni, there were still many mysteries they did not share. *All that may change*, she reminded herself, *should I succeed in becoming Briochan's Initiate. Every secret is known to him.*

She felt a thrill at the thought of it. Briochan the Wisdom Keeper, head counsellor to Bridei, the high king, and also his foster father. Briochan was a master of the dying art of weatherwork, the skill that belonged to one of the most ancient goddesses of all: the Cailleach. Keeper of death, creator and destroyer. Bringer of wind and snow, hurler of storms. Guardian of grain. Shape-shifter and protector of animals through the cold, barren months. On Imbolc she drank from the Well of Youth and transformed into Brighid. But it was her weather-making to which Angharad was most drawn.

Already the Britons had lost much of their wisdom. Their tales of weatherworkers were moth-eaten things, unraveled at their edges, and the priestesses of Isle Cailleach in Loch Lomond emerged from their hermitage only once a year in Strathclyde, to bring the people their needfire. The true mysteries of weatherwork were kept only by the Picts now. Angharad had been training with Ariane and the Daughters of the Cailleach at Woodwick Bay, but Ariane had told her it was Briochan she needed now. He was one of the few masters remaining.

The trouble was, Briochan hadn't accepted an Initiate in ages.

Every novice must train with a master before earning their robes. But while Angharad could beseech Briochan, no law bound him to accept. The bond of apprenticeship was held even higher than fosterage, and masters were unmercifully selective when it came to Initiates. Even if Angharad should succeed past the Questioning, she'd be granted only one cycle of the moon to prove herself. After which, if Briochan did not accept her, she'd be refused, sent back in disgrace to Woodwick Bay.

Sea spray beaded on her feathered cloak, and Angharad drew it more tightly about her as Talorcan sailed west along the coast, keeping clear of the golden fingers of jutting rock, famed for splintering vessels into sticks. The dark-haired warrior with the leaping salmon marking on his brow had been kind enough to offer an escort, for he carried a petition of his own to the king, though what it was Angharad could not say; Talorcan kept to himself. Moreover, he kept the confidence of Murienn, his lover, the flame-haired lady chieftain of Dùn Dèagh.

Beside her, Ariane had opened her eyes and was scrutinizing Angharad's face.

"You are full of fear, Angharad," she observed. "Briochan will know. He will see it."

Angharad believed her. She'd seen Briochan only once, many winters ago, but she had never forgotten it. It was at the slave market at Ceann Mòr, the day her friend Brother Thomas was sold. Priests were, at best, curiosities, if not loathed. Angharad had watched Bridei, the king, come down from his fortress, Briochan striding close beside him. His presence billowed like vapor. She hadn't known the multitude of tales sung of him then, the many stories of his might told by winter light. His eyes were the color of oak and his head entirely shorn, save for a shock of gray hair that streamed from the base of his skull like a horse tail. And then, from his place near the slave platform, his eyes had lit upon Angharad's. They pierced like a firebrand and left her feeling heady, as if she'd been smothered by cloud.

To know that strange, elemental power. Longing pounded in her like a mallet.

"The Crooked Path has beckoned," Ariane said. "Follow or step off. The choice is always yours."

"I do not fear Briochan," Angharad said.

"What is it, then?"

"I suppose I fear . . . the sickness." Shame heated her cheeks.

Ariane stiffened. "You have heard of it, then? Not at Woodwick, I pray. Initiates are forbidden to speak of it."

"No, not at Woodwick," said Angharad. "At Fortingall, with Eachna. Before you came for me, an older girl was refused. She returned to us pale and sickened. She was in such pain. She could not sleep and would not eat. I asked Eachna, 'Can we not heal her?'"

"And what did Eachna say?"

"She said the girl must heal herself."

"And did she?"

Angharad looked away. "No. She ate the poison of the yew. They found her dead at the foot of the tree."

Ariane scoffed. "Eachna should know better." She glanced at me, considering.

"I may tell you this much. This 'sickness' you speak of—it has been with you since the beginning," she said. "When you were a child, it was hidden in your dreams, in the creatures you saw that frightened you in the night. As you grew older, it was in the songs you would hear, in the flicker of shadow that danced between trees. Then came misfortune. Loss and death, heartache and ruin. Such are the signs that you have been Chosen. Your uncle, myself, we each had our path. For each Keeper, it is different."

"It is a test, then," Angharad said. "I have proven myself before. I will do it again."

"It is not a test. It is an invitation." Her dark hair whipped in a gust of wind from the north, and she turned as if she could see Woodwick Bay and the colony of priestesses that lay beyond it.

"It is as I say, Angharad. Your illness has come already," she went on. "It comes again and again, in different guises. But these illnesses— they are necessary. And they will not abate until you have found your teacher. The spirits, they are serious. For you, fulfilling your purpose is a matter of life or death. If you do not find your way, there is no joy in living. Life drains away."

"So the girl in Fortingall . . ."

"She did not find her teacher. But when one is Chosen, there is always another way. Eachna should have aided her," Ariane said sternly. "Likely Eachna did not care for the reflection the girl's refusal cast upon herself."

"What if Briochan is not meant to be my teacher?" Angharad asked.

Ariane looked at her. "You doubt me?"

"I do not."

"Good. Wind and weather will tear you apart if you cannot learn the way of them," Ariane said. "Only Briochan has the wisdom you seek, and you must not delay your petition. Bridei is much at war, and his head counsel is always beside him. Whether it be by age or by enemy, Briochan the Wisdom Keeper soon may be dead."

Talorcan's oarsmen stuttered at their stroke, turning in alarm.

"She makes no such proclamation!" Angharad said quickly.

Ariane tapped two fingers to her breastbone in the way of the Picts. "Gods keep Bridei, son of Maelchon, and his counsellor, Briochan," she said, but her eyes sparkled with amusement.

"You cannot speak so," Angharad admonished.

"But look," Ariane smiled. "Now they row more quickly."

I will miss you, Angharad longed to say. But Ariane was not one for such things. And Burghead Fortress had just come into sight.

"Sound the horn!" Talorcan called from the helm. A man took up the horn and sounded a bellow. They were nearing a place where the land curled into a natural harbor and a behemoth fist of golden rock jutted out, creating a headland. Four impossibly thick ramparts encircled the headland, quarried from gray stone and studded with massive oak posts. But Bridei's fortress was not only a show of military might; it boasted sophistication, too. As they neared, Angharad saw the outer walls were dressed with swirling stone carvings of bulls painted in blue, red, and ochre. Their heads were lowered in a charge: a warning to foolish men. Warriors, little more than specks, moved along the flat-topped avenues of the ramparts, spears in hand.

"Surely this is the largest fortress in Pictland," Angharad said.

Talorcan, who was readying the currach for docking, looked up with his signature frown. "It is three times the size of any fortress anywhere at all."

Seagoing merchant vessels bobbed regally at anchor alongside Bridei's warships. Talorcan angled the currach toward the quay, where mariners and traders bustled on the sturdy dock. Just beyond, on a flat spit of golden beach, a cluster of fishermen were at work resealing an overturned boat, their faces cast in shadow by the towering stone ramparts.

Traders' voices caught on the wind as Talorcan eased the vessel to dock, their foreign tongues summoning visions of caravans carrying precious barrels of exotic spice. The men tied up. Talorcan stepped lightly from the currach and turned, offering Angharad his hand.

"Come," he said. He was not a man of many words, but his smile was reassuring. Ariane stepped onto the planking as Talorcan's men unloaded the boat: gifts and tithes for the king.

"Passage to Woodwick, passage to the Orcades!" a ferryman called out.

Panic struck, and she turned to her teacher. Surely Ariane needn't depart so soon.

"You can take the next," Angharad said.

Ariane only smiled. "You must trust me, Angharad. I've said many farewells. Delaying does not make it any easier." The look she gave Angharad was steadying.

"Do not expect kindness, nor consideration for any plight," she said. "You must ready yourself for instruction. Lay yourself at its feet, no matter the cost. There is only the learning now."

"But what if something should happen?" Angharad said in a rush, fear once more getting the better of her. "What if Briochan should submit me to some trial and I should die?"

Ariane looked at her, puzzled. "Of course you will die."

"Whatever can you mean?" Angharad demanded. Didn't Ariane have a care for her life?

"Listen to me, Angharad." Ariane leaned in. "You *will* die. You must. You will enter into the earth, and you shall die. For however else can you be reborn?" She drew back with a nod, her voice gentle. "Someday you will find me and tell me what you can of this death. I should very much like to hear of it."

Angharad searched her eyes. There was constancy there—and solace. The Wisdom Keeper had come to Fortingall and rescued her from Eachna and all her manipulations. Since that day, Ariane had not led her astray.

"Last call, Orcades!" The ferryman eyed Ariane pointedly, but he was not bold enough to hurry a priestess.

"Remember, Angharad. Follow or step off. The choice is always yours," Ariane said. "May the Gods keep you."

Angharad swallowed. "May the Gods keep you, Ariane."

She watched as the priestess strode unhurriedly to the boat, lifting the hem of her blue cloak to step gracefully on board. A few paces down the quay, Talorcan stood waiting.

There are moments that are thresholds. On one side sits everything that has come before, and on the other all that is waiting to begin.

For one aching moment, Angharad imagined racing to the ferry and flinging herself aboard. Surely the shame and humiliation would fade. Perhaps she could be content offering the days of her life up in service at Woodwick Bay. And if Ariane would not have her? Well, she could give up her robes and travel back to Strathclyde. Her father would marry her off to advantage, a marriage like her mother's. Was that not a service to her people? But even as she thought it, her gut twisted. Such a life was not contentment. It was confinement. Angharad had chosen. Now she must choose again.

Take the first step, she willed herself. Angharad felt as if she were stepping from a cliff. But as she lifted her boot, to her surprise, it came down on solid planking. She turned one last time, watching as the ferry bearing Ariane rose on a gentle swell, disappearing over the top of the wave. In the sky over the boat, the gleaming white breast of a black-capped tern flashed as it soared, dipping to the west.

"Angharad." Talorcan waited at the quay's end with her little trunk, impatiently shifting his feet.

"Yes. I'm coming." As she hurried along the planking, another flicker of white caught her eye and she craned instinctively, searching the fortress's upper rampart. Another tern, she thought at first. But no. This was no bird. It was the figure of a tall man dressed in robes of pure white, his wide sleeves fluttering in the wind.

Briochan. Even at this distance, Angharad knew it could be no other. He stood motionless, forbidding, and Angharad felt his power, towering as any wall of stone.

Her boots sank into sand as she crossed the beach to join the others at the gate. A wooden guard tower skulked above the massive timber doors, but as Talorcan lifted his hand in greeting, the gate swung open.

Angharad felt a shiver as she hurried through the entryway. Warriors of old had died here, breaching the gate, and death still clung, beckoning her to remember.

No, thank you, she told it. Land possessed such memory; it could not help its hauntings. But she would need all of herself to face what lay ahead.

Beyond the gate the fortress teemed with the living: the lowing of livestock and the chattering of villagers, the clang of a smith's hammer and the shrieks of children playing at chase. A bustling town upon the sea. Scores of stone huts with tidy thatched roofs were scattered round the lower citadel, along with two large paddocks, some sort of gaming arena, and a vast stable for horses. Stone steps were cut into the rampart leading up to the warriors' walk, which was wide and cobbled as a village street.

Up ahead, a small band of warriors waited, their tunics embroidered with golden hem that branded them elite. Bridei's own retinue, the Picts of Fortriu. Their long hair was bound in the horse-tail allowed only to Pictish warriors. One stepped forward to clasp Talorcan's arm in greeting. As if sensing her scrutiny, he glanced up, eyeing her with a look of disdain, as if he could tell Angharad was a Briton.

Haughty, Angharad thought as they followed Bridei's men toward the upper citadel. All the Picts looked at her as such, for Cruithni blood came only through the mother. And although Angharad no longer felt herself to be a Briton, neither would she would ever truly be a Pict. Eachna had sensed this pain in her and at night would soothe her, whispering in the Pictish tongue.

You belong with the Cruithni, little bird. You cannot help to whom you were born.

The warriors led on up a steep hill fitted with stone steps, the wind off the water seeming to push at her back. *This way.*

Angharad squared her shoulders as the single oaken door to the upper citadel opened and they emerged onto a grassy expanse where the high rampart walls kept the whipping winds at bay. Before her, a regal lane was marked by towering upright stones leading to the High King's Hall. Ancestors. The stones held the spirits of kings and queens of long-lost winters. Each stone now bore a carving of a bull, but they felt as if they'd once been part of a great circle, and their presence lent her strength.

The stone huts in the king's courtyard were larger than the huts huddled in the citadel below. And there, at the end of the lane, stood Bridei son of Maelchon's Hall, its whitewashed walls bright against the molten silver sky. Its ornate wooden doors were carved with leaping salmon, dagger-toothed hunting dogs, and monstrous three-headed beasts. Painted in jeweled pigments from overseas, the doors were propped open to welcome the last breaths of summer air, before night blew the ocean in, bringing its chill and sea damp.

Inside, cedar oil lamps lent a smoked, woodsy char to the heavy, drifting smell of stewed meat. It was not quite evening, and the Hall was idle. Warriors sat in clusters chatting mildly, horns filled with drink or with hands beneath their chins as they played at *brandubh*. The woolen mantles pinned at their shoulders were dyed in rich colors, checkered in their weaving, fastened at their waists by artfully tooled leather belts with ornate silver buckles. Men and women varying in seasons from middling to old wore the white robes of Wisdom Keepers. But where the robes of Brythonic Keepers were simple in design, the Keepers at Bridei's court wore white robes embroidered with decadent golden thread. She knew Bridei had three wives at court, and little kinglings ran every which way, jostling and playing chase between the warriors' knees.

Angharad had not laid eyes upon the high king since she was a child. Bridei sat now on a bench surrounded by counsellors, studying what looked like a map. He looked up and she saw his eyes were the same captivating blue. They sent a shock, a douse of cold water as the warriors in the great room turned, eyeing the newcomers.

"Talorcan of Dùn Dèagh," Bridei declared upon seeing him. "I hear you and your chieftain were victorious." The king's smile did not reach his eyes.

"The Gods were with us," Talorcan said. "I have brought spoils and the promise that Dùn Dèagh remains faithful to Bridei, high king of the Picts." Talorcan tapped his breast.

"Muirenn of Dùn Dèagh went to battle without my consent," Bridei said.

"That is so, my king." Talorcan bowed. "But I would have you know that Muirenn of Dùn Dèagh acted solely with the welfare of the Cruithni in mind. Our retinue turned the battle's tide. Had we not gone to the aid of the Britons, the Angles would now sit on the thrones of Gododdin, and your lands beyond the Forth would now be in jeopardy."

"I know this." The king considered him a long moment. "Tell Muirenn of Dùn Dèagh that I see her." He tapped his breast with two fingers. "She is an honorable warrior and a strong leader. But should she disobey me again, I have many lords eager to govern Dùn Dèagh in her stead. I do not wish to see her replaced."

"You have her word and mine," Talorcan said.

Bridei nodded, and his men took possession of the spoils. With that matter concluded, the king turned to Angharad with curiosity, eyeing her feathered cloak. "And who is this in your company?"

"A novice, my king. She seeks an audience with Master Briochan." Talorcan gave Angharad an encouraging nod.

The king lifted his dark brows in surprise, and a ripple traveled the room as all of his court turned to stare. She'd been so enraptured with the high king and his company she'd failed to spy Briochan upon entering. Now the Wisdom Keeper moved from shadow as if he'd worn it as a cloak.

"Master Briochan." She stepped forward, addressing him with a bow. "I am Angharad of Fortingall and Woodwick Bay. I wish to become your Initiate."

If the king's gaze was icy water, Briochan's landed with the strike of a snake.

"I have no want of an Initiate," he said. "Scores have tried. All have failed. It has been many long winters since I have accepted a novice into training."

He gave a shoo of his hand as if he could whisk her away. As if the blood of storm and rain had not pulsed through her body. Angharad stiffened. She was a Daughter of the Cailleach. The goddess had claimed her. She would not be treated like some wayward beggar.

"It has been more than ten winters since you have accepted an Initiate," she said boldly. "But I would try all the same, if it please you."

"If it please me." The Wisdom Keeper pinned her with his dark eyes, his height suddenly towering. "*It does not please me!*" he bellowed.

Angharad did not blink. Briochan would not dismiss her out of hand. He could not. Her *hennain* Eachna came from the old line of priestesses whose prophecy had delivered the Cruithni from the tyranny of Rome. King Bridei still allowed Eachna ownership of the White Fort, which sat high on the hill above Fortingall. Like his ancestors before him, he still stationed men at the temple of the yew to protect the priestesses who dreamt there.

One of the old counsellors seated at a long oaken table drained his cup.

"The girl is a Briton," he said with disdain. "She may have trained at Woodwick and Fortingall, but her tongue gives her away."

Talorcan cut in before Angharad could speak. "You are right, esteemed Counsellor. She is a Briton, the daughter of Rhydderch, king of Strathclyde, no less. But she has lived many winters among the Cruithni. She has trained with Eachna of the White Fort. It was this girl's prophecy which led to the defeat of the Angles in the Caledonian Wood."

From his place on the bench, the high king laughed. "Do you mean to tell me this girl is to blame for Muirenn's disobedience?"

Angharad's palms went clammy.

"We have no need of foreign prophecies," Briochan said. "We have seers of our own." But beside him, the king's eyes were keen. Bridei tilted his head.

"Aedan the Scot brings ceaseless war, ever darkening our borders," he said. "Perhaps foreign prophecy is precisely what is needed. She has come." Bridei pointed. "Test her and see for yourself, Master Briochan."

She must only say the words honored by kingdoms round, be they Brythonic, Pictish, Gaulish, or Scotti. The words that began the Questioning, in which Wisdom Keepers could test any who sought a place in their court. This was the way it had been since time out of memory. It was the way it must continue to keep the learning safe.

Speak the words. Say them, and one way or another, it will soon be done. Angharad took three steps forward and, taking a breath, looked straight into Briochan's prickly dark eyes.

"Question me. I am a Keeper," she said.

"Come, then. Let us be done with it." Briochan's annoyance was plain as he strode from the great room, the other white-robed Keepers setting down their cups with sighs and looks of sheer condemnation. The eyes of court upon her, Angharad followed the pack of Wisdom Keepers across the great room toward a small chamber at the back of the Hall.

Inside the chamber, the air was close, the scent of sea blubber wafting from tallow candles filling the room. The Keepers loomed like winter mountains in the dim, flickering light.

If the Cailleach would have me, the Cailleach will find a way, Angharad thought, moving to the center of the chamber. The feathers of her cloak fluttered in a rustle, as if she were a bird. How, then, could her body feel so heavy? She closed her eyes and Ariane's voice came, an echo.

Follow or step off. The choice is always yours.

Angharad straightened, meeting Briochan's hawkish gaze.

"I am ready," she said. "Let it begin."

CHAPTER 15

Artúr

The Black Water Lands, Kingdom of Dalriada
Land of the Scots
10th of July, AD 580

They moved through the land like a courtship.

Dalriada was a kingdom of islands, bogs, and sea-lochs, its southern reaches a series of long, ragged fingers stretching into the sea. The Grampian Mountains ran along its northeast spine, and there were few ways over the mountains. It was a journey that must be done both on foot and by boat, with currachs built light enough to carry over broad stretches of moor, slight enough to draft in the shallowest of waters.

They traveled with Gogfran and Vanora, numbering fewer than two score: Artúr, Cai, Eiddilig, and Bedwyr, along with Gogfran's men—and Young Ewan, of course, who'd not wish to be forgotten. By loch, land, and river, it was three long days of travel to the high mountain pass that marked the border of Dalriada and the western reaches of Mannau. But as they took the warm hospitality of chieftains along the way, it felt more a celebration with his future bride than the mindless journey he'd become so used to, churning the leagues thoughtlessly underfoot.

Artúr found his eyes increasingly drawn to Vanora. The men liked

her good humor. And wild animals sought her, too. On the first morning sleeping out, Vanora had emerged from her tent swaddling a baby
lynx, mewing in her arms as if it were little more than a kitten.

"The poor thing's lost its mother," she said. By noontime she'd
taken some milk off a tenant and fed it some scraps of meat, too. By
dinner she'd fashioned a sling for it and it purred from her breast when
she stroked it.

"They grow quite big, you know," Artúr said.

"Oh, I'm not planning to keep her; she belongs in the wild. I'm
bringing her home to teach her to hunt."

Artúr was not used to such thinking. His own father was a collector
of wild things. He wondered what Vanora had made of his father's
cranes. As they walked side by side, sometimes their forearms would
brush, and the nearness of her was a heady thing, intoxicating.

"This land once belonged to the Epidii, you know," Vanora said, as
she and Artúr strode together looking out over the hills. "It was a land
of Picts long before the Scots laid claim to it."

"I am well aware," Artúr acknowledged. "After all, Fergus was my
forefather. But . . . it was not so much a conquering as it was a seduction, wouldn't you agree?" He looked at her sidelong until at last she
smiled.

"Go on, then," she said.

"Well," he said, rowing through midair. "They came in their vessels
across the Narrow Sea. The Picts, high on horseback, looked out over
the water and spied the strong and fearsome Scots, rowing their boats.
So impressed were they by their warrior prowess—and most noble
nature—that they invited them to their fortresses and offered them
mead. I think you can imagine what happened thereafter."

Vanora did not laugh, only cast her eyes to the sky, shaking her
head. It was a stupid thing to say, and not nearly funny. Artúr cursed

these strange new nerves. He wasn't one to feel unsettled round women.

"Were they humble, too?" Eiddilig called out.

"Nay, Eiddilig." Vanora smiled. "Humility they inherited when they bred with their betters."

"Do not talk of breeding, Lady Vanora. You will make Young Ewan blush," Artúr said.

On the second day, mist snaked over the mountains as they reached the black waters of Loch Restil that lay in the pass between Glen Croe and Glen Kinglas.

"The Black Water Lands," Vanora said. The wind tussled her hair as she stood in the tall waving grasses. "It's beautiful here. But I can still feel their ghosts."

The Miathi, she meant. Artúr had fought four gruesome campaigns against them in these glens and high passes.

"Aye," he acknowledged, coming to stand beside her. "Shades of your people and mine yet haunt these hollow places."

She turned to look at him. "Does it not trouble you to move through lands where such tragedies took place?"

"I suppose I am accustomed to it," he said. "Fighting for your land only makes it more beautiful. These lands have sheltered me. They've given me clear waters to drink to help me survive. I've slept covered in my cloak with only these tall grasses to hide me. These lands have protected me like a mother."

"You speak as if the Miathi are not deserving of her protection," Vanora said. "They fight only for what once belonged to them."

Artúr stiffened. He and his men had bled in these Black Water Lands to protect women from rape by wayward Miathi raiders. From their thievery and burning. He did not like to be made the villain.

"You and your father are allied with the Scots. Or am I mistaken?"

he asked. "Am I and my brothers not bound to come to your aid in battle if ever your father should need it? You Miathi war against one another. You raid and rustle just as we do. These lands belong to the Cenél Gabrahn. I only fight to protect what belongs to me."

Vanora considered this. "I no longer want the Miathi to war against one another. It is perhaps the largest reason I agreed to be wedded to you. Together with your brothers, Artúr, we can forge a new way."

By the time they reached the pass of Mannau, Artúr found himself wishing that the sun might slow its arc through the sky. Ahead in Mannau lay nothing but training and machinations, feasting and obligations. Here in the hills with Vanora and the men, he supposed for a moment, he'd even felt free.

Artúr had manned this pass for three long winters before his father had relented and given him charge of Mannau. It was a cold and thankless post, but a vital one, and no Pict had crossed the borders unannounced under his keep.

The hill steepened, and Young Ewan complained of aching feet. Banks of mist clung in the high places. Vanora fell back to walk with him, fixing the sling with the lynx kit over his shoulder.

"She likes if you stroke her tufty ears, just there," Vanora said. "Look, Young Ewan. You cannot stop now. She's quite content you're giving her a ride."

The men carried the currachs in a line through the open belly of the pass. Without the warriors keeping watch from their station, they'd be vulnerable as a snake might look to an eagle.

Just as he thought it, a pebble skittered down, striking Cai's boot. Artúr glanced at it, uneasy. Aye, there were goats and cattle and any sort of wild creatures that could have caused it to tumble from the steep, bouldered slopes.

But the air itself had shifted.

It pulsed with a waiting silence that raised the hair on the back of Artúr's neck.

Picts. It shouldn't be a risk with his father's men keeping watch. Then again, it had been a while since they'd passed any warriors. He signaled to Cai, looking pointedly uphill, and Cai cursed beneath his breath.

"Are you certain?" he asked, voice low.

Artúr nodded. "Soon."

"What of the lookouts?"

"It's no matter now." Artúr's blood was racing. To warn their party was to invite the strike, but even a moment's preparation was better than none. He glanced back at the caravan. Vanora was laughing with Young Ewan and her men. She looked up, her smile fading at the look upon his face.

"Attack!" Artúr bellowed. "Ewan, sound the horn! Get behind the boats!"

Behind him, Young Ewan fumbled with the horn at his belt.

"Aye, the currachs, use the currachs!" Gogfran shouted. He stepped to shield Vanora like a rampart, but his nearby warrior wasn't so lucky. The first arrow streamed like lightning, piercing his chest. His brows shifted in confusion, and then he dropped to the ground like a sack. A wild cry echoed through the pass. Vanora darted behind the nearest currach as a hail of arrows sailed and a mass of enemy Picts roared downslope from the cover of boulders. They were shirtless, their skin and hair painted like mottled gray rock.

Shite. They were outnumbered. They needed the watch, and now.

"Young Ewan, the horn!" Artúr shouted. But the boy was frozen.

"Sorry, I'm sorry!" Young Ewan blubbered. Arrows clattered off the currachs as Artúr raced back and gripped the horn at Ewan's belt, sounding three quick bellows to summon his father's men.

"*Get behind a boat!*" Artúr yelled. Young Ewan dashed behind an overturned currach as Vanora shouted something in Pictish to her father. Ducking from shelter, she slammed the tail end of the currach into the head of a charging warrior, knocking him from his feet.

Sweet Gods, she can fight, Artúr thought, blocking an axe blow with his shield as he kicked the man's feet out from under him. Bedwyr had already drawn his bow.

"Aye, Bedwyr. The archers!" Artúr called out. Bedwyr flipped a fallen currach on its side and crouched behind the shield of it, picking off the Pictish bowmen as they stepped from behind their boulders to fire.

They could not stay here. The Picts had the advantage; it was like shooting fish in a barrel. Crouching behind his shield, Artúr shouted to Cai and Eiddilig. "End it!" And then, ducking from the currach, he charged into the fray. Gogfran stepped out from behind his boat just in time to slice a charging Pict with an efficient sweep of his blade. He attacked uphill with a roar, his men pressing behind.

The attack was blistering, over nearly as soon as it had begun. Racing to the sound of the alarm, Aedan's watchmen careered downhill, attacking from behind. The raiding party's commander shouted to his men and they turned and fled, disappearing into the rocks and mist from which they had sprung.

"This way," Cai called, giving chase, but Artúr stopped him.

"Nay, Cai, leave off!" He'd not risk his own brother over some watchmen's stupidity. Turning on his heel, he scoured the slope until he caught sight of Vanora and their eyes met. Thank the Gods she'd not been harmed.

"All right?" Artúr called out. *Aye, aye,* the men returned.

"Never would've happened on our watch," Bedwyr said, slinging his bow over his shoulder.

"Aye, Bedwyr." Still laboring for breath, Artúr rounded on his father's men.

"What happened?" he demanded.

"They killed the lookouts and took two others, Lord Artúr." The warrior's face tightened with shame.

Artúr looked round at the aftermath, shaking his head. Gogfran had lost six men by arrow. Contents that had been lashed inside the currachs scattered the ground. Ten enemy Picts lay dead. The men keeping the pass had gone soft. He would never have allowed such a bloodbath on his watch. And yet, what could be done?

"I can see your regret," Artúr allowed. "You can yet fix it. They'll have left their boats somewhere near Loch Lomond. Take the men and go. Find them."

"Yes, my lord."

As the warriors raced off, Artúr cursed. Whoever the Picts had taken captive would suffer before they met their end.

Across the pass, Gogfran stood over a dead man, examining his inkings.

"Picts from Fortriu. Bridei's men," Gogfran said. "Look. This one bears the mark of the bull." He held up the man's arm, where a charging bull had been pricked in black ink.

Cai sheathed his sword. "They're a long way from the Ness. It was you they were after. I warned you, Artúr."

"He will've heard of the handfasting," Artúr said, glancing at Vanora. "He's not keen on our alliance; he's threatened."

"Aye, there's that." Eiddilig gave a humorless laugh. "But did you not see us battling to protect your hide? Ten to one they came at you, charging. And some of 'em could fight."

Artúr was accustomed to being a target. What stoked his ire was the danger in which he'd unwittingly placed Vanora. Would the Picts of Fortriu have attacked the Miathi if Artúr had not been in their caravan?

Blood pooled in Artúr's mouth from a blow to his jaw, and he leaned forward and spat. "If Bridei wants to kill me, he'll need to send more men than that."

"Young Ewan nearly shat himself." Eiddilig grinned. "Where is that little . . ."

The men stopped at once.

"Oh, no." Vanora's fingers flew to her lips as she looked round.

"I told him to stay bloody well put," Artúr said, his pulse quickening. "Young Ewan?" he shouted.

The men began their search in earnest. Across the pass Artúr eyed an overturned currach and jogged to it, flipping it up by the gunnel.

The baby lynx startled from beneath it with a yowl and Vanora darted to scoop it up.

"The sling." She pointed. Young Ewan had been wearing it. But he was nowhere to be found.

"Ewan!" Artúr shouted, stalking the pebbled ground.

Vanora caught up, touching his arm. "They've taken him. They must have. I'm sorry, Artúr."

Artúr looked away. "I should've sent him with the cavalry."

The men, for once, were silent.

Vanora moved to kneel beside a fallen Pict, one of Bridei's men, placing one hand over his forehead and the other at the crown of his head.

"Picts from Fortriu killing Miathi. Cruithni killing Cruithni," she said, her green eyes sad.

"Whatever are you doing?" Artúr asked.

"Prayers." She glanced up. "It is only right. It is what we do."

He looked at her, exasperated. "They attacked us, Lady Vanora. They were lying in wait."

"And how many times have you done the same?" she challenged. Turning her back on him, she murmured something in Pictish. Artúr stared into the retreating mist, thinking of his father.

"Perhaps you're right," he said. "It needn't be this way. It shouldn't."

He waited until Vanora had finished her prayer, then yanked out his dirk. Squatting beside the dead man, he pulled the head up by its long, gray-painted plait and sheared off the hair at the scalp. The man's hair was brown at the nape of his neck. He stood with satisfaction.

"What are you doing?" Vanora gasped. "Stop. Artúr! You desecrate the dead."

"Cai." Artúr gestured. "Toss me that satchel."

Vanora's face darkened and she swiped at the dirk, but Artúr was too fast. "You said your prayers, Vanora. Now let me get on with it."

"This man has grown his hair since the day of his first battle. Look." She thrust a finger toward the plait. "He was a great warrior. Each strand tells his tale."

"Aye." Artúr nodded. "And his king will know it was I who cut him down. Vengeance is the only peace Bridei mac Maelchon understands."

"There is no honor in this," she said angrily.

Artúr wheeled on her. "You speak of honor? Look round you. Six of your father's men lie dead at Bridei's command." His arms swept the pass, then he leaned in. "Be thankful I do not sever their heads, as Bridei did my grandfather's. Gabrahn—a hero—kept from the Summerlands, his spirit rotting forever in his enemy's keep. I refrain, for you."

Vanora looked at him a long moment. "Well enough," she said.

Bootsteps sounded in the pass, and they looked to see Aedan's warriors returning.

"Well?" Artúr questioned. The man shook his head.

"I will send an envoy for the prisoners," Artúr said. "I will get Young Ewan back." *If indeed he still lives.* Artúr turned to his men. "Leave their bodies for the corpse birds and throw their plaits in the satchel. I would send Bridei a gift on behalf of Gabrahn."

CHAPTER 16

Angharad

Burghead Fortress, Kingdom of the Fortriu
Land of the Picts
11th of July, AD 580

A servant came just before dawn, stirring Angharad from sleep, an old man whose bony fingers dug into her shoulder.

The fire had gone out. She strained to see in the shadowy stone hut where she'd been housed after the Questioning, feeling her way so as not to trip over strange stools and table ends. She did not wish to wake her hostess. The woman in the lower citadel had graciously taken her in, despite her infant's wailing at the servant's persistent knocking late last night. A fisherman's net lay slumped in a heap beside the door, and no man was present.

A widow, her husband lost at sea. One did not need a gift to see as much. Though the woman eyed her feathered cloak, she did not speak of sorrows, and Angharad was grateful, as she felt little more than a husk.

We are finished, Briochan had said in the end. Her feet throbbed from standing and her voice was hoarse from recitation. The candles lighting the chamber had burnt to stubby fingers, and yet still the counsellors sat, eyes like coals as they fired their questions in the stifling dark.

Angharad had imagined elation, but she felt hollow, as if her skull were scraped clean. A few moments more and she might have faltered. But then Briochan had lifted a hand.

We are finished.

"Hurry, mistress. He is waiting," the servant urged.

Angharad closed the door soundlessly, stepping out into the early morning dim. High on the warrior's walk, sentinels skulked like shadows, and from beyond the rampart walls came the crash and hush of the sea. The villagers slept on, the only sign of wakefulness the steady shovel and thud of the smithy as they passed, heat blasting, dragon-like, from the fiery mouth of the forge.

Angharad pressed the sleep from her face, squinting to keep the servant in sight as he trotted the narrow steps like a mountain goat, disappearing through the small oaken door into the upper citadel. The path they followed was not the grand stone-lined avenue she'd traveled the day before. This was a servant's path, worn by boots along the rim of the upper rampart. It skirted just beyond the Great Hall to the kitchen house, where Angharad smelled the hot yeast of bread, and her stomach kicked. The servant stopped at the door of a tidy stone dwelling with a roof of freshly netted thatch a short distance from the king's hall.

The servant swung the door open, ushering Angharad through. "Hurry, hurry. Just through here."

Inside, the hearth had been banked, but silence prevailed. A figure sat tall upon a sheep's fleece by the fire. It did not stir except to gesture to the servant, a long finger made orange by hearth light.

"Corc. You may leave us."

"Yes, Master." The servant ducked out the door, and Angharad stood, waiting. Silence stretched. At last Briochan spoke, his voice low, embers itself.

"You would become a Daughter of the Cailleach. I have seen such as you before. Your desperation clings like a mantle. You are prideful and self-important. Angharad, the princess, the daughter of a king. In this state, you shall never meet her."

Self-important? Angharad bristled. She'd been tossed like a leaf by the storm of the Gods and scarcely questioned it, but she swallowed the insult, bowing her head.

"I have no want of an Initiate," he continued. "I have said as much. But you did not fail the Questioning. By law, I must grant you the cycle of one moon. I warn you, your trial will be difficult."

"I am not afraid," she answered.

Briochan turned, his eyes black in the dim. "That is what they all profess, in the beginning."

"I will make no complaint," Angharad swore. "I would learn of the Cailleach and of weatherwork."

"Weatherwork?" His voice cut. "Who are you to speak of such things? You are a child. A *witless* child!"

Anger rose in a swell, but she stifled it. What good would it do to tell him what she had felt on the battlefield? He would think her boasting if she told him she'd conjured a storm. Briochan considered her a long moment before speaking.

"For the turning of one moon, I will act as your Master. And you"—he stabbed the air—"you shall become like a shadow. You will eat what I say. You will sleep where I say. You will not speak unless I desire it. To which end, I shall command you, '*Speak, Initiate*.' And only then will you answer. Do you understand?"

Angharad waited. He could not fool her. He'd not asked her to speak.

"Speak, Initiate," he said.

"Yes, Master Briochan. I understand."

"Good. You will rise each day at this very hour. You shall take your meals in the great room, but never at my table. And you shall do my bidding without question at all times, should you wish to remain," he said. "Should you, after one moon, still find yourself sound of mind and of body, and should I deem that to be so, only then will I consider beginning your training in earnest."

At the far end of the room, a reed panel creaked open and a woman emerged. She was far younger than Briochan, her hair the color of summer barley. She had thick, graceful brows and wore a deep-ochre mantle pinned at each shoulder by delicate silver brooches. She stopped at the sight of Angharad.

"She is staying, then?" she asked. Her Pictish was thick. She spoke like a Scot.

"For now," Briochan said. "Initiate. This is Imogen. My wife."

Angharad nodded.

"But I have no chamber ready," Imogen said.

"There is no need for a chamber," Briochan said. "She will sleep on the floor." He gestured to a pallet by the hearth.

"As you say." Imogen looked round. "Where is Corc?"

"I sent him away."

"Why have you done that?" She frowned. "Who'll serve the oats?"

A heavy black cook pot waited beside the hearth, bowls already set upon a nearby pine table. Angharad made herself quickly of use, picking up the wooden spoon to ladle the oats into portions. Imogen watched a moment before laying a hand upon Briochan's sleeve.

"Husband. I would speak with you."

They stepped into their chamber, closing the screen. Angharad could not hear her words, only the low murmur of dissent.

"It will be twenty-eight days, no more," Briochan said, making no effort to lower his voice. "And the girl will be but a shadow. As you know well: those who would lead must first learn to serve."

The woman murmured something low in Goidelic. So she *was* a

Scot. But the Picts and the Scots were enemies. How, then, had this woman come to be Briochan's wife?

At the table, Imogen and Briochan ate in silence while Angharad sat on her pallet. The oats were hot and speckled with bits of garnet dulse that still carried the fishy salt of the sea.

Angharad had scarcely finished when Briochan stood and Imogen fetched his white over-robe, easing it over his head. He kissed her hand quickly but tenderly where it settled at his collarbone. And then he was striding to the door.

"Initiate," he called, without looking back. Angharad sprang up, following like a pup.

Outside, beady-eyed gulls bayed from the village thatching against a milky, clouded sky. The morning was blustery: everywhere was wind and the low roar of water. In the settlement below, livestock were bleating for grain as the rest of the fortress was stirring. Briochan rounded the corner to the Great Hall, and one of Bridei's attendants thrust open the doors. Servants were rolling up the bedding of the warriors who slept in the great room as the men scratched and stretched, finding their way lazily to tables. They looked up at Angharad playfully, but Briochan admonished them.

"Do not look at her. Do not speak to her. She is not *en Cruithni.*"

Of the People. It was an expression reserved for those without Pictish blood who managed to demonstrate their belonging, their worth. Many never achieved it. The warriors averted their eyes. Angharad was to be shunned until she was declared *en Cruithni.* Briochan took his place at the king's table and pointed to a little pine stool in the corner of the room. There Angharad sat as the fortress commenced its morning routine.

Picts did not care for strangers. It was a grand inconvenience for Bridei's court to find Angharad suddenly among them—and not *en Cruithni,* no less. They carried about their business with an air of annoyance, now having to take great care not to call each other by name, and thus risk their names being overheard by a stranger.

There was power in a name.

And, so in the absence of names, Angharad used the colorful animals pricked on their faces, necks, and arms to name them herself. There was Crane-Neck, and Seal-Man. Jumping Fish and Wolf-Bearer. Bridei's three wives she called by their hair: Flaxen, Fire, and Dun.

The king spoke low with Briochan and his counsellors. The wives ate a little, then retreated to their looms, setting about their work with luxurious patience. Warriors wolfed down their meals and left for training. No one acknowledged her. Not even the servants. But Angharad had no need of conversation nor acknowledgment for that matter. Instead, she turned inward, as she had always done. Everything spoke, if one knew how to listen.

If she closed her eyes, she could feel the slate floor hum. The shields that hung upon the walls of the great room hummed, too, each in its own reverberation, for they were cracked and aged, resounding with the memories of masters long gone. But the shields soon grew too rattly, demanding, and Angharad closed herself, uninterested in elegies so soon after breakfast.

Sometime before midday, the routine of the Hall was shattered by three men-at-arms rushing through the doors.

"My king," one of them said, breathless. "The commander and his men have returned."

"What word does he bring?" It was Briochan who spoke; his voice held a flicker of worry.

"He would speak to you and the king himself."

Bridei's court issued from the Hall only to see a retinue of Pictish warriors marching a bloodied line of men whose hands were bound. Prisoners. One had a floppy sweep of fair hair and freckles on his dirt-smeared face. He seemed little more than a boy. A man with dark-blond hair bound in a thick horse's tail stepped forward, averting his amber eyes from Briochan and the king as he bowed. A black bull was pricked upon his chest, though she could see only the tip of it, its head lowered in a charge as if it sought to escape his tunic. Traces of gray paint clung in flakes to his forearms and the edges of his scalp. He looked to be their commander.

"Tell me," Bridei said.

The commander straightened his muscled shoulders, eyes fixed ahead. "We had a good position in the pass, but we could not slay Artúr. I am sorry, my king. I failed you."

Shock coursed through her at the mention of Artúr's name. Then, relief. The commander and his men had not managed to kill him. Of course they hadn't. She'd seen Artúr fight at the Caledonian Wood and on the beach of Woodwick Bay. He moved with a liquid sort of quickness, as if battle came like breathing. Bridei's disappointment was a thick and unctuous thing.

"You believed the pass would be the place," he said, looking at the commander.

"Aedan's men came too quickly. But we have prisoners." He gestured. "Slaves."

Bridei glanced at the line of men, some of whom looked to be Picts. "Take them to the lower citadel," he said.

The commander nodded and signaled to his men, and Angharad watched as the prisoners were dragged from sight.

"How many did we lose?" Bridei asked. The people in the courtyard fell quiet.

"Ten, my king."

"And their bodies?"

A shadow crossed the commander's face. "There was no time."

"We will mourn them," Bridei said heavily.

"Yes." The commander bowed, moving to follow his men to the lower citadel, but the king stopped him, laying a hand upon his shoulder.

"I am glad you returned," he said. "The Gods were not with us. But your time will come." Bridei tapped two fingers to his chest.

The king's gesture seemed too much for the guilt-laden commander. He met Bridei's eyes only briefly, then strode stiffly down the lane and out through the oaken door.

At the edge of the courtyard, Imogen touched Briochan's sleeve.

"One of them is little more than a boy," she said.

"He's a Scot." Briochan spoke the word as if it soiled his mouth. Imogen gave him a hard look.

"As am I," she said.

"You are *en Cruithni*," he corrected her. "This is what you chose, Imogen. And the Scots are our enemy."

"And what of the others, Husband? The Miathi in their company. They are Picts!"

"They are traitors," he said. "Gogfran of Stirling has handfasted his daughter to Artúr. There has always been division among the Miathi. Thankfully there are far more who remain loyal to our king."

Angharad stepped back. Artúr, betrothed? And to a Pict? She'd never put the bond she felt with Artúr into words. But to hear mention of him now stirred something secret, protective. She knew Artúr's father was Bridei's greatest enemy. Yet here she stood in Bridei's court, wishing nothing more than to become *en Cruithni* among the Picts of Fortriu.

She cared for Artúr, that was all. He'd survived the battle, and he was well. Perhaps he might even find something that resembled love with this woman, whoever she might be. And if Angharad felt sickened, it was almost certainly the dulse: her stomach was not yet accustomed to such heaping amounts.

Imogen, meanwhile, had not given up. She frowned at her husband, her blue eyes searching. "Corc is old and cranky. You have said so yourself. Speak with Bridei. I would have the boy. I will train him up. You needn't do anything."

"You are too soft, Imogen." Briochan said. "Leave it."

Briochan rode out for the day, leaving them behind, and while Imogen returned to the hut, Angharad could not forget the boy who'd been taken. He had a connection to Artúr; he had been in his party. The Cruithni would not deal with him kindly. But while Briochan had commanded Imogen to do nothing, he'd given no such orders to Angharad. What was to stop her from visiting the lower citadel just to make sure the young Scot was all right?

Angharad reached the oaken door of the King's Mount only to find the commander keeping watch there, his amber eyes fixed straight ahead.

The door stood open. She frowned and ducked, trying to pass, but he shot his muscled arm out, barring her way.

"They've told you I'm not *en Cruithni*, have they?" Angharad guessed. "Well enough. Just let me through, please. I wish to visit the lower citadel."

The commander said nothing, only planted his feet.

"The boy, the Scot," she tried. "What have you done with him? Will you harm him?"

Nothing, save, at the mention of Scots, a flaring of the commander's nostrils. Angharad expelled a breath.

"I'm not permitted to leave, I gather. I'm to be kept to the King's Mount?" She crossed her arms, not so easily put off. "And why are you here, standing guard? You seemed a commander. Is this your penalty, then?"

His jaw twitched and Angharad felt a small satisfaction in making him angry. But no sooner than she felt it, it curdled into frustration.

She was powerless here, and utterly so. She had no choice. She would have to wait to see about the boy.

It was evening, and the last boats were tying up for the day as Angharad watched the commander enter the Hall briskly, his mouth set in a line. He carried a leather satchel in hand rather strangely, his expression a mingling of reverence and disgust.

How curious.

He murmured in the king's ear, then passed him the leather satchel gently, as one might a babe. Bridei set it on his lap and slowly drew it open only to wince, as if stung. He cradled the satchel almost tenderly for a moment before looking up at the commander. The words he spoke were lost in the murmur of the Hall. But the commander's head hung low as he left. And as he passed Angharad, she glimpsed a shock of human hair poking from the satchel's opening.

It was dark in the Hall, but when Angharad looked back to Bridei, she could have sworn the king's eyes held tears.

As one day followed the next, Angharad discovered the terms of her apprenticeship. She was to wash Briochan's face, hands, and feet at the beginning and end of each day. Imogen and Briochan spoke to her only in moments, and always in the privacy of the hut. While others dined on beef and rich exotics from traveling merchants, Angharad ate only oats boiled with dulse. Unable to speak, unseen and unregarded, she lived in a world of utter isolation. Sometimes she would spy Imogen watching her from the corner of her eye before she ducked away, returning to her task. Their hut had a central room and two small bedchambers, each with its own woven reed door. In one, Briochan and Imogen slept. But the door to the other chamber remained closed, and Briochan forbade her to go near it. At night, when the Wisdom Keeper thought she wasn't watching, he would stop there a moment, head bowed, before shuffling off to sleep.

Continue, continue. There is only the learning, a voice spoke in her head; it was soft, like a mother's. Sometimes Angharad wondered if the voice was her own.

The counsellors met in muffled tones behind closed doors. But the wives, Flaxen, Fire, and Dun, kept their looms in the great room and could not keep up their guard forever. It was from eavesdropping on them that Angharad learned Imogen had once been a slave. As such, she had once ranked below even a hall servant. Briochan had first taken her as a concubine, and then, much to their astonishment, the old Wisdom Keeper had made her his wife.

"He hasn't been the same since that tragedy on the mountain," Dun whispered. "He mightn't have married her if he'd been of sound mind." Flaxen nodded knowingly, and then Fire leaned in.

"Do you think he fears it might happen again?" The three exchanged weighted looks and their eyes fell on Angharad. Realizing she'd been listening, they'd closed their mouths quicker than fish traps.

Angharad took to pacing the perimeter of the upper citadel's rampart, the boundary of her confines, her feet wearing a path in the grass.

Days passed.

Loneliness rose, and she swallowed it. All the while, Angharad looked to the sky, speaking to the growing belly of the moon. On the last eve, before the moon reached her fullest, Angharad dreamt of a fog rolling in from sea, thick and choking. She woke in a start, clutching her throat only to find Briochan looming at the foot of her pallet, considering her in the dark.

"You are not yet a shadow. Would you continue? Speak, Initiate."

Angharad had not spoken in a turning of the moon and could scarcely find her voice. "Yes, Master Briochan. I would stay."

Hope beat beneath her ribs. Yet one sundown came, then another. Still Briochan did not alter the pattern of her days.

He had not refused her.

But he was meant to begin her training in earnest after the turning of the moon. Why, then, had he not? He was still hoping she might fail. Speak when she should not, weep, dry his feet with the wrong sort of linen—the smallest infraction and her trial might be ended.

Hope become strange, and Angharad a moth, the dust knocked from its wings. In the stifling silence she screamed without sound.

What must I do to become shadow enough?

CHAPTER 17

Anghorad

Burghead Fortress, Kingdom of Fortriu
Land of the Picts
16th of September, AD 580

There was a place outside the upper rampart, high on the sandstone cliffs, where the grass was soft and mounded. There Angharad would sit with her back to the stone and look out to sea. She thought about the boy, the Scot, still kept prisoner somewhere in the lower citadel. Gulls flapped and hung in the air before her, wings outstretched, their glassy eyes unblinking, and she collected the feathers they left to add to her cloak. It was her brightness, sitting there. It was all that preserved her.

She'd been forbidden to leave the upper citadel, and this place, though unfrequented, certainly lay outside the sturdy oaken door. Were it not for the commander, she would surely never have found it.

She'd worn a narrow path pacing the interior of the rampart, passing the same guard at the king's gate, always hearing the ocean, yet never able to see it. Until one day the gate stood open a crack.

The commander stood watch as he had the first day she'd spoken to him. He still hadn't acknowledged her, only tilted his head. *Go.*

There was nothing but the cliff's edge here, between her and the sea, and the fresh smell of salt strengthened her resolve. Knowing the risk the commander was taking, Angharad was careful not to ruin their arrangement. He would appear when Briochan was traveling for the day, or when he seemed to know court business kept him to the Hall, and Angharad would slink like a cat to perch on the cliff's edge, careful never to linger too long.

Sometimes the waves struck the cliffs with such force, the ground beneath her trembled. The wind whipped, tugging at her hair, snatching up decaying, papery white stars of seed flower and scattering them like snow.

In thanks, she brought the commander gull feathers once. Another time, a snail shell she'd discovered under a rock. These she set by his feet quickly, in passing, becoming increasingly familiar with the sight of his weathered brown leather boots. Because of his kindness, she grew curious. He seemed preoccupied with metalwork. Now that Angharad had begun to seek out his wild-haired figure, she spotted him often in conversation with the smith, or before the others woke, in the hour just before morning, with his head bent in the smithy itself, dealing steady strikes to iron that sparked in the semidark.

Her days were measured by the dirt removed from Briochan's fingernails. She watched him pray. Watched him eat. Watched him pause by the closed chamber door each night before sleeping. She watched him walk the ramparts, tilting his head to the ocean as if listening to it speak.

She dwelled in shadow, just beyond hearth light, while feasts roared in the glow of the Hall. Clouds shifted and raced, thundering like cattle. On Lughnasa, Angharad had stood alone, watching the beacon fires flicker with hungry, hollow eyes. They whispered with their flame-forked tongues: *Burn on. Burn on.*

Unseen by those around her, Angharad slipped into a place where time did not pass. The only thing that changed was the weather. Soon she began to feel not like a shadow but a ghost.

And then, one unremarkable morning, something wonderous occurred.

Angharad was squeezing the water from a warm linen to wash Briochan's feet when he caught her hand.

"Enough."

Angharad froze, water dripping through her fingers.

Briochan dried his feet and stood, tugging on his boots.

Angharad could only stare after him, disbelieving. Imogen rushed from the pot she was tending on the hearth, snatching the linen from Angharad's hands.

"Hurry, then, quickly," she whispered. "Before he changes his mind!"

Grabbing her cloak, Angharad hurried after him.

Outside, rain pelted like pebbles. The sea was wild and white capped, the early chill of autumn biting with a thousand little teeth. Water streamed her face as Angharad followed Briochan down the king's path, nearly colliding with a hooded figure. Her boots slipped in the muck and she plummeted forward only to be caught by the elbows. She looked up into the commander's face. His amber eyes met hers, then shot to Briochan striding downhill at a steady clip through the rain. Worry flickered in his gaze, but still he wouldn't speak. Already Briochan was nearing the upper gate, where a rain-drenched guard stood waiting.

"Why are you holding me? Please! Let me go," she said. He released her and she scrambled down the path, arriving just as Briochan spun upon his heel to hurry her through the doorway. She glanced over her shoulder, but the commander had gone.

"Go on, then." Briochan frowned. "What do you wait for? Would you rather keep to the mount?"

Angharad shook her head and hurried out. She'd lost count of the days she had been kept to the upper citadel. Now she followed

Briochan along the path between the ramparts and through another gate into the sprawling lower enclosure. The freedom was nearly intoxicating.

The villagers were tucked in, away from the wet, and hearth smoke fogged in billows from the thatching like the breath of a water beast. She blinked rain from her eyes as Briochan strode toward a grassy mound built into the wall of the lower rampart. *Some sort of temple,* she thought, her heart drumming at her breastbone.

A narrow series of rock-hewn steps led down into the belly of the earth. At the bottom of the stairs, a heavy oaken door was framed by thick slabs of stone. Angharad did not have to descend to feel it; the narrow stone passageway was breathing. Deepness lay upon the other side of that door.

Rain made the steps slick underfoot. At the threshold, Briochan stopped, murmuring a prayer before entering. Angharad paused in the narrow alley of stairs, fingers gentle on the stones, and offered up a prayer of her own. The easing Angharad felt was slight, conditional. As if the mound and its breathing waited to see if Angharad might prove herself.

Winters of wet, salty air made the rusty latch stick as Briochan lifted it, pulling open the door and gesturing impatiently. Angharad ducked carefully beneath the lintel, stepping into the darkness of the earth.

Inside the chamber, the splatter of rain was swallowed by the silence of soil and rock. The walls were drystone and the air was damp and smelled of water. Angharad stood before a rectangular pool. Oil lamps flickered on half-moon ledges fitted into the wall at the far end of the pool, their light wavering uncertainly on its inky surface. Three stone steps lead down into the pool, disappearing into blackness, where a presence pulsed like an organ, a heart. The stone intensified the cold, chilling the tip of Angharad's nose. Behind her, Briochan bolted the door with a clank, his voice echoing in the chamber.

"*Ceist.*" *Question.* Briochan had begun the pattern used between master and student. "What place is this? Speak, Initiate."

Ni ansa. Not difficult, Angharad must say. But what *was* this place? Any fool could see it was a temple. That was not the answer Briochan sought. Angharad sniffed. The chamber did not smell of salt; rather, it smelled more of clay. She sensed a source that lay deep beneath the earth, somewhere secret. This pool was spring fed, then. It was not a welling up from the sea.

"*Ni ansa.* It is a holy place, a place between lands," she answered. "Fed by a freshwater fountain."

"*Ceist.* And what are the secrets kept by our springs?"

"*Ni ansa.* The secrets kept by our springs are godly ones: In the beginning, the Gods of our land sprang forth in innumerable places on earth, born from deep within the womb of the land. Born in multitudes, each was birthed from the belly of its own freshwater spring."

Briochan gave a tight nod, his oaky eyes almost eager. "*Ceist.* To whom does this place belong?"

Angharad's stomach pitched. The question was nearly impossible to answer. There were as many gods and goddesses as there were springs. And each settlement kept its own gods of place. One could not travel more than two leagues without stumbling upon a holy fountain. Not to mention that theirs were many-named gods, for names were given like armor: if there was power in a name, a god's true name was most powerful of all. There were few secrets guarded more closely by Keepers than a god's true name. But Angharad would not fail.

She peered into the water's murky depths. There had been a pool once, at the foot of a waterfall she loved. She had found it as a girl when she first came to Eachna. In plunging beneath its surface, Angharad had found healing. But this place felt different. There was something unnatural about entombing a spring. The dark water brooded, as if demanding a price for its keep.

"*Ni ansa*," she said. "I will seek it."

She was not certain if this was right, if this was what other initiates might do. She could only follow her knowing. It had never led her astray. She unfastened her cloak and yanked off her leather shoes, dropping them on the stone as she stepped to the water's edge. Any manner of creatures could be lurking beneath the surface. Leeches or freshwater eels. Her throat tightened as she lifted the hem of her robes and took one step, swallowed her gasp as her feet met the water. Cold burned her legs as if she'd plunged into a bank of snow. As tiny ripples traveled the water, disturbing the pool's glassy surface, Angharad could not escape the feeling that something sleeping had awoken within.

"To whom does this temple belong?" Briochan pressed. "Speak, Initiate."

Angharad could delay no longer. Taking a breath, she ducked beneath the dark water. The shock of cold pushed air bubbles from her nose as she plunged down into its icy grip. The pool was not deep; her bare feet quickly met the slick bottom of the pool, and she battled her instinct to propel herself up, clutching for the ledge. But in the land of Gods, only the bold were rewarded. She held her breath, working her arms instead to keep herself submerged.

Show me.

She did not have to wait long. The water swallowed her greedily, eager to replay its echoes. She suddenly felt groggy, as if she'd been fed a powerful draft, and her body went leaden, as if not her own. She opened her eyes in alarm, straining to look up through the murky water. *Let the water have its way*, she thought, calming herself. *It is only a vision.* Above the surface, cloaked figures stood at the pool's edge looking down on her, the fiery blur of torches in their hands. Her ears pulsed with the pounding of drums, and far through the muted water came the rhythmic drone of chanting.

It was then she felt the hands.

They gripped her shoulders, digging at her back, pushing her under, forcing her down. Her chest spasmed, desperate for air.

Sweet Gods, I cannot breathe. I cannot breathe!

Angharad fought and thrashed, yet she could not surface. Down, down, the hands drowned her. She opened her mouth, choking, flailing, feet scrambling to gain purchase upon the slippery bottom of the pool. But what had once been shallow now was fathomless. Through the black water Angharad felt a yawning in the earth like the mouth of a cave, and beyond it a watery passageway in rock.

A passageway that led to the heart of the spring. *To whom does this temple belong?* she asked.

A god of the North. A god older than land itself. A god whose kingdom was vast as the sea. Her realization sent a spark, as if some sleeping beast had stirred, hungry, rearing its head. Angharad felt a tug, like being dragged by a current.

Please, tell me your name, she beseeched it. But now the feel of the cold and wet had disappeared. The passageway spat her out into the high green grass of a summer valley, the slopes of the mountains bursting with pink heather bells.

And there among the heather stood two figures: a man and a woman. Their faces lit at the sight of her. The man was tall and muscled, his gingery beard the color of her mother's hair. The dark-haired woman was slight, but her calm blue eyes held the power of a priestess. Angharad marveled. *Why, there is Morken King and the lady Idell.*

Come, Angharad, they beckoned. Her family. *Come, Angharad. We will bring you home.* For a moment she forgot where she was, looking into the bright eyes of her mother's dead parents. But just before they reached her, they stopped, questioning.

Was this indeed her wish? For they would welcome her if she chose it. This god of the seas would gladly accept her offering.

It was then Angharad understood. Why else should she step foot in this pool if she were not a gift?

I am no sacrifice, she said.

It happened so quickly, it was dizzying—the sensation of being caught up in a whirlpool, drawn by a loud, commanding voice.

"Stand! Blast you, stand!"

Angharad scrambled and kicked, finding her footing, and pushed up in a burst from the pool's slippery bottom. Briochan clutched her robes, pulling her leaden weight from the water. Angharad sputtered and coughed, gasping for breath open-mouthed, like a fish. Her robes were twisted, tangled round her limbs like vines. There were no drums, no figures with torches. Only Briochan stood, chest-deep in the pool before her, his breath coming in foggy puffs.

"*Ceist*. The *name*," he insisted, searching her face. "Speak, Initiate."

Angharad's clammy face burned and she coughed. He looked at her. Angharad felt the familiar fog, seeking, searching, testing as if with a flickering tongue.

"And I thought you worthy of higher teaching," he said, releasing his grip. Just as Briochan turned to slog from the pool, she spoke.

"*Ni ansa.*"

Briochan froze. Turned. Angharad bent her head and leaned in, cupping her hands to his ear. She whispered the name of the god of the Picts of Burghead. The truest name there was.

Briochan stood back. Shifted his gaze to the water and tilted his head as if he were listening. Then at last he sniffed.

"Yes," he said with satisfaction. "Sometimes that is what we call him." He gestured for Angharad to grab her cloak and turned for the door. "Come, then, Initiate. We have at long last arrived at the beginning."

CHAPTER 18

Angharad

Outside the temple, the rain had passed. Fat banks of mist had settled at the foot of the stone houses, making the settlement seem a village built upon clouds, the silence reverberating with the far-off thunk of a workman's anvil. Villagers emerged from their shelters, averting their eyes upon spotting Briochan stalking through the lower citadel with Angharad slogging behind, half tripping on the wet robe clinging to her legs. The only one to pay her any mind was an old woman who looked up as they passed, humming as she sat outside her hut, her knobbly fingers working a basket.

A gust of warmth met them as Angharad followed Briochan into the great room. A bard plucked tenderly at her cruit while the warriors gathered their weapons, preparing for their morning training. Flaxen had paused at her weaving to nurse a drowsy babe at her breast. Only the commander glanced up at the sight of Angharad, his eyes flickering with something that looked like relief. He watched as Briochan drew Angharad to the center of the great room with a clap of his hands. Water dripped from the hem of her robe, puddling on the floor.

"An announcement! I have an announcement, please," he called out.

Angharad straightened. The bard paused, fingers silencing her strings as Bridei and his court turned, wives, counsellors, and warriors alike. After Angharad had spent so many days skulking through the fortress, an unseen shadow of dulse and of gruel, their gazes burned like sun on winter's skin. She'd never been much taken with vanity, but suddenly she was aware of how tightly the skin stretched over her bones and of the deep hollows beneath her eyes from long hours of sitting in contemplation and too little sleep.

The king stepped forward in his purple robe, regarding Briochan, his foster father. "Well, then?" Something in his voice sounded like hope.

Briochan smiled, the first smile Angharad had seen. It was rather confusing, like a lion rolling over for a belly scratch while still baring its teeth.

"This girl has passed her trial," he said. "Thus, I have made her my Initiate. As such, she is *en Cruithni*." He tapped two fingers to his breastbone in the way of the Picts. "We will call her Angharad *Ton Velen*."

Angharad of the Tawny Wave. She blinked, reeling. Had Briochan truly pronounced her *en Cruithni* here, before all of court? The Picts of Burghead seemed as startled as she. For a moment, no one spoke. It had been so many winters since Briochan had last accepted an Initiate. Then the king stepped forward, gesturing to his hearth with a sweep of his hand.

"We bid you a most gracious welcome, Angharad Ton Velen."

Angharad bowed, utterly speechless. Then the commander stood from his place amidst a cluster of warriors, tapping two fingers to his chest.

"*Ton Velen*," he said.

"*Ton Velen*," the company echoed, fingers tapping their chests in return. Angharad's cheeks heated as she met their gazes for what felt like the first time, and Briochan leaned in, placing a fatherly hand on her shoulder. Angharad looked at him, her heart near to bursting.

"You may speak now, lest you abuse it," he said dryly. "Go and seek dry robes, Initiate." As Angharad made her way through the crowd, the Cruithni stood, catching her soggy sleeve, offering smiles and names of their own. Words flooded her ears, sifting like sand, the heft of their regard making her shrink despite the warmth and inclusion.

Imogen stood when Angharad entered the hut as if she'd been waiting, and Angharad said the words, scarcely believing.

"I am *en Cruithni*."

Imogen's face brightened and she hurried over, kissing Angharad upon both cheeks. "I knew it would be you. I knew you could do it! You are like me, now. *En Cruithni*. Come," she said, beckoning. "There is something I must show you."

Angharad followed Imogen to the closed door of the mysterious chamber.

"Do you know anything of this room?" she asked.

Angharad shook her head.

"This chamber belonged to the last Initiate who trained with my husband."

"You speak as if something terrible happened," Angharad said.

Imogen bowed her head. "Yes, from what I can tell. The chamber has lain empty since the day I arrived. Briochan bade me only enter to clean it."

Imogen opened the door and stepped over the threshold as if into a temple. A narrow bed layered with a thick brown fleece was nestled against the back wall. Imogen had taken care to bring in Angharad's trunk. On a wooden stool beside the bed, a little clay vase sat, its withered sticks pointing like an accusation. A fine little mountain of dust on the stool top was all that remained of what must once have been flowers. The chamber did possess a feeling, though Angharad did not find it particularly holy. It was as if it contained a presence already, and the two of them were not welcome there.

"You feel it, too?" Imogen said, observing her. "I never stay long. Truth be told, it gives me the shivers."

"Yes." Angharad eyed the vase. "I feel it."

"Well. It's your chamber now, isn't it?" Imogen said with a smile. She paused a moment, her face shifting. "I would not ask questions were I you. He doesn't like to speak of it."

Whatever had happened, Briochan was still haunted. This was the reason he'd refused to take on new students. The reason he still paused before sleep at this desolate chamber door. Angharad shivered in her wet clothes, caught by a sudden chill.

"You're shaking," Imogen said. "Come. I'll help you out of those robes before you catch your death."

Imogen eased the trunk open and pulled out Angharad's spare robe, chatting pleasantly about the necessity of new robes and perhaps one or two thick cloaks for winter. But as Angharad tugged the wet robes from her clammy skin, slipping mercifully into a dry linen undershift, she could not forget the blackness of the pool and the panicked sensation of drowning. She risked a glance at Imogen.

"That pool in the temple," she said. "People are drowned there. Aren't they?"

Imogen stopped and straightened. "We cannot discuss it, Angharad. It is forbidden to speak of it."

In all the time she'd been a shadow, Angharad had never heard Imogen speak with such warning. But Imogen needn't say anything at all, for Angharad had seen the cloaked figures in her vision. She had felt the hands, forcing her down.

When she was little, her brother Cyan had told scary nighttime tales of Picts with clubs and sharp teeth who roasted victims alive in the name of their gods. It had been many long generations since the Britons of the Old Way had offered people in sacrifice. With Eachna and Ariane, she had learned only the ways of animal offerings in ritual, no different from the offerings of the Britons. If Ariane had known of this pool, she had given Angharad no warning.

"Thank you, Imogen, for showing me to my chamber," Angharad said. "And for helping me dress. These past months you have been a most gracious host."

"Aye. Well." Imogen smiled. "I'll let you settle, then."

As Imogen shifted toward the door, Angharad bent to pull the withered stalks from the vase, sweeping the decayed flower dust into her palm.

"No, no! Not the vase!" Imogen cried. Angharad froze, turning to see her cheeks flushed with horror.

"Briochan bade me never to touch that. He wanted it left as it was." She stared woefully at the clutter of stalks and dust in Angharad's hand.

"Oh, no. I'm so sorry," Angharad said. "I thought—"

"It's all right. I should have told you. You couldn't know." Imogen shook her head and reached to brush the dusty little pile into her own hand. "Perhaps it is time. I'll give these to the hearth."

Angharad nodded and dropped her hand to her side, feeling like a chastened child. Imogen made for the door, then stopped.

"You asked about the pool," she said carefully.

"Yes?" Angharad glanced up.

"There is a cave not far from here whose entrance bears the skulls of children on pikes." Imogen lowered her voice. "When first I saw it, it struck horror in the heart of me, those tiny watchers at the edge of the unseen world. But I soon learned they were not offerings; they were ancestors. Children of the First People who died many winters ago."

"Why do you tell me this?" Angharad asked, searching her face. Imogen gave a small smile.

"I only mean to say, things are not always what they may seem. Trust in the people. You are *en Cruithni* now. Someday, you will see."

That night Angharad fell onto the bed in her new chamber, wrung out. She'd lost count of the days she had slept on the pallet on the floor. The fleece smelled clean and was impossibly soft, and had been laid over a firmly packed mattress with a fine cloth ticking. There had been such celebration, she still hummed from it. And the food! Angharad had nearly forgotten the rich splendor of butter and warm, yeasty bread.

"Eat slowly, or you will sicken," Briochan warned her. "And no meat until you are through with your training. After that, you may decide."

It wasn't until she was making her way back to her new chamber that she recalled her earlier sense of unease. She hadn't bothered with a candle; at this hour it would be light soon enough. But now that she lay alone with the door closed, the chamber felt eerie. Angharad's head yet spun with all that had taken place since that morning, and though she had no fear of ghosts, today, at last, her trial had ended. She was worn to her bones and did not have it within her to seek answers.

"I know you are there," Angharad whispered into the dark. "You were Briochan's Initiate, as I am now. I beg you, let me rest. This is my chamber now. And I am going to sleep."

It may have been her mind playing tricks, but she thought she felt the unwelcoming feeling withdraw a little—a fragile sort of peace. That was enough. She turned on her side and, within moments, fell into a deep and dreamless sleep.

It was not yet morning when the shattering came. Angharad bolted upright in bed, eyes searching the pitch blackness of her chamber. She could feel her heart beating in her throat. The chamber was still, its silence unyielding. Carefully, she reached to the little pine stool set beside the bed, feeling round gently, only to find it empty.

The little clay vase with its memory of flowers had shattered upon the ground.

CHAPTER 19

Languoreth

The Forest of Strathclyde
Land of the Britons
16th of September, AD 580

The hermit's hut lay deep in the woods, at a place where the Avon water birthed a streamlet, and the clear little burn raced beneath an elm wood, coursing into a gentle waterfall. I left Brodyn and the Gauls behind, traveling only with Torin and three men.

"He has picked a lovely place, Torin," I said darkly. "You told me he lived in the woods of Partick. But these are, in fact, the outer reaches of Cadzow. My lands. This burn is the marker."

"I am sorry, my lady, I reported only what I'd been told. I had not yet visited the place."

"He seems quite well settled." No doubt Torin heard the edge in my voice. As we dismounted from our horses I noticed a need-garden sitting neatly beside another small plot where gourd vines spilled, drinking in the rare afternoon sun. A bread oven was set beside a tidy outdoor cooking pit. Beneath the cover of a shed, there was enough wood to last well through winter. These were the borders of my lands before they gave way to those of Rhydderch and his forebears. Yet somehow a monk had entrenched himself here without my knowledge?

"How long has he been here?" I asked.

"He sought petition from Rhydderch some four winters ago," Torin said.

"Four winters?" I exclaimed. "And Rhydderch said nothing. We may be wedded, but these are yet my lands!"

"Your husband the king might have failed to mention it, but I did tell you, my lady, if you recall. We spoke of it before the battle, at Dùn Meldred."

"Yes. I am sorry, Torin. Of course I remember. You are not the cause of my temper. It's only, as you know, Cadzow is a place of the Old Way. If Rhydderch granted such a petition in my absence, he should well have told me."

I looked round, gathering my wits. "So this hermit has been entrenched here four winters, drawing Christians from all reaches of Strathclyde into my wood?"

"It would seem so, my lady."

"Doesn't that beat all." Striding to the hut, I rapped on the door.

A man nearing fifty winters opened it, wearing a simple brown tunic. He had steady, light blue eyes and slightly yellowed teeth. His graying hair was shorn in the manner of a holy man, over the forehead from ear to ear. He looked at me, then my guard. I'd left my torque in Aela's care and borrowed her gray woolen cloak. With my thick auburn hair bound in a knot at the back of my neck, I was far less likely to be recognized, but these were my lands. There were none here who did not know me.

"Hello," he said. "You are most welcome, my lady."

"You do not seem surprised to see a queen standing at your door," I observed.

"Well," he said quietly. "I confess I heard you from quite a distance."

"Good. Then you know who I am."

"You are Languoreth of Cadzow, daughter of Morken." He bowed, then gestured toward the hearth. "Do come in."

I ducked into the hut's single room. It was spare but tidily kept, devoid of any comfort save some crosses hung upon the walls. He followed my gaze.

"I offer them in trade," he said, adding, "No trees are felled. I craft them only from found wood." The monk cleared his throat and set about gathering cups and retrieving a sturdy jug from its place on a wooden shelf. "I fear I do not have much in the way of seating," he said. "But you are welcome to my chair."

"There's no need. I will stand."

"As you like." He turned and handed me a cup, then passed the others to Torin and the men. Mead, from the soft, honeyed smell of it, and a fine one at that. Clearly he had visitors of influence, ones who brought gifts.

"I understand my husband granted you permission to settle here," I began.

"Yes. And I am grateful, Queen Languoreth," he said, careful to use my title.

"It was without my knowledge." I set down my cup. "I make no secret of the fact that I am not a Christian. I do not care to discover a monk has been residing, unbeknownst to me, in my own wood."

"A *culdee*," he said quietly. I blinked.

"I am sorry. I do not understand the difference," I said, no apology in my voice.

"Culdees are solitary. 'Hermits,' as you say. I belong to no monastery. My only concern is my relationship with God."

"A *culdee*, then," I said.

"I apologize if you were unaware of my presence, my lady. I sought permission and my petition was granted. My only desire was to find a new home."

"And where was it you lived before?"

"The woods I once dwelled in now lie within the kingdom of the Angles. As you may know, they do not take kindly to Christians."

"Not even culdees?"

He allowed a smile. "Not even culdees. I was told Strathclyde was a kingdom that welcomed people of both faiths, the old and the new. That I might find welcome here."

His words struck a pang of guilt. I wanted Strathclyde to be a place of refuge. And I had fought hard these many years to try to keep the two faiths in balance and peace, even though I might not agree with Christianity's tenets.

"I will not rescind permission that has been granted," I said. "But my men tell me that you draw Christians from Partick into my woods. I would like to know why."

He seemed startled by my question. "They come seeking my counsel," he said.

"That must be disturbing for a man who craves solitude."

"I am a servant of God," he said firmly. "I will not turn away any who find themselves in need. They ask questions of my faith, and I answer."

"They can find no counsel among the Christians of Partick?"

He paused, hesitant. "They are discontented with a man called Anguen. They say he has poisoned the minds of the chieftains in Strathclyde and, in so doing, has brought about the return of the exiled bishop, Mungo."

"Yes," I said. "Brother Anguen has long been a servant to Mungo. He's led the community since Mungo's exile. What counsel do you give?"

"I remind them that no soul can sever the bond between a man or woman and their god," he said carefully. "It is like the bond between mother and daughter. Father and son. That is one thing we speak of."

"I see," I said. "You may not know, for I have only recently come into power. But I am not only a queen of the Old Way. My husband won the tanistry due to the support of Christian lords and petty kings. I do not like to hear that our peaceable Christians are troubled. When I was young, before Mungo came, it was not that way. My own father had studied the teachings of Jesus; there was a good and kindly monk named Brother Telleyr whom many admired and we called a friend. Have any of your people spoken of him?"

"I cannot say," he said firmly. "I do not play in politics."

"Brother Telleyr is dead," I said. "Mungo saw to that. And now Mungo is returned."

The monk said nothing. We looked at each other. I took up my cup and took a small sip, considering him.

"I have been rude. I apologize. I did not even ask your name. Do . . . culdees have names?"

"Yes," he said, his eyes lit with humor. "Culdees have names. I am called Brother Thomas."

"Brother Thomas," I said, inclining my head. "It seems to me that some are born to live blessed, ordinary lives. They sow their crops and cut winter's wood and die at peace in their beds. I do not think you were meant to live an ordinary life, no matter how ardently you seek it. The people of Partick need you. They are seeking you in the woods. You say you are a servant of God. How can you deny them?"

Brother Thomas met my eyes. "I do my part. Here, in the wood. Those who knock upon my door know I will not forsake them."

"I am here," I said. "I have knocked. Would you forsake me, then? The mark of Christ was left in blood upon my brother's door. Mungo has been returned only a number of days and already he stirs intolerance and hate. Are these the acts of a true Christian man? I cannot believe it."

"No." Brother Thomas's blue eyes were sad. "I am deeply sorry that's happened. It should not be so."

"I cannot help but think it would be different were you in Partick. When Mungo catches word that Christians seek you here, he will send men to your door. There shall be no one, then, to stop him from taking your life. Can you not see, Brother Thomas? You shall have to face whatever it is you fear either way. What is it, then? Is it Mungo?"

"I do not fear Mungo."

"Why, then, do you hide?"

"I do not hide," he said evenly. "Solitude is the way of seekers of many faiths. It has been so throughout the ages."

"You need not lecture me on the ways of mystics. And I do not believe solitude is the only reason you have become a culdee."

I had touched something—I could sense it—but what it was, he would not give away.

"Come out from the shadows and protect what is good and right of your faith," I urged him. "Come to the capital. Mungo needn't know the king and I back you, but you shall have everything you need. We will furnish you with a hut and a small piece of land where you can plant a new garden, one sown with seeds of community. Fate has given you the chance to level the balance. You cannot stand by and watch as your people fall into darkness, and neither can I."

For a moment I thought I saw him battling, but then Brother Thomas sighed, shaking his head.

"No," he said firmly. "I have great respect for the Old Way. But forgive me, I cannot come to Partick."

"But surely—"

"My lady," he said. "I do not care to dwell in a Christian community again. Now, if that was the sole purpose of your visit, I must thank you and bid you good afternoon."

• • •

I spoke little as we made our way back through the forest, gloomy in the wake of my defeat. Stubborn man. Torin rode in silence, all too familiar with my interior weather. I had arranged to meet Lailoken at Buckthorn, and we'd nearly reached the walled gates of Partick when a movement in the trees caught my eye. Torin saw it, too. A hooded figure—a man on foot, it looked like—had been watching us and, having been spotted, slipped behind an oak. We exchanged a look, and then Torin turned in his saddle, nodding to the men. Kicking their horses, they charged off into the trees, catching the man by the collar of his cloak.

"And who are you?" I asked, riding up to look at him.

"Only a farmer," he exclaimed. "I heard horses in the wood!"

I studied him a moment. "Let him go," I commanded.

Torin looked at me, questioning.

"He meant no harm, Torin. As he says, he is only a farmer." Reaching into my saddle sack, I drew out a silver coin and handed it to him. "Men such as you should be rewarded for keeping a watchful eye on Strathclyde's woods. Your queen is grateful."

His bristle faded and he bowed with a smile. "Thank you, m'lady."

I straightened. "Gods keep you, and good day."

Torin waited to speak until we'd cleared a good distance.

"Are we in agreement that he was a spy?" he said.

"Of course we are."

"Mungo will soon know you paid a visit to the culdee, then."

"Yes, he will."

"Won't be long then before Mungo or his men pay Brother Thomas a visit." Torin considered it. "My lady, you may hope to flush him from hiding. But what if they should harm him?"

It was something I'd considered. Despite our differences, Brother Thomas seemed a kind man, one truly in communion with his god. I did not wish to see any harm befall him. Yet it was as I said: Mungo would come either way, as soon as he deemed Brother Thomas's influence too great.

"I have a feeling Brother Thomas is more than capable of protecting himself," I said. "But should he need protection, he knows what he must do."

CHAPTER 20

Angharad

Burghead Fortress, Kingdom of Fortriu
Land of the Picts
17th of September, AD 580

"Beginning today, you will care for the temple," Briochan said. "It will be swept morning and night. The lamps must stay lit and the offerings kept tidy."

"Yes, Master Briochan."

The morning was purple as an urchin shell, the only sound the gentle crackle of the hearth as Angharad sat on a fleece beside her teacher.

The Wisdom Keeper glanced at her, adding, "Perhaps this time you will not fall in." Angharad was taken by surprise as his dark eyes lit with humor. But then he grew serious, nodding to the pallet where she sat.

"Here we sit in contemplation, as you have done these past many days. *Ceist*, Ton Velen. Why do we sit in stillness?"

"*Ni ansa*. We sit in stillness because the soul resides in the head. And the head must be empty to hear the voices of spirit."

"Correct. A vessel must be empty if it wishes to capture rain."

She'd learned as much at age eight; it was a lesson for child novices. But since Briochan had named her Initiate, some of his fog had retreated. He spoke with the passion of a scholar and even seemed to regard her with the kindness of a father. Angharad would take nothing for granted. She slipped effortlessly into the silence, allowing the fire to burn the chatter in her mind. Moments melted like candle wax. After a while, Briochan stirred.

"Come, then, Ton Velen. It is time you and I pay a visit to the sea."

Angharad stood, ignoring the stab where a little clay splinter had lodged in her foot, smiling at the villagers as they passed through the lower citadel toward the harbor gate. She would remove it later, in better light. *It was only an accident*, she thought, though she did not believe it. She'd swept her chamber thoroughly, but it was easy enough to miss a sliver. She also knew at some point she must tell Briochan about the shattered vase, and she knew he would be angry. After all, he'd instructed Imogen to never touch it. Then there was the spirit itself. Surely Briochan knew a shade dwelled there. He paused at the door in the evening, yet did nothing to manage it. Imogen had told her not to ask of it, and Briochan said nothing more. Angharad would have to sort the matter herself.

They had just reached the stables of the lower citadel when Angharad caught sight of the boy. The Scot. He was tending the pigs. His hair had been clipped short and stuck up like straw. There was a purpled bruise upon his cheek and his fingernails were crusted in dirt. He'd been made a stock slave, minding the animals. A pang of guilt struck. She'd waited too long. She'd been worried about inviting Briochan's wrath by asking after the boy, and it was selfish. Now that she'd seen him, she had no choice. She'd speak first to Imogen, she decided. Otherwise, they'd stand no chance at all.

The fortress at their backs, wind blasted the rocky, seaweed-strewn shore. The season of storms would soon be upon them, making travel on open water too dangerous until spring. Angharad could feel it in the way the water churned, weather-whipped and restless, sending white, broiling waves pummeling like a giant's fist against the shelves of golden rock. Briochan looked out at the water, reading her thoughts.

"It's nearly time to leave for Craig Phadrig, our winter steading," he said. "You can feel it on the sea."

They stopped on the rocks, well away from the slap and roar of the hungry morning tide.

"You said you would know of the Cailleach," Briochan said.

"I would." Angharad tried to keep the eagerness from her voice. Briochan gave half a smile. Thrusting his arms wide, he looked into the distance and bellowed:

> I am a stag: of seven tines,
> I am a flood: across a plain,
> I am a wind: on a deep lake,
> I am a tear: the Sun lets fall,
> I am a hawk: above the cliff . . .

He lowered his arms with a smile, turning to Angharad. "Those words belong to the far-famed Wisdom Keeper Amergin, as you know. But the Cailleach. She was the first shape-shifter. She can become a pack of hinds, racing through a thin winter wood. She can change from a giantess to a forest hare in the blink of an eye, or become even an old woman outside a hut, working at a basket."

The images of the goddess sprang alive as he spoke, and for a moment the deity felt as if she hovered close—as if the simple act of speaking her name were a summoning.

"Throughout all of our lands, we are losing such ways," he went on. "This, I have been told when I sit with the Gods. The ways of dreaming are stamped out beneath the feet of the Christians, who laugh and say, 'Show me a Wisdom Keeper who takes the form of a fox!' Fools. The learning is not for them. This learning is for *you*. For you are at once a Briton and a Pict. And you, Ton Velen, shall be one who preserves our ways."

He turned, regarding her, and tapped a finger to his temple. "Shape-shifting occurs in the head. Those who cannot understand that cannot believe it to be real. But you have just told me the head is the seat of the soul. We are born and we die, all within here. So the head is the most real of all." Briochan gestured in a sweep over the wide, swelling sea. "All of this? It is only a dream."

After the lesson by the sea, Briochan said he must return to the Hall for a short while and bade Angharad visit the temple for her morning duties.

Deep in the silence of the temple chamber, Angharad's blood raced like a river, skin prickling with the closeness of the unseen as she filled the lamps with clean oil from a clay jug, tidied the offerings that had been left by the villagers, and carefully swept the wet gray stone. She had only just mounted the top of the stair when she saw the commander making his way toward her, something small and black tucked in his fist. Of the many Cruithni who'd offered their names the eve before, the commander had not.

"Good morning, Angharad Ton Velen," he said. His deep voice was calm, but his eyes shifted a little, as if he were nervous.

"Good morning." She nodded, waiting. It seemed he had sought her out, but now he stood stiff, as if uncertain. It *was* odd. She supposed she and the commander had become comfortable in their silence, and now that there could be words between friends, they only seemed to get in the way.

"Rhainn," the commander said suddenly. Confused, Angharad frowned, searching the sky.

"I'm sorry. Rain?"

"Nay, nay. Rhainn. That is my name," he said, tapping two fingers to his breast.

"Ah," Angharad exclaimed. "'*Rhainn*,' '*rain*,' it sounds just the same," she rhymed with a smile, tapping her breast. "It means spear or lance. Does it not?"

"It does."

"I'd gotten quite used to calling you 'the commander.'"

"I see."

"Well, I needed to call you something, didn't I?" she pointed out. "And you didn't give your name, even yesterday eve."

"There were already too many names."

"But yours is one I would not forget. You've been a friend—and at risk to yourself—when I needed one most."

"A commander of the Picts is never at risk," he said. "Besides, I do not fear Briochan. I respect him. But I do not fear him."

"You do not fear Briochan? Whyever not?"

Rhainn looked at her widened eyes and laughed. It was rich, almost musical.

"Because he is my father," he said.

"Master Briochan is your father?" Angharad sank back, stunned. "Are you jesting?"

"I do not jest."

"That's true," she allowed.

She looked at him, squinting. In all her keen observations of Bridei's court, she'd seen Briochan and Rhainn speak only on occasion. She felt a fool. "All this time, and I did not know?"

"You were not *en Cruithni*," Rhainn said. "As such, I could no longer visit their hut. And at court, we each have our duties. We do not disturb the other."

Angharad examined his face anew. "I suppose you share the same nose."

"Perhaps," he said. "I look rather more like my mother."

"Is she passed?" Angharad asked carefully.

"Sickness. It was long ago now."

"I am sorry to hear it," Angharad said, and they were quiet a moment. "Well. I should get back to the Hall."

"I will escort you," he offered.

As they strode along the village path, Angharad was careful to keep a distance. She had sacrificed much to become an Initiate, and, like novices, they were meant to remain chaste. She would not risk her friendship with Rhainn being misconstrued. Yet neither was she willing to abandon it. Now that they could speak, Angharad had too many questions.

"I wanted to ask you," she began. "Briochan's last Initiate . . . did you know her?"

Rhainn's answer was careful. "My father does not like to speak of it."

"Which is why I am not asking your father. I am asking you," she said. "Please, you must tell me something. I can feel her in my chamber. I know something terrible happened. I know that's the reason Briochan hasn't taken new students. All I wish to know is why."

Rhainn slowed his pace. "It is not for me to speak of," he said. "But perhaps I can tell you one thing. She, too, longed to become a daughter of the Cailleach."

A shiver traced her arms. Of course. That was why Briochan had reacted in the way he did when Angharad had first introduced herself in court. *I wish to become a Daughter of the Cailleach*, she'd announced. But what had happened to his Initiate, and why did she insist on lingering so long after death?

"Does that frighten you?" he asked, looking at her.

"No."

"Perhaps it should." His voice held concern she could not easily dismiss.

They reached the upper citadel, and Rhainn nodded to the man at the gate as they went through. As they neared the Hall's entrance, Rhainn paused at the doors, fidgeting with the object in his fist.

"Angharad Ton Velen," he said. "I am no smith. I only tinker. But . . . I made this. It's yours, if you would have it." He held out his hand. In his palm sat a black iron bird. "For the feathers you left me," he explained. "And the marks upon your wrist."

Angharad looked at it, startled as he passed it to her. The metal was warm from being clutched in his fist.

"It's lovely, Rhainn. Thank you."

Rhainn nodded and, clearing his throat, disappeared into the Hall. The bird was beautiful and weighty in her hand. Angharad stood a moment looking after him, unable to escape the feeling that Rhainn had just given her much more than a bird.

Later, Imogen came upon her as Angharad hunched awkwardly in the last of the sun's light outside the hut, a pair of metal tweezers in hand, digging at the shard in the bottom of her foot.

"Sweet Gods, what's happened, then?" Imogen asked, kneeling down beside her.

"It's nothing, only a splinter," Angharad said. Better just to tell her. "The vase broke in the night, and it seems I've stepped on a shard."

"Oh, dear." Angharad couldn't tell if Imogen was more concerned about her or the vase.

"I'm so sorry, Imogen. Honestly, I don't know how it happened. I was dead asleep."

"I know how it's happened." Imogen glanced darkly at the hut. "It's not the first time she's tossed things round."

"You mean to say she's done that before?"

Imogen did not answer, only leaned in with a frown. "Here, I can see it better. Hand me those, please."

Angharad passed her the tweezers, watching as Imogen gently lifted her foot. She'd made it clear she didn't wish to speak of the spirit, and Angharad didn't want to press her. But there was something else.

"Imogen. Do you remember that Scotti boy who was brought to court? The prisoner?"

"Aye," Imogen said, careful not to look up.

"Have you seen him?"

"No, I haven't. My husband has bade me let it be, and I—"

"They beat him," Angharad cut in. "He sleeps in the muck in the stables. Do you think Master Briochan might change his mind? Perhaps the boy could serve in the house."

Imogen looked at her, guarded. "And what importance is it to you, Ton Velen?"

"I've met Scots before," she said.

"And lived to tell of it?" Imogen's laugh was humorless.

Angharad stopped her hand. "I know the Scots are supposed to be our enemy, but there are some I consider friends."

Imogen was quiet a moment before she spoke. "I was taken, you know. But it's been seven winters now. I have a good husband, and this is my home."

"I confess I heard Bridei's wives speak of it," Angharad admitted.

"I'm certain you did," Imogen scoffed. "'Twould be bad enough to be taken a slave, but I was also a Christian."

"Were you?" Angharad was too surprised to avoid being rude. "Are there many Christians amongst the Scots?"

"A small number, but growing, I suppose. My family were stock keepers. We kept a small croft at the edge of the Moine Mhòr."

"The Great Moss," Angharad said. Imogen raised her brows.

"You know Goidelic?"

"Only a little."

"Well. My father gave hospitality to a band of monks when I was a child," Imogen explained. Angharad winced as Imogen dug with the tweezers. "Sorry." She glanced up. "The monks dwelled with us for some time and my father had us baptized. One of the monks stayed behind, and together we built a wooden church. We passed peaceful days there, listening as he shared the word and acts of Jesus, the son of God. And then I was taken in a raid by the Cruithni, sold like cattle at Ceann Mòr."

"Ceann Mòr, did you say?" Angharad asked. "I've been to the slave mart at Ceann Mòr. I stood upon the grass and witnessed the selling of a friend. He, too, was a Christian."

"It's true, the Picts do not suffer Christians well," Imogen said. "But it came to pass that Briochan was kind. I might've been his slave, but in truth he wanted a companion. I think he was lonesome. It was my choice, you know, when I went to his bed."

Angharad blushed, but Imogen did not seem shamed. "There, I've got it."

Imogen held the bloody shard delicately between the prongs of the tweezers, dropping it into Angharad's palm.

"What sort of man was your friend?" Imogen asked. "The Christian."

"He was a culdee."

"Ach, then . . ." Imogen trailed off sadly.

"No, no," Angharad smiled. "Brother Thomas is not dead. He was bought and then set free by the priestess at Fortingall."

"A priestess?" Imogen raised a brow. "Whyever would she do that?"

"She could see that I cared for him. And I was her kin."

And Eachna wanted no other to possess a bond to me, she thought. With Brother Thomas's voice in her ear, Angharad might not have done her bidding.

Angharad drew out a salve from her healer's pouch and smeared a little on the bottom of her foot.

"Do you ever wonder what became of him?" Imogen asked. "Your Brother Thomas."

"I do wonder sometimes," Angharad said. "But Brother Thomas was a kind and clever man. Wherever he may be, I'm certain fortune follows him still."

Imogen stood. "I'll speak to Briochan about the boy. Make him see. I'm the wife of Bridei's head counsellor. I should in the very least be granted my choice of servant."

"Thank you," Angharad said.

That night, the chamber felt watchful as Angharad came in and undressed. As she crawled beneath her fleece, she placed the little black iron bird on the pine stool beside the bed. She slept undisturbed that night. When she woke in the morning, the little figurine still sat where she'd left it, steady as the man who had made it.

CHAPTER 21

Gladys

Dùn Rheged, Fortress of Urien, Kingdom of Rheged
Land of the Britons
25th of September, AD 580

"It is good for the babe to walk by the sea," Penarwan said, nodding at the round swell of Gladys's belly. "He shall hear the call of his ancestors and come out."

The wife of Owain, one of Elffin's elder brothers, Penarwan had borne him four children and thus considered herself an expert.

"Yes, indeed," Gladys said agreeably, though she much preferred the loamy forests of Cadzow to the ocean, and rather wished she had kept to her bed. They had been walking the beach for only a short while, and despite having urinated before Penarwan had collected her, the way the babe pressed upon her bladder, Gladys felt the necessity again. Penarwan was small, with sharp blue eyes, a rather pointed nose, and fair hair that was always neatly plaited. Her body was tight with muscle, for it seemed she was always moving at a purposeful pace, and her children— all boys—had been born in perfect order: less than two winters apart, they already marched at their mother's command like tiny warriors.

It was late afternoon and the tide was low, exposing the flat belly of sand all the way out to Ard Bhaile island, where the Wisdom Keepers dwelled, strewing the mucky shallows in between with watery treasures: crab husks and swirling shells in washes of violet blue and creamy white. When the water was high, Gladys could hear the Keepers' voices carrying across the short expanse of sea. Behind them, past the sprawling, fading autumn grasses, Urien's fortress loomed on a gorse-clustered hill.

"You think it will be a boy?" Gladys asked her, trying to be amiable more than anything. She spoke lightly, as if the thought of a boy did not stir her, as if it did not stab at her stomach, summoning her brother's peaceful green eyes and the way he would ruffle her hair at bedtime. *Nos da, blodyn*, he'd say with a smile. Good night, flower.

"Of course," Penarwan said. "Look how high you carry. It'll be a boy, and any day now."

It was best to ask Penarwan for advice, for as long as she felt she was the most knowledgeable, she'd not root round to find things to pick at, like Gladys's hair or the way she spoke to her girls ("Truly, Gladys, you are far too indulgent!").

"If it please the Gods," Gladys said, wishing Penarwan had kept to the fortress and her spindle rather than insisting upon dragging her here, far beyond the merse. She couldn't help but feel it was bad luck to speak of the babe. Let the Gods bring the newborn in their own time. Healthy and strong. Gladys would wait.

Gladys eyed the bright copper pin capped with a thistle that Penarwan wore in her cloak, eager to change the topic. "That's a lovely pin. Is it new?" she asked.

"A gift from Owain. I can scarcely wear them all, I told him, but my lord insisted this particular piece caught his fancy and could belong to no other than me."

Indeed, for you are a good match for a thistle, Gladys thought, glancing back to the clump of rocks where Fendwin stood, his weathered face scanning the bay. Where she'd first found Fendwin an annoyance, his presence in the span of the last few months had become reassuring.

Penarwan bossed. Elffin fussed. So near to birthing, Gladys moved as if weighted by boulders and had little patience for anything save the old Dragon Warrior's stories. Each night before sleep she'd beg yet another tale from his adventures, and he, failing at appearing irritated, would always provide.

Up ahead, Penarwan's wiry legs moved along the shore fast as a sandpiper's. "Come, Gladys! You're falling behind."

Gladys looked at her darkly, the press of her bladder now coming in stabs. At the sound of Penarwan's voice, Fendwin turned and, spotting the look upon Gladys's face, strode resolutely toward the two women.

"Lady Penarwan, Lady Gladys. We'd best get in now. Tide's coming back," he said.

Penarwan turned with a frown. "Is it? It doesn't appear so."

"Ach, aye," Fendwin said with authority. "It'll be rolling over these flats like a speeding horse, and you wouldn't want to get caught out. It would muck up your cloak."

"Very well," she said, put out, as they turned back the way they'd come. It was true—the tides came quickly here, a fact that Penarwan might know if Owain's fortress were not such a great distance inland. But not so quickly as all that. Fendwin knew Penarwan took pride in fine things, and her cloak was pure luxury. He waited gallantly for them to pass, and Gladys flashed him a grateful smile.

It *had* been nice to walk out of doors. Weaving and embroidering Elffin's garments—"Good luck to be done by a wife," Penarwan said— had Gladys nearly weeping with boredom. She cursed her mother and the intelligence she'd handed down. If only Gladys were dimmer, she might be more content with her lot in life. What was the good of learning to read both Latin and Greek if one could scarcely use it, save for conversing with merchants once in the span of a year?

Up ahead, Penarwan was going on about seven different sorts of cloth and the prices she'd haggled for each, and Gladys wanted to bash her own head against a rock. Or perhaps wade with soggy skirts into the water and drown her ears with the sound of the sea. Instead, she shuffled her way back along shore toward the place they'd left the horses, where hungry tides had eaten the fertile land, exposing fissures of lichen-and-algae-covered rock. Beyond the beach, salt marshes drained in channels eroded by the flush of tidal waters, and the river Fleet reached the end of its course, flooding the ocean. Here the land became merse, rich pasture for cattle.

They rode past the cattle on horseback; black with furry white belts round their middles, they grazed under the keen-eyed watch of the cattle-keeps. One of Rheged's forefathers had bred his midnight-black cows with Cadzow's pure white, and the distinctive belting had been born. It had since become the pride of Rheged. And it now served as a reminder to the Angles of nearby Deira that the great kingdom of Rheged did not stand alone. The Britons of Strathclyde and Rheged were united.

By the time they reached the base of the fortress, it was nearing twilight. Now that summer had gone, the sun fell faster, leaving a new chill in its wake. Beyond the pastures, trees stood in shocks of color, and as Gladys peered into the beckoning depths of the forest, she caught sight of a stag standing at the edge of the river.

Penarwan, ever hurried, had charged ahead. Gladys stopped her horse, certain even a breath might startle it. But the beast stood regal and unafraid, regarding her, its great antlered tines opened skyward like an invocation. Like a blessing.

Fendwin drew his mount up beside her, and they looked at each other, knowing. Gladys's hands went by habit to the taut round of her stomach. They watched until the stag heard a sound and turned with a flash, disappearing into the wood.

It was no surprise, then, in the early morning hours, when the wetness woke her from an already fitful sleep. Her nightdress was soaked beneath her bottom. Elffin stirred.

"It will be hours yet," Gladys said, urging him back to sleep. But he woke and dressed.

"I'll send for the Keepers," he said.

"In good time," Gladys said firmly. "Wake Fendwin. I'd have his company for a while."

"If it please you." Elffin's voice was somewhat clipped in the dark. He did not understand.

"Fendwin reminds me of home," Gladys said, reaching reassuringly to stroke her husband's bearded cheek. Moments passed. Her serving-woman came and helped her ease on a fresh linen nightdress. Then Fendwin appeared in the door holding a candle.

"You asked for me, my lady?" He looked uncomfortably stiff, and Gladys realized he'd likely never attended a birth before.

"You needn't stay," she said, trying to sound as if she might not care. He looked at her, then bowed his head, entering the chamber. Setting the candle down on the chest at the far end of the room, he crouched at the hearth, tossing in more fuel. A wave of cramping came, shocking in its bite, and she gasped, doubling over. She must have reached out her hand, because the old warrior took it.

"Breathe, my lady." Fendwin leaned in. "It will soon be done."

"Soon be done?" Gladys blinked at him wide-eyed, her knuckles white. "You haven't any idea."

The laboring lasted an eternity, until Gladys felt the entirety of her body had been pulled inside out. And then came the cry every mother hungers for: the shrill little fury that splits the chamber, a new soul entering the world. Gladys held the tiny, slippery baby boy to her breast as the Wisdom Keeper dealt efficiently with the final birth matters at hand. Safe on his mother's chest, the boy's cries ceased, and Gladys's pain dulled to a low hum as her son's miniature chest rose and fell in the quiet euphoria of sleep. Elffin came, looking down on him, reaching a trembling finger to touch the velvet of his impossibly round cheek.

"Will you send word to my mother?" Gladys asked. "Tell her I've given birth to a boy."

"I will, my love." Elffin beamed. "She'll be ever so pleased. The Gods have smiled upon Rheged."

More visitors came, ducking into the darkness of the room; King Urien's wife, then Penarwan. All the while Fendwin stood like a shadow at the wall, his presence sturdy as a boulder. And yet, Gladys could sense an unease in him, like a fly at a tent flap buzzing in search of escape. When at last the Wisdom Keeper packed her satchel and left, the Dragon Warrior stepped forward, a satchel of his own held loosely by his side. He shifted his weight.

"Apologies, my lady, but I have been called away to an errand, one that cannot wait."

Gladys frowned. "An errand? But you are in my service. What sort of errand could you be called to? Who commands it?" Her face felt hot, stung by abandonment.

"'Tis an errand of a personal sort," he said evenly. "My mother is ill. I must pay her a visit."

Gladys narrowed her eyes. "You're too old to have a mother."

"Every man has a mother."

"Tell me the true reason."

Fendwin had the gall to ignore her. "A fortnight," he said. "Then I will return. The babe's born and hale, as are you. My errand can wait no longer."

"You say you serve me, yet you abandon your obligation," Gladys protested.

"You should not call yourself an obligation," he said, his blue eyes sparking with humor. And with that, Fendwin turned and strode out the door.

CHAPTER 22

Lailoken

Buckthorn Hall, Partick, Kingdom of Strathclyde
Land of the Britons
25th of September, AD 580

Word came at night from my sister in the way of a simple white seashell, still warm from its grip in the messenger's hand. "A gift from your sister the queen," he said.

"A lovely shell," I told him. "Give her my thanks, and tell her I received it."

I looked down at the hard bit of sea that lay, innocuous, in the palm of my hand as he departed. We'd agreed upon a shell. But it might've been anything.

The less significant a symbol of Ebrauc, the better.

For months now, men and women in the service of my sister had been laying the groundwork in shadow. In the bathhouses, inns, and brothels of Ebrauc, the warriors of Gwrgi and Peredur—those Torin thought most likely to turn—were sought with sweet whispers. Discontent was already rife. It was a slow and gentle seduction: land, cattle, silver, and places secured in the ranks of Strathclyde or Rheged. Though Rhydderch and Urien knew nothing, once it was done, neither king would refuse them. But my journey was long, and to slip from Strathclyde unnoticed I required the black mantle of night.

Having heard voices at the door, Eira came to stand beside me, watching the messenger ride away.

"It is time, then?" she asked.

"It is time."

"But must you leave now? It's night, and there's been too much rain. The rivers will be running high at the crossings."

"I know these rivers and their high waters well," I assured her.

"Yes, but alone? Can you not take Brodyn and the Gauls? Surely they are ripe for adventure."

"A band of men draws too much attention. Mungo has men who are watching. Besides, I am a Wisdom Keeper and may travel at will. Brodyn and his men invite too many questions."

She moved to stand before me, her face half-cloaked in shadow. "There is a curse on Gwrgi's head. The Gods are with you," she said. "But you must promise me you'll be careful. If anything should happen . . ."

"My love." I drew her to me, nodding to the open door. "The moon is high. Look how she glows to light my way. It is a good night for travel. I know these lands better than most, and Fendwin will be waiting."

"Well enough." Eira stood on her toes and, burying her fingers in my hair, laid a gentle kiss upon my forehead. "To keep you safe. Come back to me, Lailoken."

I looked into her eyes. "I promise you, I will return."

Eos was waiting for me in the stable, tacked and ready. I nodded my thanks to the groom and then we were out, racing through the night, her gray flanks glowing dim under the light of the full moon. I brought down my hood only briefly, at Partick's gates, and Rhydderch's warriors nodded, releasing me into the open.

I'd been training with Eos, had slept some nights over the summer in the straw of the stable, and she and I had built a bond stronger than I'd had with any mount before. I felt safe having her along with me. She was an exceptional warhorse—and now she knew all sorts of clever tricks.

The moon lit the road like a beacon, and I could travel at a good clip. But I had traveled less than a league when I felt another presence behind me. I glanced over my shoulder. A distance back, three riders had appeared.

Who was to say they were following me?

But who was to say that they weren't?

There was an unmistakable prickling at the back of my neck. A warning.

"Eos. Show them how you run." I urged her into a gallop with a squeeze of my legs. But fast as she was, I knew I could not lose them in the open.

I pulled Eos from the road and we streaked across a field, leaping over the hedge-woven fence into the dark wood. I heard them shout, and the rumble of hooves as they took off after me into the forest.

The trees blocked the moonlight, casting shadows of leaves as we coursed through the brambled forest, ducking low-hanging branches and vaulting over fallen trunks. Behind me I heard a tumbling crash and a curse. One less rider. A stumble at this speed meant a horse's broken leg. We dodged a close-knit stand of birches and changed course, but the two riders were gaining, close on my heels. We moved like one, leaping a burn where the water had risen high, nearly bursting its bank.

I risked a quick glance over my shoulder.

Only one rider now. Where had the other gone?

Turning again, I urged Eos on faster, only to feel a sudden whack of what felt like a tree branch. The wind rushed out of me as I sailed from Eos's back, landing in a heap on the cold forest floor.

That's where the second rider had gone, I realized, gasping to pull air into my lungs. He'd circled round to cut me off, launching me from Eos. But my speed had been enough to send him hurtling, too. I scrambled to my feet just as he charged me, blade drawn. My breath came back just in time for me to yank my sword from its sheath, blocking his strike. We traded blows, the moonlight playing tricks on the eye, casting darting shadows. But even as I held him off, I knew the sound of our clashing metal would draw the other rider. I'd fought two men before. Skill wasn't enough.

"Eos!" I called for my horse. She couldn't be far. If I could get her back, she could be a help.

"Eos!"

I leaned in, making a show of positioning my sword as if to fight, then turned tail and ran. It was enough to catch him off guard. Sprinting to a hillock, I reached higher ground just as the other rider galloped into the clearing, swiveling to block his blade just as it came down upon my head.

Sweet Gods. My arm shook from the force of the blow. I readied myself to take on the two of them, but then a voice came at my ear.

"Drop your blade." The third man. I lifted my arms in surrender, craning my neck to regard him.

"You must've run fast," I said, reluctantly dropping my sword.

The rider on horseback dropped from his saddle and the three men circled me. I could not die; Eira would kill me. And I would miss my meet with Fendwin. A Dragon always kept his word. I eyed their coarse woolen cloaks and dark trousers, trying to stall them.

"Mungo, I suppose."

"Doesn't much matter," the one who'd been on horseback said. "Let's get it done with."

Just my luck. They were not verbose. My stomach sank as one of the men lifted his blade, ready to strike.

"There are few others who might wish to kill me," I said quickly. "Mungo's a fool if he thinks this won't come back on him. And you are foolish to trust him. He'll be the first to give you up. Rhydderch will see you dead."

The men paid me no mind.

"No, not the blade," the one on horseback said. "It's got to be a hanging. That's what *he* wants."

I hadn't seen the length of rope he gripped until he stepped into a shaft of moonlight and tossed it over the nearest branch. There was a sinking in my chest. They could not know how it struck me—but Mungo did. He could not resist the chance to pry at old wounds. I thought of Eira and my sister, saw their faces, grief-stricken, as they heard how I'd swung and purpled, how I'd been left dangling in the wood. Just like Cathan.

"How unoriginal," I said, not giving them the pleasure of my fear.

"Come on, then." The rider beckoned. I'd die a thousand deaths before Mungo got his way. It lit a fire in me. I glanced at the rope with disdain.

"No, thank you. I don't much care for heights."

"Get him, then! Bring him here," the rider shouted, impatient. He still held one end of the rope in hand; he'd need to send it over the branch one more time to be able to secure it. Just then, a flicker of movement caught my eye at the edge of the clearing. Eos had come. But she stood at the edge of the glade, watching, uncertain.

"Eos," I called gently, nodding toward the men.

The men swiveled, searching the dark. "What's that? Who's he talking to?"

It was my chance.

I charged the first man with all my might, catching him off guard and sending him crashing into the second, then snatched up my blade, which they'd stupidly left on the ground. The rider cursed and dropped the rope, but now I was armed. The other two men recovered too quickly as I clashed blades with the rider, backing up and angling, so all three couldn't close in on me. Eos stood somewhere at my back now. As they ran at me, I commanded her.

"Eos, strike!"

Her gray flanks caught the moonlight as she came barreling into the clearing, rearing up and knocking the rider to the ground. He cried out as she crashed down on him, pummeling with her hooves.

"Good girl." Eos backed up, wild-eyed, her ears flattened against her head, and I rushed in with a stab, finishing the rider off.

The second man charged, and Eos reared up again. "Strike, Eos. *Strike!*" I called out, turning as the third man lunged at me.

"Yahhhh!" I shouted, meeting his blow as Eos's opponent let out a howl: she had bitten his neck. He held it with one hand, blood gushing. I arced my blade, slashing his heel tendon, then his throat as he fell.

"Back, Eos." I stepped in front of her. The third man held a dirk in one hand and a sword in the other, and she'd done more than enough.

"Come, then, let's finish this," I said. I tightened the grip on my sword. He glanced at the two prone bodies on the forest floor. And then he turned and ran.

We'd not see him again. My shoulders sank in relief as he disappeared into the black of the forest on foot, and I turned to Eos. Blood stained the velvet round her mouth, and her eyes were yet wild.

"Good girl, Eos," I soothed. "Good girl." I reached out and she snorted, then lowered her head so I might stroke the smooth plane of her forehead.

"Are you hurt?" I asked, running my hands over her in the dark. By some miracle, she was unharmed.

Across the clearing, the rope lay in a heap. A reminder of what nearly was.

I bent, picking it up, and coiled it, knotting it at my chest.

"Come, girl," I said, pulling myself astride. "We've got leagues yet to travel, and we cannot be late."

CHAPTER 23

Lailoken

"Nearly gave up on you." Fendwin turned as Eos and I approached in the dark. The torches of Gwrgi and Peredur's fortress of Caer Greu burned bright in the black night from our vantage point on a nearby hill.

"There was trouble on the road," I said.

"What sort of trouble?"

"Later," I promised.

Fendwin nodded, securing a length of rope over his shoulder. "Brought you a rope, but you've got one, I see."

"Aye. I do now." I tethered Eos to a nearby tree. "How is Gladys?"

"She had her babe. A boy." There was tenderness in his voice. I stopped, turning to him.

"Did she? A boy . . ." I was unprepared for the feel of it, the way it struck me. My niece had two other children I'd never laid eyes upon. Life was passing too quickly, and my kin felt so far away.

"Is she healthy? And the boy?" I asked.

"Aye, aye. Both hale."

"Thank the Gods. And how are you two getting on?"

Fendwin grunted and I smiled.

"She never used to be difficult. Good for her."

We stood side by side, eyes fixed on the fortress. The Angles were coming for Ebrauc; the light of their campfires could be seen from the heights in the pastures below the fortress, a sea of glowworms burning in the dark. They would attack at dawn. The women, the frail, and the children had already found shelter at a western fort. At least Gwrgi and Peredur had seen to that, when their scouts had caught wind of the Angle king Ælle of Deira and his forces marching on Caer Greu.

Gwrgi and Peredur planned to fight. They had summoned their allies to come and save them. But men and women—spies of my sister's—had been whispering since summer, sweetening the hearts of Ebrauc's warriors with cattle and coin, promising refuge in Strathclyde for the men and their families. Ælle was bent on attack, there was no changing that. And once Languoreth's whisperers had seeded the knowledge that Strathclyde would not answer Ebrauc's call to battle, any man of sense came to see that fleeing in the night was a far better fate than sunrise and death.

The signal—the rhythmic waving of a torch—came at last from the watchtower of Caer Greu.

"Ready, then?" Fendwin asked.

I glanced at him. "You are certain we can trust them?"

"The warriors of Ebrauc want no battle. They've sworn it and will be richly paid. Only slaughter awaits them at dawn. Their commander has assured us we'll find no resistance within the fort."

"That's it, then," I said. Our eyes met briefly in the dark. "It has come to you and me to finish it."

"Aye." His mouth was a thin line as we moved silently toward the fort.

Fendwin and I, we had waited so patiently. There were times when I thought this night would never come, that Gwrgi of Ebrauc would live out long days in the comfort of his Hall upon a fleece-lined couch while I watched Eira twist and cry out, flinching in her sleep.

Gods grant her justice, I'd begged.

Some deeds could not be undone by the payment of cattle. The viciousness of Gwrgi sullied the laws given to men. This night we risked our lives not only for Eira but for all the lives Gwrgi and Peredur's Battle of Arderydd had churned beneath its feet. Gwenddolau. My nephew Rhys. Countless fallen Dragon Warriors.

"Come," Fendwin whispered. "Quickly—this way." He cupped his hands, sounding a dove call to the watchman, and we crept beneath the outer rampart. A moment passed, then the heavy oaken gate opened a crack.

"Would that every raid were this easy," I said.

Yet as we crept through the fortress, I kept my fingers light, close to my blade. There need be only one young Ebraucian foolish enough to think himself heroic and we'd be dead.

The guards did not meet our eyes as we slipped inside the fort. Perhaps they felt guilty. Or perhaps it was only that our arrival was their signal to depart.

They had been waiting.

The latches of the hut doors had been oiled, and they opened now without a sound. Any dissenters had already been silenced. As the warriors of Ebrauc spotted us, they gathered their belongings, signaling one another. They slipped downhill as one body, like a school of fish, as Fendwin and I crept uphill as if swimming against the current of a moonless sea.

The formidable wooden gate of the upper citadel lolled open. The huts were abandoned, the grass scattered with forgotten things and dirty cook pots. As we neared the Hall, a monk some winters older than I opened the door holding a torch, and a cluster of servants issued out silently behind him. He looked at me, eyes catching upon my tonsure and then my scar.

"Here. Take this," he said, offering his torch.

I was thankful, for inside the great room the oil lamps had long been snuffed as the men sought one last sleep before battle. Cups still lay on tables. Soon it would be a hall inhabited by nothing but shades.

We knew in which chambers the brothers of Ebrauc slept. Fendwin split silently off to the eastern room. The western chamber was mine. My heart raced as every muscle coiled. It was so quiet, I could hear the blood beating between my ears. There was a soft but surprised choking sound. Fendwin had woken Peredur. It must be now.

I slid open the door, heard him breathing in the dark only long enough to realize it was not the breath of a man in sleep but one pressed beside the door, waiting. Before he could strike, I slammed my torch at his face, blinding him long enough to strike his stomach with the pommel of my sword.

I was no fool. I did not expect Gwrgi of Ebrauc to go without a fight. But against my rage, he stood only a fool's chance. I tossed my blade aside for the satisfaction of my fists.

Grabbing the collar of his tunic, I pushed him up against the wall. It was then that something on a nearby chest caught my eye. A blade I'd know anywhere.

"This does not belong to you," I said, reaching to take up my sister's golden dagger.

I dragged Gwrgi into the great room where the two wooden thrones of Ebrauc sat side by side. Fendwin waited with Peredur, bound tightly to his seat with rope.

Gwrgi let out a growl as he caught sight of Peredur's bloodied face, his body slumped as if sleeping and tied to his throne.

I looked at Fendwin. "Dead?"

"Not yet," he said.

Gwrgi's breath was coming in short, bull-like bursts. As he looked round the great room, I saw the knowledge dawn on him that his men had given them up.

"Aye, your army has left you, and no allies come," I said, studying his face.

"You bluff," he exclaimed. "The Britons would never sacrifice Ebrauc."

"Your reign is now over." I leaned in close so he would not mistake me. "We've seen to the safety of your men and your people. The Britons have severed you like a festering limb."

Gwrgi's eyes skittered like a badger in a trap.

"Kill us, then," he goaded, craning his neck. "That's why you've come, isn't it? Go on, Lailoken. Take your revenge."

"Nay. It won't be so easy for you," I said.

Fendwin came to grab him, pinning him to his seat as I bound him up. Yanking the knot, I stepped back, giving him one last look.

"Your evil is a rot," I said. "But as much as I'd like, I'll not be the one to strike you dead. It's a nasty feud you've got with the Angles. King Ælle of Deira will be far more artful than I could ever be."

Peredur did not stir, though I imagined he would before the last. The black banner of Ebrauc hung limp in the great room. I stopped long enough to wipe my blade upon it.

We jogged downhill. The fortress was a husk. In the valley below, the lights of the Angle camp winked in the darkness, waiting. For we had made a bargain with the Angles, too.

We'd offered them the lords of Ebrauc.

Though I could not escape the feeling that our actions this night had served only to feed the hunger of the insatiable Angle beast, we were rid of Gwrgi, Peredur, and their poison at last.

Only one man stood waiting by the gates. Our messenger.

I looked at him with a nod. "Go and tell the Angles: Now they may come."

CHAPTER 24

Angharad

Burghead Fortress, Kingdom of Fortriu
Land of the Picts
27th of September, AD 580

The boy's name was Ewan.

He had been a steward to Artúr, what the Scots called a *ghillie*.
The way his eyes lit when Angharad had told him the story of their
meeting! The rush of hope that came to his face when he and Imogen
spoke in Goidelic, even if it was only for her to tell him, *Mind the cook
pot and don't you let it burn!* He kept the hut far cleaner than old Corc
had ever done, eager to keep his place in his newfound home.

Master Briochan will come round, Angharad assured him. For she
had learned that the Wisdom Keeper's bark was far worse than his
bite.

Angharad's days were consumed by teachings. Prayers. The recitation of new kennings. *Ciest. Ni Ansa. Ciest. Ni Ansa.*

She devoured it, hungry for more. At night her dreams were made
of water, wide, undulating waves that claimed her in their current.
She saw water beasts with slick, sinuous bodies and fish with glowing
white eyes and razors for teeth.

And then, one night, came a dream that was altogether different.

Angharad dreamt she was a gull, skimming high above the gray-blue waters of the sea. Her lungs were full of the thick, kelpy smell of ocean, and the sun was bright, warming her feathered back. All could be seen from this height: the fickle silver flash of fish, the gentle rise and misty spout of a mother whale with her calf. It was a lovely dream. Sunshine and the wild buoy of wind beneath her. But even in dreams, where there is light, there is always shadow.

The air went damp as clouds blotted the sun. And suddenly the sea was churning, waves drawing up, curling like a fist. She spotted, bobbing in the water, what at first seemed only a little black fleck, rising and plummeting at the will of the waves. But, wheeling more closely, she saw it was, in fact, a man being tossed by the sea, struggling to keep his head above water. His pale face was aged and his hair unnaturally dark.

Gwrgi of Ebrauc's eyes narrowed as he battled, his chin tilted up. But you cannot fight water.

Angharad watched as a swell rose, towering in its hunger.

And then the wave crashed down, swallowing him whole.

CHAPTER 25

Lailoken

Glasgu, Kingdom of Strathclyde
Land of the Britons
1st of October, AD 580

The salt smell of the Clyde blew in gusts off the river that twisted in the distance as Eos and I entered the familiar forest of elm, river ash, and oak. The sky was gray, but the leaves overhead were an autumn glory of copper and gold.

When Languoreth and I were little, the villagers of Cadzow had told us the veil between the worlds was spun so thin on Bright Hill, you could hear the Gods breathing. Now the hill was pricked with grave markers and stuffed with bodies of the Christian dead.

I'd sworn I would never return to this place. But I had stopped at my waterfall in the Borderlands as I journeyed home from Ebrauc. I had dreamt with the Keeper of the Falls, and he had shown me visions. I was ready to return.

Besides, the Gods have a way of making mockery of oaths. For this was where our story had begun, at the place once called Bright Hill. This was where the first fine threads were set in the web of fate that bound me and my sister to Mungo.

I knew I would find him here, at the monastery built at the foot of our once sacred hill.

I stopped at the old wooden bridge that arched over the gurgling burn, dismounting to let Eos drink before tethering her at the old sycamore that still stood sentinel there. But the bridge was haunted with echoes.

Come on, Languoreth, I'll race you!

You are about to enter a sacred place, said Cathan. *For when you step off this bridge, you step out of our world and into another . . .*

I bowed my head, whispering the prayer he'd taught me so long ago, and crossed the bridge.

It was Brother Telleyr who'd cleared this small place in the forest beyond the spring—who'd first raised the lofty wall of timber stakes that encircled the monastery. The gate stood where it had always been. Mungo worked in shadows, with hired puppets. He would not harm me here. He could not touch me.

I knocked, and a small hatch opened in the door, revealing the stubbled face of a guard.

"Let me in," I said.

The guard looked at me, wary. "What are your intentions?"

I thought a moment. "I would kill him if I could. But to do so would spark war between the people of your god and the people of mine—something your master seems to desire above all. Given my dedication to the safety of the people of Strathclyde, sadly, I cannot kill him. So for today, it will have to suffice simply to speak with him."

"Hmmph," the guard grunted. He slapped the hatch closed. A reluctant clunk came, then a groan as he opened the gate. A monk with faded auburn hair stood behind the guard. He'd once been quite handsome, but he now looked rather sickly and pale.

"Brother Anguen," I greeted him.

"Your sword," the guard demanded. I turned to him.

"I have just survived an attempt on my life, so you will understand that I will keep it. But you have my word, I will not harm him."

Brother Anguen nodded to the guard.

"Come," Anguen said. "I will take you to him."

"You've kept his flock all this time," I said as I followed him past the two long whitewashed buildings that served as the monks' quarters. Brother Anguen did not turn.

"I did what any good servant would do."

"Is that how you conceive of yourself? You are his servant, not your god's?"

"When God speaks through man, they are one and the same. The people rejoice at Mungo's return."

"Do they?" I said no more. A scattering of rich Christian chieftains rejoiced because they and Mungo shared the same thirst for influence in Strathclyde. But there were a fair number who sought Brother Thomas and the measured faith he offered in the woods.

Not far past the kitchens, the timber-and-stone church still sat.

"He is in prayer," Brother Anguen said, opening the door. I stopped at the threshold.

"I will wait here."

He'd not make me wait long. Rather, like Gwrgi, Mungo thrilled to a game.

He emerged from his church, his graying head yet bowed in contemplation.

"Why have you come?" he asked. I tossed the coiled rope at his feet.

He looked up at me, his blue eyes keen. "You bring me rope? A strange gift. Is this an offering of peace, perhaps?"

"You talk of peace," I said. "Is murder, then, your peace offering?"

Mungo's face hardened, but I held up my hand. "Do not waste your breath, for we both know you are a coward. You will never admit to your shadowy dealings under the broad light of day."

He looked at me a long moment before speaking. "You do not

understand me, Lailoken. I shall attempt to explain, though a pagan mind is unlikely to grasp it."

"By all means," I said, giving a flourish of my hand.

"It is my duty to lead people to the light," he began. "The Old Way is one of fickle gods, of darkness. The Son of God is peace. He offers a way to deliver us from the dark. Let the people come to the light, and Strathclyde shall be united. There is no Angle army that could come against us then. God shall be on our side. Darkness always shrinks in the presence of light."

I nodded, considering. "Before you arrived in Strathclyde, we had peace," I said. "Peace is a grace long offered by Wisdom Keepers— those who possess intellect enough to debate in philosophy, and who hold freedom of thought in the highest regard. We had such peace with the Christians of Strathclyde. Your first act was to dismantle it by felling a sacred grove. I cannot debate the virtues of peace with a man who is blinded by narrow thought, ruled by ambition, and driven by hate."

"Men, women, and children have been martyred, persecuted, and enslaved by Britons, Scots, and Picts alike," Mungo said. "There would be no place for a new religion if the people of this great isle were content with the old. Was Brother Telleyr not a Wisdom Keeper before he heard the word of the one true God? Perhaps you should look to those who have come before you."

"If Christians are persecuted, it is due to their intolerance to any way of thinking but their own." I leaned in so he could not mistake me. "And I have not come to harm you, so you would be wise to keep the name of Brother Telleyr from your mouth."

Mungo stepped back. "It would seem we are at an impasse."

"No," I said. "*You* are at an impasse. I have come to say this: you will cease in your wicked and underhanded dealings. In turn, I will concede to counsel with you in peace. You shall minister to the Christians, and I shall minister to the people of the Old Way. Advise the king how you will; he has requested both our counsel and will receive it in fair measure. I will give my word if you will give yours. Will you agree?"

Mungo seemed startled by my offer. Insides revolting, I extended my hand.

"Very well. I agree," he said. Our grip on each other's arm was painfully firm. I used it to draw him close.

"In parting, I will say only this. The next time you threaten me or my sister, you had better have an army at your back. For this is *our* kingdom, *our* home, and these are *our* people. It may be winters yet, but I promise you, the Angles are coming. And when I lift my sword for Strathclyde, I lift it for every citizen, man or woman, Old Way or new. Are you indeed holy? If that be so, then I challenge you: Live by your word."

"I have given my word," Mungo said dismissively. "I believe we are finished."

"Aye," I said. "That we are." Giving one last look at the rope by his feet, I turned and took my leave.

Insides roiling, I left the gates of the monastery behind me.

Yes, I had sworn I would never return to this place. But as I neared the burn, something in my chest pulled, rousing an ache I could not deny.

It had been so long.

I could not leave without visiting what had once been the White Spring.

The same narrow spout of clear water issued from a crack in the rock where the hill had broken open, spilling into a pool below. Now a heavy stone incised with a cross stood at the spring head, and the ancient, gnarled blackthorn that had dug its roots into the slope above the spring was dying. Even trees could not live forever. The wind stirred, fluttering the ribbons of cloth tied to its branches as if with a sigh.

Cathan had always told us that water holds memory.

Once, I had stood on this very bank, casting a wish for greatness and wisdom. I had since sought spirit in deep places, yet still I battled that impetuous boy.

I sat back on my heels now beside the smooth stones at the edge of the spring, gazing down into the clear water. Did the honeyed bits of amber my sister and I had tossed as children still lie buried somewhere in the sediment of the pool? The trickle of cold water resounded with my sister's young voice.

And what of the lady of the spring? Would you abandon her, too?

I had been so certain about the spirit of this place. *The lady of the spring is sleeping. They call her by another name—a name that is not her own. And so she may become it, if she chooses, and her true name will be lost.*

As a boy, my fear had led me to believe it. But perhaps the lady of the spring had indeed granted me a measure of wisdom. For I knew now that spirits of land were not so easily displaced. Gods answered to so many names.

What did it matter what the people of Strathclyde called her, so long as they still believed?

I closed my eyes, listening. A bird called in the forest. I could still feel that same thrumming in the land like a heartbeat. She was yet here.

I sat with her a long while, Bright Hill behind me.

I thought of the ancient oaks that had stood there and the genera- tions of Wisdom Keepers who had worshipped among them. And for a moment I could have sworn I heard a deep, familiar laugh.

It was as if Cathan still stood by my side.

CHAPTER 26

Angharad

Craig Phadrig, Ness Lands
Kingdom of the Picts
1st of November, AD 580

At the head of the Great Glen, on the gently sloped shoulders of the steep hill fort of Craig Phadrig, a village had grown up, just as seeds, over time, sprout and then spread, windblown, from their mother.

The fortress sat at the meeting place of a river and two saltwater firths. The winter steading of the high king, the village had long been a center for trade, known to possess the finest cattle, horses, wool, and furs: marten and beaver, weasel and fox. Timber, too, was plentiful, and oak was floated by river for the halls and ramparts of chieftains who kept watch over the barren uplands, the treeless places.

It had been twenty-four winters since Bridei son of Maelchon had first become high king of the Picts, and his promise of wealth and protection had been kept among all his Cruithni, but there were perhaps no people more loyal to him than those of the Ness.

Their company arrived in a fleet of ships late morning. The waves had been bestial leaving Burghead, as they had left it rather late for sea travel, but as they sailed west along the coast, the Moray Firth became increasingly sheltered by land. By the time they reached the place where the Moray met the waters of the Beauly Firth, the salt waters beneath them were nearly smooth as glass.

The people of the Ness rushed to the shoreline at the sight of boats, cheering and singing, their cheeks bright with cold. From their turf-roofed huts, the comforting smell of peat smoke drifted, and as Angharad gazed up at the wooded hills, she was surprised to find herself suddenly standing beside the king. Bridei's face creased into a smile at the sight of the gathering crowd at the wooden quay and turned to her, his blue eyes proud.

"Welcome to the Ness, Angharad Ton Velen," he said. "You have seen the head of my kingdom. Now you shall see its heart."

"It's beautiful." Angharad smiled as the boat jostled with men tying up to the quay. Overhearing her, Briochan leaned in, his arm round Imogen's waist.

"You have not yet seen the river Ness and her loch," he pronounced. "There are many sights to behold here."

Briochan seemed happy here, winters falling from his face.

"It feels like a festival day," Angharad marveled as she and Imogen were rushed by the crowd onto shore behind the king and his company.

"Aye, there is always celebration," Imogen called over the noise, bowing her head to accept a wreath of yew and dried rowanberries. "The people are delighted to have their king returned for winter's keep."

Young Ewan walked beside them; he'd been wide-eyed the whole journey. It reminded Angharad of her first glimpses of Pictland. It was like slipping through a cave yet emerging into a corrie. A whole world she'd never seen. Angharad brimmed with it all, barely resisting the urge to pinch herself. Here she was, *en Cruithni*, in company of the high king, Initiate to the great Wisdom Keeper Briochan. She could scarce remember a time when she felt so much happiness.

At a gentle tug on her robes, Angharad looked down to see a little girl with sprays of frizzy, straw-colored curls offer her a wreath of her own.

"Did you fashion this?" Angharad asked. The girl nodded shyly and Angharad crouched, so the girl might flop it onto her head.

"Thank you," she said. "It's beautiful."

Angharad stood only to catch Rhainn eyeing her from his place beside the king. He balanced a wreath, too small, with one hand on the crown of his head, and he was smiling. His amber eyes lingered on hers a moment. She smiled and glanced away.

Donkeys hitched to waiting carts and a handful of graceful horses stood ready for the king and his company. There were vessel-loads of trunks to be carried uphill to the fortress, but Bridei and his wives waved away the horses, eager to walk alongside the villagers in cheerful company, heads bent as they listened to news of harvests and new births and squabbles between neighbors.

Thin shafts of early winter sun filtered through the bare-fingered oaks as they began to climb, brown leaves shuffling and crunching satisfyingly underfoot. At last, nearing the top, they rounded a bend in the path and Angharad stopped, catching her breath.

The Beauly Firth stretched like a shimmering blue mantle, its fertile outskirts a rusty autumnal patchwork of turf-roofed roundhouses and thickly wooded forests stretching all the way to a thrust of distant mountains. Crannogs and basket weir fish traps dotted the firth, where fishing boats and seagoing merchant vessels skimmed like water striders. But it was the mountains in the distance that beckoned, tugging at some invisible cord in the center of her chest.

"What hills are those?" Angharad asked, gazing into the distance. Their pull was stronger than a current, so insistent it nearly ached.

"Those are the lands of west Ross, and the hills, the Gray Mountains," Briochan said. "Beyond the peaks which you see, there is a mount which may well interest you. It lies farthest to the west. That hill belongs to the Cailleach. She who has always been."

"Is it quite far?" Angharad asked.

"The distance is of no consequence if you are not ready," Briochan said.

Angharad's cheeks heated. Why tell her, then, if she was forbidden to go? As if she did not already feel shamed by the ferocity of her own desire. She had helped to turn the tide of a battle. She had felt thunder thrum in her veins. The Cailleach had claimed her. Even now, the Crooked Path laid its stones at her feet.

"What if I am ready?" she asked.

"Put it from your mind, Ton Velen," Briochan said sternly. "You behave as a novice might, with no idea the dangers that wait."

His insult stung, and Angharad was unable to hold her tongue. "Tell me, then, if you would have me be afraid. What dangers await? Tell me why you refused an Initiate for all these long winters—carrying blame and grief like boulders! You fear I will die just as she did!"

The villagers stopped and turned, gaping. Briochan dealt her a sharp look, but Angharad had stifled her frustration for too long.

"As I thought, you'll tell me nothing," she said. "All the while behaving as if I do not share my chambers with a shade."

She wished she could swallow the words even as she spoke them. Briochan straightened, towering over her, his face tight with anger.

"You would do well to keep the counsel of your silence, Angharad Ton Velen," he said, "As I seem to remind you far too often of late."

For a moment Angharad thought he might strike her. But his anger faded as quickly as it had risen, leaving only sadness in its wake. She watched the morning's joy drain from his face as Briochan fixed his dark eyes on the mountain.

"As I said. The distance is of no consequence when you are not ready. When the Cailleach summons, you will know."

• • •

Angharad had not realized how accustomed she'd become to the tumble of the sea until it was absent, though over the sheer crush of people the first eve, it was difficult to hear anything at all. Craig Phadrig was intimate compared to the vast upper citadel of the fortress at Burghead, and the winter fortress left little chance for solitude. She soon learned this was why the village and the court seemed so bonded: with only a hall, a stone well, and six small huts that made up the fortress, many warriors and court members alike lodged with families in the settlements below. Even the king himself seemed to spend little time in the confines of the ramparts, preferring to check the winter stocks, visit the leather makers, and ride out among the tenants. Angharad thought of the shade from her chamber, languishing in the shell of Burghead while the wicked winter storms rolled in, hoping the girl found company in her fury.

The following day Angharad and Briochan kept a careful peace as they began their contemplation followed by a lesson, this one upon horseback. Rhainn had insisted Angharad borrow his mount, Cysgod, a beautiful black horse with a smooth, gentle gait.

Outside it was cool and overcast, the sky a dull gray. Cysgod was quick beneath her, eager to escape the confines of the fortress, and Angharad leaned forward to stroke his neck, breathing in the comforting smell of hay that lingered on him from the stable. It was a scent that reminded her of childhood, of her mother.

The horses took them down the steep path from the fortress and along the edge of the firth until Briochan drew his mount to a stop, stepping down onto a rocky beach strewn with red weed.

The water was choppy gray metal as the wind belted from the north. As they stood side by side, Briochan bent, picking up a stone, and smoothed it with his thumb before gently offering it back to the water.

"*Ceist*," he said, with the tone that signaled a lesson about to begin. "Tell me the Twelve Winds."

"*Ni ansa*," Angharad began. "The four chief winds blow from north, south, east, and west. Between each of these, there are two subordinate winds. The Gods also gave the winds color, so that each is different from the other."

"Continue." He motioned impatiently. She took a breath and recited the kenning.

"The white, the clear purple, the blue, the strong green. The yellow, the red, sure in their knowledge; in their gentle meetings, wrath does not seize them. The black, the gray, the speckled, the dark. The deep brown, the dun. Darksome hues, they are not easily controlled."

"Well done, Ton Velen. You can chirp out the kenning," Briochan said. "But what do you know of the *winds?*"

"Of the winds I know too little. I am learning to listen," she said.

Briochan tilted his head to the water. "Always we are listening. What do you hear?"

Angharad closed her eyes. The wind was bitter, yanking at her hair and tossing her cloak. She waited, asking. But it did not speak in the way other things might.

"I cannot hear anything," she said at last, feeling like she'd failed. But Briochan only nodded, seeming relieved.

"Then this wind is not for you," he said.

"Do *you* hear it?" she asked, looking at him.

"Yes. I can hear it."

"What does it say?"

Briochan looked north into the face of it for a moment. "It speaks of dark things," he said at last. "Things that needn't concern you."

He blinked as if returning to himself, then glanced at the horses.

"Come then, Ton Velen. I will show you the Ness. There is someone I should very much like you to meet."

Away from the firth, the wind dropped in the shelter of the hills. They followed the narrow road that led from Craig Phadrig, the one that skirted the broad channel of the river.

They rode a while without speaking, Angharad absorbing the grace of the swiftly moving water. Then Briochan glanced at Angharad from the corner of his eye, breaking the silence.

"Her name was Alys," he said.

The Initiate, he meant. At last he would speak of her? Angharad held her breath, worried that the slightest movement would clamp him shut forever.

"She, like you, showed an aptitude. Those who would be weather-workers do not come to me in search of Brighid; they are not all soft-ness and spring. It is the crow women who come. The ones who have seen death. Alys was such a one. As are you. But Alys did not come to me grown. I found her, a tottering, helpless babe in the fiery ruins of a Scots' raid, still trying to nurse from her dead mother's breast."

The memory deepened creases at his eyes.

"I speak of things that happened long ago. Long before Imogen," he went on. "My first wife and I were not destined to bear many children as others were. I had been foster father to Bridei, who'd grown to a man. We were blessed by Rhainn, a tottering boy himself. But as much as my wife's eyes brightened at the sight of our son, she had always longed for a daughter. It seemed Alys was given to our care by the Gods, and we loved her as our own. As she grew, the wind danced round Alys. I realized she was Chosen. One day, she heard the Cailleach call." Brio-chan looked away. "Alys left to seek her and never returned. She died on that mountain."

"You blame yourself for what happened to her," Angharad said carefully. "But I'm certain you were not at fault."

Briochan frowned, disappointed. "Blame and fault are the ways of a child. Nay, Ton Velen. You do not understand."

He waved his hand in the familiar way that meant he would say no more on a subject, and Angharad clenched her jaw in frustration.

Up ahead, a hill caught her eye, thrusting from the flats like a fist. Briochan followed her gaze.

"Tomnahurich, Hill of the Yews," he said. "It is our sacred grove. The Gods keep it close. We light the festival fires there and administer to justice when need be. At midsummer it is home to horse races round the bottom."

Passing along the foot of Tomnahurich, they wound back to the river Ness, and Angharad spotted a chain of wooded islands in the middle of the water, the river flowing gently round them. As they neared the ford, Angharad looked up to see a sparrow hawk perched on a tree above the water as if keeping watch.

"That will be her bird," Briochan said. It flew off as if hearing him, disappearing into the tree-sheltered islands.

"What is this place?" Angharad mused. She felt dreamy and disoriented. The land here was strong.

"The islands and the hill are governed by Aislinn, high priestess of Inverness," Briochan said. "It is she I bring you to see."

Nerves kicked in Angharad's chest. She'd been raised at Fortingall, a place of yews and dreaming. But while Fortingall's high priestess Eachna might've been her kin, power had twisted her. It gave Angharad pause to think of encountering such a woman again.

At the gently rushing ford, the water was no deeper than the horses' knees, and Cysgod crossed on steady feet. As they stepped onto the isle, however, Angharad's trepidation dissolved. Here, between the Hill of Yews and the eager push of the river, something was swirling.

It was a thin place. Undeniably so. A thrill hummed through her at the sensation—better than the elated sort of spinning one gets from drinking too much mead.

"Aislinn is a great prophet," Briochan said. "One of the most gifted I have known."

"I'm humbled to meet her," Angharad acknowledged. "I am grateful you arranged it."

"One does not make arrangements with Aislinn." Briochan laughed. "She seeks an audience with you, Ton Velen. Though I cannot imagine why. Do not allow it to fatten your head."

"Impossible whilst you are my teacher."

The Wisdom Keeper's eyes sparkled, and Angharad went on, encouraged. "She has heard Briochan, the Great and tortured Keeper of the north, has at last accepted an Initiate, and must see as much to believe it, more like."

"That's enough talking from you," he said.

Tall trees stretched their fingers skyward, and leaves scuttled under the horses' hooves in a sudden breeze as they found themselves standing on a narrow woodland path. Spotting them, a woman clad in flowing black robes and a thick black woolen cloak appeared, her hood drawn up against the cold. She had the bearing of a holy woman, but not quite a high priestess.

"Master Briochan," she greeted him. "We are expecting you. Come, this way."

They slid from their horses, reins in hand, following the priestess along the forest path. The isle held the peace of a temple. A realm of broad-reaching oaks and leaning silver birches; everywhere was the cold feel of water, its rush and soft trickle. Angharad felt the pulsing of the place that marked it as holy—gentle but persistent. Small timber huts were scattered throughout the woods, where hides were stretched or a butter churn stood, objects bearing witness to daily life, but everything was spare and tidily kept. Women clad in matching black cloaks stopped at their duties and looked up as they passed, offering small smiles. A man dressed in freeman's clothes walked, hobbled over, leaning on a priestess's arm.

"There is a powerful spring here that flows near Tomnahurich. Many come for healing," Briochan said.

The priestess slowed as they reached a small clearing. In the clearing's center sat a stately stone altar, and beyond it a round house with a small wooden door.

"Come; she is waiting."

They crossed the clearing, but Briochan stopped at the threshold.

"Go, then, Ton Velen," he said.

"Are you not coming?" She turned with alarm.

"Nay." Briochan shook his head. "What lies beyond this door is not for me. It is for you, and you alone."

From beyond the door came the soft, hollow sound of a bone flute. Briochan raised his brows, expectant, shooing her in.

Angharad opened the door gently, peering into what at first seemed to be utter darkness as her eyes adjusted to the dim. Scents overwhelmed her: vetiver and pinesap, meadowsweet and a certain musk she could not place. As her eyes grew accustomed to the dark, she made out four figures seated on woven mats round the dying embers of a hearth, as if in contemplation. Each was dressed in the same black robe of the other priestesses, but thick black veils covered their faces. Above the hearth, a cauldron steamed from an iron pothook, filling the room with the aromas she'd breathed in. She heard the rustle of feathers and glanced up to see the brown-and-white-speckled sparrow hawk perched beside the door. Beneath the bird, a young priestess sat cross-legged, a drum leaning idly against her thigh, her lips pressed to a flute. The tune was like a moan in the wind, a whispered, haunting song.

"Welcome, Angharad of Fortingall," a woman's voice said.

Angharad bowed deeply. "I am humbled by your summoning, Lady Aislinn," she said, not quite certain whom to address.

"Come in." The voice was gentle but firm, though Angharad could not tell which figure had spoken it. The four sat, spines straight as spears, their veiled gazes fixed ahead. A reed mat lay at the edge of the chamber. Beside it on a low wooden stool sat an empty cup. The priestess's voice was warm, and the air within the chamber somehow soothing.

"We are Aislinn," they said, for when they spoke, the voice might have issued from one's lips or another's, but each sounded nearly the same. "Welcome to the Ness Lands."

"Thank you," Angharad said, bowing again.

"You needn't bow to us, child," Aislinn said. One figure turned, inclining her head. "Go on, then. Bring us the cup."

Angharad took it and moved to the hearth, offering it up. Aislinn took it from her, one of the women rising gracefully to ladle some of the cauldron's liquid into her cup. Aislinn's pale fingers glowed in the gloom as she passed it to Angharad.

"Drink, Daughter of Fortingall. You have come so we might grant you a vision. For seers are often born blind to their own destinies. Such is the way of the goddess's gift."

Angharad blinked. She'd imagined Aislinn might simply deliver a message; she hadn't expected to undergo a sleep. She knew all too well the potency of these drafts made for dreaming. After all, she'd prepared them countless times, though no two drafts were the same. The drafts were prepared for the dreamer, and while some elements were essential, each dreamer required a medicine that was somewhat unique. Yet the presence of Aislinn sparked a hunger inside her, this chance to glimpse what the goddess held in store.

She brought the cup to her lips, breathing in the astringent steam of mushroom and herb. Then, tilting her head, she drank.

Too soon, the chamber round her began to spin, her lids pulling as if made of lead. Or was it the low and hollow echo of the flute that left her feeling drowsy? She should lie down upon the mat, she knew—that was the way—but her legs would not take her. She slumped down beside the hearth, her head dropping into Aislinn's waiting lap.

Angharad woke in darkness, gasping and disoriented, her tongue dry as fabric in her mouth.

A voice came, rich and calm, drawing her back from the blackness. "You are with Aislinn, Angharad, our child. You are safe."

She felt hands, arms, gently lifting. Slowly, Angharad opened her eyes. It was impossible to tell how much time had passed: the hearth was still embers. The four who were Aislinn still sat erect in their circle. The girl who'd been playing the flute had helped Angharad to sit up.

"How long was I dreaming?" Angharad asked.

"Long enough," Aislinn replied. "It is a new day. It is morning."

"I—I don't remember." Angharad rubbed her eyes, searching, trying to catch even a scrap of her dream. She looked at the women clad in black, panic mounting. "I cannot recall anything," she said.

"Hush, child, hush," Aislinn said. "All in good time."

But Angharad had a sinking feeling in the pit of her stomach. "In all my days at Fortingall, there was never a dreamer who could not remember . . . ," she said softly. It had been such an honor to be summoned here. They had given her a draft, a medicine all her own. And she could remember nothing.

"Just as a falconer blinds the bird with a hood, so do the Gods from time to time blind us to the essence of our dreaming," Aislinn said. "You dreamt deeply, Angharad. Dreams that are deep cannot always be summoned, but return when you have need of them. In this, we trust. And so then must you."

Angharad swallowed, and her tongue stuck to the roof of her mouth. Aislinn called to the girl.

"Water, little one."

The girl fetched a cup of cool, clear water that tasted slightly of chalk, as if from a spring. Angharad drank deeply. Aislinn waited patiently as her grogginess faded, though Angharad could sense the closing; their time was finished. Angharad stood.

"Thank you, Aislinn."

She could not see Aislinn's faces but felt their smile. "You are most welcome, Angharad. We will see you again, we are certain."

"Yes." Angharad offered a smile and moved toward the door.

Aislinn stopped her: "Angharad of Fortingall."

"Yes?" She turned.

"Do not return to the fortress. Follow the road instead, upriver. You are a newcomer here. There are so many people yet to encounter, so many miraculous sights yet to see."

"But Briochan—"

"Briochan knows you are with Aislinn," they said. "And this is what Aislinn commands."

"Of course." She bowed. "As you say."

Aislinn nodded, dismissing her. As Angharad ducked out through the door, the little girl at the edge of the chamber laughed, a joyous tinkling sound that rang in her ears long after she mounted her horse, blinking into the brightness of the sunny November morn.

CHAPTER 27

Angharad

Angharad rode Cysgod along the tree-lined path that followed the river. Fishermen and farmers with creels slung over their backs bowed at the sight of her in her robes, careful not to gawk at a Keeper. Huts studded the land, livestock chattering behind sturdy woven fences. The river was wide here, with sloping banks of dying grass.

Nessa. She did not feel like other rivers. Then again, what two rivers were the same?

Clota of the river Clyde—the river of Angharad's youth—was a forceful, salty river, one of sea kelp and queens. But Nessa possessed a more deep-rooted magic. Rich with salmon and sea trout, seals and otters, Nessa was the piney smell of living things and deep, forgotten places.

Nessa was a keeper of secrets.

As she rode, Angharad remembered a story she'd heard in Strathclyde as a child, a story of the Cailleach.

The Cailleach had two wells she looked after. Each morning, she would uncap the wells so that the people might draw water, but she was always very careful to shut them at dusk. However, the two wells were a great distance from each other, and the Cailleach grew tired of traveling between them each day. She entrusted a maiden named Nessa to look after the farthest well. But one languid summer day, as Nessa sat beside the well, she grew sleepy and lay down beneath the cool shade of a tree to dream. She woke at dawn only to find water gushing from the well she had forgotten to cover. Frightened of the Cailleach's wrath, Nessa ran away, but she could not escape the watchful eye of the Cailleach. The goddess caught sight of the fleeing maid from the top of her mountain throne and cried out: *You have neglected your duty! Now you shall run forevermore.* With a wave of her staff, the Cailleach struck the maid, and Nessa was transformed into the river, cursed to flow ever on from the loch.

Angharad smiled, remembering how her mother had delighted in telling the tale at nighttime under lamplight. But even as a child, Angharad knew the story made no sense.

What goddess would punish a woman for dreaming?

The thought of it stirred shame—that Aislinn could have summoned her, yet she came away with no memory of her vision. Angharad had visions that plagued her, even in waking. And yet, somehow she had failed to capture this dream.

Have faith, she consoled herself. After all, when had the Gods not shown her the way?

The river bottom was mead-stained from peat washing down from high places, but Nessa's water was clear in the shallows. A speckled seal bobbed in an eddy, its dark eyes observing her, and Angharad nodded to the creature. Sometimes a seal was not merely a seal. She rode for some time, until she came to a place where the river stretched, and in the distance she could see its joining with a loch.

A wide pebbled bank beckoned, and she dropped from Cysgod's back, drawn to the water's edge. Delicate waves slapped at the shore, and she sat on the dry stony bank, overlooking the water. Stark blue hills brooded in the distance. A tune rose from her belly and she sang it: an offering to Nessa, the goddess of the river.

She did not know how long she'd been singing when, out in the deep, a flicker of movement caught her eye. It was a ripple—a great, long ribbon, traveling like a wave trails a fast-moving boat. A *trick of the light*, she thought. But as she watched, a strange animal rose to the surface.

The creature was slick, slate gray and shining. Its long, sinuous body arched from the river, looking for a moment like the underbelly of a currach, but the height of its back equaled that of a man.

What are you? she wondered. It moved as if drawn to the shore by the low call of her song. Angharad had seen all manner of whale and dolphin in her day. This creature was no such thing.

Beside her, Cysgod gave a whinny, shifting his dainty black feet.

"Hush," she whispered, worried he might break the spell.

It must have been so, for the beast stopped, as if listening. Then it slipped back beneath the water, disappearing once more into the amber-bottomed deep.

Sweet Gods, she thought. *I have just seen a monster.*

A monster. And yet . . . it did not feel as such. For Angharad had felt exhilarated, not afraid. She sat, searching, hoping it might reappear, but the river felt eerily vacant. The creature had gone.

Every river had its kelpies and serpents, urisks and nuckelavees. It was not unusual for folk to tell stories. There wasn't a glen, burn, or loch that didn't have its tales—nearly all of which were told to keep willful children from dangerous waters. But there were still more mysteries than one could explain. Angharad could not help but suspect that Aislinn knew of this beast. Perhaps the sighting was some kind of omen. But an omen of what?

Angharad stood and stretched, easing back into Cysgod's saddle. But no sooner had she turned back to Craig Phadrig than the quiet of the river was shattered by a scream.

"Someone's hurt," she said aloud. "Come, Cysgod. Let us find the source of it."

She did not have to go far. A short way down the road they arrived at a village—a fisher's settlement, truly, only a cluster of turf-walled huts nestled along the river. Outside the houses, people were gathered, heads bowed in ceremony. Then the cry came again, followed by a low, dismal chanting, and Angharad patted Cysgod's neck.

"Nothing to fear. It's only a keening," she whispered. The people of the Ness were burying a loved one. It was the Keener who'd been crying out, mourning the dead.

The villagers were circled round a freshly dug grave, the Keener clad in torn gray robes, her white, wiry hair like a halo round her head. Keeners were elders, cunning women. But they were not full priestesses. She looked up, eyeing Angharad's robes. "Greetings," she said.

"Greetings to all. I do not wish to disturb you," Angharad said.

"Nay, do not think it," the Keener said kindly.

"I would pay my respects, if you would have me?"

"Yes, come and join us, Initiate. You are most welcome."

"Who is it that you mourn?" Angharad asked quietly. An old man shuffled forward, his face lined with grief.

"My boy," he said roughly. "Though he were well grown to a man. I told 'im to keep from the water. But he wouldn't leave off, ever since he seen it."

"Seen what?" Angharad asked, glancing between them.

"The beast," the man said. "It moves between her river and her loch. As a lad I'd heard tales, but no one had e'er seen it. 'Til now."

"The water beast?" Angharad echoed. "And you mean to say it killed your son?"

"Aye. I saw the white o' his arms flash as he were dragged 'neath the water w' me own two eyes!" Color rose in the old man's face, and Angharad lifted her hands reassuringly.

"I do not doubt you," she said. "I, too, have seen it. Longer than a vessel and quick as an eel. One moment there, the next moment gone."

"Aye," the old man said. "He were swimming in search of it when it took 'im. I heard 'im shoutin' and brought the boat quick as I might, but when he rose up again, he were half-eaten, drowned."

Angharad bowed her head. "I am so very sorry," she said, but she truly hadn't felt the creature was harmful.

The old man looked at her beseechingly. "Will y' speak the death prayer? I canna help but think it's the Gods wh' brought you."

Angharad looked at the Keener. "If it is all right with your Keener."

The old woman nodded. Angharad stepped carefully round to kneel at the grave. Placing her hands over the mound, she closed her eyes. Angharad could feel the man beneath the earth, curled as if in the belly of his mother. Together, she and the Keener intoned the words for safe passage. But even as Angharad prayed, her sight searched the deep waters, calling to the beast.

There, she felt it—a flash of anger and the darting of one eye.

Angharad pulled herself from the vision and stood. What could have angered the creature?

One by one, the mourners offered their sorrows to the man beneath the earth and then, wiping their faces, guided his father back to the settlement.

A large metal cook pot stewed over an open fire not far away; the funeral feast. That's when Angharad saw it, just beyond the huts. Racks upon racks of fish drying in the open, far more fish than was needed to sustain one settlement, or even three.

The old man stood beside a long pine table, seeming uncertain what to do as his kin prepared the feast. She reached out, taking his hands in hers, and he let her. They were rough from winters of lines and nets. She could feel he was gentle, a lover of river, loch, and sea.

"Why do you think the beast has come now?" she asked. "You say in all your years you had not yet seen it."

He seemed bewildered. "Why'd it come now? I canna say."

"I could not help but see you have many fish there, stretched out to dry," Angharad said carefully. "More than is needed to provide any one man a living."

The old man's eyes darted to the racks and he shook his head. "Ach, my son. He had a mind to trade beyond the next villages! I told 'im as much, but m'lad didnae listen. The fish would oft go to rot afore we could trade it! A waste, and I told 'im. But we made offerin's, every morn, same as we always done."

"It is good to make offerings," Angharad said. "But the fish are Nessa's children. And the beast in the river, the guardian of her waters. Man is not the only creature who depends upon fish to survive. By taking too many, you upset the balance. Perhaps this is why the beast attacked your son."

The old man nodded, squinting over the river. "I should ha' done more when he did'na heed my warning."

"You mustn't blame yourself. Beasts, too, must live and eat," she said. "In some ways the beast was serving itself. That is the way of the Gods. But when next you make an offering, tell Nessa you have seen the error in your ways. Nessa will see to it you and your family are never without fish, as she has always done. So long as you and your kin never again take more than you need."

"We'll heed y' words, I swear it," he vowed.

"Good." Angharad released him, glancing back at Cysgod. She was worn from this journey and longing to return home. "I am sorry, but I must go," she said. "Gods give you strength in remembering your son."

The old man nodded. "Gods keep you."

"And you."

Angharad lifted a hand in farewell to the Keener and hurried to her horse.

"You're a good boy, Cysgod," she said, untethering him and giving him a tickle. He leaned into her hand, but then his ears pricked as he gazed over her shoulder.

"What is it?" she asked, turning.

Along the road, a company of men approached. But they were not Bridei's men. Curious, Angharad drew Cysgod behind a stand of trees. Something about them made her want to remain out of sight. They were armed like soldiers but lofting a white banner of peace. Their hair was shorn in the manner of Keepers, yet they did not wear robes. They wore instead thick brown hoods, and the long woolen tunics of freemen stuck out beneath their cloaks. A bearded man with curling blondish-white hair strode in the center of their caravan, his tunic bearing an ornately checked border and his cloak luxurious, rich purple in hue. Purple was a color allowed only to nobility. He carried a tall wooden staff like those used by shepherds, crooked at the end, and his feet were clad in a pair of sturdy leather boots.

Christian monks, and the man looked to be their leader. What in the name of the Gods were they doing in Pictland?

Pulling herself noiselessly onto Cysgod, Angharad turned back toward the fortress before they caught sight of her, urging him into a trot.

CHAPTER 28

Angharad

The fortress of Craig Phadrig was stirred the next morning by the sound of singing.

At first Angharad slept on, so winsome was the melody, but there was a chill on her nose where her face stuck out from the bedding, and she sat up with a start. Dressing in a hurry, she followed the drifting chant into the cold morning air to find that curiosity had dragged nearly half the fortress to the height of the warrior's walk, where they gawked down at the monks gathered at the foot of Bridei's impenetrable gate.

Imogen was wrapped in a fur, standing amongst the others and looking as if she'd seen a shade.

"You told us you saw monks, Ton Velen. You did not say it was Colmcille himself!" she said as Angharad came to stand beside her.

"Colmcille? I do not know him," Angharad said.

"Colmcille is a high nobleman of the Uí Néill, one of the most powerful *clanns* across the Narrow Sea," Imogen said. "He was a monk of great learning, but he was banished from Scotia for stealing a book."

"Banished for stealing a book?"

"Well, he refused to return it, and begot a war."

Angharad frowned, moving along the platform to have a look for herself. The monks below were wrapped against the cold, fourteen

SIGNE PIKE

in all, their voices lifted in song. Colmcille's deep voice carried over them all. He stood straight as a pillar in his thick purple cloak, his clear blue eyes cast skyward.

There were men and women who knew power: kings and queens, Wisdom Keepers and warriors. Theirs was a presence unique among others, an emanating force. Colmcille was such a man.

"What does he sing?" Imogen asked, having no knowledge of Latin. It was a praise song, promising glory, the sort a Keeper composes for his sovereign. Angharad listened, putting it into the Pictish tongue.

"*My song is of a king. May my tongue be the stylus. You are the most handsome of the sons of men. Gracious speech flows from your lips. That is why God has blessed you forever. Strap your sword on your side, O mighty one, in your dignity and your splendor. And in your splendor go on to victory . . .*" Angharad stopped. Imogen had lost interest.

"They've been singing since before dawn," Imogen said. "They first sought entry, but Bridei will not open the gates." She tapped two fingers to her breastbone in naming the king.

In the great room of Craig Phadrig, the king and his council argued over breakfast.

"Colmcille goes by another name," Briochan said. "Those who have met him call him 'Crimthann'—'the Fox.' I would not see you loose this fox amongst your chickens."

"He comes on a matter of politic," another Keeper said. "You saw his white banner."

"He comes on behalf of Aedan mac Gabrahn," yet another counsellor said. "What is there to speak of?"

The king shook his head. "Colmcille is no friend to Aedan. Theirs is an arrangement built upon necessity. Colmcille was appointed by the previous king. Aedan may be of the Old Way, but Christendom has taken root in Dalriada. Now one cannot rule without the other.

We cannot know the nature of his mission. It may serve Aedan, or it may serve himself. Foxes are nothing if not clever."

"I say we let him come and argue his point," the first counsellor said. "This is the way of Keepers. None shall be moved, and we'll be rid of them sooner."

Briochan rose from his seat. "*Rid* of them?" he scoffed. "Nay, my friend, we shall never be rid of them. Even now, Britons suffer the desecration of groves and the theft of sacred waters. And from across the sea come tales of far worse! Ancient scrolls set alight. Temples toppled. Masters of renown flayed open by mobs on cobbled streets!"

The Keepers were silent.

Briochan sighed. "Colmcille's god is a jealous god, one whose worship demands wrath upon those who do not seek his 'salvation.' Nay, my friend. I fear we shall never be rid of them."

"They will *leave*," Bridei said with a thump of his fist. "Until then, the gates will remain shut."

On the second day, rain swept in curtains over the firth, as if the sea god himself wished to wash the monks from the slopes of the fortress. But for three days and three nights, the singing did not cease. The monks of Colmcille did not stop in their prayers even for sleep. By the third day, the people within the walls began to grow irritable. Angharad was certain the droning in Latin was worse than being stretched upon a wheel.

She was bemoaning that very thought to Rhainn in the great room when at last Bridei stood and put an end to it.

"We have unwittingly submitted ourselves to a siege," the king said angrily. "There are things that need tending beyond these high walls. Let this 'Fox' speak his piece. I am curious to meet this man. And the sooner we see the back of him, the better."

Rhainn motioned for the men to unbolt the gate, then turned to Angharad. "This shall be interesting."

He leaned against the wall beside her as the doors to the Hall opened and the monks ushered in. They'd stood three days and three nights in the bitter of early winter, yet there was no sign of relief on their faces as they entered the Hall's warmth.

Colmcille strode before Bridei with heavy steps, clearly less than pleased at the king's lack of hospitality. But the bow he offered was gracious, and his tone was pleasant enough.

"Bridei son of Maelchon. I am Colmcille, abbot of Iona and cousin to Aed, high king of the northern Uí Néill." Colmcille tapped his breastbone stiffly. Bridei regarded him with a measure of disdain.

"Welcome, Colmcille." He did not tap his breast.

"I must say I am gladdened to hear our presence is welcome," the abbot said. "For as we traveled the Great Glen, we found only fire in our wake."

Angharad leaned into Rhainn. "What does he speak of?" she whispered.

"I burnt their boats."

"Ah."

His shoulder brushed hers as he bent closer. "And the huts we imagined they were sleeping in. But as you can see, we missed on that count."

Angharad lifted her brows.

"Pictland is a dangerous place for any Scot," Bridei was saying. "No less a Christian one. But you stand before me unharmed."

"I suppose that is so. I have brought gifts, of course." Colmcille gestured and two monks came forward with a satchel, emptying its contents and offering them up to the king. Bridei gave a nod of acknowledgment.

"It would please me to learn the reason you have traveled to my kingdom," he said.

"And I would not delay your answer," Colmcille replied earnestly. "But we are heartily grateful for a meal and some warmth. I pray we may speak afterwards."

"Well enough. Dine and take your comforts. You are my guests."

Bridei waved his hand and decadent platters appeared, accompanied by goblets of fine Gaulish wine. The king may not have wished to host Colmcille and his company, but he would impress them. Colmcille was cousin to a high king in Scotia, after all, not to mention he would likely carry word of the luxuries of Bridei's court back to Dalriada. Bridei would have Aedan know that he was by far the superior king.

Music was played, and then from the Song Keeper, a story. Each time the king sought to draw Colmcille into conversation regarding the purpose of his visit, the abbot found some gentle delay or diversion.

At last, the hour had grown late, and though the king would not reveal it, Angharad knew he'd grown tired. His wives directed the monks to the settlement below to seek the shelter they'd arranged, and the king bid all a good night.

The following day, Briochan's mood was foul.

"Colmcille seeks a friendship with the king, yet ignores his advisors," he said. "He delays in hopes of making himself more affable. But I will have it out of him. We will speak with him now, and I would have you there."

"Of course," Angharad said. "I'm most eager to hear what the abbot might say."

They arrived in the great room to find it already emptied of all but Bridei, his advisors, Colmcille, and his monks, all sitting round the king's table.

"Ah." Bridei nodded. "This is Briochan, my Head Counsellor. Now that he is arrived, we may begin."

Briochan threw Colmcille a black look as he took his seat next to Bridei, and Angharad moved to stand by the wall, watching.

Colmcille began at last. "King killing. The Battles of the Black Water. Now this business of a raid at the pass. It is needless bloodshed."

"King killing?" Bridei's eyes sparked. "You refer to Gabrahn, who brought war? Kings kill other kings. It has always been so. The stronger man prevails. I see nothing needless in the defense of my sovereignty and the protection of my people."

"I have come in hopes of building a bridge," Colmcille said. "There must be a way in which our two kingdoms might find peace."

"I have no need of your peace," Bridei said simply. "Neither yours nor your king's. I do not worry over Aedan mac Gabrahn. Let him bring war. I will ride to the forefront with the head of his father strapped to my horse."

Briochan, who'd been watching the abbot shrewdly, leaned forward, placing his hands upon the table. "I believe it is you, Colmcille, who needs peace. You may be abbot of Iona, but Aedan mac Gabrahn keeps no Christians at court. I wonder how much influence you truly have. It is a long journey home through perilous glens. Perhaps you should not have ventured into Pictland in the first place."

"I can assure you I am here by his sanction," Colmcille said. "If there can be no peace, we would propose, for time being, an exchange."

"Slaves?" the king asked.

"Aye. The prisoners you have taken. Innocents."

"Innocents?" he scoffed. "Nay. Warriors are whom we have taken."

"I would argue respectfully that is not so," Colmcille said. "There is a boy I know of. Young, and only a ghillie. And there is a daughter of a stockkeeper: her ailing father traveled to Iona to beg my aid in the matter. I'm told her name is . . . Imogen? There are countless others."

Angharad's eyes widened.

"This Imogen you speak of is my wife," Briochan said.

"She is Dalriadan," Colmcille said. "And as such, we demand her return."

Briochan stood, nearly upending the bench. "She is *en Cruithni*."

Colmcille ignored him, turning to the king. "In exchange, we will return the same number of innocents Aedan keeps behind his walls.

And the bodies of your men from the raid at the pass. Along with their heads."

Bridei glanced at his foster father, and Angharad could see the steadfastness of their bond. Neither presumed to control the other. Nonetheless, Briochan smoothed his robes and sat.

"I will consider giving you the boy you speak of, along with others," the king said. "But the woman is *en Cruithni* now."

"The woman belongs with her people. She was taken forcibly, and she will return with me," Colmcille said.

"You come to this court and make demands?" Bridei said. "You are no king. You are a guest here, and only by our pleasure."

Colmcille was unfazed. "Let me at least speak with the boy."

The king thought on it. "Well enough. You may." He looked to his men. "Take him to the boy."

"I thank you." Colmcille and his monks stood. But before taking his leave, he stopped and caught Briochan's sleeve, his voice low.

"Release the woman to my care. If you do not, you shall suffer the worse for it, for Christ is a warrior on behalf of his flock, and I would not see you come to any harm."

Briochan shook him off. "You dare threaten me? Neither you nor your god hold any power here."

"I suppose we shall see." Colmcille stepped back and turned to the king. "I am grateful for your hospitality and will await your answer."

"'*We shall see*,'" Briochan echoed with disdain as they watched him leave.

Angharad looked at him with concern. "Will you tell Imogen?"

"Of course I'll tell her," he said roughly, but his dark eyes were sad. "Imogen is free to go. It has been so."

"Perhaps they treat their slaves differently," Angharad said. "They do not understand."

"Yes, Ton Velen. They treat their slaves differently. Aedan of

Dalriada digs pits for Cruithni slaves on feast days, and there they must stand, waist-deep in cold earth, a fire built between them. They must hold the roasting spit upon their shoulders for the many hours the swine cooks, their flesh burnt as well. This is how Aedan mac Gabrahn deals with slaves. These are the people Colmcille would return her to. *Scots*," he spat.

Angharad fell quiet. She knew Briochan could not bear for any Cruithni to suffer, and now he might secure their release. But so, too, did he love his wife. He murmured something to the king and then left. He would be going to the hut to speak with Imogen, no doubt, and Angharad did not wish to disturb them.

She went to the kitchens instead, to speak with the cook and perform her inventory of their remedies. The Keepers possessed three shelves in the kitchens that no one else was to touch that held the medicinal stores for the people of Craig Phadrig, and it was Angharad's responsibility to keep them stocked.

"That's odd," she said, squinting at a shelf. "Cook, have you seen the charcoal powder?"

The woman frowned, wiping her hands on her skirts. "Nay, m'lady. Why, it's gone missing?"

"I could've sworn it was here the other day." Angharad sighed. "Truth be told, I've been so busy with teachings of late, I've neglected the stores. I just haven't the time."

Still, it was her duty to replenish it. It was cold outside, but not raining. Angharad walked to the smithy to burn the wood she required in a small metal cauldron, then set it to cool before powdering it. She returned to the hut a good while later to find Imogen in a chair beside the hearth, gazing thoughtfully into the flames.

"He told you," Angharad ventured, setting her supplies on the table.

"Aye."

"What will you do?"

"My father is ailing. It may kill him if I don't return. It may kill my husband if I do. You've not seen him when he's sick with grief as I have." She sighed. "Five or six winters ago, my choice would be different. But I've no desire to return. I am *en Cruithni*. I love this land, and its people. My husband is good to me. It has been many winters since I have been Imogen the stockkeeper. This is my home."

"But what of your father?"

Imogen's face fell. She held out her hand. "Will you come and sit with me? I would send him our prayers."

A few days passed. The presence of Colmcille and his brethren felt like a splinter beneath a nail as the king and the counsellors deliberated.

"If Imogen does not wish to leave, perhaps she might tell Colmcille herself," one of them suggested.

"It would not matter," Briochan said. "I was a fool to tell Colmcille that Imogen was my wife. I have long been an enemy of Aedan and am chief counsellor to the king. Colmcille has no care for her. He would bring devastation only because he can."

At midday, Bridei left to visit the chieftain at the neighboring fortress of Torvean, and Briochan waved down a servant, lifting his glass.

"Haven't we anything stronger? This wine is too watered. I am in need of a drink."

The servant nodded and disappeared for a moment, returning with a new amphora in hand.

"Ah." Briochan drank with a nod. "Much better."

Angharad had never seen him drink to excess. A man of measure and discipline—if not in temper, always in action—he did not care to lose control of his faculties. It was worrisome but, despite his bleariness, Briochan insisted that they not miss their afternoon rhetoric.

They were sitting in a far corner of the Hall, Imogen nearby at work on her embroidery, when Briochan looked up suddenly, blinking.

"I am sorry, Ton Velen, repeat that again." He wiped his forehead, which was damp with sweat.

Angharad stopped and looked at him. "Perhaps we should—"

"Nay, nay, keep on," Briochan said, then winced.

"What is it?" Angharad asked, suddenly ill at ease.

"Perhaps we have been sitting too long." The Wisdom Keeper stood, almost puzzled. He wiped his forehead again with his sleeve, then pressed his hand to his stomach. "I do not feel well. I do not feel quite like myself." He coughed.

Imogen looked up from her weaving in concern. Frowning, she stood and fetched Briochan's cup. "Here, my love. Take some drink," she said.

Drink is the last thing needed, Angharad nearly said, but Briochan nodded gratefully, lifting the cup. No sooner had he sipped it then he doubled, sickness spewing onto the floor.

Angharad and Imogen glanced at each other in alarm.

Then Briochan's knees gave way. The glass shattered in his hand as he fell convulsing upon the floor.

Imogen screamed, dropping to take his head in her lap.

"What is the matter, love? What is it?!"

Angharad looked between her teacher and the cup.

She saw it dawn upon Briochan, too, but as he tried to speak, his eyes rolled back and a foamy white bile issued from his mouth.

Angharad scrambled for the shattered pieces of his cup and picked one up, sniffing. It still held the faintest smell of carrot. She knew that smell. It had no place in wine.

Cowbane.

"Briochan has been poisoned!" she exclaimed.

CHAPTER 29

Artúr

Kilmartin Glen, Valley of the Stones, Kingdom of Dalriada
Land of the Scots
1st of November, AD 580

They brought him to the grave at sunset on the first eve of the
new year.

For three days and three nights, Artúr had been kept to the mount
of Dunadd, the fortress of the Wisdom Keepers, the fortress of the
kingmakers. Hunger had passed in waves, animal in its want. On the
first day, it fought hardest. On the second day, it bit fiercely two or
three times, then retreated to its cave. By the third day, as he and
Chaorunn set off along the path through the Moine Mhòr into the
valley of the stones, Artúr's head felt light, as if made of feathers. His
body felt hollow, as if it were merely a gourd.

His father and his grandfather had each made this journey before.

Artúr shifted on his horse, his free hand on the bull skins that lay
folded between the horse's neck and his saddle. A chain of Wisdom
Keepers trailed their way through the marsh, seven in all. His shoulder felt strange without the company of his sword, his back exposed
without the trappings of his shield. In their place he carried a satchel
full of offerings.

As they reached the stone circle, Chaorunn held up her hand and they stopped for a moment. Artúr eyed the circle of stones, twenty-odd, their roots buried in cobbles, bowing his head respectfully.

"A place of the moon. Built by the First People," Chaorunn said, and drew out a flask. In the beginning, all of these lands belonged to the Picts.

"Here, Artúr. Drink this."

The honey in the mead did little to mask the draft's bitterness as he drank it down. It was a concoction made for seeking, its making the secret of Keepers.

"You may sicken," she warned. "Then again, you are strong."

There had been a fortress once, now long since abandoned, on the hill that rose beyond these stones. Its ruins sloped in shadow as Chaorunn nudged her horse on. They followed the narrow lane awhile in silence, Artúr's uneasiness mounting until at last they reached the cairns.

The flanks of Chaorunn's mottled gray horse were speared by the last sinking shafts of light as the Keepers dismounted in the forecourt of the tomb, gesturing for Artúr to do the same. Sweat pricked his brow. Over Chaorunn's shoulder, the entrance to the burial mound yawned cold, black, and foreboding.

Artúr peered into the darkness as the Keepers knelt before the rectangular stone entryway, chanting their prayers and laying offerings on the threshold. In the silence that followed, an owl hooted, as if the landscape had ears.

"I hope they will have you," Chaorunn said, glancing back at the cairn. "Go on, then, Artúr. Take off your shoes."

Artúr made quick work of them, half-frozen mud seeping between his toes.

"Your clothing."

Artúr pulled his tunic over his head and unbelted his trousers, trying not to shudder in the brisk evening breeze. The Keepers struck up a chant as he stood before the mound naked, holding only the two folded hides and his satchel.

"Enter," Chaorunn said. "And no matter what you might see, what you might feel, or what you might hear, I must warn you: Do not cross this threshold until morning. To do so is to fail."

"Aye, Chaorunn," he said.

Artúr paused at the threshold, took a breath, then stepped in. Pebbles pricked his feet beyond the stone lintel. The air was watchful and his heart clenched like a fist. Inside this cairn was no place for mortals.

Bird flesh pricked from head to toe.

Speak your name, Chaorunn had told him.

"I am Artúr, son of Aedan, son of Gabrahn." His deep voice was small in the emptiness. In the land of the living, the Keepers droned on in their song, yet here in this chamber, Artúr was utterly alone. The passageway to the main chamber was no more than ten steps. The constriction lessened slightly as Artúr stepped from the confines of the passage deeper into the earth.

At the entrance of the tomb, the Keepers moved in shadow, their chant never ceasing as they gathered up their stones.

Spreading the first hide, he sat carefully in the cairn's chamber, wrapping the second hide round him like a cloak.

He took his offerings from the satchel and set them on the bull hide.

Down the narrow passageway, Chaorunn was stacking rocks. Artúr took another breath, battling to keep his panic at bay as the Keepers worked to seal him in.

Twilight fell, and stone by stone, they interred him.

• • •

It was warmer than he'd thought it might be in the shelter of the tomb, and so still he could feel the pulse of his heart against the cavity of his chest.

Night came, clear and cold. Through splintered gaps in the stone-capped roof, Artúr could catch only slivers of stars. His offerings sat before him, but the air round him bristled. To linger here was to issue a challenge, and Artúr could not escape the feeling he would be put through the paces. He blinked, his eyes going bleary. The draft given to him by Chaorunn made the stone behind him feel like a gateway and the ground beneath him feel porous, as if it would suck him forever in. The watchfulness of the chamber was soaking into his skin. He began to hear voices, distant in the dark.

What was that?

A touch upon his neck?

No, it was breath—his own, or another's?

Artúr blinked in the dark, swatting at his ears. Then a thought crept in like a haunting.

In all his questing for fame, this was all that waited.

Cold stone and darkness.

You're dead, dead, dead.

Had he heard it aloud, or was it only in his head?

The air felt too close, too thick in his chest.

And then, the feeling he was no longer alone.

Spirits came flooding through the stones, feeding on his fear. Terrifying demons dashed in the dark. The spirits were circling, hungry, devouring. Panic took him. He was surely going mad. He need only race down the passageway and claw his way out.

To do so was to fail.

Artúr had faced armies and never felt so much fear. He pressed his palms to his eyes until they ached. Shook his head, trying to clear it.

"I will not flee," he said, his breath coming short.

This is only chaos. This is only fear.

Frustration flooded and Artúr roared, casting it out, his warlike cry reverberating in the black.

Only silence in its wake. His chest heaving.

He curled onto his bull skin, watchful in the dark.

Stars traced their paths overhead. After a while, Artúr drifted into dreaming, the power of the draft still ruling his head.

The demons, at last, grew bored and retreated.

And then it happened, the visitation he'd been waiting for. He looked up to find a man in the chamber. The man stood, regarding Artúr with the solemness of the dead. A little boy stood at his side. Somehow Artúr knew this had once been their land.

The man was bearded, a bow slung over his shoulder. He looked like a king, but kings wore a torque. This man, instead, wore a black collar of beads.

The man squatted to look at him. Took Artúr's face in his hands. Artúr felt safe, and breathed out with a sigh.

There were no words, then, for what passed between them. A conferring of wisdom.

Eons in an instant.

Battles and droughts. Kin and *clann*. Spirits and land.

He must have faded from dreaming and into true sleep, for when Artúr opened his eyes, the old king had gone. From ten paces away came the soft clacking of stones.

Though the first light of morning streamed in through the gaps, Artúr did not stir from his place on the skin.

The cairn and its secrets were part of him now.

Too soon, the world of the living invaded. Chaorunn appeared, calling down through the dim.

Slowly, Artúr stood, moving to meet her at the mouth of the cairn.

His body was blue, chilled beyond shivering, and the Wisdom Keepers helped Artúr step into his clothes.

Chaorunn questioned him softly, examining his face. "Artúr, did you see him? Tell me, did he come?"

It felt a violation to speak it.

"Aye, Chaorunn. He came," was all Artúr would say.

CHAPTER 30

Anghard

Craig Phadrig, Ness Lands
Land of the Picts
10th of November, AD 580

Rhainn raced through the doors, stopping dead at the sight of his father sprawled upon the floor.

"Quickly, Rhainn," Anghard said. "Fetch me the black powder from your father's hut. It's on the table. Please! Fetch it now!"

In a flash he returned with it, Ewan at his side. The boy looked stricken.

"I need a clean pitcher of ale," she told Rhainn. "Draw it from a sealed barrel, and do it yourself." She'd rather have water from Aislinn's spring, but they hadn't the time. Emptying her own cup, she dumped the charcoal powder into it, stirring hastily as Rhainn brought the ale.

"Lift his head, Imogen," she said, kneeling. Briochan was no longer convulsing. He was not moving at all.

"Drink, Briochan," she commanded, putting the cup to his lips, but the dark liquid only leaked from his mouth. "He must drink!" she exclaimed.

She had only so much powder. Rhainn squatted beside Briochan, taking the cup in one hand and his father's head in the other.

"Father. Father. Can you hear me? You must drink. Drink!"

Briochan's thin lashes fluttered and he moved his lips. Rhainn eased the cup to his mouth, tipping the black remedy down.

"Thank the Gods, he's taken it," Imogen breathed.

Angharad turned to Rhainn. "Send men for Colmcille. And Rhainn, do not harm him."

Rhainn's face darkened but he nodded as he eased up from the ground and made for the door.

"Come, Imogen, help me," Angharad said. "We must bring him to your bed."

Imogen stayed with Briochan while Angharad returned to the Hall.

The counsellors came with warm words, commending her quick action, telling her a messenger had been sent to the king: he would want to know the state of his foster father. But Bridei had not yet returned by the time Colmcille was brought through the doors in the company of Rhainn and his men.

"I dare not trust myself," Rhainn said, nodding to the men who gripped the abbot by his shoulders. Colmcille's monks stalked after them with tight, angry faces, but their weapons had been taken; they could do nothing but abide.

"Unhand me. I have done nothing," Colmcille demanded. "In fact, I was hastening here already, the moment I heard something ill had befallen your Keeper."

"Briochan, you will call him." A counsellor leaned in, looking hawkish. "That is his name."

"Briochan, of course. You all bore witness, did you not? I warned him this might happen," Colmcille said.

The only thing Angharad could not figure was how he'd arranged it. Then she thought of Ewan. Of course. Colmcille had spoken with the boy only days ago and must have given him the poison. But Briochan had been kind to him, and Imogen like a mother. Angharad did not want to believe that Ewan had agreed. It was no wonder he'd looked stricken. He was a good child. It did not seem in Ewan's nature to try to kill a man.

Colmcille was rummaging through the pouch at his belt. "Quickly, you may give him this," he said, pulling out a creamy white-and-brown stone.

The counsellor frowned. "You bring us a toadstone?"

"As you know, they are rare, but I always keep it on my person," Colmcille said, offering it up.

"Ton Velen," the counsellor said. "You may take it."

Angharad gave the abbot a hard stare. "We have no need of your stone; I have provided a remedy already."

"Take the stone," the counsellor said. Angharad bowed and did as she was told. Colmcille studied her as she plucked the stone from the palm of his outstretched hand.

"What remedy has healed him, pray?" the abbot asked kindly.

Angharad met his eyes. "Charcoal powder," she said.

Consternation flickered in his eyes before he could prevent it. So he'd told Ewan to get rid of the powder store, too.

"You seem surprised," Angharad observed. But she did not give him leave to answer, only dropped the stone in the hand of the counsellor and turned for the door.

"I would see to my teacher," she said, and left the men to play at their politics.

Ewan sat on his pallet in their hut, knees tucked to his chest. He looked up as Angharad entered, his face markedly guilty.

"Why have you done it?" she asked, kneeling beside him. "It was

hateful, Ewan. Colmcille has come for you. You were going home any-
way. Why would you try to take a man's life—one who has been kind?"
The look she gave him was heavy with disappointment.

"I did it for Artúr. I did it for the Scots," he said. He could not meet
her eyes.

"I had the chance to harm Artúr once. Perhaps you were not
aware," she said. "He cut down good men on the beach of Woodwick
Bay. He slew Cendaleath, our king; he killed the warriors who guarded
us, many who were friends. And then it was I put in charge of his
healing. My heart was full of anger and hate. But I did not harm him.
I healed him instead."

"Why?" Ewan looked up.

"Because in every moment, I have a choice. I can choose to hurt
the world or I can choose to help heal it. And I am a healer, Ewan.
What are you?"

"I am a warrior," he said resolutely, but he glanced away, fidgeting
with his fingers.

"Are you?" Angharad peered at him. "Is that truly your role, or do
you not bring goodness and comfort to Artúr and his men when they
need it most?" Angharad touched a hand to his knee. "We must seize
the chance to make our little peace, Ewan. You may think it does not
matter, but I tell you it does. It is we who can make all the difference."

Ewan blinked and a tear escaped. "Will Briochan die?" he asked.

"It's too soon to tell. We'll know more by morning."

"Will you tell them?"

Angharad sighed. "No, Ewan. I will not. I know what it is to be held
captive. I would see you safely returned to Dalriada, where you belong."

She stood and opened the door softly to Briochan's chamber. Imogen looked up. "He's still sleeping," she said.

"Good. Let him rest."

Rhainn came sometime after, trailed by servants with plates of food for supper, but no one was hungry. He stayed and sat with his father so Imogen might sleep.

Angharad took the last watch, just before dawn. She sat upon the floor with her back to her teacher, watching the single candle burn beside his bed. This was the hour she and Briochan would sit, two empty vessels. He would be angry to think she had neglected the discipline on his account.

"*Ceist.*"

Briochan's voice rasped, startling her in the silence. She turned to find his oaken eyes open a slit, his pale hands planted and lifeless by his sides.

"Master Briochan, you should not—"

"*Ceist,*" he said hoarsely, coughing from the force. Angharad bit her tongue, not wishing to distress him. "What force on our land gives power to a storm?"

"*Ni ansa,*" she said softly. "Wind is the storm bringer."

"You are all storm," he said. "You build strength like a storm rises, but you do not know how to send it. *Crash!* You send mayhem. You must send it with wind."

Briochan was so weak. He should not even be speaking. Yet this was the teaching she'd been waiting for. Angharad sat, fearful to move, torn between reason and her hunger to learn.

"Weather always comes with good reason," he said. "It is not easy persuading weather to change its mind. This is why it is so very dangerous. It must only be undertaken in times of great need, else foul things arise. Drought, Flood. Fire. Such things can bring about the ruin of your people."

"I understand," Angharad said.

"You do not. Not yet," he said. "But soon I will show you."

• • •

"Help me to stand," Briochan demanded the next day. Angharad bent and looped his arm round her neck, pulling as he labored to draw himself from bed. It had been only two days, but she knew better than to argue. He claimed it was the spring water Aislinn had sent, but Angharad knew it was because Colmcille was due to depart the following day, and Briochan would face the abbot standing on his own two feet.

"Your cloak," Angharad said, reaching for it with one hand. The poison had weakened him. "You must keep warm."

"Bah," Briochan declared. But he allowed her to prop him up against the chamber wall so she might fasten it over him. They stepped outside and he squinted into the brightness, sniffing like a hound into the wind.

"This will do." He nodded. "Come. To the warrior's walk."

He leaned heavily upon her shoulder as they slowly climbed the stair, emerging onto the guard platform. The view was magnificent. The glittering blue water of the Beauly Firth stretched all the way to the fortress of Ord Hill. Beyond the firth, the Gray Mountains of Torridon rose in the west. Briochan, having just recovered his breath, pointed to the peaks.

"The Cailleach's Mount. There. Do you see it?"

"Yes," Angharad said.

"Would you still learn the way of weatherwork?" he asked.

Angharad's heart tripped in the cage of her chest. "Yes," she said.

"Good." He nodded. "For I would do some weatherwork to send Colmcille off on the morrow. The best sorts of storms take time to grow."

Briochan smirked at the sight of her eagerness. "Well enough, then," he said. "Now, close your eyes. Picture the Cailleach's Mount," he instructed. "Can you see it yet in your mind?"

"Yes," Angharad said, squeezing her eyes harder. Though she'd never stepped foot on the mount, she could imagine it clearly now, before her, as if she stood upon the rocky path to the summit surrounded by hills of old pine. She felt that same familiar tugging, as if some force would pull her from the rampart if only to have her nearer. A northwest wind huffed a gentle breath against Angharad's cheeks.

"Do you feel that?" Angharad heard Briochan's smile. "The wind, it is listening. It knows we come seeking. Now we must only summon the strength."

"I don't know how," Angharad said, fluttering open her eyes.

Briochan paused. "You saved my life, Ton Velen. Tell me, do you care for me?"

Angharad blinked. Briochan was gruff and so often wry, she'd imagined he would sooner drown in a puddle than speak of such things. But he had asked, hadn't he?

"I do care for you," she said earnestly. "Though I will admit, I did not much care for you at the start."

Briochan snorted, the closest he might've come to a laugh. "Fine, fine," he said. "And do you *anger* at Colmcille for what he has done?"

Heat rose in her face at the thought of it. "Of course I do."

"Good," he said. "I anger, too. There is you, there is me, and there is the Cailleach's mountain. We hold our anger and injustice before her. Together, we build it. Together, we will raise it. Breathe, like this," he said, sucking in through his nose and blowing out from his mouth. He turned to watch her, then frowned.

"No, no. From here." He smacked a hand to her belly. "Like this!"

He stood exaggeratedly taller, protruding his stomach like a sheep bladder, breathing in.

"Now grow it," he said. "*Grow* it, Ton Velen!"

Angharad fixed her gray eyes on the distant mountain, feeling the rumbling storm in her belly. Feeling the strength of their bond. As clouds mounted and towered, heavily it built, stacking.

"More," Briochan said.

Inside her skin, the swirl and churn pounded like an anvil. Her chest began to tighten as the storm within her whirled, coiling as she battled to keep it in. Angharad felt the wind dodge and tickle at her cloak as if waiting.

"See it before you. Show the Cailleach what you're seeking. Mist, fog, and wind. Rain, blinding boats! Waves whipping! Beckon it. Draw it in. Now send it, Ton Velen, send it to the loch! Send it on the wind!" Briochan shouted, thrusting his hands.

The wind stood before her on fast feet, fickle. But then out of the north blew a gust. Angharad thrust out her own hands, sending the storm from her body. She felt the moment it hovered, then caught, snatched up by the wind.

They stood for a moment in silence, feeling empty. Then Briochan turned, clapping a hand upon her back.

"How do you feel?"

Vacant in the wake of it, reeling. Angharad's head ached and she felt suddenly drowsy, as if she might very much like to lie down and sleep.

Briochan read her face. "A bit of honey should aid you," he said.

Her senses yet heightened, she could feel someone watching. Turning from the firth, she looked down from the warrior's walk to see Rhainn. He stood as if transfixed, his spear by his side.

Their eyes met, and this time, neither looked away.

By the next morning, it became clear Rhainn had not been the only one who'd seen Angharad standing upon the rampart, arms lifted, invoking the Gods. Word had traveled beyond the walls of Bridei's fortress down to the settlements below that something exciting was afoot: Briochan the Wisdom Keeper and his Initiate Angharad Ton Velen had summoned a storm.

And the Cruithni knew enough to know that whatever Briochan had stirred, should it come to pass, would be wondrous indeed.

So it was, on the morning Colmcille was due to depart with his monks, there was a festival-like feel to the air. The abbot had succeeded only in persuading Bridei to release Ewan and three others. In exchange, four Cruithni would return, but they would not be granted the bodies of their dead from the raid at the pass.

Imogen handed Ewan a satchel with cheese and bread and whispered a blessing in Goidelic, brushing his forehead with a kiss. Angharad had fashioned him a Brighid's cross, which she pressed into his hands, worrying over his safety in the coming storm. But what good would it do to tell him if he had not already heard? The boy was fixed on returning to Dalriada.

"Travel safely, Ewan. May the Gods keep you," she said.

As the gates opened into a misty but mild November morn, the entirety of Bridei's court issued out on horses and on foot, save only the watchmen required to mind the gate. Even they, despite their solemn natures, seemed gloomy about being left behind. It was the sort of event from which stories were made. No one dared miss it.

At the foot of Craig Phadrig, Colmcille and his monks stood waiting. He beamed as he saw the vast crowd come to see him off, and all the while Angharad's heart thudded in her ears.

Briochan rode proudly, erect upon his horse. She could not bear to see her teacher made a fool. But as they followed the river ever steadily toward its source at the loch, the air did seem to possess a new and sudden chill. She glanced over her shoulder to see a tenant wipe the tip of his nose, pink with cold. And was that not a gentle but steady breeze that had begun to build, blowing strands of their hair against their faces?

With each settlement they passed, the number of Cruithni trailing their caravan grew like pebbles rolling downhill until, by the time they reached the place where the river sprang from the open mouth of the loch, more than one hundred people had gathered.

At the small wooden quay, boats rocked against their moorings in the gently chopping waters of the loch.

Briochan and Colmcille, two mages of differing faiths, had succeeded in ignoring each other so far on the journey, but now that it was time for Colmcille and his monks to board their boat, Briochan stopped before him, crossing his arms over his chest.

"Briochan. You seem much recovered," Colmcille observed.

"Yes. In fact I feel quite hale now that I have come to watch you leave."

Wind gusted, ruffling Colmcille's heavy purple cloak, and Briochan looked mildly out over the water.

"Though I do wonder. It looks as if a bit of weather comes this way."

Colmcille looked to the water, a hint of a shadow darkening his face. Briochan leaned in. "You may be a child of Christ, but I am Briochan, son of the Cailleach, and these are our lands. You shall see that the Cailleach does not deal kindly with either man or gods who threaten her kin."

At the end of the quay a ferryman waited, his boat set with oars and a sail, but it bobbed and slapped now in growing waves. The monks glanced up as a hard rain began to fall, and the Cruithni shouted at them.

"Briochan the Wisdom Keeper has summoned a tempest!"

Briochan's mouth twitched in amusement. "You had better leave before it gets worse. Look, Colmcille, the water whips white. You are a Scot. I needn't tell you how quickly the weather can turn."

The ferryman looked anxious. Colmcille called out to his men. "Come, then, bring the innocents. Let us depart."

Rain gusted, pelting. The ferryman met them halfway along the quay.

"Abbot. There's a contrary wind and the water's gone chopped. I cannot set sail."

Colmcille set his jaw, blinking into the rain. "Nay. We leave now. Put your men to oar."

"But—"

"Put your men to oar!" he roared, turning. "Come, brothers, quickly. Board the boat."

The monks clutched their hoods as they leaned against the wind, stepping onto the precariously rocking vessel with Ewan and the other slaves.

"But the wind—" the ferryman protested.

"Row," Colmcille demanded. "Row, I say!"

Angharad's eyes fixed upon Ewan as the men at oar bent their backs to the wind.

Cailleach, Mother, keep him safe; he's only a boy, she prayed.

The men rowing were white-knuckled as a wave took the currach, nearly toppling it, and Angharad held her breath. But then the boat righted. The rain did not cease, but Angharad felt the wind shift direction. She watched as Colmcille's boat hoisted its sail, slipping farther and farther into the distance.

A cheer rose up from the rain-drenched crowd. Around them the storm whipped and wailed. Clothes were clinging. The people were smiling. The people were singing.

They clustered round Briochan and hoisted him in the air, laughing like children as the rain puddled in their mouths.

Angharad tipped her face to the sky, letting the rain wash her clean.

The Cailleach had come.

She looked out over the stormy waters of the loch and thought of Nessa and the story of the wells.

Just before she turned back to the crowd, she could have sworn she saw a flash of gray rise and then sink beneath the tossing white waves.

CHAPTER 31

Artúr

Dunadd Fortress, Valley of Stones, Kingdom of Dalriada
Land of the Scots
2nd of November, AD 580

The din of the crowd sounded from the mosses of Dunadd, kicking life into Artúr's hollow bones.

After the ceremony would come the feast. His warrior's body was not used to starvation, and Chaorunn had warned him he must take food slow.

A gentle rap came at the door and Lailoken ducked from the light into the firelit hut. His long sandy hair was loose about his shoulders and he wore his white robes, the ones reserved for ceremony.

"The Gods have given us a windless day," he said. "They would have the people hear each word of your oath."

Artúr nodded. "The Gods are good. When did you arrive?"

"Yesterday eve, on the incoming tide. It is an honor to come to Dunadd." Lailoken stepped back, appraising him. "That'll catch the sun's gleam on a battlefield," he said, nodding at Artúr's golden torque. "It would seem this is a year of new torques. First my sister, now you."

"I'm glad you could be here to stand with the Keepers up on the mount," Artúr said with a smile.

"I was glad for your summoning. It's not every day one's named tanist." Lailoken grew serious. "You shall be a good leader, Artúr. Of that I have no doubt."

The door opened and Chaorunn entered, her white hair in high coils fastened with gold. "Come, Artúr. It is time," she said, adjusting the brooch that pinned the folds of his cloak.

Artúr stepped from the oblong confines of the hut, following Chaorunn out onto the mount. His father waited a short distance ahead, beside the Rock of the King. Beyond Aedan mac Gabrahn stood three veiled figures clad in robes of dark blue.

"Daughters of the Cailleach," Chaorunn explained. "They come bearing a gift."

A *gift?* he wondered. They had traveled a good way from their isle on Loch Lomond. Far below, between the dark twist of the river Add and the rocky root of the mount, firepits dotted the moss, bringing warmth and good cheer, and a horde of people erupted into a roar as Artúr stepped into sight. He looked out across their faces, caught unawares by a swell of emotion as his father strode forward, taking his hand.

"Aye, Artúr. Let that fill your sails. For there will be plenty of windless days where you'll find you will need it."

Three blasts of the horn silenced the crowd. The drums struck up and a slight wind rose, rustling the robes of the Daughters of the Cailleach. The Wisdom Keepers of Dunadd struck up their chant.

Artúr bowed at the feet of the Daughters, and one of them reached out, gripping his hand. She led him to kneel before the small rock-cut basin carved in the King's Rock as the second Daughter came forward, a vessel in hand. Blood, viscous and garnet, splattered into the rock's hollow as she tipped its contents into the basin.

"The blood of the bull. The blood of the mother. The blood of the land."

Dipping a pale finger into the basin, she marked his forehead and nose. Dragged two fingers along the planes of his cheeks.

"Artúr mac Aedan. Now you may stand," the third Daughter said. She moved toward him bearing a long, slender packet in her hands.

It could only be a sword.

The Daughter unwound the weapon from its packing. Its rich leather scabbard was pristine and finely tooled, its golden scape studded with garnet and red enamel. The priestess held the weapon before him, bellowing so that all those assembled might hear.

"This sword was given to our waters upon the death of Gabrahn," she called out. "Down it dropped, to the belly of the loch, where it dwelled a long time. But then a storm came. The waves of the loch frothed and tossed. And the sword was washed up upon the pebbles of our shore. Gabrahn's sword had risen. Aedan, son of Gabrahn, has seen it reforged. Now, Artúr, son of Aedan, the sword of Gabrahn finds a new master in you."

Artúr looked to his father, questioning. Aedan gave a small smile, nodding at the sword. Carefully, Artúr took it, holding it flat between his hands as the priestess guided him onto the platform of rock.

Before him a footprint lay, chiseled in gray stone. Within its impression, his father had pressed his boot; his grandfather had planted his too, lofting this very sword.

Now it came to Artúr.

Chaorunn lifted her arms to the heavens, her voice ringing to every ear of Dalriada.

"Artúr son of Aedan, son of Gabrahn, son of Domangart Réti, son of Fergus Mór. Second only to your father, you shall be the head of the kingdom of Mannau and the kingdom of Dalriada. Every head defends its people, if it be a goodly head. Of keen intellect, of sound morals, of good deeds. Do you commit to be their servant?"

"I do."

Artúr's heart was beating in his ears. He took a breath and placed his right foot in the footprint.

The Land.

Down below, the Moine Mhòr swelled with their people.

The Children.

Gripping the sword in his right hand, he drew it smoothly from its scabbard. With a warlike cry, he thrust the sword into the sky.

The cheers were deafening as they rang through the glen.

Artúr mac Aedan had lifted the sword from the stone.

It felt as if he were spinning. Then he felt the welcome grounding of his father's warm hand.

"It is done," Aedan said. He grabbed Artúr's face and kissed him, guiding him to the edge of the rock.

Artúr looked out over the sea of faces. Never before had Artúr been able to imagine what it was to be a father.

Now each and every soul before him was granted to his care by the Gods.

Each and every soul was one of his children.

The tenderness he felt was a kick to the ribs.

The weight of their love was a thousand boulders.

CHAPTER 32

Angharad

Craig Phadrig, Ness Lands
Kingdom of the Picts
Late January, AD 581

Winter had come, bringing its mantle of ice and early darkness. It was the time of the year for thick furs and the tales of Song Keepers spun by fire ember, their tellings a ritual meant to bring safety and harvest enough in the days of the dawning year.

And yet, in the middle of the night, Angharad had woken from a sound winter's sleep, a singsong voice still ringing in her head.

You must go find the Cailleach on the mountain. That is where she lays down her head. And you cannot seek her unless it be winter, else why would she deign to be there?

Briochan had been quiet a long time after she'd told him of the rhyme that had woken her from sleep. At last he looked at her, his face full of shadow.

"It is an old Cruithni children's rhyme. As a girl, Alys would sing it at bed."

"Then she must think me ready," Angharad said.

Briochan smiled softly, considering, and nodded. "Yes, Ton Velen. Alys is right. You are ready. I shall prepare you the best I know how."

The Crooked Path, the Wisdom Keepers called it, for there was no single way to become a Keeper. The path rose in twists and forks, unique to each seeker. But there was one trial all Initiates must undergo. They must all undertake a journey to present themselves to their chosen god.

Now at last it seemed the Cailleach had summoned. Angharad would not refuse her.

There are places that hold no care for human survival. Where rock can give way and there is no longer earth beneath your feet. Where wind can flick you from the face of a mountain like a cattle tick. A bog can swallow you. A rising river can sweep you away. The mountains of Torridon were such a place.

The children were right. Where else would the Cailleach choose to dwell?

Angharad was attempting to fit the supplies she would need in a sturdy leather satchel when a sound came at the threshold of her chamber. She turned to see Rhainn standing at her door.

"It was this time of year that she left," he said.

"Alys, you mean."

"Yes."

"I know. But I shan't be like Alys."

Rhainn leveled her with a stare. "Do you imagine Alys left to seek the Cailleach planning never to return?"

"Of course not. But what would you have me do?" Angharad stopped gathering her things and turned. "The Wisdom Keepers call it the Crooked Path with good reason," she said. "Those who seek union with the Gods understand that no two paths are alike. We may go to schools to learn our rhetoric and the movement of stars, or the hundreds of thousands of Triads and kennings. But to truly know the Gods, we each must follow where our Crooked Path leads. This is my journey, Rhainn. This is how I must earn my robes. Triumph or fail, I must go."

Rhainn watched her a long moment, his amber eyes troubled. She hated to see him distraught. She fumbled through her belongings until her fist closed on a small piece of cold metal and she drew it out, holding it for him to see.

"Look," she said. "I am bringing my bird. Surely it will protect me on my long, snowy journey."

He glanced at the bird in her hand. "You asked what I would have you do," he said. "I would ask you to stay. Yet I know you cannot."

Angharad did not think this was only about the danger. She set the bird down gently on her bed, summoning the strength to say what she must. To carry on this way was only to delay the inevitable. She could not offer Rhainn what she knew he desired, nor did any yearning for him stir within her heart.

"Rhainn, do you not think it is time that you settled with a wife? I mean to say, if that is what you wish."

Rhainn blinked as if struck.

"A wife," he echoed.

"I am not blind to romance," she said. "I see the way women look at you. You are powerful and intelligent. Honorable and kind. You are my friend, and so very dear to me. I want nothing more than to see you happy. Do not grow old waiting round for me. I . . . am not built in the way of others. I do not think I shall ever love any earthly woman or man."

Rhainn swallowed. Her words may as well have been arrows. A moment passed. Then he stood taller, clearing his throat.

"Of course. I understand."

She watched as a wall came up between them, feeling both his hurt and her own.

"Rhainn—"

"Bridei wishes to speak with you," he said, cutting her off with an efficient double tap upon his chest. "That's why I've come. He waits in the Hall."

"Oh, I—" she said. But he did not wait for her so they might walk together. He turned on his heel and left.

"Bridei king. You wished to see me?" Angharad bowed as she entered.

"Angharad Ton Velen." The king looked up with a welcoming smile, ushering her in. "Briochan tells me you leave for the mountains at dawn."

"Yes."

"There will be warm huts along the way, and the Cruithni are a good people for hospitality, even in winter months. But should any question your errand, I give you this."

Bridei held out his hand. In it sat a circular brooch smaller than her fist. Fashioned in its swirling silver was a charging Pictish bull with a gleaming eye of garnet.

"You travel under my protection, Angharad Ton Velen. No one would dare trouble you whilst you are wearing this."

The silver bull glinted in the lamplight as he passed it to her. The weight of the silver alone was worth more than ten cattle.

"It's magnificent. I don't know how to thank you," Angharad said.

Bridei waved away her gratitude. "Thanks are not necessary. Meet your fate and return. That is all we ask, Ton Velen. For we have grown fond of you. We are proud to call you *en Cruithni*. May the Gods keep you."

"And you, my king."

Briochan paced the hut the next morning, fussing after Angharad as if she were a child.

"And you have a spare fur," he asked for the second time that morning. "In case one should get wet. One never knows if one might fall into a river."

"Yes."

"And the flint."

"Yes."

"Good," he said firmly. "One never knows if one might need to kindle a fire."

Imogen cast him a pitying look. If Angharad hadn't known better, it might have been funny.

But last night she'd dreamt of Alys. The snow outside the hut had been piling, wind banging at the shutters. Angharad had heard a sound at the door and opened it only to see a girl lying lifeless in the drifts, her fingernails bloody from trying to claw her way in. She shuddered now at the thought of it, and Briochan tsked.

"Already cold? For the sake of the Gods! And you would seek out the Cailleach? Put on the woolen trousers underneath your robes. One never knows if one might get sunk in a snowdrift."

"Hush, now, Briochan. You'll drive the girl mad," Imogen said.

Briochan only frowned. "Remember. It is four days travel by foot at a slow pace. At Loch Glascarnoch there is a ferryman who can take you the length, providing it's not frozen. From Lochdrum you shall see the slopes of Sgurr Mor. A' Cailleach is the mount that lies just beyond."

"I remember," she assured him. "It'll be less than a fortnight, then I shall return."

Rhainn did not come to see her off. But as she left the heights of Craig Phadrig behind, Angharad heard the solemn bellow of a horn. She looked over her shoulder to see his figure standing high on the ramparts, his sights fixed upon the mountains that jutted up past the sea.

It was a dry, mild morning for winter, and Angharad could not help but think it boded good luck. The first day took her through farms and settlements set upon the outskirts of wide, sweeping moors. At the edge of a wood, she found a dead branch that had fallen from a bird cherry. Long and straight, it was good for a walking staff; bird cherry kept one from getting lost in the mist. As she walked, Angharad sang to the goddess, filling the space between steps with her chant.

"*Stone mother, bone mother, bringer of snow, queen of the dying, keeper of storms.*"

As she traveled west, the distance between settlements grew. Brio-chan's worry had forced her to bring far more than she needed, and after a few tiresome leagues of the heavy satchel chafing her back, she left some of her spare clothing with a pair of beggars she met on the road. They wanted food, too, but she hadn't any. Her walk was a pilgrimage, and she would be observing a fast.

The second day was bleak and bitter, and as she stopped at midday to rest, snow began to fall. She passed through quiet woods and bare winter trees, the mountains of Torridon rising white capped in the distance. The snow settled and stuck, night falling as if someone had snuffed out a candle. Stopping in a hut for the eve, Angharad prayed for a dream, but with more than ten leagues passed beneath her feet, her sleep was a hibernation deep as the land's.

On the fourth morning, she left the last settlement behind, fol-lowing a slim, snowy track that led out of the village. Angharad knew she'd not see people again. She walked until the land rose, folding into broad ribbons of hills.

At last she had reached the foothills of the Torridon mountains.

Icicles hung from the water-carved banks of a narrow winter river. Beyond it A' Cailleach hunched like a slumbering bear. Angharad pulled her furs more tightly around her. The air here was colder, she noticed, as she forded the shallows of the half-frozen river.

She'd just reached the opposite bank when, out of the corner of her eye, she caught sight of a figure. There, moving past a thin stand of trees in the winter bog ahead, a woman was trudging, wearing an old Pictish cloak.

Angharad stopped, watching her. It could well be a tenant's daughter in search of stock that had escaped into the cold, or perhaps it was another Wisdom Keeper embarking on a journey of her own.

As Angharad began the trail up the mountain, she noticed the woman also seemed to be climbing, though she managed to keep a fair distance ahead.

Cloud closed in. The snow deepened.

Angharad quickened her pace, but as briskly as Angharad strode, she could not seem to get nearer, nor could she overtake the woman. Her cheeks went hot with exertion, sweat springing in the pits of her arms beneath the heaviness of her furs.

Snow had fallen harder here in the heights, and the farther Angharad climbed, the deeper the snow became, until she was stumbling in hollows that sank her up past her knees. As she slowed, so did the woman, but scarcely enough for Angharad to keep her in sight.

The path disappeared, the way becoming only a vast, exposed shoulder of snow and ice. The sky darkened and thick, downy flakes began to fall. Winds kicked up, tugging at her furs. Angharad flexed her fingers in her thick wool mittens, stiff from the cold. The distance to the top of A' Cailleach had not seemed nearly so far from the frozen moor below, and her legs were weak from leagues underfoot and four days of fasting.

Angharad pressed on until she came to a place where seasonal streams had carved a broad gully into the mountain. On the other side of the gully were the stony ruins of a shieling, no longer fit for housing cattlekeeps, having lost half its roof.

The woman had gone. Here there was nothing but the slap of wind and wet tickle of snow on her cheeks. Angharad had last seen her crossing the gully, stopping a moment to glance back as she'd passed by the shieling.

The snow was pelting harder now. Whiteness closed like a fist.

Angharad thought of turning back in favor of safer weather, but what if this was some sort of test?

It was still early enough in the day, she reasoned. The cloaked woman had crossed at the bottom of the gully, favoring the open slope of the mountain. But traveling up the gully itself was no doubt the quickest way to the top.

Angharad blinked through the thick veil of snow and began trudging her way up the mouth of the gully. But something was needling her. Something did not feel right. She stopped midway up the slope, listening, looking up into the white.

There. An ominous rumble was sounding. Angharad knit her brows. Thunder in snow? She supposed it was possible.

But then, to her horror, a crack rang out high on the mountain.

The ground beneath her trembled as her ears filled with a violent rush like the torrent of a river. Angharad glanced uphill to see a towering cloud of snow thundering down the gully.

She would not make it out of the chasm in time.

She stumbled knee-deep in snow as she raced toward the shieling. The rumbling roar was so close it was hard to keep her feet beneath her. Any moment she would be swept from the heights, crushed beneath the speeding wall of snow.

Placing her life in the Cailleach's hands, Angharad leapt the last of the distance, throwing herself against the outer stone wall of the shieling, pressing herself beneath the short overhang of the roof.

A hissing cloud of ice rained over her as a wave of snow and rock collided with the structure, shaking the stone, cascading up over the roof. Ice and sticks pelted, stinging her face. Angharad tucked into a ball, covering her head with her hands as the pummeling tower piled up all around her.

It might have been moments, but the barrage felt never-ending. She crouched powerless beneath the might of the cascade, entirely at its mercy. And then, as fast as it had come, the rumbling roared on downhill.

Trembling, Angharad dusted the snow from her face and looked up.

The avalanche had buried everything in its path, swallowing the shieling. She was trapped in an odd little cave, thanks only to the shieling's stone wall at her back and the shelf of roof overhead. She reached out, poking the confines of her icy tomb with her walking stick, but it was impenetrable, hard and smooth as melted rock.

Were it not for the shieling, Angharad would surely have been buried alive.

She remembered the cloaked woman, how she'd stopped at the shieling to look back, and a shiver coursed through her in the growing cold. What if the woman was not a woman at all but a spirit?

Could the figure have been Alys, giving her a warning?

The roof gave a sharp snap under the weight of the snow overhead, and Angharad cried out, bracing for collapse, but there came only a fine sifting of snow. There was a fracture in the support beam of the roof. She did not know how long it might hold.

The roof had afforded her an icy chamber the span of one arm's length on each side, but it was only high enough for her to crouch; she could not stand upright. Her breath clouded in the cave as she grappled with what had just overcome her.

She hadn't made it to the summit. Angharad was trapped, and soon it would be night.

Alys had gone in search of the Cailleach, never to return. Had she died on this very mountain in a tomb made of snow?

Angharad still had her satchel and her walking staff, useless as it was against the snow. She shimmied the pack from her shoulders and searched it. A skin of water she'd filled from the half-frozen stream. A small hand axe. At Briochan's insistence she'd also packed the flint and, before leaving her host hut that morning, she'd added two narrow splits of wood. She tugged them out. Praise the Gods, they were still dry. Perhaps the snow was not set too deeply on top of her. If a fire's heat could warm it, she might be able to dig herself out come morning.

But a long night loomed. With so little fuel, eventually her fire would go out. And any fool knew that lighting a fire without a place for the smoke to go could be deadly. Her only hope was that there were cracks enough in the drystone for some of the smoke to escape. For if she did not get warm soon, she would not last the night.

As Angharad tried to puzzle out her survival, another thought crept in.

What if the cloaked figure had not been Alys but the Cailleach herself, hoping to bury Angharad in this wintry bed?

She'd brought mugwort and yarrow. She could still make her offering here, on the mountain. Setting her mittens aside, she set to work to kindle a small, flickering fire, feeding it some flakes of splintered wood from the fractured roof beam. The fire made a hungry, hissing sound in the quiet of the cave, orange light casting ghoulish shadows on snow.

She could feel the weight of the avalanche squeezing its heavy fist on the roof overhead. She crushed the herbs with stiff fingers, offering them to the flames, then added the last split of wood to the fire.

Be still, she told herself, wrapping herself more tightly in her furs. Time passed. She closed her eyes, dropping deeper.

An Cailleach an Cailleach . . .

The air in her little cave was growing thicker with smoke, the smell of cold and burning leaves filling her nose. Perhaps if she lay down, she might breathe better. Of course she felt drowsy. She had walked so far only to survive an avalanche, after all. Angharad tried to fix her eyes on the wavering flames.

An Cailleach . . .

Had she struck her head when she'd leaped to the safety of the shieling? It ached now, splitting.

No, of course. The fire—it was choking her.

But it was either choke or freeze.

She blinked, dizzy, trying to rise, but a dagger of pain stabbed at her chest and Angharad rolled over and vomited, nearly choking on sickness. Her chest labored, fast and shallow, even as she tried to slow it, conserving her breath.

The walls of ice round her went a grim winter's hue. Night had fallen.

The snow entombing her was as blue as the skin of the Cailleach herself.

Angharad swallowed the dryness in her throat. Briochan would find her body in a puddle of spring snowmelt.

Darkness closed in from the corners of her vision. Soon it would take her. What was that she heard? A woman's voice?

The answer came in a whisper.

Yes, child.

Come to me.

I am the Cailleach.

CHAPTER 33

Angharad

Angharad was cradled in the arms of her mother.

Visions rose, growing in the dark, and she listened, nodding, fingers stroking the earth. How could she doubt that she would find her way? There was no cold, no suffering, no fear of death in the snow.

I am here. I am listening, Mother. Please, show me more.

Hours slipped by as Angharad lay on her side, drifting in a spell. Eons flashed before her in what seemed only a moment. Time shifted as she traveled to a place that, upon waking, she would not recall. All the world's sorrow, sunk into the earth from days beyond memory, came rushing in, filling her until she could feel it all: the generations of children grown to men and women, each with their bloody, shattered dreams.

Tears streamed, dripping over her nose into dirt and snow.

Some people claimed that the Gods had no mercy. Now Angharad knew. The Cailleach wept for her children.

Angharad grieved until she was all wrung out.

From that moment on, she would never be the same.

After that, peace came. And then, sometime toward morning, the lone cry of a bird.

Angharad coughed and stirred, blinking.

No. No! She did not want to leave.

She was still so tender, so close to the goddess. Safe here in her tomb from all the hurts that waited, the unavoidable wounds caused by living.

But something gentle in the stillness urged her: *Look up.*

Slowly, Angharad lifted her throbbing head. A tiny hole had melted in the snow at the roofline of the shieling, letting in just enough air to reveal a sliver of blue morning sky.

The storm had passed.

Angharad pushed herself onto her knees. Standing half crouched, she thumped her walking stick just above the hole. The snow around it had thinned now, fragile as glass, and it shattered, ushering in a gush of crisp, cold air.

Angharad drank it in, letting out a whoop that sounded more like a croak.

Collapsing back against the drystone wall, she let the fresh air fill her. When she felt strong enough, she gathered her things and, with a will she hadn't known she possessed, clawed her way from the avalanche's icy womb, blinking as she emerged into the glittering white, the slope lit vermillion by shafts of morning sun.

She could see the way to the top now.

The gray stacked rock of the Cailleach's cairn at the peak stood sentinel, as if waiting.

Hers were the only set of footprints in the snow as she climbed.

But beneath a small, flat rock at the top of the cairn, someone had left a fistful of dried flowers.

Angharad went to touch them but they collapsed into dust, scattering like ashes in the frosty winter wind.

CHAPTER 34

Languoreth

Cadzow Fortress, Kingdom of Strathclyde
Land of the Britons
Late September, AD 584

Three winters passed, and three battle seasons with them. On the fourth year, autumn came early to Cadzow. I felt it, the day something shifted, as I walked the land given me by my father.

There wasn't a season I did not love at Cadzow, but autumn was unsurpassed in magnificence. Summer was the season for warriors: everything hot and languid—for if the men were not fighting, they could be found making love, and the world became too wet and verdant for my liking. As a girl, I had thrilled to midsummer, rising at dawn to wash my pale cheeks with dew. I had loved a warrior then.

Now it was when blackberries withered and the autumn leaves lit the beech trees like torches that I felt most alive.

I was forty-four winters and had borne four children. Perhaps this meant I was becoming a crone. Or perhaps this was simply how it felt to stand at the helm of a kingdom. I was forty-four winters, yet I had lived a thousand lifetimes since I was a girl.

As the seasons had passed, we found ourselves in a rare time of peace. My brother and Eira were happy at Buckthorn. Brodyn had resumed his position as captain of my guard, along with his Gauls, giving Torin leave to roam, and our watchers now brought news from far beyond our kingdom's borders. Brodyn and Elufed spent long days together, very much in love.

Since Lailoken had escaped Mungo's hired men, Mungo had kept his word not to stir further discord, but the peace we kept was brittle. That is not to say that he and my brother did not clash, for their hatred for each other was a palpable thing. But despite the strength of my spies, we could not find reason enough to exile Mungo once more. So it was that we continued in our game, watching, each ever trying to catch the other out.

Lailoken assured me it was only a matter of time.

In the south, Maelgwn Pendragon and his Army of Stags had strengthened as they battled alongside the Selgovae and the Britons of Rheged in raids against the Angles. I had swallowed the news that Maelgwn had taken a wife—a daughter of Lord Archer—now becoming Selgovae himself.

Angharad had risen to high esteem in the court of Bridei, king of the Picts, and had been entrusted as one of his own counsellors, along with her teacher, Briochan. Gladys had born Elffin a son. But in the winters since, it seemed her womb had gone barren, and she spent much of her days traveling to temples of healing in search of a cure. Cyan had taken up the study of warfare and weaponry with the doggedness with which he'd formerly studied books. There was muscle on his frame now, and he had even gone east with Morcant to train alongside the Gododdin.

But Rhydderch had yet to name our only living son his tanist.

I escaped the tide-washed isle of Clyde Rock and the busy capital of Partick whenever I was able, retreating to the shady refuge of Cadzow's forests. Here, there were no matters of politic, no lords or ladies to entertain.

And where is your queen? Mungo's watchers would ask, their hungry eyes searching out any weakness. But it was accepted by most that I must manage my estate. We had the mill and the brewing to mind. The shearing, spinning, and weaving of fabrics. We had the granaries to fill to help support the king and his retinue. And of course there was the managing of my family's creamy-white cows, the pride of the Britons.

The most scandalous thing they'd managed to discover was that when I was in residence at Cadzow, I'd taken to wearing trousers.

I wiped my hands upon a set of them now as my chamberwoman Aela entered the Hall bearing a small scrap of parchment.

"A message from the king," she said, handing it over.

"Thank you, Aela." I tipped it to the light.

My lady Queen. I would have you prepare Cadzow for a hunt. It is time we gather the Selgovian lords with the lords of Gododdin. I have summoned them. All shall arrive within three day's time. My gratitude and my love. Rhydderch.

"What is it, m'lady?"

I looked up. "We are to host a hunt," I told her. I'd known it was coming, but had not thought it would be so soon.

"For the king and his men?"

"Yes. I'm afraid this will be a bit more elaborate than usual. The king wishes to remind the Selgovae and the Gododdin of our bonds of friendship. Everything must be perfect."

Aela nodded. "Then it will be so."

"I will speak with the cook. We must ready the guest quarters and tell the villagers; they must help shelter those traveling in our visitors' company."

"Well enough," she said. "And what of the healing hut?"

She regarded me frankly. How many winters had Aela been nee-

dling me to set it to rights? Now I could no longer deny my mother's
hut needed tending.

I'd been relying upon a healer who traveled from Cadzow village
for any incidents, not wanting to disturb the place that, to me, was my
mother's only tomb. But the lords would be traveling with healers of
their own, as hunts came with danger. We might well be in need of
remedies and a place to treat the wounded.

"I'll see to it," I assured her. "Tell the healer from the village she
may bring her supplies. We'll need all her stores. I'll go and make a
place for them."

"Surely the servants can do it. There'll be dust, m'lady, and creep-
ies!" Aela waved her fingers.

"No," I said more sharply than intended. That was not the way it
had ever been done. It had been tended by my mother, then me and
Ariane. And then no one at all.

"I'm sorry, Aela. But I should like to do it myself. Look." I gestured
to my clothes. "I am quite ready for cobwebs."

Two of my Gauls stood guard at the rampart, and I smiled at them as
I stepped onto the forest path. The hut stood beside the mound where
my father lay buried, surrounded by a grove of ancient oak trees. They
rested together in this way—my mother and father. We had scattered
my mother's ashes when I was a girl. This hut was all I had of her, the
only place where I could still feel her near, pressing upon the veil that
had dropped so thickly between us.

The door groaned as I ducked inside and pulled it shut behind me.
The air inside was dank and smelled of moldering herbs, and splattered white droppings scattered the floor. Swallows had nested in the
thatching.

I'm so sorry, Mother, I could not bear to disturb it, I thought, looking
round.

A fire in the hearth chased away the dampness but did little to dispel the ghosts. The hut was haunted by the selves we'd once been: my mother, cheeks bright, in good health, her dark hair falling into her eyes as she worked the mortar and pestle. Lailoken swinging his gangly legs as he sat watching her from the bench. Me stocking roots and hanging twine-bound bushels from the rafters to dry.

Do you see? Here in this hut, I could move through time like a worker of miracles.

For a moment I wished I could hide here, unseen. Tuck myself back into my mother's skirts and be her child again. Regretfully, I had kings and chieftains arriving at my gates in three days' time.

I opened the shutters and took down the cobwebs, then swept, pushing winters of neglect over the threshold of the door. One by one I took the clay pots down from the sturdy wooden shelves and emptied them outside, setting them on the table to be scrubbed.

The stillness was a temple.

I was just stepping down from a rickety old stool when I heard the scuff of boots on the path outside. The healer with her stores, or Aela, no doubt. Sooner or later, someone always came looking.

"I'm here," I called out.

The touch on the latch was hesitant. I strode to thrust it open myself, only to find myself face-to-face with Maelgwn Pendragon.

"Oh!" I blinked as if he were some trick of the light. Or perhaps he was a ghost of this place, fashioned from my wanting. But then a breeze gusted through the open door and I caught the familiar scent of him. Leather and pine. He was all too real. He squinted as his green eyes adjusted to the dim, taking in my dirt-smeared trousers and linen tunic. I swiped at my hair and came away with a cobweb stuck between my fingers.

"I didn't mean to startle you," he said. "Aela said I would find you here."

"What . . . whatever are you doing here?" I asked.

"Your husband the king requested I join him for a hunt," he said, eyeing me as if I'd gone simple.

"Yes, yes. Of course. You would be the Selgovian lord, then. He did not say which. But you were to arrive three days hence," I said carefully, not wanting him to feel unwelcome.

"I had other business nearby. Lailoken assured me it would be no trouble. I apologize if—"

"It's no trouble. You've surprised me is all."

"Again, I apologize." He stood rather awkwardly.

I smiled with a sweeping gesture. "Please. Do come in."

Maelgwn stepped over the threshold, ducking to keep his dark head from hitting the lintel. He eyed the broom and the jars cluttering the table. "You were . . . tidying?" he asked.

"Unbecoming of a queen, is it?"

His smile was only a flicker. "You have never been like other queens. The first time I saw you, you were training with a knife."

"This knife?" I patted the golden hilt where it hung from my belt.

"That very one." He looked at it. "I thought you had given it to Angharad."

"It was taken from her. Lailoken returned it to me. He discovered it in Ebrauc, of all places."

We exchanged a look. There was little that Maelgwn and his stags did not know.

"You must be happy to have it back in your company," he said, looking round. "This was your mother's hut, if I remember."

"Yes. It's been too long out of use, and with so many coming for the hunt . . ." I paused, setting down a jar I'd forgotten I was holding.

"Well, I won't prevent you from finishing your task. I'll leave you to it," he said, turning for the door.

"Maelgwn?"

He swiveled. "Yes."

I met his eyes. "I heard you had married," I said. "Lord Archer's daughter." She was young, I knew, far younger than I, dark-haired and pretty.

"Yes," he said. "It's been three winters now."

"Three winters," I echoed. "Yes, that's right. Have you . . . have you any children?"

I still had not told him of Rhys—that my firstborn had been his child. Our child. Each time I'd seen him, it had pressed at my guts. *But why cause Maelgwn any more suffering?* I'd thought. Each moment we'd spoken had been the wrong time. Now I was uncertain he ever need know, but it dug at me still.

"A child? Yes, we have." Maelgwn's smile was contagious as his green eyes lit. "A boy called Gareth. He's two winters now."

"Gareth." My heart brimmed at the news. "How wonderful, Maelgwn. I can tell you are happy. Tell me, has your wife traveled with you?"

"Nay, she has not. I've brought Diarmid, though. He's gone on to the Hall."

"Goodness!" I smiled at the mention of the old Wisdom Keeper. "We mustn't keep him waiting. I'm finished here, if you'd care to accompany me?"

"Of course," he said.

"That's good"—I smiled—"for I'm stuck with cobwebs and must make myself presentable. It would seem I have some important guests for dinner."

● ● ●

"How's your brother, then?" Diarmid asked through a mouthful of mutton. His gray-speckled hair had gone white and he had one milky eye ever since Arderydd, but other than that Diarmid the Keeper was wonderfully unchanged. "Still hasn't managed to get rid of that Mungo?"

"I'm afraid not," I said, signaling my servant to refill his wine. "The monks at Bright Hill have tripled in number, and Mungo's established churches all across Strathclyde. It seems every week I witness new baptisms."

Diarmid ceased chewing. "And what have you done about it?"

"What can I do?" I replied, not put off by his directness. "We keep the turnings of the year. I host the chieftains of the Old Way with lavishness. I travel the kingdom fashioning Brighid dollies with the children at Lughnasa. Lailoken blesses the granaries. There are the same rituals and handfastings. And still the number of novices at the White Isle dwindles with each passing year."

"Youth are forever chasing novelty," Diarmid declared. "We have no such troubles among the Selgovae. Their traditions are strong. Christians do not bother us in the deep of the Caledonian Wood."

"I'm sorry, my old friend," I said. "But I fear it is only a matter of time."

Maelgwn glanced at me across the table. "The Old Way is yet strong among the Britons. The Selgovae of the Wood speak of you highly in the south."

"You sound weary," Diarmid snapped. "You are far too young for all that. Liven up!"

"I do not feel young," I told him.

"Pish-posh. Smart and still pretty. And you've got two good eyes, haven't you?" he said, waving at his milky one.

"I have many more eyes than two these days," I said.

"And what do they tell you?" He leaned in. Maelgwn set down his spoon, also keen.

"The Angles are growing restless again. Rhydderch's brother, Morcant, cannot help but incite them to skirmishes. And the descendants of Ida are fighting amongst themselves. Hussa will have to prove his strength to keep the throne of Bernicia. He will bring war, and soon. That is why you are here. Rhydderch seeks to build a confederation under my brother's advisement. The Selgovae and the Gododdin are only the beginning."

"Why not summon a Gathering?" Maelgwn asked.

"Why not call the Angles with a blast horn?" Diarmid shouted, then winked at me. "The strongest walls are built stone by stone. Isn't that right?"

"Yes, that's right," I said. "This is only a hunt, you see."

Later that eve, Maelgwn had retired to the guest quarters, leaving Diarmid and me cradling our goblets of wine by the fire. I'd sent the servants away, and we sat in a rare moment of absolute isolation in the great room. Soon my hall would be spilling with nobles and their retinues. But for this eve, it was only the two of us, and there was something about Diarmid that made me want to confess all my secrets. I risked a glance at him.

"Maelgwn told me he had business near Cadzow," I said.

The old Wisdom Keeper raised a brow. "Business, was it?"

"So he said."

"Hmph," he said, gazing into the fire.

"He seems quite happily wedded," I went on.

"Happily? Who can say? Certainly not me. Happy to have children to carry his bloodline at least." The look he gave me was pointed but not unkind.

I bore him a son, I wanted to say. *I bore him a child and we lost him.* But the truth only dug at the scab on my heart.

"I am glad for him. Truly," I said.

"You envy his wife."

"I have no right to envy."

"But you feel it the same," he said.

"I suppose I do." I shook my head, watching the flames a moment, then turned to him. "Tell me, Diarmid. Have you ever loved?"

The question caught him unawares. He looked up from his goblet with a laugh. "Aye, of course I have loved."

"Sometimes it feels that love is only suffering." I did not speak only of romantic love. This I think he knew. "Sometimes, I wish I could dam its stream so it cannot flow and therefore drown me. So I cannot be broken when someone is taken from me. I grow so tired of breaking open again and again."

"Nay, nay." Diarmid turned his brown eyes on me. He spoke as a father might admonish a child. "Life is suffering, my lady. It is only love that makes it worthwhile."

It was easy to avoid Maelgwn in the days that followed. The impending arrival of my other guests kept me racing from the kitchens to the great room, checking the guest quarters and the readiness of the stables for all the noblemen's horses. Lailoken and Eira rode ahead of Rhydderch's retinue, arriving midmorning on the appointed day.

"Mungo rides in the company," Lail said, dropping from Eos's back. "I wanted to give you fair warning." His voice was even, but bitterness leached as he helped Eira down from her horse.

Some hurts, I'd found, faded with time, but the thought of Mungo standing in Cadzow's courtyard made my very innards burn. This place was nothing less than our beating heart, and his presence despoiled it. He knew this; he reveled in it.

"I knew he could not resist it," I said.

The thought of poison crossed my mind, but Cadzow was a place of the Old Way. If Mungo died here, it would bring riot to my gates and divide my kingdom besides. Lail handed his horse off to a groom, raising a brow.

"I know that look," he said. "His food and drink?"

"Shall remain untouched," I said.

Eira leaned to kiss my cheek. "You mustn't let him rankle you. That's what he wants, Sister. To twist the thorn."

"He'll see nothing upon my face," I assured them. "Thank you for the warning."

As Aela readied me for the arrival of the lords of Strathclyde and the men of Gododdin, I stared at my reflection in the bronze.

My heart felt wasp-stung, a swollen and tender thing. But it was not only thoughts of Mungo that seeped as Aela pinned my hair back in combs, smoothing oils into its lengths. It was the dawning that, once again, it was my own husband who invited my suffering.

Warring against my brother. Granting my land to a Christian culdee. Summoning Mungo from exile. Bringing him here to Cadzow, where the soil still remembered the weight of Cathan's feet.

This Hall belonged to my father, the man Mungo made his enemy.

Now I must serve him from our finest platters and watch him drink our sweet heathered mead.

I'd felt such guilt for the tug of my heart toward another man, for straying from our marriage bed. For the word of Christians said, *Wives obey your husbands as you obey your Lord*. But their lord was a stranger to me. And the master I was meant to obey was far too often the cause of my pain.

"Are you all right, m'lady?" Aela leaned in, her face creased in concern.

"Quite," I said.

From the stillness of my chamber, I heard Maelgwn's low voice drifting from the great room. Just the sound of it, his nearness, brought me some peace.

Life was suffering.

All I had done was love.

CHAPTER 35

Angharad

Burghead Fortress
Kingdom of the Picts
Late September, AD 584

Angharad stood on the rampart looking out over the sea. The wind played in gusts, billowing her white robes. Far below in the cobalt-blue waters, the warships were at anchor, their ivory sails tethered.

Lughnasa had come and gone, the hay in the fields had been harvested and stacked in the byres. Beyond the walls of Burghead, calves lazed, blinking sleepily in the grass beside their mothers, and the moors yet bloomed, scattered with white tufts of bog cotton.

The growing seasons had been good to the Cruithni; there was little sickness, and the granaries were well stocked for yet another winter. They'd had no need of the drowning pool since Angharad had arrived. Weatherwork, it turned out, was not all swirling wind and the summoning of storms. It was the practical minding of a people and their food. The rain, the sun, the droughts, the blights. To be a weatherworker was to carry a white banner of peace from the people while begging the benevolence of the Gods. And these days she spoke with many. Though Angharad mightn't worship the Cailleach alone, it was the Cailleach who was her true patroness.

It was the Cailleach who sent her dreams.

A horn blast from the guard tower startled her and she looked to the water, spying three small vessels cutting along the coast. Her shoulders eased. Rhainn and his men had returned. She'd had an unsettled feeling about their journey, though it was nothing if not routine, going round as they were, collecting tribute for the king. Still, she'd ensured they left on a day that was *mat*, lucky, for collecting. She'd offered a blessing for safe travel. She'd even tacked a talisman under the gunnel of each boat.

You see? she told herself. *All is well.*

She was turning for the steps when a woman's shrill voice called up from below.

"Are you up there, Ton Velen? Can you see, is it him? Have they come home?"

Angharad moved to the edge of the warrior's walk to look down at the curvy woman with waves of brown hair. She bounced a drooling babe on her hip, her face pinched with concern.

"Yes, Carys. They've returned," Angharad said evenly. Rhainn's lover Carys was a silly woman, prone to fits of hysteria and a devotee of the dramatic. Imagine if she'd known of Angharad's worries.

"Oh. Praise the Gods!" Carys exclaimed, her eyes shimmering with tears.

"It was only the taxes," Angharad said.

Carys covered the babe's ears as if Angharad had cursed. "One never knows what can happen at sea."

How she tried Angharad's patience. But the babe was looking up at her, grinning, and Angharad could not help but smile.

As Angharad climbed down, Carys passed her the little girl. "There, now. Go to your auntie," she said.

Angharad pulled the child close. She smelled of sweet autumn grasses and the salt of the sea.

"Hello, little one," she whispered into her hair. "Your da's returned."

At home in Angharad's arms, the babe reached for an auburn lock of Angharad's hair, gripping it with chubby fingers. And yet there was still something unsettled in Angharad's chest. She stopped, listening.

Why were the guards barking orders at the gates? If Carys had been worried, her face now was stricken.

"Come," said Angharad. "Let's see what's the matter." Hefting the girl more solidly onto her hip, she hurried toward the lower citadel, Carys trotting alongside her.

The men were just entering the harbor gate.

Rhainn looked up and Angharad saw his tunic was spattered in blood.

"Rhainn!" Carys crossed the grass at a run, thrusting herself into his arms. "Oh, my love. What's happened? Are you hurt?"

"It's not mine." He nodded behind him. A muscled warrior with a bloodied face was being dragged into the fort by two of Rhainn's men.

"We came across enemy scouts. They escaped, save this one," he said to Carys, but his eyes were on Angharad. "They were Scots. Artúr's men."

Many seasons had passed since she'd last seen Ewan or Artúr, but her heart still skittered as she looked again at the man's face.

If he was a warrrior of Artúr's, she did not know him.

"Where did you find them?" Angharad asked, passing Rhainn his daughter. He pulled the little girl to his chest, murmuring something sweet in her ear.

"In the province of Circenn," he said.

Angharad knew it well. Murienn of Dùn Dèagh's lands lay within its bounds, a Pictish territory that spanned the southern reaches of the Grampian Mountains to the Firth of Tay. Circenn was deep into

Pictland. It was worrisome that any enemies could have penetrated so deeply before being caught. And from the indignant look upon the warrior's face, he hadn't imagined they'd be found out at all.

Angharad eyed the blood on Rhainn's tunic and glanced at the Scot. His lip was split and his face badly beaten. Rhainn had failed to kill Artúr four winters ago. He'd lost good men and still blamed himself. He wanted revenge.

As the prisoner was taken to an outbuilding in the lower citadel, Angharad turned to Rhainn. "Do you know for a fact this is one of Artúr's men?"

Rhainn scoffed. "What Scot would be fool enough to send scouts into our lands without the sanction of Artúr or his father?"

"You're right," she admitted. "You think they're planning something."

"I don't know—not yet." Rhainn looked after the prisoner and his face hardened. "But I am going to find out."

That night, the soothing roll and hush of the sea was shattered by horrible cries. Angharad lay awake in her tiny hut in the lower citadel until she could bear it no longer. Wrapping her cloak hurriedly over her shoulders, she crossed the grass in the dark, moving toward the light of torches that marked the outbuilding where the prisoner was being kept. Two guards stood watch at the door, but they would not deny a Keeper.

"Let me in," she said.

Rhainn whipped round as she entered, his face contorted with rage.

"I said leave us!" he shouted.

Angharad shrank back. He stopped at the sight of her. He had a wild look in his eye, and he gripped a knife. The Scot's body was a tortured mass of tiny cuts, weeping blood. Rhainn must have seen the look of horror upon her face, for he stepped closer, blocking her view.

"You should not be here," he said, his voice low.

"On the contrary, I should have come sooner," she said. "What has he told you?"

Rhainn's jaw was tight. "He says nothing."

"I would speak with him. Alone."

Rhainn dealt the man a hard look, considering. "No," he said.

"You mistake me. I was not asking." Angharad planted her feet. "Your lessons in pain are not working. Let me try another way."

They stood toe to toe a long moment, then at last Rhainn gave in.

"Well enough," he agreed. "He's bound. He cannot harm you. But I will wait by the door."

Rhainn stepped aside. The man had been bound standing, his arms stretched out. His body sagged against the ropes, his head lolling to one side. For a moment she thought he might be dead. But then, as Rhainn moved toward the door, she noticed his chest sink almost imperceptibly. Relief. No more pain, at least for the moment. Angharad swallowed and moved closer.

"Can you hear me?" she asked. "Please. Open your eyes. I would speak with you. You needn't suffer any longer."

The man opened his swollen eyes slowly, regarding her.

"You need only tell me why the Scots have sent scouts to Circenn," she said. The Scot opened his cracked lips as if to speak, then spat a mass of clotted blood. Garnet flecks spattered Angharad's white robes.

"Warriors," she muttered. She closed the distance between them.

"Do not mistake my practicality for pity," she said, lifting her hands to the crown of his head. He jerked away.

"Be still, you stubborn man!" she said. He mustn't know it, but of course she was stirred by the sight of him. She was a healer. Her innards recoiled at the sight of what Rhainn had done. But now she was flustered, and nothing would come in this way.

Blowing out a shaky breath, Angharad reached again, closing her eyes, searching for stillness.

She touched the man's skin, and then she saw Artúr.

Briochan stood beside the hearth in his nightclothes.

"He stood at the head of a great army," Angharad told him. She had woken him from the depths of sleep, and he looked at her now, blinking as if to better see her.

"What else did you see, Ton Velen?"

Say it. Angharad closed her eyes. She knit her fingers together, pressing until they stung. "I saw the standard of the bull, trampled and black with blood."

He looked at her a moment, then sat heavily upon the bench. "You do not know the significance of Circenn, do you?" he asked.

Angharad shook her head.

"A fortress lies in Circenn, where the river Tay meets the Earn. The fortress is called Asreth. It was there, twenty-six winters ago at Asreth, that Bridei son of Maelchon defeated the Scots in battle . . . and took Gabrahn's head. The battle became known as the Battle of Circenn. At the time, both Aedan and Bridei were but young men. Now they are seasoned kings, enemies, rivals, in their full power."

Angharad's voice sounded small in the dark. "Aedan and his sons come at last for revenge."

"Yes. Given your vision, now we must fear it." Briochan's sigh could have sailed ships. "Aedan and his sons march to Asreth for the head of our king."

"Then we must prepare," Angharad said. "We have warning enough—"

"Nay, Angharad. Can you not see? There is too little time for preparation. Aedan will strike, and quickly. Already they are marching, of this I am certain. We must ready the boats and set sail for the Tay. We are already too late."

He stood. "I will go and wake Bridei."

It was the way that he said it—with the tenderness of a father. But he stopped at the door, turning.

"We are at war, Ton Velen. Tell the Keepers to ready themselves for ritual. We must make a sacrifice. Prepare the draft in the way I taught you. We shall meet at the temple at first light."

CHAPTER 36

Angharad

Angharad bathed, as was expected, and pulled on fresh white robes.

It was still hours before morning, yet the fortress hummed like a nest of angry bees. Somewhere in the blackness, warriors sharpened their blades on whetstones. Servants hurried between the huts and the water, packing currachs with supplies to be rowed to the deep-anchored warships. Children, woken too early by the commotion, fussed in their nightclothes or stood in hut doorways, moon-eyed, watching.

All the while the prisoner sat in the outbuilding. Perhaps the Scot had heard stories of the Picts, as Angharad had. Perhaps what clamped his lips was the thought that his fate was inescapable.

Fresh torches were made, their fiery wrappings dipped in sacred oil. The drummers were summoned. Angharad tucked her little iron bird into her feathered cloak and folded it into her waiting trunk.

A human being was the costliest gift that could be offered to the gods. Angharad had never killed a man before. At least, not with her own two hands. But she had killed with her words, with her power, had she not? She'd cursed the oarswoman, cursed Gwrgi of Ebrauc, and both now lay dead.

The Scots were coming for Bridei and his throne. And the Gods did not suffer injustices done to their children. Was the protection of these good people, her people, not the purest reason for sacrifice of all?

The coming of dawn felt like a speeding horse. Angharad knew she must come round to it. And yet. Was this prisoner not someone's child?

She did not want to kill the man, but neither could she let him live.

She could, at least, do him a kindness. It was only a pinch more of this root, a few more drops of that. She knew where the man was traveling. She had been there herself, after all. The Summerlands waited. On the other side of momentary pain, he would be greeted by his kin. Why, then, did she feel so sickened?

A knock came at the door of her hut. Briochan stood in his ceremonial robes, his dark eyes regal, his gaze heady as a high mountain fog.

"Come; it is time," he said, extending his hand. In it was a goblet of delicate green glass. She took the cup and filled it with the draft from her pitcher.

"You made it as I've shown you?" Briochan asked. "It must not kill him, only dull his wild senses. It must be the water, in the end."

"Yes," she said.

Drums echoed into the yawning black, foreboding. Angharad walked barefoot through the cold night grasses, Briochan at her side, her hood drawn and her eyes painted black. Behind them came the other Keepers bearing their torches.

The villagers had gathered and stood waiting in silence, their forms lit gold by the fire pits illuminating the lower citadel. Rhainn and his warriors stood ready for battle, their shields by their sides and their spears in hand. Across the courtyard, the temple was nestled in its womb of earth, its narrow stone steps leading into another world.

There the high king stood, waiting. Bridei was barefoot and dressed all in white, the heavy silver chains of his torque his only ornamentation. His wives stood beside him in creamy linen shifts, their long hair set loose, each holding a garland of flowers.

The air was weighted with the sorrow of a funeral as the prisoner was brought out and forced to kneel. Beyond the open door of the temple, only darkness. The drums did not cease but softened in their thrumming as Angharad stepped toward the prisoner, the fragile green goblet between her hands. The Scot was bound, but he had been bathed and his cuts washed clean. He was dressed in a scarlet tunic embroidered in gold threading.

Angharad leaned in as she offered him the cup.

"Drink," she said in Goidelic. "It will help ease your passing."

At the sound of his mother tongue, the prisoner looked at her in disdain. "You are a traitor," he said.

"No," she said softly, this time in Pictish. "I am no traitor. But I was once a friend."

Their eyes met. He gave the slightest nod. Then, as Angharad brought the goblet to his mouth, he tipped his head back and drank the draft down.

The Keepers' chant droned on. The wives of Bridei came forward, bowing to their sacrifice, draping their garlands round his neck.

The Keepers were singing.

Angharad murmured a prayer, following the torchbearers down into the chill of the temple's inner sanctum. The air smelled of incense and the stones round the pool were dressed with harebell, bog asphodel, and sprays of dried heather. As she stood before the steps leading into the dark water, torchlight wavered in fingers on its skin. Behind her, Briochan was speaking, his voice sounding in ricochets off the cold stone, but Angharad's ears were full of the whoosh of her own thudding heart.

The Keepers brandishing torches moved sunwise round the pool, lining the water's edge in a wall of white robes and hungry flames.

Angharad took a breath and stepped down, into the water. She did not feel the cold, though it seeped into her robes as she submerged just below her chest. The stony bottom of the pool was solid beneath her feet, but the pulsing was there, ancient and deep.

In the beginning, the Gods of our land sprang forth in innumerable places on earth, born from deep within the womb of the land. Born in multitudes, each was birthed from the belly of their own freshwater spring . . .

The water made ripples as Angharad turned to look at the Scot. He was descending the steps into the pool now in the grip of two Wisdom Keepers, one on each side.

But his eyes were soft focused and bleary, as if he were dreaming.

CHAPTER 37

Artúr

Stirling Fortress, Kingdom of Mannau
Land of the Scots
Late September, AD 584

Sunlight streamed through a crack in the door. Artúr turned to look at Vanora, still asleep, the bare curve of her shoulder familiar as his own. He traced a finger along its outline and she shivered a little, stirring.

"It is morning," Artúr said.

"Shhh. Do not wake me. If I do not wake, you cannot leave." Vanora tried to make light, but beneath her voice was sadness. She rolled over to look at him. Freckles scattered like stars across the bridge of her nose from the afternoon some days ago when they had sat too long by the river.

"I would come," she said. "I will keep to the heights and safety of a nearby fort."

"No." Artúr drew her close, pressing his forehead to hers. "You must stay here in Stirling. I will see Gartnait's throne won, then I will ride home to you."

"To us," she said, looking to the cradle at the side of the bed.

"Look. He sleeps still," Artúr said. "He is just like his mother."

Vanora swatted him. He caught her wrist. Kissed it.

A banging came at the door and their son woke with a start, then burst into tears. Vanora hurried from bed to console the babe, putting him to her breast.

"Hush, then, Llachen."

Artúr yanked on his trousers as Cai and Bedwyr opened the door. They were already armored, wearing their swords.

"Come; it is time," Cai said.

Vanora glanced at them, then at Artúr.

"Only a moment," Artúr said. Cai nodded and turned, but did not go. Artúr crossed the chamber to hold Vanora and Llachen, kissing his son.

"I'll send word," he promised.

"May the Gods keep you safe," Vanora whispered, pressing his hand. He stood back, looking at her.

"Manannan rides with the Scots," he said. "I am certain of that."

He would keep Vanora and their son far from harm's way. But that was not the only reason he'd insisted she stay. The words she'd spoken in the Black Water Lands echoed still. Vanora loved the Pictish people. In the winters that had passed, they had gained the allegiance of a dozen new Miathi chieftains whose lands abutted Artúr's and his brothers'.

Gartnait had won the allegiance of the Pictish lords halfway through Circenn. But the other half, and all along the northern borders of Dalriada, were loyal to Bridei still. The raiding and warfare would not cease until the Picts were united under one king.

Bridei's reign must end. And Vanora might never be the same if she should see it. For today, Artúr and his army marched to Circenn. From there, they would burn their way to the fortress of Asreth, leaving nothing but blood and ashes in their wake.

Young Ewan waited beside Artúr's horse. The boy had grown tall in four winters, now a man, but he had never taken to fighting, and Artúr could tell this battle, more than others, troubled him.

"You all right, then, Young Ewan?" Artúr asked.

Ewan pushed a blond shock of his hair from his eyes.

"It's only, I wonder," he said, eyeing the road, "do you ever feel . . . afraid?"

Artúr felt Vanora and his infant son at his back. Never had he felt so mortal, so exposed. "Fear is a trick," Artúr advised him. "There is no sense in it. There is only doing what must be done. Commit all your senses to the task at hand."

"Right," Ewan said. Then swallowed. Artúr's words were hollow. They were the words of his father. And though Artúr loved his father, and paid him all respect, he was beginning to understand he wanted to be a rather different man.

"Listen, Young Ewan," he said, lowering his voice as he mounted his horse. "Look at these warriors all round you. Murderers. Masters. The best in the land. Somewhere deep down, every single one of them knows fear."

He looked at Ewan, nodding at him to pull astride his own horse.

"Nay. I'll tell you the truth of it," Artúr said. "Fear isn't a trick. Fear is a friend, come to try to save you. Listen to your fear. Heed its warning. Use it to fight, and it'll act like a fuel. But never let fear rule you. That's the way you wind up dead."

CHAPTER 38

Languoreth

Cadzow Fortress, Kingdom of Strathclyde
Land of the Britons
Late September, AD 584

"It's a fine morning for a hunt," a Christian lord of Strathclyde said pleasantly, coming to stand beside me in the courtyard. He was an honorable man, and kind. His father had been a follower of Brother Telleyr.

"Yes, glorious," I said, squinting into the sun. Crisp and cold. Something of the morning, the quality of the air or the way the light shimmered off the Avon, made me think of the stag Lailoken and I had visited far below on the riverbank as children, but the thought was sobering. The stag was long dead now, somewhere in the woods, his nine-tined antlers buried in leaves, his soft parts dissolved back into the earth.

"Are you certain you'll not join us?" he asked me.

"Oh, no, I mustn't. There is much to do to ready for the feast, after all."

"Of course," he said politely. Any meat from the hunt would need to hang; it would be days before it was ready. Thankfully, I had meat from a steer that I'd been aging a fortnight.

The warriors stood in clusters wearing their finest tunics. Rhydderch's head was bowed intently as he spoke with a petty king of the Gododdin. Mungo stood in the company of two monks in their hooded robes at the courtyard's edge, waiting to give the blessing of the hunt.

Maelgwn stood beneath our old crab apple beside my brother, a bow strapped over his shoulder and his black hair loose about his shoulders. Already the dogs were whining, straining at their leads.

As the grooms raced between the courtyard and the stable, bringing the men's horses, one passed Mungo, who reached out, catching his arm. Leaning in, he murmured something low in the groom's ear.

I turned to my guest. "If you'll excuse me."

He nodded, turning to a companion as I crossed the courtyard to Mungo.

"Is something the matter?" I asked him.

"No, no. It is nothing," he said amiably. "I only noticed the king is in need of his mount."

"The king receives his horse last as a grace to his company," I said. "It would be best to leave the management of my grooms to me."

"As you say." He bowed. But as the groom returned, Mungo's eyes flickered with an unsettling satisfaction: the groom held two horses in hand, one belonging to the king and the other to Maelgwn. What was he playing at? Both men looked up and strode from where they stood in the courtyard to the place where their horses were waiting, side by side. Mungo studied my face as the two men exchanged pleasantries. I turned to him.

"You must excuse me. I would kiss my husband for good luck." I started off, calling to my brother. "Lailoken, we are ready. Would you give the hunt the honor of your blessing?"

Mungo stiffened as Lail smiled broadly, lifting his hands to address the gathered crowd. It was not until he'd finished Cadzow's traditional call to the hunt that Mungo and his monks stepped forward to offer theirs.

"And now we beseech the favor of Christ . . . ," Mungo said, intoning a prayer in Latin.

I stood beside Rhydderch, my face a mask of decorum. My husband was an intelligent man. Surely he must see the levels of machinations leveraged in every waking moment to secure his insisted balance, this delicate peace?

"May your god keep you safe on the hunt, husband," I said, leaning to kiss his bearded cheek. Maelgwn turned his head as if studying something in the distance.

"And good luck to you, Maelgwn Pendragon," I said to him.

"Thank you, Lady Queen." Maelgwn's brown mare shuffled impatiently.

"She is more than ready for the hunt," Rhydderch declared.

"Indeed," Maelgwn said, bending to check her girth. As he did, a trinket slipped from beneath his tunic, dangling in the air a moment from the cord round his neck, catching the light. A glint of green and gold.

My ring.

I blinked. I'd returned it four years ago. Had he worn it all this time? There I stood beside my husband, but the sight of the jewel I'd carried close for so many winters ensnared me. I had stared too long.

This is how they happen, those moments that change one's life, that thrust open the door into a waiting storm. It's always these small moments, when one least expects it.

I recovered too late and looked up to see Rhydderch's gaze shift between us, his gray eyes settling on the ring as Maelgwn tucked it back into the safety of his padded leather vest. He looked at the grass a moment, then up at my face. But I could not speak.

"We must be off," Rhydderch said tightly. "I will see you for supper."

My ears hummed with his unspoken condemnation as the men kicked their horses off to the triumphant blast of the horn.

I had kept the ring a secret for so many seasons. Or so I had thought. But from the look upon Rhydderch's face, he had recognized it. Cheeks burning, I hurried from the courtyard toward the isolation of my chamber, but just as I reached the door to the Hall, Mungo stopped me, catching my wrist.

"My lady queen, whatever is the matter? You look quite upset. Is there anything you would confess? Let me bear your burden."

"The men are gone yet will soon return, and there is much I must see to," I said evenly.

"Ah." Mungo nodded, tilting his head. "For a moment I imagined you were distraught that the king has spied the ring you have given to your lover. He wears it round his neck, does he not?"

He wanted to see terror, regret, or panic. I would offer him none of those to delight in.

"I don't know what you imagine you saw, but I would be careful, were I you," I said, my voice low. "You haven't any idea what you speak of. Step too far beyond your bounds and you are destined to fall."

Shaking free of his grip, I pushed past him into the Hall.

It was damning enough that Mungo had somehow learned of the ring. Not only that, it was clear he thought Maelgwn and I were yet lovers.

But all I could see as I closed the door to my chamber was the look upon Rhydderch's face. Yes, he had seen the ring.

And he knew it was mine.

"Maelgwn wears it round his neck?" Eira whispered as we readied in my chamber for the hunting party's return. "And you're certain Rhydderch saw it? But how would Rhydderch know the ring belonged to you? You told me all these long winters you had kept the ring hidden."

"I suppose it's impossible to know. I suppose he must have seen it once or twice, all these winters sharing a roof. The look upon his face, Eira." I glanced at her. "It was horrible to see."

"Be that as it may, you must tell your brother as soon as they return. He in turn will warn Maelgwn. Perhaps Lail can also reason with Rhydderch."

"I cannot be seen conspiring with my brother," I said. "Not now.

Not with Mungo and his hidden eyes watching my every move. Someone most loyal to me must have told him."

"We cannot assume," Eira said. "In the meantime, I will speak to Lailoken as soon as I'm able."

"And we must send word to Torin."

"Of course. You may trust me to do it." She looked at me. "You must speak with Rhydderch before Mungo has occasion to drip more poison into his ear. Your love affair has long since ended. You need only explain."

I felt I might be sick all over my delicate leather shoes. "You mistake my husband," I said.

"But you are his queen," she said worriedly. As if that were armor.

"Yes," I said softly, staring blankly at the wall. "I was his queen."

Divorce. Banishment. Exile. These were the punishments by law for adultery. Perhaps I should be grateful that Britons were civilized: I could not be put to death for being unfaithful to my marriage bed. I'd heard tell of kings from foreign courts who'd murdered their wives for far less.

The men returned drunk, with three glassy-eyed does on the back of a sledge. I smiled beside the cheering villagers as they rode into the courtyard. The hounds' muzzles were covered in blood. The lords were happy enough, but they could have fared better: stags were a prize. Does were expendable.

"Hang them!" Rhydderch said to the footmen, gesturing to the sledge. But his eyes were on me.

Guilt wracked like a sickness as the men filed into the Hall. I had never meant to hurt Rhydderch. When I approached him, he looked away. I knew he was angry, felt wounded and betrayed. And he'd not decided what to do with me yet.

The feast was a haze of music and drink. Maelgwn was under the mead's spell more than I'd seen him. Lail had spoken to him, then. Rhydderch's smile was too easy, save when he looked at me. I kept busy playing lady hostess, trading a quip with a lord, nodding to the servants to clear up the courses. Each time my path collided with Rhydderch's, Mungo's eyes tracked to us like a hawk. Across the hall, I noticed Lailoken had not touched any drink. Though he spoke brightly with our guests, I knew in my core my brother's mind was fixed upon me.

Rhydderch had never asked me to be faithful. But now my actions had put all of us in jeopardy. What was there to prevent Rhydderch from setting me aside, sending my brother back to the Selgovian lands, and choosing Mungo as his chief counsel?

And beneath all the guilt, beneath even my fear, lay a desolate sadness. Not only for the hurt I'd caused my husband but for the shame this cast upon something that had once been so shining.

The love I had shared with Maelgwn.

For so many years it had been a beacon burning on a far-off hill, even just a glimpse of its brightness consoling me in the dark.

Our gazes caught briefly across the crowded room. That same sadness reflected upon Maelgwn's face.

I could do nothing but watch as Mungo, then my brother, both took their turns speaking quietly with their king. Rhydderch's face betrayed no emotion, but I could feel his patience wearing thin.

At last the night wore on to the moment it would be acceptable for me to take my leave. I crossed the hall to bid my husband and our company good night. And as I leaned stiffly in to brush Rhydderch's face with a kiss, he caught my hand, pulling me close.

"Do not expect me in our chamber," he said, low-voiced. "Tomorrow this shall be dealt with. There will be guards at your door. Do not try to flee."

CHAPTER 39

Languoreth

I did not see Maelgwn or even my brother the following day. Rhydderch sent Brodyn and the rest of my guard away. I was to be watched by his men now. I heard my husband announce to our guests I was ill. I was kept to my chamber as the lords departed, promises made and gifts exchanged: Rhydderch had forged a strong new alliance. He could not punish Maelgwn because he needed the Selgovian forces. I was at least thankful for that.

I was taken from my chamber sometime in the early afternoon, straight into the back of a waiting cart. Cadzow's courtyard was emptied of my servants. It was there that they bound my wrists. From inside the cart I heard the sound of horses and men's voices but could not tell if I traveled alone or in Rhydderch's caravan. All I knew was that we traveled back to Partick.

I should have expected he would not keep me at Cadzow, for Rhydderch did not want blood on his hands. My power was too strong there, and imprisonment could mean riots.

I hadn't slept the night before; my insides felt scratchy and my head ached.

I woke to a jostle and the slowing of the cart.

We'd arrived at Partick, then.

I expected he would not let me roam freely, but I did not expect him to take me to the prisons. At least he could not toss me in the pits. That would be too vulgar a treatment for a queen. Such behavior had been tolerated from his father, but Rhydderch was much beloved, and such savagery would have been unbecoming of their king.

My cell was a windowless hut with a bench and a blanket and a short, sloping roof. Just beyond it lay the pits.

Time passed. Flies buzzed at the thatching. No one came. Not Eira, nor Brodyn, nor Elufed, nor my brother. It occurred to me that my only living son would now find me a disgrace. But while Elufed and my brother might not be permitted to visit, it did not mean they weren't lending their help. Elufed and Lailoken would be speaking with Rhydderch. Somewhere, Torin had been alerted. He would be finding out all that Mungo knew. It was only a matter of time.

I closed my eyes and prayed to Clota, the goddess of my childhood. I had stood on her salty banks gathering seaweed the day I learned that I was to be Rhydderch's bride. She had taken the tears I'd shed for the loss of my children. I had felt her steady hand at my back as I'd grown to become a queen.

Sweet goddess, see me through this.

Some hours later, I heard voices outside my door.

The guard fiddled with the padlock and Rhydderch stepped in.

His gray eyes were cold and ringed in dark circles. His strong shoulders slouched. I dared not be the first to speak.

"Maelgwn Pendragon wears your ring," he said. His look was pure condemnation.

"I will not deny it. But our love affair ended some years ago."

"Have I not been good to you, Wife? Have I not shown you kindness and due respect? Have I myself not kept the sanctity of our marriage bed?" he asked.

"You have been a steadfast and loyal partner," I said. "I am shamed I could not be the same."

"I knew when I took you for a wife that you were of the Old Way."
He shook his head. "But you, too, knew you had married a Christian.
You knew what was expected of you. You betrayed me, and you have
made me look a fool. Why? Why have you done it?" he demanded, but
could not look at me.

"Do you truly wish to know?"

A waiting silence was my only answer. I looked down at my hands,
white-knuckled in my lap. "I was a young woman and I fell in love
with a warrior. There were times, in the beginning, when I dreamt of a
different life. As I grew older, I learned such sentiments were selfish. I
had wedded myself not only to you but to this land and our people. We
were not intimate so many times. But I will be truthful and say that for
many winters I did possess a longing in my heart. One that, as much as
I hoped, our love could not fill. You and I are so very different."

"And you and Maelgwn Pendragon are the same?" he challenged.

"We are both dreamers." I said. "But dreams fade upon pillows. It
is the living that matters. And I have long since made my choice: to
live out my days with you."

Rhydderch was quiet a long moment, considering. The logician in
him always came forth before too long.

"What might have been a private matter has been put about the
kingdom," he began.

"And who do you think has put it about the kingdom? Mungo
set his spies upon me, determined to undermine my influence. The
people of the Old Way look to me as their scion now. Can you not
see? Mungo does not bend your ear out of love for you. He would use
anything—or anyone—to destroy me."

"He is my counsellor and seeks to protect me," Rhydderch said.

"It is not like you to be blind, Rhydderch."

This was the wrong thing to say.

"You are right, Languoreth. I have been blinded for far too long.

And as for you, the Christian lords—not all, but many—are insisting I set you aside. Some have suggested worse."

"Rhydderch, I—"

"No, you will not speak. Gossip and speculation now travel through Strathclyde," he said. "The people are raising questions regarding our son."

Rhys, he meant. I swallowed. So it would be now?

"I wanted to tell you, Rhydderch. All of this time. I wanted to tell you that Rhys—"

Rhydderch flinched, holding up a hand. "I beg you, do not say it."

I watched, gutted, as he sat down upon the bench, gazing at his hands. "I loved that boy. I loved my son."

Tears rose and I turned my head; he had no care to see them. "He loved you," I said. "You *were* his father."

He gave the slightest nod.

"I do not know what it is I must do," he said. "And no more can I go to you for the answer, for you are the cause of it now."

Never had I heard Rhydderch so lost. I did not think I could bear it.

"I will not deny I loved Maelgwn," I said. "There is a place in me that loves him still, for love does not die, but it can change. And my love for Maelgwn changed as *our* love grew. There was a time, Rhydderch, when I could not reconcile our differences. But in time I came to realize that together, you and I are like two trees that have twisted together to form one single body. Throughout these many years, your roots and mine have become inextricably intertwined. And it is our roots together that nourish the divided halves of a kingdom. Together we have grown a mighty forest. Rhydderch, our love lives beyond ourselves. I beg you to trust in me. Do not allow Mungo to do to us and our people what he did to Bright Hill all those years ago. He has come once more to slaughter our trees."

It was as if he did not hear me.

Rhydderch stood slowly and moved to the door, rapping on it to alert the guard. Only when the door opened did he turn. My husband's eyes were those of a stranger.

"The people are always in search of a scion," he said. "You speak as if you are the only woman in Strathclyde who keeps the Old Way. Perhaps it is time you were replaced. There are many noblewomen who would gladly fill your role, and they are not spent, as you are. They could yet bear more children."

Food was brought that I had no stomach for.

Then, on the second day, my brother came.

Lailoken found me sitting on the floor, blanket spread beneath me, my back against the wall. Worry wore him like its puppet. He came to sit beside me, taking my hand.

"We are through with Mungo," he said angrily. "And by this time tomorrow, mark my words, you shall be free."

I looked at him, baffled. "Have you gone mad? Brother, surely you have not spoken to Rhydderch. I'm afraid he is in a terrible way."

"Oh, aye, he's in a terrible way," Lail agreed. "But this cannot go on. Do you not know why Maelgwn left in such haste? He left to summon your Army of Stags."

"What?"

"An army nearly five hundred strong marches even now, as we speak. They are coming to Partick. Men and women. Warriors of the Old Way—of our way. They are coming to save their queen."

"No. Lailoken, no." I sat up from the wall. "Brother, you cannot do this, I beg you. There will be riot. There will be bloodshed! It will be worse than what happened when we were just children. You're not thinking clearly, Lailoken. Our people will be slaughtered, and what of the innocents trapped in the chaos? People will die!"

"Lower your voice, Languoreth," he whispered fiercely. "We should have done this winters ago, but we hadn't the cause. This is our show of strength. Rhydderch cannot afford a battle of this measure with his worries over the Angles. Such news would send them racing for Strathclyde, and well he knows it. He will have no choice but to see that he must release you and send Mungo away. I will win the sole counsellorship and you will be reinstated as his queen."

Lailoken's blue eyes were clear. I wanted to bash my head against the door.

"Brother," I tried again. "You may control our Army of Stags. But you cannot control the Christians. And there will be no stopping the battle once it should start. One errant rock thrown, or Gods forbid a stray arrow, and you will bring about the ruin of our kingdom. There must be another way."

"There is no other way." Lail turned to me, reaching a hand to smooth the hair upon my head. "You must trust in me, Sister."

CHAPTER 40

Lailoken

Partick, Kingdom of Strathclyde
Land of the Britons
Late September, AD 584

I did not go to the chamber Eira and I shared. I could not sleep for thought of Languoreth locked in that dank, dirty cell. At dawn I stole out to the stables to saddle Eos only to find my wife standing there, already dressed in her riding cloak.

"Surely you did not think you were going without me," she said. I opened my mouth, but she shook her head. "Nay, Lailoken. Let me speak. You say there are women in this Army of Stags. Well, then, I am one. I'll not let you stand before the gates of this capital on behalf of your sister without me by your side."

This woman.

I looked at her a moment, then nodded. "Very well, then, my lady. But hurry. They wait for our signal. You and I must lead them to the gates."

The morning was stark and gloomy. We took the familiar road through town and were followed by a man who looked to be Mungo's, but that did not matter. Maelgwn had argued we should undertake this moment in darkness. But for me there was no question: we must commit this act in the brightness of day. For only then could

Rhydderch see that we could reach him anywhere, even within his own walls. Only by daylight would Rhydderch comprehend the true nature of our might.

By the time we reached the gates of town, it had started to rain. The merchants were opening their stalls for the day. The marketplace of Partick was filled with the smell of freshly baked bread. I took a breath as we neared the gates.

Languoreth thought me headstrong, but I had weighed this risk mightily: I knew this maneuver put us all upon a knife's edge. What I would not tell her was that my men had caught whispers of Christian lords under Mungo's sway who would see her strung up. Enough was enough. And my sister also did not know that three days ago, Torin and I had hatched a plan.

The guard watch was empty for the slightest spell, as Torin had arranged. Just long enough for Eira and me to unbar the gate and push open the massive timber doors. I looked to the wood, just over the bridge, and sounded the call.

Then they came striding, emerging from the forest, weapons in hand. Five hundred strong, they were a mass of people of the Old Way.

Our Army of Stags.

Just as a stag knows the power of his antlers but will rake his en-emies only if forced to, they moved peacefully, but with purpose. I searched the crowd for the faces of our friends. Diarmid and Maelgwn. Brodyn and Old Man Archer. Dragon Warriors and wayward warriors from Scotia. Those who had come to me in my exile, in my wilder-ness years. The men and women of Cadzow. Their faces were solemn and drawn in determination, their gazes fixed on Partick's gates. They came because their queen was in need. The sight of our army nearly brought me to tears.

How many kings and queens found comfort outside of their mar-riage beds? There were laws for first wives and concubines. A man could divorce a woman if she sought Keepers to compose slanderous songs. A woman could divorce her husband if he became too fat to pleasure her.

It was only the Christians who sought to dictate how we could love.

The Army of Stags filed into the capital, filling the market. By the time they were spotted by the guard, it was already too late. The watchmen might have charged, but I was their high counsellor, perched high on Partick's walls.

"Listen to me! Listen!" I said. "This army you see before you belongs to your queen. We do not wish a fight. Please, I would ask you. Summon the king."

Villagers came, curious, and were sent to the safety of their homes. As we waited in silence, I could not escape the feeling we stood as if upon kindling. One good strike of the flint, and fire would erupt. At the sound of horses galloping through town, I climbed from the battlement to stand at the front line, Eira by my side.

Rhydderch had come dressed for war.

In his retinue rode the Christian lords and chieftains. Mungo and his monks followed, and marching only a short distance behind them were scores upon scores of angry-looking Christian men.

I turned to the Stags. "Do not let them incite you to fight," I warned. "If we battle, it shall be only by my command."

Rhydderch yanked his mount to a halt, and I stepped out to meet him. His gray eyes flashed beneath his war helmet.

"What is the meaning of this?" he demanded.

"Brother, I do not wish to fight," I said. "We can come to peace on this day. Release the queen and return that creature to exile, where he belongs."

Rhydderch glared down on me. "This is betrayal, Lailoken. I could have your head."

He rounded with his horse, addressing both crowds. "The Angles would love nothing more than for the Britons of Strathclyde to battle amongst themselves. We Britons must remain united. Have we learned nothing from the senselessness of Arderydd? I have grown wise, for I lost countless lives. I lost my own son. And I will not see this kingdom torn apart. Not whilst I rule it."

"Nor would I, my king," I told him. "These people have come only to ask that you do what must be done. This man and his whispers have clouded your head."

"That's enough." Mungo stalked forward, pointing to me. "You brought raiding and slaughter to our warriors at Clyde Rock. Now you bring your warmongering here. My king, it is he who should be exiled. This kingdom cannot sustain the influence of this violent and barbarous man."

It happened then, just as my sister said it would. A rock was thrown. It sailed across the distance between our two armies, pelting me on the head.

I blinked, somehow surprised, and when I raised my hand to my temple, found my fingers smeared in blood. My army bristled at my back. But they knew their order. They would not break. Mungo's mob, however, was not so particular. Rhydderch turned just in time to see them charge. They barreled toward us in a mad rush, weapons raised.

"Hold!" I shouted. "Hold!" I glanced round the marketplace, growing worried now. Where in the name of the Gods *were* they? Torin had assured me all was in hand. Just as I thought our cause would be lost, a long, low blast of a horn came, followed by a voice.

"Stop!" he commanded. But it was not the king.

A man in the coarse brown robes of a culdee strode into the space between the rushing mob and our army, his arms lofted in the air. "Stop, I say!"

Something in his presence billowed like thunder. The mob, seeing his face, held one another back, tripping and then righting themselves, halting in their tracks.

"It's him! Do not harm him," I heard a man say.

"Stop, men, stop. Listen to what he might say," said another.

Mungo, too, sensed his power.

"Who is this man?" he demanded. "What is the meaning of this?"

The man in the brown robes moved slowly toward the former bishop until they stood face-to-face.

"My name is Brother Thomas," he said. "And I have come to minister to the good Christians of Partick."

CHAPTER 41

Languoreth

I sat in the dark hut in stillness, battling the thought that whatever happened beyond the locked door was beyond my control.

I had begun to lose sense of time passing, of night or of day, when I once again heard voices beyond my cell walls.

This time, it was many.

I closed my eyes. This was it, then. My brother had failed. The Christian mob had come to carry me away.

"Open the door," a deep voice commanded.

I would not fight, nor would they see my fear. It would only feed their satisfaction.

The door was thrown open. But it was a familiar face that appeared. I rubbed my eyes against the light.

"Torin?"

He strode in and helped me stand. Taking my arm, he led me toward the door.

"Whatever has . . . Can someone please tell me . . ."

"All will be revealed, my lady," he said.

I stepped out into the early evening. Firepits were lit and servants were hurrying round the grounds as if preparing a feast. A tremendous crowd—hundreds, more—were gathered in the courtyard and as far as the eye could see. As I stopped and stood there, staring, they erupted at the sight of me into a magnificent roar.

My brother, Eira, Diarmid, Maelgwn. The servants from Cadzow. Aela and countless scores of other bright, smiling faces. I blinked as their cries washed over me. Rhydderch stood at a distance beside his mother, Elufed. The look she gave me was one of reassurance.

The crowd fell silent as Rhydderch approached and slowly extended his hand.

"You cannot forgive me," I said. "That is how it seemed. I—I don't understand."

"Perhaps all cannot be forgiven," he said. "At least, not on this day. But a man has come forward who has helped me see reason. We have spent many hours in conversation, since this very morning. He has reminded me of the virtue I once found in the true Christian way." Rhydderch inclined his head and I turned to see Brother Thomas, the culdee, standing not far behind. He bowed, giving a soft smile. He had stepped from his shadowed forest, and not a moment too soon.

"Moreover," Rhydderch went on, "he told me a story involving our daughter that you may need to hear recounted yourself before you believe it to be true."

I soon learned the details of all I had missed whilst locked in my cell: how the Army of Stags had stood in a righteous peace before the king; how Mungo's mob had nearly roused a battle, but they were put down and sent off by Rhydderch and the Christian lords who stood with Brother Thomas. Those who had favored Brother Telleyr had been backing Brother Thomas all along, carefully planning the moment he might at last step in and rid us all of Mungo.

Mungo, in turn, had fled with his monks. Torin had it on good authority that he planned this time to run all the way to Rome.

The eve had become a festival, with people bringing food and kindling. There was music and dancing, and we had just carried out our twelfth barrel of ale. People of the Old Way and the new together, making peace, offering a hand. As it had once been.

Somewhere in the trees, beyond the music and laughter, an owl hooted as Brother Thomas and I sat by a fire in the cool autumn air. I sighed to release the tension of it all, leaning in.

"Why did you not tell me you had met Angharad when I first came to see you in the forest?" I asked him.

He was not a man to speak quickly just because one sought an answer. I waited as he considered it, weighing his words.

"I had promised to see your daughter returned safely home. But the priestess granted my freedom only upon the condition that I flee. She warned that if I dared return, her warriors would kill me. I came to Strathclyde intending to see you and tell you of her whereabouts. But it was your husband who granted my audience instead. I was cowardly, and full of shame for having abandoned your daughter. I said nothing, offering my penance daily to the forest instead. By the time you came to me in the wood, years had passed. I'd heard the bright news that Angharad had returned. It seemed, then, there was little to say."

"She spoke of you fondly, but she never mentioned your name," I said.

"Ah," he said. "When you arrived at my hut, I realized perhaps you were right. I'd been far too long in hiding. Since that day, I doubled my efforts and began offering a sermon in the wood. More and more people came in secret. Lords and their ladies. They helped keep me safe from Mungo's foul dealings."

"And Rhydderch has agreed to keep you on as his counsel?" I asked.

"Yes." Brother Thomas smiled. "It would seem our gods work in mysterious ways."

Across the grass I spotted my brother and Maelgwn.

"If you'll excuse me, Brother Thomas?"

The culdee nodded and waved his hand.

I could feel Rhydderch's eyes on me, but I wanted to show my husband he had nothing more to fear. Crossing the courtyard, I looked down on Maelgwn where he sat, his familiar sloping shoulders, his strong, familiar hands.

"Thank you for all you have done for me," I told him. Hoping he would know all that I meant and more. Maelgwn's green eyes lit with understanding.

"You are welcome, Languoreth of Cadzow."

"Will you return to the Caledonian Wood now that the stags have seen the day won?"

"Yes," he said. "For a while, at least. Until we are needed again."

"You are a hero of the ages, Maelgwn Pendragon."

With that, he smiled. "A hero of the ages? That remains to be seen."

CHAPTER 42

Angharad

The Northern Sea
Land of the Picts
Late September, AD 584

The war fleet of Bridei raced eastward by sea, carrying Angharad back toward the place where her journey had begun. The Firth of Tay in the land of the Picts. First as a child, taken by raiders. Then as a novice, seeking her teacher.

Now, as a Wisdom Keeper, the Gods delivered her here.

She had survived two battles in her lifetime. But survival did little to quell her fear. Once again, Angharad found herself in the midst of a battle with people she loved on both sides. Somewhere beyond the water, Artúr mac Aedan was on horseback, driving his men through the kindgom of Circenn. Cai rode beside him, with Ewan in their company. Poor Ewan. Even grown, she could not imagine he'd found a stomach for war.

Rhainn and Briochan stood at the helm of the ship, heads bowed as Briochan placed a talisman gently round his son's neck. She watched as Briochan pulled Rhainn's forehead to his own, the blessing he murmured carried off by the sea.

As the fleet turned south, she spotted Pictish warships skulking the coastline, patrolling. Boats joined their fleet in growing numbers, and Angharad felt a shiver of hope as their massive fleet angled west, entering the wide mouth of the Tay.

Talorcan and Muirenn of Dùn Dèagh manned one of those ships. But when Angharad thought of her friends, she could not escape her vision of blood. She could not see beyond it. Soon they would be marching in a horde of soldiers, marching to meet the Scots in a battle made to end the era of Bridei and his kingdom forever.

They reached the harbor of Asreth in a race of rope and sails.

Warriors rode up, breathless, reporting that Artúr and his forces had decimated the lands to the west, leaving hundreds, if not thousands, dead. The Picts of Fortriu did not have the luxury of rest. Artúr and his army were closing in, and they would not submit themselves to a siege. They would march to meet the enemy on the sprawling plain below. There would be Wisdom Keepers on both sides, perched like battle ravens, calling down curses, offering the warriors their strength. This was the role of Keepers, who were, by law, exempt from war. They were not to be harmed.

Angharad had busied herself that morning in anointing each shield with sacred oil that she had blessed with a battle charm. Her weapons were her words, their power like arrows from the land of the Gods.

But Artúr's Keepers had curses, too.

Artúr's god, Manannan, was only another name for the same god honored by the Picts in their drowning pool.

Both sides held a rage equal to the other.

This was not like any other battle Angharad had seen.

In the Battle of the Caledonian Wood, she and Ariane had summoned foul weather. Now, in this battle, she sought only to keep the powers of the Cailleach at bay.

No mist must snake the fortress walls, disguising attackers.

There must be no fierce rain or wind. Our arrows must fly true.

Just ahead, Rhainn spoke to the king, low-voiced.

"We will keep the Wisdom Keepers on the ramparts, just behind the archers," he said.

"Good," Bridei agreed. "If anything should happen, they shall be safe there."

Angharad startled nearly from her skin at the grip of a hand on her shoulder. But it was only Briochan, leading his horse.

"Are you frightened, Ton Velen?"

It seemed one hundred years since Angharad had been a young woman sailing to become his Initiate, terrified that the Wisdom Keeper would know her fear. Now she looked up at him, her eyes speaking the truth.

"The Gods grant us visions so that we know what may come," Briochan said. "Your visions are a blessing. You must always let them guide you."

"Why do you speak as if saying goodbye?" she said.

Briochan looked at her, his brown eyes pooled with warmth. "Because I have lost those who had no opportunity to say goodbye. And you have been dear to me, Angharad Ton Velen."

"The men cannot know that Briochan, of all men, has given up before the battle has yet to begin," she whispered fiercely.

"Oh, I have not given up, Ton Velen." He smiled and reached to draw out his sword. "Mark my words: the Scots have come, and before this battle is done, I will spill their blood."

"No, you will be beside me, upon the ramparts," Angharad said. "That is their plan."

"Your place is on the ramparts, Angharad. We shall seek out your strength. Shower them with curses and think well of me. For I ride into battle beside my two sons."

Panic roared. They'd reached the outer ramparts of Asreth, where warriors were charging this way and that, readying the fortress for war. The towering gates stood open, heavily manned. Drums pounded in the distance, ominous in the hills, and Briochan looked toward the sound.

"This is it, then. They come," he said.

The king kicked his horse into a trot, barking out orders. "Archers will post on the ramparts above! Keepers, stand with them! Hurry, now! Go!"

Nay, this was not like any other battle Angharad had seen.

It was all happening so fast.

As Bridei and Rhainn directed the men to the battlefield, Briochan turned to her, his eyes steady on her face.

"Call and I will answer, Angharad Ton Velen. Even when I am gone, I will be with you still."

Her teacher's words undid her. But he did not need her pain.

He'd asked for her strength.

Angharad nodded, tears choking her throat. And with one last look, Briochan was gone.

War horns were blasting. The din was deafening. In the autumn grasses beneath the fortress, Bridei son of Maelchon and his army of Picts would make their last stand.

The Cruithni screamed, beating their shields. Just as Angharad reached the fortress gate, Rhainn turned and glanced back.

"Gods keep you, Ton Velen," he called, straining to see over the spears of his men.

"Rhainn," she shouted, tapping her breast. "Commander of Fortriu. The Gods guide your blade."

Reaching into her cloak, she snatched out the iron bird, holding it aloft in her fist.

Rhainn smiled then, a rare, beautiful thing. And then, tapping two fingers to his breast, he disappeared into the fray.

"Hurry!" a guard barked. "We must close the gates!"

Angharad ran to join the scores of archers along with the Keepers, her robes tangling at her feet.

"Steady, now, Ton Velen," said an old Keeper as he caught her. "Steady as the sea. The day is long."

Tears blurred her vision as she raced up the guard walk, emerging on the heights of the fortress of Asreth. Angharad smelled the chalky tang of quicklime from the buckets that lined the rampart's edge, ready to scald skin from bone. Along the walk, archers stood as far as the eye could see, bows in hand, ready to draw. She was meant to be their strength, too. They must not see her weep.

Stepping up behind the archers, she took a breath and peered across the broad expanse to where the Picts were massed in the field below. Bridei drove his warhorse along the line in a gallop, his shouts carried away by the wind. In the front line, she caught the bright white of Briochan's robes. He sat, back straight, his gaze fixed on the approaching army. Beside him stood Rhainn, his sword at the ready.

The Keepers on the rampart stood shoulder to shoulder. As Angharad lifted her eyes to the horizon, she saw the Scots in a clouded mass, coming over the rise. Far across the valley, she swore she could see the banner of Artúr.

Angharad closed her eyes, summoning her strength. The force that came was stronger than the tides.

The two armies stopped at a distance, the hills resounding with a deafening cry.

Bridei turned and, with a flick of his hand, signaled the archery commander.

"Loose!" the commander shouted.

Angharad reached her hands to the sky, building her curse. Arrows arced safely overtop Bridei's warriors and the Scots ducked or dropped as the archers set fresh arrows in their bows.

The battle had begun.

"Loose!" he commanded again. A thousand spears glinted, raised at the ready. The footmen charged. The armies collided in a clatter of metal.

And then, out of the corner of her eye, Angharad spotted movement to the west. She dropped her lofted arms and turned, squinting. It could not be. Another army appeared from the cover of hills, speeding on horses as if born on their backs, their long hair dyed lightning white.

Miathi Picts.

Traitors.

And there, to the east: a second retinue of Miathi, cutting toward the outer line of Bridei's forces, flanking them! The two new armies wrought chaos, pressing from either side, forcing Bridei's men on the wings to turn from battle to meet their blades.

Bridei's army was pinched, forced into the middle.

Then came the charge.

Angharad could only watch as Artúr's cavalry charged through the center of Bridei's line like a scythe, men dropping in sheaves. Down below, at the foot of the rampart walls, a line of Miathi Picts crouched beneath their shields like beetles, warding off the sailing arrows as they tried to mount the defenses.

And then a grappling hook arced over the rampart wall, its prongs sinking with a clunk into the timber lacing.

"The quicklime!" an archer shouted as one hook became ten.

He leaned over the lip of the rampart, leveling his arrow at the Miathi attackers, but no sooner had he drawn his bow than he cried out and fell back, stuck by a half dozen arrows. Artúr's archers were supporting the enemy Miathi, targeting the archers now.

"Grab the lime buckets!" Angharad cried as the Miathi began to shimmy up their ropes. She dashed to the rampart edge, lifting a bucket in hand, and leaned over, scattering its contents in a powdery mist down on the attackers. She heard screams as the lime burned, men dropping like ants flicked from a wall. But there were more, too many. Battle-painted faces were popping up over the rampart wall with shocks of white hair as more archers began to fall. Stabbed, pierced, and dragged by a grappling hook. Halved by a sword. Warriors rushed to fill the vacant spaces. Those Keepers not dusting lime down hurried to pick up fallen weapons and joined Angharad at the wall, whacking at the attackers' heads.

Angharad's bucket was empty, and lime was scarce. She turned from the wall in search of something—anything—to use to defend herself.

"Ton Velen!" a Wisdom Keeper shouted. "Watch out!"

That was the last thing she heard before everything went dark.

Angharad woke in a panic, still in blackness, the terror of battle still pounding through her veins. Her head throbbed in stabs of hot pain. Her nose stung with the musk of body odor, and she was being crushed and jostled every which way. She thrust out her arms in an attempt to scramble to her feet only to hear a muffled cry as she struck what felt like somebody's ribs.

"You're all right, you're all right. Try to open your eyes. They've gone crusted shut," a woman said.

Chest heaving, Angharad sat up and rubbed at her eyes. Blinking and pulling the crusted bits, she looked down at her fingers to find they were covered with rust.

Blood. From her head, judging by the feel of it.

"I was struck on the head," she said.

"I can see that," the woman said.

People sat round her in all states of misery, wounded and softly weeping. A prison cart. Its rough planks beneath her pricked splinters into her bottom as they rattled over a bump. She sat at the back of the cart, closest to its bolted door. Angharad had the sense that they were traveling in a caravan. The woman who had spoken was elderly and, save for a bruise, looked mostly unharmed.

She searched the cart for familiar faces, but saw no one.

"Do you know where we're going?" Angharad asked.

"Nay."

Visions from the massacre charged through her head. "Is Bridei—"

"Dead," she said.

"And what of the others? What of Briochan the Keeper or Rhainn, his son?"

The old woman's face creased; she shook her head. As the weight of it sank in, Angharad buried her face in her hands, her mouth stretching with a sob.

"There, there," the woman said. "You're lucky to be alive. It's not often that Keepers are harmed, but the Miathi who took the fortress seemed to make an exception. I am sorry to tell you, many are dead."

Angharad pressed the heels of her hands to her eyes, taking a breath. "Who's got us?" she asked, straining to see between the slats of the cart. "Picts or Scots?"

"What does it matter?" The old woman laughed.

Angharad looked at her as if she might be deranged.

The old woman was quiet as the day wore on. The air grew cold. The Cruithni in the prison cart huddled together for warmth, their wounds mingling. There was nowhere for anyone to urinate except where they sat, and soon a sharp stench gagged at her throat. The cart jerked to a stop sometime before dark. Angharad looked up, her head still pounding, her thoughts coming muted and bleary, as if traveling through water. She listened to the voices of the warriors as they moved about, setting up camp.

Picts. They'd been taken by the Miathi.

A shudder trailed along her arms as memories of their garish, leering faces flashed. Who was to say what they'd do? She drew her knees to her chest, readying for a long night of bitter cold. But then, to her horror, she heard the grassy trample of boots approaching. The prisoners pressed together as if that might make them invisible. But the warriors were not targeting their cart—not yet. Someone cried out as the warriors barked orders, dragging the prisoners from the cart ahead.

"Move aside!"

"Line up!"

"Do it now!"

"Please," one of the Cruithni rasped. "I can't hardly stand!"

"Do not speak!" a warrior shouted. There was silence, then the sound of a single pair of boots, as if moving along a line, inspecting.

"Nay," a voice said at last. "She's not here."

That voice . . . she knew it. But her mind was addled, her insides warring between guilt and hope.

"Load them back in!" one of the Miathi commanded. His voice held an edge, as if he had tired of his directive.

The Miathi were nearing their cart now, and Angharad sat pinned closest to the door. There was a fumbling and a clang, and then the bolt slid open. Angharad pressed herself back against the slats.

"Come on, then." A Miathi warrior appeared, his battle paint smeared and cracked from the fight. "Let's see who we've got."

She glanced round at the wounded. "How in the Gods' names do they expect these poor people to move? Some of them are half-dead," she said.

The warrior's eyes flashed at her nerve, and he lifted his hand. Angharad braced herself for the blow she knew was coming. But then that deep voice—one no man dared disobey.

"Stop. Move aside."

Angharad blinked, unwilling to believe. But there before her, his curly reddish hair flattened by sweat and his battle armor bloodied, stood Artúr.

His blue eyes took in the state of her, touching on her bloodied head, crusted eyes, and soiled clothing.

"Angharad."

She nodded, trying to speak, but no words came out.

"Here," he said. "Come out of there."

He reached out as she moved stiffly, dropping from the back of the cart unsteadily into high grass.

"This is her. We've got her," he said to the men. "Lock it up."

Angharad pressed her lips, fighting back tears. The prisoners began to shout and wail, banging their fists against the side of the cart.

How was this right? In these carts, people suffered. Her face burned with anger, with shame. Yet the animal part of her wanted to weep in relief. Artúr took her arm, helping her.

"We've been looking for you," he said. "You healed me, lady priestess. I told you I would not forget it."

Warriors turned to stare as Artúr led Angharad gently through the maze of tents that covered the fields. Horses stood, asleep on their feet, their hooves black with mud and their knees stained by blood.

"Young Ewan!" Artúr called out. "We've found her."

"Ewan?" Angharad echoed. It all seemed a strange dream.

"Young Ewan told me you'd be among the Keepers. We've searched every prison cart." He glanced at her head. "How did that happen?"

Artúr was speaking too quickly, and Angharad's thoughts oozed like honey from a jar. She opened her mouth just as a lanky man with a shock of pale hair jogged toward them.

"You found her, my lord?"

He was so grown that if it hadn't been for his hair, Angharad mightn't have recognized him. "Ewan?" she said.

At the sight of her, Ewan's shoulders slumped in relief. "Aye, it's me."

Artúr was still looking at her wound. "The men were not to harm any Keepers. How did this happen?" he demanded, as if it were her fault.

Angharad reached gingerly to explore it. "The Miathi," she said.

"Gartnait's men." Artúr's face darkened. "They disobeyed me."

Angharad stopped, head spinning, and drew away. It was all too much. "And what of the others?" she demanded, her sluggish mind gaining pace with her tangle of emotions.

"I'm sorry?" said Artúr.

"I said what of the others?" she repeated, growing hysterical. "What of Briochan and Bridei? What of Rhainn and his child, who is now without a father? What of all the prisoners who suffer, wounded in the carts?!"

Artúr frowned. Hurt flashed, and his blue eyes went stony. "She needs rest," he said to Ewan, as if she did not stand there before him. "Take her to the tent and send for the healer. See that she gets cleaned up. I'm going to scout."

Artúr ducked into the tent only long enough to pull out a cloak, handing it to her almost roughly.

Then, spear in hand, he slipped off into the woods.

CHAPTER 43

Artúr

Hadn't Angharad any idea the lengths he had gone to find her? Artúr stalked off into the forest, exhausted and fuming. He needed a moment alone, to breathe. To think.

Here in the wood, the trees wove their spiderweb of branches, snuffing out the fading autumn sky. The forest was rich with the smell of rain. His men were shattered from battle and badly in need of rest. But something within him marched on, restless. The Battle of Asreth had cost him dearly. Artúr still did not know how many men were dead. And then there was Angharad. He'd saved her life, and gone to great lengths to do so. In return, she'd been ungrateful. She hadn't any idea the dealings of war.

Small sticks snapped beneath his feet as Artúr headed deeper into the wood. He breathed in the stillness and felt a stab in the ribs. Cracked from a shield slam. But the smell of autumn leaves and the gilled underbellies of mushroom caps filled his nose. He sank into the quiet as he would the embrace of a mother. *There, now.*

The trees, too, were breathing. Birch and elm. Hazel and ash. A slender deer trail meandered through the scrub, following the path of a burn, and he struck off to follow it.

As he moved through the wood, the squelch of flesh impaled by spears and the weeping splits from thrusting blades played patterns

behind his eyes. The gore never left you. Not truly. But he trained his
eyes on what was before him: shriveled red berries in animal scat, broken acorns, bark mauled from a tree. He listened to the forest speak.
Bear. Squirrel. A roebuck testing his antlers. There was no sign of
men. For a moment Artúr's shoulders eased, but then he spotted it. A
narrow path, man-made by the looks of it, an earthen memory of many
feet. Not caring for surprises, he followed the trail dutifully through
the brush until it spilled into a lofty clearing of oaks. Old ones, by
the look of them. They were mossy and thick boughed, their trunks
gnarled with age. He narrowed his eyes, blinking. For a moment it
almost seemed as if there were faces looking through the bark in the
twilight. Gods of the glade. Or a trick of the light? A recumbent stone
altar in the center of the trees left little doubt: Artúr had stumbled
upon a sacred grove. Bird flesh pricked his skin.

It can be no accident, he thought. Anyone who'd ever witnessed the
chaos of battle knew survival was not based only upon merit. Survival
was bestowed. Gods-given. And here was a temple. Artúr could not
pass it by. Bowing his head, he stepped carefully into the center of the
grove. The altar stone was bluish gray and flecked with yellow lichen,
but a cuplike depression at its center was smooth and clear of fungus,
waiting.

Damp seeped into his trousers as he knelt in the leaf loam. He
closed his eyes a moment, praying. Then, pulling his dirk from his belt,
he pierced the pad of his third finger. Blood beaded, then dropped,
splattering the stone. He watched as it seeped into the carved depression as if the old stone were thirsty.

He thought of the men he had lost, sleeping in the dark earth.
Chaorunn had spoken the rites. They had found their way to the Summerlands. He let the battle memory swell, filling him, and thought of
the Gods who had kept him alive.

Thanks in blood for blood I've not shed. I will not waste the time I've been given. As if in answer, a breeze rustled the dying leaves overhead. Standing, he wiped his dirk on the hem of his tunic and sheathed it. He should get on. The men might worry if he lingered too long and send hounds out after him. But just as Artúr turned to follow the path back in the direction of camp, a voice caught his ear, drifting.

A woman's voice. Singing.

Something beyond himself compelled him to follow. He softened his boot steps, listening for the far-off strains as he traveled deeper into a thickening wood. The burn began to dwindle, its trickle hinting at a source that bubbled up from the earth. And then, through the trees, he spotted it: a small, dark forest pool.

A spindly hawthorn bowed over the pool's edge as if curious to see its own reflection. And there beside the pool stood a woman in a coarse brown dress, her long, thin hair white as ash. A tattered gray shawl hung from her shoulders.

"Shite," Artúr mumbled, cursing his curiosity. Song Keepers warned of such encounters in the wood. Of women such as this. White-haired hags at forest pools were better left alone. What child had not listened to Songs of the Cailleach on black winter nights? A touch of her finger could freeze a man's heart. Shape-shifter, weatherworker, giant. She roamed the glens and high places, minding red deer and wild creatures, taking their shapes as it pleased her. And twilight was a tricky time: things were not always as they seemed.

Don't be daft. It's only an old woman, Artúr thought. And her voice. It was soft and ephemeral, full of memory. It summoned the cool and papery touch of his grandmother's hand. Artúr watched as the old woman ceased her song. Leaning over the leaf-strewn pool, she seemed to be mumbling. Artúr took a few steps nearer, trying to catch her words.

"Look at my skin, stretched tight on the bone, where kings have pressed their lips," she said. "The pain, the pain. The sun gives its youth to everyone, touching with gold. In me, the cold. The cold! Yet still a seed burns there. For when I loved, I loved young men."

She tossed her head back with a cackle of delight. But then her eyes must have caught the sight of her own reflection, for her face fell at the sight.

"Oh," she wailed. "Oh."

Tears rolled down her furrowed cheeks and she swiped at them like a child. Pity swelled in Artúr's chest. When she spoke again, her voice had gone brittle.

"Now still the sea rears and plunges into me. Shoving, rolling through my head, images of the drifting dead."

So enraptured was Artúr that he scarcely noticed the old woman look up with a start, peering into the dim.

"Who's there?" she barked.

His stomach twitched in hunger. The hour was growing late. But he did not wish to frighten an old woman alone in the wood. Artúr stepped from the shadows.

"Greetings, grandmother. I mean you no harm."

"Eh?" The old woman narrowed her eyes. "Young men ought to be wary, spying on women in the wood. They might see such things they mightn't wish to see." She shifted her weight between her feet, then threw up her hands with a huff.

"Well, now that yer here, ye needn't just stand there. Canna you see? I need help wi' my boots." She made a show of hunching with a grunt, struggling to reach her battered leather booties.

"Well enough, grandmother. I'll lend a hand," Artúr said, closing the distance.

As he neared, he saw her face was a map of a thousand creases. Her pale eyes were cold, weak as winter light, and something warned Artúr he must not look too deeply.

"Your boots," he said gallantly. He bent to aid her but recoiled just as swiftly, his nostrils stinging with the sharp tang of shite.

Aye, it was shite. The soles of her booties were crusted with it.

"Er—you seem to have trod through a fair spot of cattle muck," Artúr said. A whole pasture, more like.

"Aie me." The old woman blinked, her blue eyes playful. She knew of it, then. She plopped unceremoniously on the ground with a grunt, crossing her arms over her thick woolen shawl. "Well. Will ye help me or no?"

Artúr bit back his displeasure, setting aside his spear. "Aye. Aye."

Squatting at the spring's edge, he gripped the booties as best as he could above the muck, tugging them from her stockingless feet with some effort, only to find the evil stench was like that of a hydra: it had sprung another head! Her feet themselves were yellow-toed and smelled of spoiled innards.

An old woman after all, for surely Gods did not stink as such.

"There, now," he managed, setting the booties aside. The old woman grinned and sighed in relief as she scooted to the water's edge, plunging her feet into the clear little pool.

"Ahh, but that's lovely," she murmured. "It pains me, you know, walking the land. I've been walking the land such a terrible long time."

She peered at Artúr from beneath wisps of white lashes. "I canna bend, y' see. Be a good lad and give 'em a rub."

Artúr's laugh was astonished, making him cough. A servant's task? Surely the woman's weak eyes left her blind to his torque. And yet, something of the old woman did bring to mind his grandmother, gone now many winters. And he had only just given thanks for his life at the grove. Showing a kindness would not be the end of him.

"Rub them. Aye," Artúr said gruffly. Kneeling, he reached for the woman's feet beneath the water. The spring was clear, cold enough to sting his fingers. Veins covered the tops of her feet like tree roots, winter's blue beneath pale white skin, and the gaze upon him pierced like wind.

He thought of her mumblings. *Where kings have pressed their lips.* Kings were wedded to the goddess of the land, were they not?

Ach, Artúr, don't be a fool. They're twilight tales is all. These were the feet of an old woman, bones fragile beneath his grip. How his men would laugh to see him spooked by the presence of a little old hag. As the bits of dirt and grime floated away, the old woman smiled, contented. Artúr prayed no unsuspecting traveler found their way to this spring in hopes of a drink.

"There, now." He took her feet from the water, folding them gently into his cloak and patting them dry.

"*Go raibh maith agat,*" she thanked him, drawing her feet from his cloak.

"*Sé ur bheatha, seanmhair,*" he replied. *No need to thank me, grand-mother.* He made to draw away, but the old woman reached up, catching his sleeve.

"Y'r a good lad." She smiled, wistful, revealing her gums. "A fair lad, and strong. I'll give y' a gift of thanks in return."

"Nay, nay," Artúr said, but the old woman was leaning already, brow furrowed, narrowing her eyes as she looked into the pool.

Curious, he watched, waiting as her hand drifted over its surface, dipping a gnarled finger in. Leaves shivered and swirled on the dark skin of water as she traced round in circles, pale eyes shifting as if she saw something before her. As if she were scrying.

"What is it, *seanmhair*? Is there something you see?"

"I see . . ." She closed her eyes a moment, then opened them in shock. "There ye stand at the head of a great host," she pronounced, her voice deep with the knowing of a Seer. "*Ceannasaí.* Commander, they'll call ye. Mark me, there's no other so fit. And ye'll have all your triumphs. 'Tis you, lad, who'll hold back the wave. Eleven, eleven . . ."

The old woman trailed off.

Artúr peered over her shoulder into the pool, but to his eyes the surface remained unchanged.

"Eleven?" he prodded. The old woman frowned crossly.

"Aye. E'ery acorn must drop," she said.

She looked into the pool's depths another moment. Then at last she withdrew her hand. The old woman blinked and turned, looking up at him. Her pale, wintry eyes were deep now with pity.

"E'ery acorn must drop. But thine will fall sooner than others. Beware Camlann."

The sorrow in her voice made his chest tight.

"*Seanmhair*," he said. "You would foretell my death?"

The old woman bowed her head. And then, from a distance, the trill of a bird sounded through the forest. A thrush, of course, and wrong for the hour. Cai was calling, awaiting his return. Artúr straightened and stood, smoothing his cloak. He felt as if he'd been kneeling at the pool's edge for ages.

"I fear I must go," he said.

For while she mightn't be a god, the woman was a Seer. And although she might seem motherly, something pricked his skin, as if there could be a danger in lingering too long.

The old woman nodded, but her snowy eyes had gone distant. And as she watched the water's surface, Artúr quite suddenly felt small, as insignificant as an ant.

Above the clawing branches of the hawthorn, the sky had grown dark, and it seemed the old woman's weather was shifting.

"Farewell, *seanmhair*." Artúr bowed. "I am grateful for your warning."

The woman did not stir. Artúr drew his cloak about him, its hem still damp from the old woman's feet, and took his leave, moving briskly across the clearing.

Beware Camlann. Her words echoed. Suddenly, at his back, her presence seemed a mountain, an ancient, rocky giant with a wind-blasted peak.

"Lad!" she called out, her voice deep and commanding. "Lad!"

But Artúr did not stop. He pressed on quickly through the under-brush.

He did not look back for fear of what he might see.

CHAPTER 44

Artúr

He returned to camp expecting to find Cai scowling with worry. But as it was, the men hadn't seemed to notice his departure at all. They were gathered round the fire, enraptured by Angharad as she told them a story. Her head was bandaged but her gray eyes were bright, her auburn hair lit like gold in the burn of firelight.

"An ancient legend tells of a great flood." She leaned in. "Forget what stories you have heard from the Israelites or the Christians. In the end, there was only one salmon who survived, and her name was Fintan. Fintan, Flood-Survivor. The waters carried her eggs across vast distances. The eggs traveled the coursing waters until they were pushed into all the fresh places. They settled and nestled into decaying leaves and cool-bottomed pools. They hatched in the belly of every spring . . ."

He did not know what lay ahead, but he wondered, for the second time, if the fates had somehow drawn them together. Perhaps this time their paths would converge.

As Angharad spoke, Artúr found a log and sat, closing his eyes to the smooth sound of her voice. His mind soon drifted from her story to floods yet to come. To fame, and the warnings of old women. He thought of his son, their own seedling, tucked safe in Vanora's arms. He thought of his brother Gartnait, now king of the Picts.

He wondered how many battles his body could fight before it was broken.

He was feeling warm and drowsy when something small and hard pelted his head, then rolled onto his lap. Artúr squinted in the firelight, picking it up.

It was an acorn, cold from the night air, smooth and brown.

Every acorn must drop. He considered it a moment. His father had once told him that an acorn was a talisman that brought good fortune and wealth. But looking at it now, he knew it meant so much more. *Beware Camlann.* Artúr took the acorn and tucked it safely into the small leather satchel he wore at his belt.

From this tiny pebble of wood, a mighty oak could grow.

Artúr did not know when he might fall. He could only hope that, in seasons to come, the splitting of his shell might nourish something far greater than himself. Perhaps even something as strong and everlasting as a tree.

A NOTE FROM THE AUTHOR

Anyone who has really lived will tell you that lives are like rivers: fast flowing in some places, rushing toward a fall, and at other times, when obstructed, they broaden and slow. There are blockages that must be overcome, trials and initiations. The river then moves at the pace it requires, content with its shadowed eddies. This is what writing this book has felt like to me.

Four years in the making, this novel reveals moments in the "becoming" of more than one character. It's the gathering of strength and the creation of foundations needed for any legend to last. To me, these books are not so much separate entities as they are simply different sections of one long river. A journey through the entirety of a life in installments, offered in however many sessions it takes to travel from beginning to end.

The Shadowed Land is the first novel to tell the story of the historical figure Artúr mac Aedan. King Arthur has captured the hearts and pens of writers for more than a thousand years. Most early medieval historians believe Arthur to be a mythical figure. Scholars more willing to risk their academic reputations have spilled innumerable pots of ink trying to work out the locations of Arthur's twelve battles as listed by a monk called Nennius (a Welsh Briton credited with writing the *Historia Brittonum*, c. AD 830), to no avail, or tried to pin Arthur to Wales or England. Ties to Cornwall were invented in an attempt to please a lord who had just acquired property there. Any ties to Glastonbury are similarly false: in a clever ploy to draw paying tourists to the abbey, the monks of Glastonbury Abbey dug up a pair of skeletons in 1191, claiming they were the remains of King Arthur and Queen Guinevere. That's long since proven to have been a hoax.

However, with the publication of *Finding Arthur: The True Origins of the Once and Future King* (Abrams Press, 2013), Adam Ardrey proved beyond any reasonable doubt that there is indeed a historical figure who inspired the legend of King Arthur. But he was not a man of Wales or of England. He belongs to Scotland. Artúr mac Aedan was a historical warlord who led a coalition of Britons, Scots, and Picts to victory against the Angles from the 580s until the end of the sixth century. His father's existence is not contested: Aedan mac Gabrahn was the king of Dalriada and Mannau from AD 574 to 609 and was active in several successful military campaigns.

Why academia has continued to turn up its nose at the convincing argument of a Scottish Arthur—not to mention its lack of interest in the historical existence of one of early Scotland's most powerful queens, Languoreth of Strathclyde—I cannot say. Rather than rehash Ardrey's research here, I will direct you to his books, which many of you familiar with this series know provided the initial inspiration for my own work.

By popularizing these figures in fiction, I hope to direct more attention to the validity of Ardrey's discoveries. Meanwhile, there has been some encouraging progress in regard to Artúr of late. The first biography of his father, Aedan mac Gabrahn, was published in 2022: *Áedán of the Gaels: King of the Scots* by Keith Coleman (Pen & Sword). But there is a long way yet to go.

Digging for Artúr

So who was Artúr mac Aedan? He is not the King Arthur of myth from popular film and fiction, living in castles with a round wooden table and jousting knights, cuckolded by the handsome Lancelot. The real Artúr was a warlord who lived in wooden halls, at ease with navigation by land and by water. To re-create the real Artúr, we must strip away the centuries of magnificent nonsense layered upon him. I began with the works of Geoffrey of Monmouth and Sir Thomas Malory, two early writers who created the cornerstones of the Arthurian legend, both of whom wrote many hundreds of years after Artúr's death, in the twelfth and fifteenth centuries respectively.

The legitimacy of Geoffrey of Monmouth (author of the *History of the Kings of Britain* and two books on Merlin) was questioned as early as 1150, when the twelfth-century historian William of Newburgh wrote, "It is quite clear that everything this man wrote about Arthur and his successors, or indeed about his predecessors from Vortigern onwards, was made up, partly by himself and partly by others." Scholars today consider the *History of the Kings of Britain* a "literary forgery" containing little reliable history.

Le Morte d'Arthur by Sir Thomas Malory is one of the best-known pieces of Arthurian literature. It has been repurposed by countless authors to create their own Arthurian tales, from Alfred, Lord Tennyson to Marion Zimmer Bradley. But this work, too, lacks integrity. Written nearly one thousand years after Artúr's death, the work comprises translated poems from the thirteenth-century Old French Vulgate romances and the *Alliterative Morte Arthure*, a Middle English poem derived from Geoffrey of Monmouth's *History of the Kings of Britain*.

The twelfth-century French writer Chrétien de Troyes invented the character of Lancelot, along with Lancelot's affair with Guinevere.

Prior to Chrétien, Lancelot does not appear in any of the Arthurian tales. A noblewoman named Marie de Champagne had assigned Chrétien the task of writing *Lancelot, the Knight of the Cart*. Known for her keen interest in courtly love, it is believed that Marie suggested that de Troyes incorporate the affair into the story.

Faulty cornerstones dismissed, it was time to dig deeper.

Ernest Hemingway once said, "The writer's job is to tell the truth." We may not always know a truth, but we can feel it in the core of ourselves, humming and plucking at our inner strings. Human truths in a story resonate; they are things that make us smile, fear, and weep. It wasn't until I dove even more deeply into the Arthurian source material that I realized why, despite nearly a decade of attempts, I had been unable to connect with the writings of Monmouth or Malory: I could appreciate them, but they didn't feel true.

The earliest mention of Arthur is in the *Book of Aneirin*, in the poem "Y Gododdin," which reads:

He fed black ravens on the rampart of a fortress
Though he was no Arthur.

While the *Book of Aneirin* manuscript dates from the thirteenth century, "Y Gododdin" is believed to have been composed in the year 602, and there is linguistic evidence to support this.

Both the *Annals of Ulster* and the *Annals of Tigernach* of Ireland detail the military campaigns of Aedan mac Gabrahn and his sons, listing Arthur as a son of Aedan. Both annals record Arthur's death and the name of the battle that cost him his life. (The tenth-century *Annales Cambriae* also mention Arthur.)

Arthur's twelve battles are listed by Nennius, author of the *Historia Brittonum*, as noted earlier.

Finally, there is the *Life of Columba* by Adomnán (625–704), in which Aedan mac Gabrahn and his sons are widely featured. In it, Columba prophesies that Arthur will never be king but will "fall in battle, slain by enemies."

Saint Columba was the abbot of Iona and a tremendous political player in early medieval Ireland and Scotland, a contemporary of Aedan's and Artúr's. Written only one hundred years after the saint's death, it incorporates elements from a lost earlier life of Columba (*Liber de virtutibus sancti Columbae*) written as early as 640.

Study of these earlier sources reveal Aedan to be a warlike, incredibly ambitious father whose power by the end of his lifetime eclipsed many of the kings who had come before. Rather than painting Artúr as his lone celebrity child, the early sources indicate Artúr was one of many sons vying for power and marching off to battle at the behest of their father.

That Artúr managed to stay alive as long as he did, through multiple military engagements, indicates he must have possessed some extraordinary prowess both as a warrior and as a leader. His father, nicknamed Aedan Bradawc (Aedan the Wily) by the Britons, certainly seemed a brilliant strategist. Nobles of the warrior class in early medieval Britain and Ireland were well educated. In a highly artistic society where wit and intellect were prized, familiarity with the songs, histories, and linguistic arts was expected, alongside demonstrated proficiency in gaming, swimming, horse racing, cattle raiding, and the like.

Whoever the real Artúr was, I emerged from my research with the understanding that he was far more complex than most of his fictional portrayals suggest.

Saint Columba and the Loch Ness Monster

The first historical mention of the Loch Ness Monster comes from Adomnán's seventh-century *Life of Columba*, in which the saint confronts a man-killing water beast in the river Ness (not the loch). The event, "Concerning a certain water beast driven away by the power of the blessed man's prayer," is attributed to the year 565, and I ask the reader's forgiveness in shifting it to 580 for the purposes of bringing the encounter to life in this book.

Colmcille is the Irish name of the saint better known as Saint Columba. His diplomatic visit to Pictland is thought to have been made under the reign of Conall, Aedan mac Gabrahn's predecessor, but for the purposes of this narrative, I edited the historical time line.

The funeral, the water beast, and Columba's meeting with Bridei and his "magical" battles with Briochan (mentioned below) are all included in Adomnán's text for any who care to read them in their original states.

Toadstones and Early Medieval Poison

Briochan, foster father and chief druid to King Bridei, emerges from Adomnán's *Life of Columba* as a major adversary of Colmcille. In the episode where Colmcille demands the release of Briochan's slave (Imogen, in my book), I found it rather curious that Colmcille threatens Briochan and then, shortly thereafter, Briochan is drinking when the glass suddenly shatters in his hand and he falls to the ground, foaming at the mouth.

That sounded less like God's wrath and more like poison.

Perhaps even more curious is the fact that Bridei's men run to beg Colmcille for a remedy, and the saint offers them a stone that is to be put into water and drunk. Some research into poison and stones turned up "toadstones." In later medieval times, toadstone, also known as bufonite, was a stone believed to be an antidote to poison. Loose toadstones were found in the Cheapside Hoard, which dates to Elizabethan times, and an example of toadstone set into jewelry survives today in a ring found in the British Museum.

Poison has been a common way to dispose of people for thousands of years across many different cultures, from the imperial Asians to the Egyptians, Romans, and Greeks. Many poisons were known to the Celts, and we do have historical records that cite the use of them.

Weatherworking

As late as 1814 in Orkney, a woman named Bessie Miller of Stromness still earned a living by summoning fair winds for mariners. Her usual charge was sixpence. For this sum, Sir Walter Scott tells us, "she boiled her kettle, and gave the barque advantage of her prayers, for she disclaimed all unlawful arts. The wind, thus petitioned for, was sure to arrive, though sometimes the mariners had to wait some time for it."

R. M. Fergusson tells of another windworker, Mammie Scott, also of Stromness: "Many wonderful tales are told of her power and influence over the weather."

In ancient times, curses were believed to hold as much power as prayer, for both Christians and pre-Christian people. A legend from the Isle of Lismore still recounts how Saint Columba/Comcille cursed the isle after losing a boat race to Saint Moluag, for example. Both Christian and pre-Christian religious figures were believed to be endowed with the power to beseech their gods for winds and weather. Briochan threatens to summon foul weather as Columba is departing Pictland, as illustrated in this novel. But Adomnán's *Life of Columba* includes several stories of the saint's influence over weather, too. Saint Mungo was credited with the ability to raise the waters of the river Clyde in order to convey King Morken's grain to his own grain stores. (See *The Lost Queen*.) And Saint Patrick also had weather at his command: when a chief druid of Ireland called Drochu challenged the celebration of Easter, Saint Patrick prayed that his God would punish him. A mighty wind picked Drochu up off the ground and threw him to his death.

Shamans in cultures across the world were responsible for rain dances and ceremonies in times of drought. In Asia, monks were responsible for dealing with land spirits that caused disturbances in weather. I mention this to help illustrate the fact that the inclusion of weatherworking elements in this book does not make this novel a fantasy. It simply makes it illustrative of the times and mindsets of the people living in early medieval Scotland.

Historical Names

Names were often reused throughout generations. There is more than one Bridei in history, for example. The one featured in this book is now known as "Bridei I." There was an earlier Maelgwn, Maelgwn of Gwynedd, who died of yellow fever in Wales prior to the time line of these books. This is not who I intend the Maelgwn in these novels to be.

The spelling I chose for Artúr is not widely represented in translated literature, if at all. But much like my use of the term "Wisdom Keepers" when referring to druids, the choice was made in an effort to help the reader see past any previous encounters they may have had with the mythical figure of "King Arthur." As Oxford scholar Mark Williams writes, "There is no doubt Arthur is a Celtic figure but . . . the development of the legend has ferried him far from [his] roots."

In searching out the most authentic name for Artúr's wife, a Pict, I discovered a burial site in Meigle, Scotland, called Vanora's Mound. "Guinevere" has countless spellings. The name "Vanora" is an ancient variant of "Guinevere," and Meigle is located in what was formerly the heartland of Pictland. Place names near Meigle only further the Arthurian connection. There is the nearby farm of Arthurbank, and the Arthurstone on the grounds of Belmont Castle, and on Barry Hill there was a quern or grinding stone known locally as Vanora's Girdle.

Burial mounds such as these were used and sometimes reused from the Bronze Age through the early medieval period. Vanora's Mound could well represent the earliest phase of Pictish burial on this site, and sixteenth-century references describe the mound as being decorated by a number of Pictish stones. The informational marker at Vanora's Mound is tantalizing: "This mound is by tradition the burial place of Vanora or Guinevere, the legendary queen of King Arthur . . ."

The Battle of Asreth

The battle of Asreth in the land of Circenn, between Picts
on both sides; and in it fell Bridei, Maelchon's son.
—*The Annals of Tigernach*

It was important to establish in this book that the Picts were as much a threat as the Angles could ever be, if not more so, for Aedan and the Scots. I hope readers have come away with a better understanding of the blood feud that existed between King Aedan and King Bridei, one that sees a dramatic development in Bridei's subsequent death at Asreth, a historical event.

Circenn was the Pictish region near the east coast of Scotland, north of the Firth of Tay. Several hillforts can be found in that area. It is Adam Ardrey's belief that this battle was fought at the old Roman fortress of Carpow, near the rivers Tay and Earn. However, the Roman fort of Carpow is known to have had a very short occupation, and the Celtic people did not prefer to occupy old Roman sites. (A rare example is the "dark age" reuse of Birdoswald.) The general pattern is the abandonment of Roman sites throughout Britain and the reoccupation of more ancient tribal hillforts, several of which show evidence of refortification and reoccupation directly following Rome's departure from Britain. Excavations at Carpow turned up only Roman coins and other distinctly Roman artifacts and demonstrate no evidence of use past the year AD 220.

A more convincing candidate for the fortress of Asreth is the site of Moredun hillfort, which also overlooks the meeting point of the rivers Tay and Earn. Moredun was built nearly two thousand years ago, and, unlike the Roman fortress at Carpow, Moredun shows no sign of abandonment—quite the contrary. At Moredun we find evidence of use well into the early medieval period. Moredun was quite possibly the later site of a battle fought for control of the Pictish kingdom in AD 728, between kings Angus and Alpin.

What was a vital site for Picts to control in 728 was likely a vital site for Picts to control only 150 years earlier. In Moredun, I think we have at last found the site where multiple battles for dynastic control occurred. And where at least two great kings, Bridei and Aedan's father, Gabrahn, lost their lives.

This may not be the last you see of Asreth/Moredun, so it was important to get the location right.

Locations

I receive a number of emails from readers planning trips to Scotland, hoping to visit the sites from the book. For those whose fingers are hovering over their keyboards—and I love hearing from you—if you're looking for travel tips, I always include the locations you've read about in the author's note of each book. Please look there first.

For those who can undertake their own adventure, the sites featured in *The Shadowed Land* are below. But armchair travelers are encouraged to look them up and explore them virtually, too.

Pictish Sites

Burghead Fortress. Located in Burghead, a small town in Moray, Scotland, this Pictish fortress is the largest known promontory fortress in Britain. It was a major Pictish power center from AD 500–1000, and it is thought that the historical figure Bridei mac Maelchon operated from this fort throughout the long years of his reign. Intriguing archaeological discoveries at Burghead include a long house in the "Upper Citadel" with a stone hearth, dress pins, hairpins, and an Anglo-Saxon coin dating to the ninth century.

The Burghead Well. The fortress at Burghead was first excavated in the 1800s during the construction of the modern town that stands today. Stone carvings of bulls were discovered, along with an ancient well and a carving of a stone head. Though much of the fort was destroyed in the course of building the new town, the ramparts and the remaining grounds, including the well, are maintained by the dedicated people of the Burghead Headland Trust. A visit to the Burghead Visitor Centre is a necessity: you can learn more about the Picts and the site as well as view one of the original bull stones.

The Burghead Well is the only well of its kind in Scotland. Whether the well was used as a water source or as a ritual site is debated. Fortress wells are ordinarily shafts dug into rock, not broad pools with steps. There was mention in the early excavation record that some sort of frieze, now entirely faded, once decorated the back wall.

According to historical sources, a traditional method of execution among the Picts was by drowning. Given this, and the fact that springs and wells were often places of worship, the use of the pool as a temple and site for ritual drowning seems likely, in my opinion. A church was built later near the well, so—given Pope Gregory I's policy of consecration and reuse of pagan sites—the well might have been used for baptisms as the Picts moved into the Christian period.

Inverness. Known as the "Capital of the Highlands," the modern city of Inverness is home to multiple sites in this book. Craig Phadrig, the fortress that was likely home to Bridei, where Columba ventured in a diplomatic visit to the Picts, can still be found via a pleasant uphill walk not too far from the city center. An incredibly important site, it is the original Inverness, and a known tribal center of the Picts. The original name of the fortress has been lost, as Craig Phadrig means "Rock of Patrick," seemingly to do with the Irish saint, who has no known association with the site. But I used its modern name so readers might better find and visit it.

In Inverness, I found it disheartening to see Craig Phadrig labeled as the site where "St. Columba converted the Picts."

There is no evidence that Bridei was converted on this visit, or at all.

Even Adomnán, writing in 690, does not assert this: he was writing too close to the time, and readers would have known it to be untrue. The Venerable Bede, writing later, is the first historian to claim that Columba converted Bridei to Christianity, but Bede provides neither evidence nor sources. The picture painted by Adomnán in his earlier *Life of Columba* is that Pictland was staunchly pagan. The incidents in the *Life* show combative relations at best: at the end of Columba's stay at Bridei's court, he is rather maliciously sent packing by Briochan and his fellow druids.

The Ness Islands. There are enchanting paths and a series of foot-bridges that take travelers through the Ness Islands, which struck me as incredibly atmospheric. The river Ness is named for an ancient goddess local to the Picts. Given that the pre-Christian people of Ireland and Scotland held islands to be sacred, and given the river island's proximity to both Craig Phadrig and the ancient site of Tom-nahurich, I had little doubt after visiting that there would have been some pre-Christian religious presence on at least one of the islands. While the Ness was prone to flooding in years past, evidence of weirs have been found just upstream of the islands. (A weir is a barrier built across a stream or river to control the height of the water level and prevent flooding.) There is also a holy well nearby, another clue that points to spiritual significance. The well is known today as the "General's Well," after a landowner who lived nearby and drank from it daily.

"Tomnahurich" means "Hill of the Yews." The hill is adjacent to the Ness Islands and has an ancient heritage. Home to a cemetery today, it is still thought to be one of the main locations in northern Scotland where the Gaelic *sìthichean*, or faeries, dwell. A great tale of two fiddlers from Badenoch who played for the otherworldly dancers within the faerie hill is still told. It deserves much more space on the page than I was able to give it.

Scottish Sites

Kilmartin Glen. Kilmartin Glen is home to the burial cairn in the book where Artúr underwent his initiation. Nearly 350 ancient monuments can be visited here—chambered cairns, round cairns, cists, standing stones, and rock carvings—all within six miles of the village of Kilmartin. The glen is a site of supreme spiritual and historical significance for both the Picts and the Scots, going back millennia. The ceremonial and religious significance of Kilmartin is no doubt why the kings of Dalriada were inaugurated at Dunadd.

Dunadd Fort. Located just north of Lochgilphead, Dunadd is an Iron Age fortress that became the power center for the kings of Scottish Dalriada in the early medieval period. The carved stone footprint found on its mount, along with a basin carved in the rock, are believed to have been used in coronations. Evidence of metalworking, curious ancient stone balls, fine pottery sherds, and pigments used for manuscript illumination have been found there. The ramparts and natural stone gateway can still be made out, along with the fortress's well. When Artúr placed his foot in the footprint and lifted his sword at Dunadd, he was effectively, according to Adam Ardrey, "pulling the sword from the stone."

Historians and archaeologists have long assumed that any site with evidence of metalworking and fortified walls must be home to a sovereign. But I think this way of reimagining Iron Age and early medieval society excludes the acknowledgment of one of the most powerful forces of this society: their druids.

Dunadd is an ancient ritual site. The river Add twists at its feet, and slightly uphill, between the fort and the river, a standing stone looms. Michael Parker Pearson, the famed Stonehenge archaeologist, believes that the ancient people of Stonehenge traveled by river to the site of a wood henge, where they would disembark and do ceremonies having to do with life, death, and the turning of the solar seasons before progressing on to the circle made from stone. Similarly, I believe the standing stone downhill from Dunadd marks the processional point from the river Add up to the mount. The mount itself exists within a vast funerary and ritual landscape, one of the most concentrated in all of Scotland.

We know from texts that druids *were* the metalworkers. It was a specialized craft, not to mention an alchemistic one. Weapons and jewelry were not just produced; they were imbued with protection or with power in their very making. These sites were fortified because druids were of high political and social status, the sites possessed deep spiritual significance, and there were valuable items being crafted on site. Not to mention the fact that such fortified sites functioned as the designated refuge for any community members living in unprotected settlements during times of raiding or war.

Kings came and went; in Christian times, sacred sites were kept by bishops, abbots, and monks. In pre-Christian times, sacred sites were kept by druids. In a society where druids were given the honor to speak even before a king, I think it is an error to claim that Dunadd was the citadel of Aedan mac Gabrahn. Dunadd was a spiritual and thus cultural power point of a people. The fortress where Aedan and Artúr would have more likely dwelled lies buried in a forest today, only a seven-minute drive from Dunadd, and it deserves to be remembered. Today it is called Dunardry. But in ancient times, I believe it was called Dùn Monaidh.

Dùn Monaidh. Dùn Monaidh is recorded as an early seat of the Dalriadic monarchy in the seventh century. But no one has proven conclusively where Dùn Monaidh might have been. Dunadd has been put forward, as has the site of Dunstaffnage Castle. In *The History of the Celtic Place-Names of Scotland* (William Blackwood & Sons, 1926), William J. Watson wrote, "The old literature, it is to be noted, gives no hint of the position of Dún Monaidh." It was the nineteenth-century historian William Forbes Skene who suggested that Dunadd was the Dùn Monaidh of old. However, there is a fortress in the Dunardry forest park, only a short distance from the sacred mount of Dunadd. The informational sign there reads: "Welcome to Dunardry, the fort of the high king."

From the summit, Cruach Mòr, it's easy to see why this site is the best candidate for Aedan's fortress. It offers eagle-eye views of the Argyll coast, and prior to the modern creation of the Crinan Canal, "in the sixth century the most important route in Argyll was the portage road that ran east–west . . . in the shadow of Dunardry" (Ardrey, *Finding Arthur*).

Today it is difficult to locate the site of the actual fortress due to a dense wood, and to my knowledge the site has never been excavated. A pity, as I wonder what might be found.

• • •

At the time of publication, I have been dedicated to the research and writing of this series for twelve years. What began as a fierce desire to tell the story of a historical queen has become a life's work. I am so appreciative for the readers who have come along on this journey. Thank you for your patience and your companionship as I have worked these many long years to research and write this story.

The final stretch of the river is yet to come.

ACKNOWLEDGMENTS

In Burghead, Moray, I'm grateful to Cath Millar, secretary of the Headland Trust, for taking time in the offseason to help me visit the museum and the Pictish Well. The team at Bothy Bistro in Burghead offered a warm welcome and unforgettable food. My Burghead-set scenes were made much more accurate thanks to the University of Aberdeen and their 3-D reconstruction of Burghead Fort. Elsewhere in Scotland, I'm grateful to Simon and Jane Paul for their hospitality in Edinburgh, and, as always, I'm thankful for Adam Ardrey's expertise, which he bestowed during my travel to sites that were pivotal locations in this book and the next.

In the United States, Pastor Carl Hofmann offered his kind assistance with Psalm 44, cited by Adomnán, which I used in the recreation of Columba's historical scene outside Bridei's gates. I'm grateful to Mark and Nancy Liebetrau for helping facilitate, and for their love and support of my work.

I'm incredibly grateful to my writing community—authors and booksellers—in Charleston and throughout the Southeast, who are more than colleagues. You make the oppressive heat worth living in. It has been fifteen years, and this little world is the reason I stay. To Mary Alice Monroe, for wisdom and the communal writing days that helped me keep going. To Corrie Wang, for the very helpful early read. To Kathryn Budig, for her friendship, and for making *The Lost*

Queen an Inky Phoenix book club pick, and to Kate Fagan, for her care and writerly camaraderie. Kristin Harmel, Genevieve Gornichec, Janet Skeslien Charles, Patti Callahan Henry, J. T. Ellison, and others have also offered huge measures of support just when it was needed. And to all my friends and family members who have given so much love and support, especially in these past few years, thank you for sharing your light.

Tobias Tillemans offered his mountaineering expertise for the avalanche scene set on A' Cailleach. Marshall Messer and Becky Saletan were on the other end of the line—and often appeared in person—with unwavering encouragement. Three Liebetraus—Ben, Cameron, and Eric—all pitched in so I could get the writing done.

In New York, I owe volumes of thanks to the incredible team at Atria, who continue to champion these books, from publisher Libby McGuire and former editorial director Lindsay Sagnette to executive editor Kaitlin Olson, who read these pages as many times as I have, offering the encouragement, patience, and guidance that helped shape the book into the story it became. I also owe big thanks to Ife Anyoku, senior publicist Megan Rudloff, marketing manager Dayna Johnson, senior production editor Benjamin Holmes, and my copyeditor, David Chesanow.

I'm incredibly lucky to be represented by Faye Bender at the Book Group, who as a literary agent wears one hundred different hats and somehow makes it look easy. And to the legendary (now retired) former vice president and executive editor Trish Todd, who acquired these books initially and has believed in my stories from the beginning.

I'm so grateful for my son, Asa Pike Liebetrau, for his daily word-count encouragement and his interest in all things historical. He was a bright presence on hard days, and this book is better for having been written in his orbit.

My mother passed away during the writing of this book, and two people stepped in to help fill her giant, irreplaceable shoes. Jim Jenkins was a receiver of endless text messages. He helped me better pin down the character of Artúr and offered insights on both early pages and the Author's Note. My sister, Kirsten Pike—who knows a great deal about literature—made herself available for endless brainstorming calls at all times of day or night, and read several early versions of the work in progress. She was with me on the phone as I wrote the final lines and helped bring the novel home. I don't know if I could have picked up these pages again without you both.

Lastly, to my mother, Linda, without whom my writing would not exist. She read all my manuscripts countless times, offering intelligent insights, new ideas, and vital constructive criticism. She caught countless typos and grammatical mistakes and spent hundreds of hours on the phone with me discussing my work. She traveled to Scotland to throw rocks into rivers with my son so I could visit sites. If it was within her power, she never let a call go to voicemail. I felt her with me on the toughest days, even if I could no longer see her. The hole she left is forever. But our grief is a measure of how much she was loved.

She told me she did not want her cancer to be my excuse for not finishing this story.

This book is for her.

ABOUT THE AUTHOR

S igne Pike is a former book editor and the author of three novels in the Lost Queen series, recently optioned for television, as
well as the travel memoir *Faery Tale*. She has researched and written
about Celtic history and folklore for more than a decade. Visit her at
SignePike.com.